THE
MISSING
GIRLS

THE MISSING GIRLS

CAROL WYER

Bookouture

Published by Bookouture
An imprint of StoryFire Ltd.
23 Sussex Road, Ickenham, UB10 8PN
United Kingdom
www.bookouture.com

ISBN: 978-1-78681-268-1
eBook ISBN: 978-1-78681-267-4

This book is a work of fiction. Names, characters, businesses,
organizations, places and events other than those clearly in the public
domain, are either the product of the author's imagination or are
used fictitiously. Any resemblance to actual persons, living or dead,
events or locales is entirely coincidental.

CHAPTER ONE

At first, Amber Dalton thought the drumming sound was coming from outside, but when she drew herself up from the hard mattress, she realised it was in her own head. Darkness wrapped itself around her like a thick blanket. She couldn't make out any walls or see the outlines of bedroom furniture. Her forehead throbbed so much it made her wince. He'd doped her.

Amber wondered if he had raped her while she'd been unconscious. She dropped her hands to her thighs, then hesitated as she felt unfamiliar rough material beneath her fingertips. She'd been wearing her short, pleated, black skirt. Her best friend, Sam, called it her 'foxy skirt'. 'It makes men's tongues fall out of their mouths,' Sam had said. 'You've got great legs. Team it with a silk shirt, and you've got a winning combination.' The lousy son of a bitch had removed her clothes and she was wearing a garment that smelt of antiseptic. She tugged at it and felt it give behind her. She wriggled about, running her hand down her backside and feeling the flesh of her buttocks. It was open at the back, tied with strings in a few places. It was a hospital gown.

A flash of pain in her forehead made her cry out. She seemed to be in hospital, but why? She hadn't been involved in an accident. She turned her head left and right to see if she was injured. This couldn't be a hospital ward. It didn't smell like a hospital. The bed was pushed into a corner of the room and she felt the wall on her right. Under the tips of her fingers she could feel the raised flock of the wallpaper. Her bedroom had wallpaper – flowers and swirls that she and her mother had chosen together. Amber would often trace the patterns while lying in bed wishing she didn't have to go to school.

Amber had a desperate urge to call for her mother and cry on her scrawny shoulder. Her mother wasn't exactly the maternal type, but right now Amber wanted nothing more than to be sat on the comfy sofa, listening to her mother tell her off for being such a stupid cow.

She sat on the edge of the bed, her head spinning as she felt for a bedside table and a light. Her splayed fingers discovered nothing but air. She pushed up onto her feet, bare soles touching cold floorboards, and began crabbing along the wall, seeking a light switch, each step cautious in case she trod on a sharp object. She found a wooden surround – a doorframe – and traced her fingers to the handle and turned it. The door remained resolutely shut. She tugged with both hands, tiny uh-uh-uh noises escaping her as her panic grew, and she questioned why she was in a locked room. She fumbled in vain for a switch. She needed to see where she was and work out how to escape. She would have to venture further and hope she didn't stumble over any furniture.

Fingers outstretched, she searched the space, arms waving up and down and sweeping the area in front of her. The room appeared at first to be empty apart from the bed. She met another wall and, resting her back against it, caught her ragged breath, which was coming in tortured, frightened gasps. Now disorientated, nauseous and confused, she dropped to her knees and shuffled on all fours, hoping to find the bed once more. Instead, she banged her knee on the sharp edge of a piece of furniture and cried out. She could not understand what was happening. Blood trickled down her head. She touched it and wondered if she had actually been involved in some sort of accident. That would explain the situation. She was in a hospital and needed to rest. She began to mumble, 'It's okay. It's okay.' There was no other explanation, she reasoned.

'Nurse,' she croaked, her voice no more than a faint whisper. 'Nurse,' she called, louder. Her voice sounded strange and hollow. The pain had started afresh in her forehead, stripping her mind of all other thoughts. She needed painkillers. 'Nurse!' The sound of her own desperation frightened her. She had to be in hospital. She couldn't be anywhere else. Her temples drummed and the sound of her own heartbeat filled the room. She lifted her arms again and found the wall. Pushing against it, she located the door again and tugged without hope on the handle. Exhausted now with the effort, she stumbled against the bed and slumped onto it.

She touched her head with her fingertips. The slight pressure was too much to bear. A sound, a cross between a moan and a scream, escaped her dry lips. It was a nightmare. That was it. She was asleep. When she was smaller, she had suffered a recurring dream about a stranger, in which she would enter her bedroom and spot a dark outline through the window. The banging would make her jump, and in that instant she would know that the man standing the other side of the glass was coming to kill her. She would be rooted to the spot, eyes fixed on the door handle, which would gradually move down. The door, which was nearly always locked, would open inch by inch. The man was coming to get her. A large carving knife would be pushed through the opening and a screaming Amber would wake up under her bed. Her mother would rush in and cajole her from her hiding place, and then sit with her, stroking her hair and making soothing noises. This must be one of those realistic nightmares, and she would soon awaken to the sounds of the television blaring downstairs and her mum yelling it was time to get up and go to school.

She wanted to wake up more than anything. This blackness and the intense silence was scaring her rigid. 'Mum!' she shouted. 'Help me!'

She held her breath but the thrumming in her temples obliterated any other sound, then she heard it – a soft squeak.

'Hello?' She regretted calling out. An icy chill filled her veins. There was a slight shuffling of feet then silence once again. Somebody was already inside the room but they weren't answering her, and that was *even scarier. She had nothing to defend herself with. Sliding to the floor, Amber wriggled under the bed and curled up, fist in her mouth as she had often done as a child.*

Briefly, a shaft of light illuminated the floor, making her blink rapidly. Amber saw a pair of trainers. They belonged to him. He had been wearing them when he answered the door. It all seemed a lifetime ago. She had stood on the doorstep, brimming with confidence, shaking her mane of dark hair in a flirty fashion and pouting her full lips, knowing he wanted her. She couldn't remember much more. The inviting sitting room with a huge leather sofa… the lights so low she could barely see his face… the sensual smell of him… the glass of champagne waiting for her on the table. His whispered words, 'Make yourself comfortable, drink the champagne and I'll be back in a minute to refill your glass.' The bubbles ascended in tiny circles and exploded into her mouth as she sipped it, pretending she often drank champagne. The memory of tumbling from the sofa, sliding helplessly onto the carpet… a dark shadow laughing… then oblivion. Her shoulders began to shake with fear as she tried to suppress sobs. They threatened to erupt and give away her hiding hole. Go away. Please go away. Please leave me alone. The light went out and the room was once again plunged into darkness.

'Come out, come out, wherever you are.'

She tried to swallow the fear rising in her throat.

'I know where you are, Amber. Come out now.'

Her entire body trembled. She repeated the mantra in her head. Go away. Go away. Go away. A sudden rush of air and a puff of stale breath. He had dropped down to the floor.

'I can see you,' he whispered.

Her keening became louder and louder. His voice lost its playfulness. 'Come out or I'll drag you out by your hair.' The last two words came out louder and higher in tone.

Amber couldn't move. Instinct made her retreat from his hands. There was a growl and the bed was lifted clean away. She curled into a tight ball and squealed as he yanked on her hair, dragging her head backwards until she thought her scalp would pull away from her face. Pain like knives dragging down her forehead made her gasp.

'Not so cocksure now, are you, Amber?'

The honeyed voice that she had found so attractive, now made her cringe. It sounded so false.

'Oh dear, you seem to have made a puddle.'

She felt the urine trickle down her leg. His voice began to fade and she felt a warmth as a numbness began to take over her head. Nothing seemed real any more. Now the voice sounded like her mother's.

'I ought to rub your nose in it. That's what they do to naughty little bitches.'

She collapsed onto the floor at his feet.

'Get up, Amber.'

She tried to stand, her legs unwilling to cooperate, her back aching and her heart hammering. She fell towards the wall, put out her hands and steadied herself. She swallowed the lump in her throat and faced him.

'What do you want?' Her words barely more than a squeak.

'Not anything you have to offer,' he hissed.

'Why are you doing this to me?'

'So many questions. Aren't you the inquisitive schoolgirl?'

A light snapped on. His hands shot out and grabbed her shoulders. She yelped as he turned her around so she faced a mirror. Her bottom lip dropped and her eyes filled. The girl in the mirror no longer looked like a sexy, flirtatious woman. She looked like a sixteen-year-old frightened schoolgirl. Her mascara, so carefully applied for him, was now streaked under her eyes like a tragic clown's. Her hair, matted with blood, had stuck to her head and her cheeks were stained brown-red. Carved into her forehead was a word that made her gasp loudly.

Behind her, with night-vision goggles covering most of his face, he grinned, a smile that made Amber scream and pull away. She beat at him, hands flapping in fear.

He turned off the torch and the room fell into complete darkness again and she fell against the wall.

'It's too late, Amber. You're mine now.'

CHAPTER TWO

DI Tom Shearer tipped several coloured sweets directly into his mouth, then offered the packet to PC Anna Shamash. She pulled a face and shook her head.

'Please yourself,' he mumbled, popping the remainder into his mouth, screwing up the packet and chewing noisily. The aroma of fruit chews filled the Porsche. Anna stared out across the dark buildings towards the mammoth Amazon distribution warehouse in the distance. She had read it was the size of eleven football pitches and stored every item you could possibly think of. She wondered how many of the thousand-plus employees were currently buzzing around the shelves like demented bees, stowing, picking, packing and shipping the hundreds of thousands of items that they moved every single day, at this ungodly hour. At least they weren't crammed in next to Tom Shearer, staking out a self-storage facility in Rugeley. She would happily swap with any of them at the moment.

Tom picked at the gap between his front teeth with a fingernail, extracted a piece of green sweet and sucked on the sticky substance. 'What?' he said. 'Never seen anyone get bits stuck in their teeth before?'

Anna turned her head away. It had been a long night. She was still annoyed she'd drawn the short straw and got stuck with Shearer in his cramped, boy-racer Porsche. He wasn't good company at the best of times and his car was an embarrassment. They all joked about it at the station, coming out with hackneyed quips about cars compensating for penis size. 'Here, Anna, what's the difference between a porcupine and a Porsche?' She had shrugged. 'On a porcupine, the pricks are on the outside.' David Marker had almost choked on his cheese roll at that one. Anna wished David was sitting in the car instead of her. It was most uncomfortable. Shearer had insisted on bringing it, claiming it would be the last car any criminals would expect a policeman to be using.

'If they spot us, they'll assume we're a couple making out.'

Anna had cringed at that thought. He was old enough to be her father and twice the curmudgeon.

Four giant power station cooling towers loomed beside them, each surface decorated with red lights to warn aircraft of their presence. The iconic towers that had been part of the Rugeley skyline for decades were now out of commission and would eventually be demolished. She peered into the moonlit sky and watched a couple of clouds skit across. The wind had picked up and the temperature had dropped. She rubbed some feeling back into her hands.

'You want the heating put back on?'

'No, I'll be fine.' She sat on her hands to warm them. There was no point in starting the engine and drawing attention to the car. They'd been parked on the verge next to the towers and opposite the self-storage warehouse for hours. One of the pool cars was in position by the roundabout entrance into the Towers Business Park, the other at the far end of the road, by the entrance to the Amazon distribution centre and near the all-night McDonald's. Anna's stomach rumbled. She hadn't eaten since teatime, when she'd only had a few minutes to grab a sandwich. She could murder a hamburger. She wondered if vegetarian Mitz had nipped in and bought anything while they were waiting. He had been sympathetic when he learnt she was on the stakeout in Shearer's car.

'An entire night spent in Shearer's babe magnet with the old man himself. I can't think of much worse, other than a night in a pool car with Gareth Murray.'

Gareth, one of the newest recruits, was incredibly overzealous. It would be like being in a car with an excited puppy. At least Shearer wasn't a big talker. If his car was a babe magnet, it must only attract rather dim ones, she mused. She shifted uncomfortably in the low sports seat and knocked her knees against the dashboard for the umpteenth time that night. Outside, the self-storage unit remained in darkness. The information received had been so promising. Drug dealers were supposed to let themselves into the warehouse and collect several kilos of top-quality heroin hidden in one of the units. At approximately fifty grand a kilo, it promised to be an outstanding haul, and would garner recognition for all of the team. Shearer wanted it so badly; the smell of determination mingled with his aftershave and permeated the entire car. It was no secret Shearer was ambitious. He wanted to further his own career, and a successful result tonight would help him on his way to promotion. This annoyed Anna. In her opinion, Robyn should be here with them, not Shearer. Robyn deserved the same opportunities as Shearer.

They'd all been pumped up when they arrived and spread out some eight hours ago. That initial enthusiasm had waned. So far, it had been a wasted night. She wondered what her mutt, Razzle, was up to. Probably asleep on her bed, which was where she should be. She stifled a yawn. Shearer would only make some comment if he spotted her struggling to stay awake.

He sighed and flicked through a few radio stations before settling on Heart FM and began singing along to Queen. Anna raised a dark, well-groomed eyebrow.

'Don't look so surprised. This is my era. Best music ever came out of the eighties,' he said.

'There were some good artists but I prefer today's music.'

'You would. You're a good few generations younger than me. You can't be much older than my son.'

'I'm twenty-five.'

'Really? You look about twelve.' His mouth curved upwards, making him look more attractive. 'That's it for compliments. I just ran out of my daily quota.'

He whistled along to the music for a while, then sat bolt upright. 'Movement.'

Anna peered out of the car window and saw what he had noticed. A figure in a hoodie was making its way along the cycle pathway. Anna held her breath. The man loped past them, neither veering off nor looking in their direction.

'Just a jogger,' she said.

Shearer checked his watch. 'It's five forty. Bit early to be out running on a Monday morning in January, especially when it's two below freezing out there.'

'They change shift at Amazon in twenty minutes. Maybe he's headed there to work.'

Shearer nodded. 'Yeah. Possible. Mad jogging in this weather, but possible.'

He drummed his fingers and Anna wanted to slap his hand. He leant forward and rubbed the steamed-up window with his sleeve, watching the man making his way past the distribution centre at a steady pace.

'I've had enough of this. Units one and two, anything?'

Sergeant Mitz Patel's voice came back over the radio. 'Negative. Nothing apart from a huge tabby cat that hawked up a half-digested mouse in front of McDonald's half an hour ago.'

'Nothing, guv.' PC David Marker, sitting with Sergeant Matt Higham, sounded his usual calm self.

'Hang on. The jogger's returning.' Anna sank further into the passenger seat to avoid detection. 'He's going to spot us.'

'Don't move,' said Shearer, his eyes trained on the man outside.

She banged her elbow on the gearstick and grimaced. 'I can't. I'm too big for this car. I think I need the next size up.'

He gave her a wry grin, then pulled a face. 'Blast. He's stopped. He's doing up a shoelace.' A crease appeared on Shearer's forehead. 'He's talking to someone. He must be on a hands-free mobile. This doesn't feel right. Shit! He's moving towards the housing estate. Unit one, he's headed in your direction. Apprehend him and check him out. He might have nothing to do with this but I'm taking no chances.'

They continued staring at the self-storage warehouse. Car headlights approached them. The traffic would begin to build up as the shift workers left the distribution centre. A black Audi drove past them, headlights on full beam, making Anna shut her eyes. Shearer grumbled beside her. 'I have a horrible feeling this is going to go belly up.'

No sooner had he spoken than Matt shouted over the radio, 'Guv, a black Audi's pulled up and the suspect's jumped into it, registration oscar, bravo, six, six.' The radio crackled loudly. 'It's headed in the direction of Rugeley town centre. We're in pursuit. I repeat, in pursuit.'

Tom weighed up his options. 'Unit two, we're going in. Can't wait any longer.'

He flung open the door and marched across to the warehouse, puffing out small clouds of air. Anna followed. Cold air like freezing fingers grabbed at her cheeks. Shearer was right. Nobody would be jogging in these temperatures. The man had to be linked to the gang. She hoped Matt and David had caught them. Mitz and Gareth arrived clad in stab vests and huddled like dark beetles in front of the huge metal shutters.

'Remind us which units we're looking for?' Shearer stamped his feet on the frosty ground and scowled.

'Numbers 127, 128 or 129. The source wasn't sure which one the gang was using.'

Tom let out a hiss of annoyance. 'He also claimed the gang would drop off more gear, and since it's now almost six and there's no sign of them, I'd say he was pretty bloody unreliable. Still, we have to give it a go.'

Gareth Murray spoke up. 'Do we need the Enforcer for this, guv?'

'For crying out loud, of course not. The owner won't thank us for destroying their property with a battering ram. You watch too much television. I have the entry code. The battering ram is for the storage units. We haven't got keys for those. Don't they teach you anything about using common sense at police school these days?' Shearer punched in some numbers on a panel beside the shutters and waited. Anna threw Mitz a look. He shrugged. Shearer was in one of his lousy moods. They'd better find these drugs or he'd be impossible to work with. The mechanism whirred into action and the shutters lifted with a squeal. They slipped inside. Shearer flicked a switch and strip lighting spluttered into life, revealing the enormity of the place. Storage units, accessed by roll-up metal doors, flanked corridor after corridor.

Gareth's mouth flapped open. 'Crikey, how many units are there here?'

Mitz glanced about. 'Several hundred. Some are the size of walk-in closets and others as big as two-car garages. The owners charge per size and you can store just about anything in here. The renters have twenty-four-hour access to this place and each unit is lockable. They can request individual door alarms too.'

Shearer growled at Mitz. 'Enough chatter. Find the units. You take 127; Anna, 128, and I'll go through 129. Murray – stay outside and keep watch.'

They followed behind Shearer in single file, their footsteps echoing in the vast space. They could still hear the sound of cars passing on the road outside. The shift changeover had begun. Shearer's radio crackled.

'Lost the car, guv. Put out a call on it. Got the suspect. He was tossed out onto the road. He's okay. We're taking him in for questioning.'

Shearer kicked at a nearby shutter. The explosive sound resonated down the corridor.

'Sod it. Okay. Keep me informed. See you at the station.'

The trio continued searching for the units, finally stopping outside the rolled shutters. 'Padlocked, as we suspected. We'll need these.' Mitz lifted the bolt cutters he'd been carrying and cut through the padlocks on unit 129.

'What the fuck?' Shearer's mouth dropped open as he gazed into the unit. A huge Dalek stared back at him, its massive form filling the entire space. 'First person to say "exterminate" gets my full wrath. Don't even think it.' A Cyberman's costume was propped next to the Dalek, and behind it, against the far wall, stood a slightly tatty Tardis, clearly used as a prop in a show.

Mitz swivelled around in the space, avoiding the armour-clad Dalek. 'I doubt there are any drugs in here.'

'I think someone was on drugs when they bought this lot,' mumbled Shearer, flicking through *Doctor Who* magazines. 'I'd better check it out thoroughly.'

'You can climb inside the Dalek,' Mitz said.

Shearer's eyebrow raised high. 'How do you know that?'

'There was one exactly like it on the news a while back. Fetched a load of money. The news presenter drove it about on television.'

Shearer smiled humorously. 'I think I'll try and resist driving it about the warehouse, tempting though it seems. Go on. Check the other units. I'll deal with weirdo world here.'

Mitz opened the unit next door for Anna. It was empty compared to the first one. Over a hundred shoeboxes were stacked on the floor. On one wall was a mirror and in front of it a red carpet.

'Somebody likes stylish shoes,' said Mitz as Anna unpacked the first box and extracted very expensive high-heeled Louboutin shoes. He pulled out his notebook and checked his information. The Dalek unit is rented by Julian Fisher and this unit, oh, it's rented by Jeremy Gubbins.'

Anna held up a pair of sparkly silver stilettos. 'Looks like Mr Gubbins has a shoe fetish. Shame, none are my size. Maybe they're stolen goods. Or his wife rented the unit in his name and puts them here for safe keeping. Oh well, better check each box. There might be drugs hidden in them.' She dug into the inside of a pair of glittering red stilettos with cold fingers, checking for packets of drugs. Judging by the number of boxes, it was going to be a long job.

Mitz left Anna in the unit and broke into the third unit. The light wasn't working in this one. Inside it was dark, in spite of the strip lighting outside. He directed his torch beam around to see it was empty apart from a large wooden trunk, the sort used as luggage, at the far end of the room. Holding the torch in his teeth, he attempted to break open the padlock.

'Anna, could you come in here a minute and hold the torch?'

She appeared at the door. 'Lucky you. Only one box. I'll be all morning opening that lot.'

'Can you shine the light on it while I get it open, and then I'll give you a hand?'

Their long shadows danced against the tin walls as Mitz dropped to his knees and struggled to remove the padlock from the trunk. The clasp wouldn't give at first, but he teased and prised until it finally lifted away with a satisfying clunk. He tugged at the heavy lid which remained resolutely shut. Anna joined him and together they sought leverage, and with grunts, eased it off then pushed it back on its hinges with relieved sighs.

'That was way more difficult than I expected.'

An earthy, cheesy aroma rose to greet them as they peered in. The trunk contained sheets.

'Oh please don't tell me we went to all that effort for a trunk of bed linen.'

Mitz removed the first sheet: cheap cream cotton that had been neatly folded. Under it were more sheets, haphazardly thrown in.

Mitz felt the sheets. 'There's something under this one.'

Anna wrinkled her nose. 'Smells like rancid butter.'

A palpable frisson of excitement passed between them as he lifted the material in anticipation of revealing the stash of heroin. Anna shone the beam into the trunk and gasped. There were no bags of drugs under the sheet. Wrapped in plastic, arms folded across its ribcage, was a body.

CHAPTER THREE

Robyn dug deep. She pushed into the sprint, feeling the warm pull on her quads and anticipating the relief she'd experience when she reached the end. She ignored the mild burning of lactic acid and flew along on autopilot, air rushing in and out of her lungs.

Her mind was not on running. She couldn't shake the irritation hanging over her like a noxious cloud. Tom Shearer was out for promotion. Ever since the new detective chief inspector, Richard Flint, had arrived at the station, Tom had been toadying around the man. She suspected Shearer had talked Flint into letting him take over the drugs case, even though the informant who called the station had spoken to her, not Shearer. She replayed the conversation she'd had with the DCI.

'You were not singled out by the informant, DI Carter, you merely happened to be there when the phone rang. DI Shearer has more experience with such cases. He was involved on several busts with Derbyshire Police.' For a moment she yearned for Louisa Mulholland to be sitting in the chair and not the ginger-haired man, whose face was so smooth and plump that he looked like an overgrown schoolboy. His manner was brusque, but unlike Louisa, he would not look Robyn in the eye, instead focusing on some speck to the left of her. 'I'd prefer you to deal with Stephen Hobbs. There's been a burglary at one of his shops. A range of expensive mobiles have been taken.'

Stephen Hobbs was a high-profile entrepreneur with a chain of mobile phone shops. He was well known for his charity work and held an annual charity ball at his estate, attended by some of the UK's best-known movers, shakers and celebrities. No doubt Flint wanted to ensure Hobbs received the police's full assistance to further his own ends.

Rankled more by his condescending tone than his words, Robyn argued her corner. 'I agree DI Shearer has more experience in this field, sir, but it'll be a catch-twenty-two situation if you don't allow me to lead this investigation. I'll never get the necessary experience and you will always pass drug-related cases to him.'

Flint's thin lips disappeared into his face.

'I won't let you down. The informant, Freddy, is calling me back with the dates and times of their movements.'

Flint took a noisy, deep breath and spoke as if she were a simpleton. 'DI Carter, I can assure you that you won't be passed over in the future, but when a large amount of heroin like this is involved, it's logical to put my most experienced officer on the case. I refuse to discuss the matter any further. If you want to take it up with the super, go ahead, but I can assure you he is behind my decision.'

She had wanted to argue further but it would have been pointless. DCI Flint's mind was made up. To be fair to Tom, he hadn't gloated. However, it should be her at the storage warehouse, not him.

Around her, faces contorted with exertion and soles slapping on treadmills drowned out the pumping beat of 'Eye of the Tiger'. Her friend Tricia wasn't among the regulars. If she had been, they'd have buddied-up and matched each other pace for pace. As it was, with her mind elsewhere, Robyn had set off too quickly and was paying the price. Her legs felt heavy and her heart was beating too fast. She urged herself on, the room a blur, her focus only on the rhythm of her breathing. Her vest stuck to her back, and beads of sweat dripped into her eyes, stinging and blinding her. She wouldn't break stride to wipe them away. She was too close to the finish. The treadmill's screen showed one hundred metres remaining. She

drove her legs into the speeding treadmill, feeling a pull at the top
of her thigh but ignoring it, and pounded the last few paces, her
breath coming in ragged gasps. The pain intensified, like a knife
burrowing into her hip. She swallowed a cry and decreased the
speed rapidly to a halt before limping off.

'Hey, you okay?' Jay, the gym manager came across.

'Just a strain. I'll be fine. Need to stretch it. I wasn't concentrating. I had a bad day at work.'

'I know those days. If you need a massage, shout out. Kath is
free. She'll sort you. Try icing it.'

'Cheers. I'll be fine.'

Robyn attempted some gentle stretching. She was now not only
annoyed with Flint and Shearer, but with herself. With several
marathons and triathlons behind her, she knew better than to let
emotions distract her when training. She hobbled into the changing
room, swallowed a couple of ibuprofen, and took a shower, all the
time reflecting on her career.

It had been a struggle to return to the force after losing Davies,
her fiancé. Louisa Mulholland had been pivotal in getting Robyn
back on track. Louisa had recently taken up a new position in
Yorkshire, leaving Robyn with an open invitation to join her, and
although Robyn loved her job and most of the team at Stafford,
she wondered whether she should consider transferring. The rivalry
between her and Shearer caused a bad atmosphere, and it seemed
Flint had taken an instant dislike to her.

She slumped onto the bench, resting her head against the
locker, eyes shut. She was almost forty, unmarried, had no parents
and no boyfriend. She could go wherever she wanted. Of course,
if she moved away, she'd be leaving behind her cousin and best
friend Ross, and his wife Jeanette, who mothered her at every
opportunity. She wouldn't see much of Amélie, Davies's daughter.
She was due to go to the cinema with Amélie and her best friend

on Thursday. The thought made her smile. No, as long as she had
Amélie, she'd stay in Staffordshire. The girl was growing up quickly
and was what they called a 'tweenager' – she'd be thirteen in six
months. Robyn couldn't deny that she loved the girl. If Davies
had lived, Amélie would have stayed over regularly. Robyn would
have been her stepmother, a role she'd have relished. Bugger Flint,
she thought as she shook her head and rose, wincing as she put
weight on her hip. She had better get home and ice it. If she
wasn't in decent shape, Flint would pass her over for a lot more
than a drugs bust.

She pulled her mobile from her kitbag and texted Amélie:
*Looking forward to the cinema on Thursday. What do you fancy
watching? Heard La La Land is good.*

The reply came back almost immediately:

> *Rather watch Street Cat Named Bob. Florence said it's sad.*
> *Okay, I'll bring a box of tissues in case we all cry.*
> *Florence says we will cry.*
> *I'd better bring two boxes then. I'll pick you up at about
> four thirty.*
> *Great. See ya then.*

Florence and Amélie had been friends for years and were always
at each other's houses. Florence's parents lived near Uttoxeter and
trained racehorses. Robyn remembered Christine Hallows, Florence's mother, telling Robyn it didn't matter that Florence showed
no interest in horses – as long as the girl was happy and healthy she
could be whatever she wanted. She would be proud of her daughter
no matter what. Robyn admired Florence's parents, who thought
the world of their only child.

Robyn mused that she too would have allowed her child to
follow his or her dreams and been there to support them. As it was,
she only had the sad memory of what might have been, having
miscarried her and Davies's baby after his death. She pushed the

memories away. There had been too many tears. Now she had Amélie and, by association, Florence. She might even treat them both to a pizza before the film.

She turned the shower thermostat to its top setting and let the steaming water wash away all negative thoughts; when she emerged, she felt better about life. The pills had numbed the pain in her hip and Amélie had helped her mood. She could face Flint and Shearer again.

As she flipped her car boot to throw in her kitbag, her phone rang. It was Anna Shamash.

'Boss, you have to come in straight away.' Anna's voice oozed excitement.

'Did you find the drugs?'

'No. There weren't any.' The phone buzzed angrily. There was another caller on the line – DCI Flint.

'Hang on, Anna. Got to take another call.'

'DI Carter, I know you're off duty but there's been a development and I need you back at the station immediately.'

Robyn felt a pull at the edges of her mouth. 'Is it regarding the drugs case, sir?'

'It's related to it.'

'Then surely that's DI Shearer's department.'

There was a hiss of irritation. 'DI Carter, I require your expertise on this matter.'

Robyn resisted the urge to wind Flint up any further. 'I'll be there in fifteen minutes.'

She ended the call and flicked back to Anna. 'I'm on my way. Fill me in while I drive.' Robyn started up the Golf and, ignoring the dull ache in her hip, drove out of the gym car park, her mind beginning to whir and her heart thumping with the anticipation of what was to come.

CHAPTER FOUR

The overnight frost had left artistic swirled patterns on the car windscreen. They looked so pretty that Ross was reluctant to remove them. He had a job to do, however, and couldn't stand around waiting for the sun to melt the white glaze. He pulled out a credit card and ran it down the screen. Tiny white flakes spun off in all directions, and over his black shoes. He stamped them on the pavement before climbing into the vehicle, scarf still wound around his neck. He started the engine and turned the heating up full blast. The display revealed it was minus three outside. At least it promised to be a bright day.

It was just as well it was sunny because he wasn't in the best of moods. He'd just taken a call from a woman, Susanne Carlisle, who could hardly talk for tears, and Ross hated it when women cried like that. Some lowlife had stolen her puppy and, although she had alerted the police, she wanted Ross to hunt for it.

'She's a Staffordshire bull terrier and she has such a sweet nature. She wouldn't hurt a fly. I hope whoever's got her is looking after her properly. I couldn't bear it if anything happened to her.'

She had dissolved into more tears. Ross had made encouraging noises and told her he'd set to work immediately. He'd found lost animals before. He hoped this one hadn't been stolen to order and taken to another part of the UK.

The sun dazzled him as he joined the dual carriageway, making him screw up his eyes. He fumbled about in the glove box for some sunglasses, then remembered he'd taken them home to clean them and left them there. He swore and dropped the sun visor. It was going to be one of those days.

He wasn't sure he was at the right place, even though his satnav had directed him here. Gallow Street, hidden within a labyrinth of roads on the edge of Derby, was one of the dingiest, most depressing streets he had ever visited. The brick wall on the left as he entered the street was covered in obscene graffiti, as was the one remaining glass pane of the bus shelter, further down the street. He drove slowly, hunting for number forty. The houses were a hotchpotch of 1950s architecture and various modern extensions. Some had porches, cluttered with bikes and paraphernalia; others had paved, oil-spattered driveways rather than gardens. The house numbers descended. The one he wanted was much further along the road.

Two young men, hands deep in low-slung jeans pockets, scowled in unison as he drove past them. Brown rubbish bins, haphazardly strewn, dominated both sides of the street. Semi-detached houses gave way to matching terraced properties with brown-painted doors and no frontages; grimy glass that hadn't been washed in many months; broken appliances and abandoned cars, rusting outside on the street. Ross wondered if he shouldn't park his car elsewhere and walk. He finally spotted number forty, and, after driving to the far end of the road, he parked next to a convenience store and returned to the house on foot.

He pressed the doorbell. The muffled tune of a song he didn't recognise rang deep inside. He shuffled uncomfortably. A shifting behind the door and the sound of bolts being dragged back. The door opened and a stone-faced girl in her late teens surveyed him from behind a safety chain, hand on the door, ready to shut it at a moment's notice.

'What d'ya want? Me mum's not interested in no double-glazin' nor nuffin' if you're selling.'

'Hi, I'm here about your dog. I'm Ross Cunningham from R&J Associates. Your mum rang me.'

The girl pulled away and shouted, 'Mum, did you call that bloke about Princess?'

There was a howl from a small child and the response, 'Yeah. Is it him? Let him in.'

'Hang on.' She shut the door with a bang. The chain was rattled several times, then the door reopened and the girl waved him in. Ross followed her through a hallway, cluttered with two children's bicycles and several coats thrown in heaps on the floor, to the kitchen. A woman with bleached blonde hair and a frazzled expression was trying to feed cereal to a toddler. The small child shook his head angrily. 'No!' he yelled. 'No, no, no.'

'Brandon, stop it.' The girl moved in front of the child and scooped him up in her thin arms, holding him tightly until he calmed. 'Come on. I'll take you to the shop. We'll get some chocolate. Let's get your coat. Mum, I'm gonna see Veronica while I'm out. I'll be back for me dinner.' She acknowledged Ross with a quick nod and carried the boy off to the hallway. Ross held out his hand. 'Ross Cunningham.'

'Oh, Mr Cunningham. Thank you for coming round. I'm worried sick about Princess and I didn't know what else to do or who to call.' Her face was a crumpled mess, eyelids heavy and red-veined from crying. 'I know she's only a dog, but she means so much to me.'

Susanne Carlisle was in her late forties but with the shadows under her eyes, sallow complexion and sunken cheekbones, could pass for a woman in her late fifties.

'The coppers came but I don't hold out any hope. The PC scribbled summit in his book then dashed off. He said he'd ask about but he probably had better things to do,' she sniffed.

'What happened, exactly?'

'I let Princess out back to do her business. I was on the phone to the health clinic cos I need some more meds, and when I called her in, she'd gone. I called and called her but there was no sign of her. I went round to the old misery next door and asked if she'd seen anything, but of course she hadn't. Funny that. She always notices what goes on.'

'How old is Princess?'

'She's only a baby. I got her three months ago from a breeder. She's beautiful.' Susanne pulled out her mobile and passed it to Ross. The screensaver was of a Staffordshire bull terrier looking up at the camera, a soft toy in its mouth. 'Isn't she gorgeous? She's got the nicest nature too. She's even nicer than Dolly.' She looked through the pictures, a sad smile on her face. 'Dolly saw me through some really rough patches. I suffer from depression and she was my lifesaver. That's why I got Princess.' She stood up abruptly and walked across to the kitchen worktop where she pulled out a tissue from a box and blew her nose. 'Want a coffee or anything?'

'Coffee would be great. No sugar. My missus has me on a permanent diet. Thinks I'm going to get diabetes if I have so much as a teaspoon.'

She filled the kettle and reached for two pink mugs. 'Princess helps me stay on top of it, or I'd give up and top meself. I had to have Dolly put to sleep six months ago. Worst thing ever.' Her hand hovered over a ceramic jar marked 'Teabags'. 'I bloody hated it, saying goodbye to her. It's like losing your best friend.' She drew out two bags and dropped them into the mugs. 'Oh, bloody hell! You said coffee, didn't you?' She took out the bag and spooned in some coffee.

Ross threw her a smile. She returned it, weakly. 'I know Staffies get bad press, but honestly they're playful, good with children and have got super temperaments. I wouldn't have any other breed. Princess is perfect. She's a loyal companion. I can't face being without her, Mr Cunningham.'

'Call me Ross.'

She nodded vaguely, as if only half-registering his voice. 'You will find her, won't you?'

'I'll certainly do my best.'

'You've found missing pets before. I saw on your website. My Lauren found it for me. She's been out asking all the neighbours but no one's seen anything. Mind you, they don't think much of us so would probably say they'd seen nuffin' even if Princess was in their front room. We've had a few run-ins over the years. My old man, Trevor, was one for speaking his mind. He offended just about everyone on this street. He had a gob on him and a temper.'

'He no longer with you?'

'Nah, did a runner six months ago. Pissed off with some tart he met. Can't say I was that upset. He wasn't the easiest bloke to live with. I don't know how I stuck it so long. Left me hometown to come to this rathole. I'd go back in a heartbeat, but I can't afford it.'

'So, you're not from Derby?'

Her eyebrows rose in surprise. 'You havin' a laugh? Can't you tell by me accent? Course I'm not from round here. I'm from London. Lived here the last four years. Came here in 2013, when Lauren was fourteen. I don't know how I'll manage without her, Mr Cunningham. She helps me cope.'

'Ross,' he insisted. 'I'll start with the neighbours.'

'Lauren asked everyone in the street, but I can't believe they didn't see anything. They're a right nosy bunch here.'

'They might open up to me. It's got to be where we start. Let's see how I get on with them and then we'll try and narrow down what's happened to Princess.'

She regarded him with light-grey eyes that seemed to have all the colour sucked out of them. Susanne needed his help. She was a woman on the edge and Ross hoped he could help save her.

CHAPTER FIVE

Robyn limped into her office and dropped onto her seat with a faint groan. The hip injury was giving her grief. She would have to ice it again.

Shearer appeared from nowhere, his chin unshaven. 'You look rough.'

'Looked in the mirror?'

'Somebody got out of the wrong side of bed this morning,' he quipped. 'I always look this rough. It comes with the job. So, you heard about our find.'

'DCI Flint has been filling me in. No drugs?'

He shook his head. 'I'm about to question the bloke we brought in again. He claims he knows nothing about any gang and was just out for a jog when the car stopped next to him. He says he went to see what the driver wanted and was yanked inside, then chucked out after they lost the squad car. I don't believe him. He got in that Audi pretty smartish. I'm going to try and convince him to chat to me.' He gave a tight smile that didn't reach his cornflower-blue eyes. 'Get all pally with him and make him understand it isn't worth keeping schtum for a bunch of scumbag drug dealers.' He cracked his knuckles and stretched his fingers.

'Arthritis? Must be your age,' she said.

'Oh, we are being scathing today. Thought you'd be pleased to be getting your teeth into a juicy case.'

Robyn sighed. 'Yeah, sorry. I'm being snarky. Hope you get a result.' She knew she shouldn't be taking her frustrations out on

Shearer, as irritating as he was. It wasn't his fault her hip hurt, or that she felt needled every time she spoke to DCI Richard Flint. She ought to get a grip.

'Right, I'm off to crack a hard nut. Good luck with the body.'

Shearer disappeared as quickly as he had arrived, leaving behind a not unpleasant smell of aftershave. He passed Anna Shamash outside the door and mumbled something at her. She answered, then slipped into the room and shut the door behind her. Her eyes were two deep hollows and her full lips were set in a grim line. 'Afternoon, boss.'

Robyn raised her head and took in Anna's appearance. 'I guess a night in the babe magnet with Shearer was as bad as I imagined it would be.'

'Worse. He's not exactly Mr Charismatic at the best of times, and his car seats have to be the most uncomfortable I've ever sat in. I still can't straighten up properly.

'Interesting Monday morning though?'

'It wasn't what any of us expected.'

'I've got to speak to the pathologist. Fancy a ride? You can fill me in on it all.'

'I'm supposed to write up a report for DCI Flint, then I'm off duty.'

Robyn gathered up her car keys, shrugged on her coat and stood by the door, hand poised to open it. 'I'm sure he'll understand if you slip off early. You can brief me on this before you go home. Have you had any lunch?'

Anna shook her head. 'Been no time for any. We had to wait for forensics and examine the area. Mitz bought burgers and a Happy Meal for Shearer. I didn't fancy anything.'

A smile tugged at the corners of Robyn's mouth. 'A Happy Meal?'

Anna chuckled. 'Yeah, he ate it too and attached the Super Mario toy that came with it to his car dashboard. I suppose he's not all bad.'

'Come on. Let's go grab a coffee and sandwich next door.'

*

The coffee house along from the station was quiet, with only a few customers and Craig the barista cleaning the spouts on the coffee machine. He acknowledged them with a wave of his cloth. Robyn placed an order for them, leaving Craig to carry it over.

'Forensics reckon she'd been there a few months. She was wrapped in a plastic bag and bundled up under sheets.' Anna wrinkled up her nose. 'She was mostly dried out but her body was covered with a grey wax.'

'It's called corpse wax,' replied Robyn. 'Technically it's known as adipocere. It's made up of saturated fatty acids.'

Craig arrived with the coffees and sandwiches. Anna ripped the top off a sugar packet, tipped the contents into the cup and stirred. Froth and chocolate topping swirled together.

'Yes, Harry McKenzie told me the same. I'd not come across it before. It was all a bit gruesome really and quite a shock. There we were, expecting a stash of heroin, and suddenly we had a pair of sightless eyes staring up at us.' She unwrapped her submarine roll, bit into it and chewed slowly. Anna swallowed. 'Harry McKenzie was thorough.'

Robyn sipped her coffee, simultaneously nodding in approval. 'One of the finest pathologists we've had. He's expecting me in an hour. You want to join us and learn a little more about forensics and how the girl died?'

'It beats writing reports.' Anna cricked her neck from side to side. 'How do you do it?' she asked.

'Do what?'

'Keep going? I've been out all night and I'm done in, ready to crawl into bed, yet you and Shearer, you always manage to pull twenty-hour shifts and keep going like you're powered by Duracell batteries or something.'

'Coffee and adrenalin. That's what works for me. I can't vouch for Shearer.'

'Sweets, I suppose. He chomped his way through three bags of them while we were out.'

'There you go.'

'I'll have to change my diet.' She finished the sandwich with one last bite, then licked her fingers. 'I needed that. Thanks, boss.'

Robyn pulled a piece of her own cheese sandwich off and popped it into her mouth. The cheese was flavourless; soft, rubbery goo. She forced it down and sipped her coffee again. She didn't fancy the food but it was always best to have something before going to the pathologist's. Some officers preferred an empty stomach but Robyn had found quite the opposite worked for her. She had seen many cadavers, and although death didn't frighten her, she would never become oblivious to it. These bodies, life now sucked from them, had been living souls at one point. She drained her cup of the remnants of chocolate-covered froth.

Anna tipped back her own cup and, smacking her lips, pointed at Robyn's sandwich. 'You not hungry?'

'It's a bit tasteless. I should have chosen the chicken like you.'

'If the offer's still open, I'd like to come and see Harry McKenzie with you. I don't feel so tired now and I'd like to know more about the victim.'

'Spoken like a true police officer.' Robyn stood up, waves of pain through her pelvis making her wince.

Harry McKenzie moved nimbly around the table. On it lay the girl from the trunk. Her hands were slightly clenched, flakes of bright-pink varnish still visible on her nails. The skin was badly decomposed and had peeled in many places, exposing bone on her forehead and high cheekbones. Her full lips, shrunken slightly in death, were parted to reveal even white teeth, and above her high forehead, dark, short hair that had once shone with health and even now retained its corkscrew curls. Robyn sighed gently. The girl had been beautiful.

Harry was in his element, explaining everything to Anna who soaked up every detail, her pupils dilated, mouth slightly open. Robyn listened to the pair of them, Harry with his round, owl-like glasses perched on his head, explaining with wild gestures how he had ascertained that the body was that of a teenage girl.

'The main indicator is the pelvis,' he began, long fingers pointing at the hips of the girl on the table. 'A female's pelvis is a different shape to a male's. And an examination of the symphysis pubis, the joint where the bones meet,' he said, noting Anna's frown, 'along with other bones in her body, helped estimate her age.'

Anna nibbled at her bottom lip, keen to understand more.

'How can you tell someone's age from bones? I don't understand.'

Harry pointed towards the clavicle visible through parchment-dry skin. Robyn stared at the girl, skin peeled from her face like wisps of tissue paper, perfect teeth grinning as if waiting for a camera shutter to fall. Harry continued, 'Bones grow throughout a child's development. They start growing in the womb but don't fully form until adulthood. The development of this girl's bones is not yet complete. I would put her at about sixteen years old.'

Robyn dragged her attention away from the yellowed corpse. 'Has she been dead long?'

Harry's head wobbled from side to side. 'Her body has been protected from insect activity and scavengers, so that along with the adipocere has helped with its preservation.'

'I thought this substance didn't occur unless a body was in water.' Anna's eyes were huge in the dim lighting of the morgue. Harry shook his head.

'Normally, but the plastic bag she was found in must have provided a moist enough environment. There's also evidence that her body had been kept in cold storage – frozen. When it defrosted droplets of water would have formed around it.'

Robyn circled the table. Although the remains were in a better state than if they had been buried, the girl's face was still unrecognisable. Her mind churned the information. The body had been frozen before it was moved to the trunk. Robyn wondered if it had no longer been safe to keep her hidden in cold storage. Such freezers could be found in restaurants or places where meat was kept frozen. Had the girl worked in such an establishment?

Harry gave a cough to clear his throat. 'In this case, death occurred approximately five or six months ago. I'd say sometime between mid-July and mid-August last year.'

Robyn cocked her head to one side. 'Any idea of how she died?'

'It's difficult to be accurate, given the level of decomposition.' He peeled back a piece of diaphanous skin. 'There appear to be superficial wounds to the forehead and other marks on her body, but they could have occurred after death. A sharp implement might have caused the wounds or she might have cut her head through falling against a sharp surface. This is what actually killed her.' He pointed to the wound in the lower part of the front of her neck. 'The trachea, both the carotids and the oesophagus have been severed,' he said. 'I believe the cause of death is a cut-throat injury by a sharp-edged weapon.'

Robyn crossed her arms and studied the body one more time. Could she have worked in a restaurant and been attacked there, then hidden in a large freezer? Or had she been murdered and secreted in a home chest freezer, big enough for a body this size? They were both possibilities.

Anna spoke slowly, as if still processing all the information. 'So, our victim is a sixteen-year-old girl, who had her throat cut five or six months ago, was wrapped in a plastic bag, frozen for some time, then removed from cold storage and placed in a sealed trunk in a privately rented storage unit.'

Harry pulled his spectacles down from his forehead and covered the body with a sheet. 'That's pretty much it. I'll have a full report sent to you as soon as possible. I've requested dental records for identification, so you should get a name soon. Now, if you'll forgive me, I must get on.'

Outside, weak rays of sun pierced through the grey sky.

Anna, in a pensive mood, glanced up and blinked as they left the hospital. 'My gran used to say sunbeams were ladders from heaven. I never understood if the ladders were for people to climb into heaven or for those in heaven to be thrown out and land here.'

Robyn breathed in deeply. The smell of death had permeated her nostrils and left its taste in her mouth. She understood that it was never easy dealing with death and Anna had done well.

'Want a lift home?'

Anna looked at her watch. 'Thanks. That'd be good. I haven't seen Razzle since yesterday. I'll pick him up from my mum's and take him for a walk. It'll help take my mind off that poor girl.'

'Good idea. Then get a good night's sleep and come back in tomorrow, ready to catch whoever did this to her. Direct your energies into helping me track down her killer.'

Anna stared out at the road. 'I shall. I just don't know how you can do all of this, day after day.'

'Motivation. Once you feel like that, you always keep going. From what I've seen of your work so far, you'll do well. You need to harden up a little, develop a thicker skin.'

'Is that why you wanted me to come to the morgue – to see the body?'

'I hoped you'd experience what I experience when I become involved in cases like this.'

Anna thought for a moment, then spoke earnestly, her face filled with concern. 'I want to do right by her. I want to seek justice for her and for her family. Standing there, looking at her broken body, discarded like it was rubbish, I got to know her better. She was just a kid, probably at school or just out of school, with a life in front of her, a life that was taken by someone. Now, I want to track them down and bang them to rights.'

'Then you're motivated.' Robyn winked at her colleague.

CHAPTER SIX

The traffic was beginning to build, heavy for a Monday afternoon, as they left the hospital and joined the A50 out of Stoke-on-Trent and headed towards Cheadle where Anna lived.

Anna fell silent on the journey home, pulling absent-mindedly at a wisp of dark hair that had escaped the twisted ponytail style she wore. Stern-faced as ever, with clear almond eyes and dark eyebrows, she exuded an air of sadness. No doubt she was digesting what she had seen and heard. Robyn admired her pluck and the fact she hadn't flinched at the sight of the body but instead asked pertinent questions. She left Anna to her thoughts, grateful she was part of her dedicated team.

Anna's home was a semi-detached brick house with a decent frontage laid to lawn. It was at the end of a road of properties that looked identical.

'Thanks, guv. See you tomorrow. Best go collect Razzle. That is if he hasn't been so spoilt by my mum that he refuses to come home.' She strolled up her path, pausing only to turn and lift a hand in thanks.

It was getting close to 5 p.m. so Robyn decided to drive into Uttoxeter and head back to Stafford on the A518, a more scenic route, although there was little to see now other than the soft glow from houses dotted along the roadside. It was more appealing than jostling with lorries on the dual carriageway again. She wasn't in the mood for the radio so selected a CD of piano concertos and let her mind wander as Beethoven's fifth floated through the speakers.

It was Davies who had got her into classical music. She had an eclectic taste in music, her collection filled mostly with various artists from the eighties and an array of more modern artists including, ironically, The Killers, something that had always amused him. Davies, whose radio was always tuned to classical stations, had encouraged her to listen to his favourites. He maintained classical music was better for the brain – a claim she could never be sure was fact or fiction. Robyn was no longer sure if she listened to the music these days because she really liked it, and believed it enhanced her thought processes, or because it reminded her of Davies…

Davies, head back in his chair, eyes closed, a pen in his hand and the crossword open on his knee. Mozart's Piano Concerto No. 23 is playing and his head nods gently in time to the music. It is one of his favourite pieces. She lifts the paper and his eyes open sleepily.

'Hello. Didn't hear you come in,' he says.

She slips onto his knee and wraps her arms around his neck and kisses him.

They sit for a while, entwined as the music serenades them. Her heart feels light. Life couldn't be better.

Streetlights flooded the pavements, and huddled figures scurried against the cold to get home to their warm houses. She was thinking about the girl in the trunk when she spotted a figure she recognised. It was Florence Hallows, in school uniform with a large backpack on her shoulders and carrying a couple of plastic bags. Robyn slowed the car to a halt, wound down her window and called out. The girl's head pulled up with a jerk and she wandered across to the Golf.

'Hey,' said Robyn. 'Bought anything nice?' she asked, pointing at the bags. Florence blushed.

'Just underwear,' she replied. 'Needed a new bra.'

Robyn nodded. She didn't want to embarrass the girl. Growing up could be difficult. 'Your mum with you?'

Florence shook her head. 'Working.'

'How are you getting home?'

'Bus. I usually catch the bus,' Florence replied.

The idea worried Robyn. Rosy-cheeked Florence was so young and vulnerable, and about to walk alone to the bus stop. The image of the girl in the trunk flickered in her mind. 'Hop in. I'll drive you home,' she said. There was no way she wanted Florence to go home alone in the dark even if it was only 5 p.m.

Florence hesitated for a second, then threw her backpack onto the back seat and climbed into the front where she clutched the plastic bags.

'Thanks. You didn't have to,' she said. 'I could've caught the bus. That's what I usually do.'

'It's no trouble. I'm looking for a good excuse to stay away from the station,' said Robyn with a grin. She liked Florence, who usually had a cheerful face and bubbly personality to match. This Monday afternoon she was more subdued.

'How's school?' Robyn asked.

Florence shrugged, a typical teenage gesture. Robyn mentally chastised herself for asking such a dull question. She changed the subject. 'Amélie said you fancied watching *A Street Cat Named Bob* this Thursday.'

'Yeah, it sounds good. Everyone's talking about it on Facebook. Besides, it has to be good – it's got a cat in it that's ginger – a ginger cat that saves a drug addict.' She shook her own strawberry-blonde hair. 'Ginger saves the day.'

Robyn smiled. Florence often joked about being ginger, although this time her smile was tighter than usual. In the past she had been teased about her hair colour. Robyn wondered if that were still the case.

'It's based on a true story, you know?' Florence looked down at her iPhone that had flashed up a message. She read it and put the phone down in her lap. She carried on talking. 'There's a book too but I'd prefer to watch the film version.' She wrinkled her nose at the thought of reading.

'Bob,' said Robyn. 'That's a great name for a cat.'

Florence agreed. 'It's sort of funny, isn't it? If I had a ginger cat, I'd call it something like Amber or Apricot.'

'Or Apricat,' said Robyn, waiting for a smile. Florence managed one. She fell silent and fiddled with her mobile, pressing keys with a dexterity Robyn could only dream of. Robyn turned on the radio, tuning it to Radio 1. Florence gave her a smile.

'I like this song,' she said. 'It's Ed Sheeran. His latest album's really good. He's pretty cool too. Did you know, he used to wear glasses, have a stutter and was teased about his ginger hair? Now he's a famous pop star and loads of girls fancy him.' She looked out of the window into the darkness. Robyn guessed she was busy drawing parallels, and wondered again if the teasing had stopped. Maybe Amélie could throw some light on the matter.

She sang along, and for a while she was the cheerful Florence that Robyn knew, but as soon as the song drew to an end she returned her attention to her phone and began thumbing another message.

Robyn turned into the dark lane towards The Stables, on the outskirts of Doveridge, only three miles from Uttoxeter, but in the opposite direction she wanted to travel. The large farmhouse was in darkness, but the stables and riding arena beyond were lit up with huge floodlights. Several riders were trotting, backs ramrod straight, bouncing up and down. The horses obediently responded to their instructions, clouds of warm air puffing from their nostrils. Robyn recognised Christine Hallows leaning on the fence, dressed in jeans and Barbour jacket, watching the riders and calling instructions out to them. She had no idea her daughter had just come home.

'Thanks, Robyn,' said Florence. She twisted around to grab her backpack and hauled it over the seat onto her lap.

'Not a problem. Looks heavy. You got a lot of homework?'

Florence nodded. 'Science and English. Not my favourite subjects.'

'Get some food and then tackle them,' said Robyn.

'I had a sandwich in town. I'll get on with it straight away. Thanks again. See you on Thursday.'

'I'll look forward to seeing Bob,' replied Robyn with a smile.

Florence got out of the car and headed for the front door, let herself in, and disappeared from view. Robyn reversed the Golf, turned it around and drove away. She checked her rear-view mirror and noticed a light come on upstairs and wondered if it was healthy to let Florence have such a free rein. Christine and Grant adored their daughter, but a small voice in Robyn's head disapproved of the fact they weren't around for the girl. It didn't seem right that Florence was so independent. She was only thirteen. She shook her head. She was becoming a fuddy-duddy in her old age. It wasn't for her to judge Florence's parents. They had to earn a living and they were at least on site with their work.

Robyn left the lane and with it all thoughts of Florence. The car gave a growl as she accelerated down the main road towards Stafford. She'd spent more time than she intended away from the office and needed to get back. The girl in the trunk had to be identified and a killer had to be brought to justice.

CHAPTER SEVEN

DAY TWO – TUESDAY 17 JANUARY

The next morning saw the office full of uniforms, and the air thick with sweat and testosterone. Thirty-year-old PC David Marker, wide-shouldered like a rugby-player, rubbed at the dark stubble on his chin and punched at the coffee machine buttons, grumbling loudly as thick black coffee spluttered into his paper cup. Mitz Patel was on the telephone, face screwed up in concentration, scribbling in a notepad. Sergeant Matt Higham, dark circles under his eyes, struggled to remove his stab vest in the small space and then threw it with an exasperated sigh onto his chair.

'Bloody lying little toerag,' said Matt for the third time. 'I hope Shearer rips his balls off when he locates him.'

'For goodness' sake, calm down, Matt.' Robyn pushed her way to her desk. 'Shouldn't you all be in Shearer's office? He's running the Towers drugs case, not me.'

David spoke up. 'Thought we'd be better off here. He's not best pleased with the operation. That little shit we picked up gave us false information. That's the second load of crap info we've had on this case, and another ridiculously early start to the day. I'm rapidly becoming sleep-deprived. Someone is giving us a right runaround.' He thumped the coffee machine.

Robyn raised her voice. 'Pack it in. You'll break it. I know you're unhappy, but taking it out on my machine isn't the answer.'

'Boss, this is for you.' Mitz passed a piece of paper over.

Robyn's lips set in a thin line as she read it. 'Okay, you lot. I've got work to do here, so unless you can settle down, go outside and let off some steam. Anna, check this name out for me. The usual social media sites, all that sort of thing. I want to know everything you can find out about her.'

Mitz sat down. 'Need a hand? I don't think we'll be needed for a while.' As he spoke, Shearer bellowed down the corridor.

'Matt, get your arse in here and bring David with you.'

Matt grabbed his jacket.

'Action stations again. Come on, David. Let's see what his lordship wants now.' The pair clattered down the corridor. Mitz shrugged.

'Looks like I've been let off.'

'In that case, can you check this name out for me, instead of Anna, and give me all the details you can about the self-storage warehouse – how it operates, how many units there are, owner, users. Everything you think is relevant. I want to talk to the owner. Anna, you'd better come with me. We have to visit her family and break the news.'

Robyn drove in silence wondering what she was going to say to the deceased girl's family. The bored voice of the satnav said: 'Turn left in one hundred yards.' She seemed to have been driving down similar roads for ages, with endless terraced houses painted in a miserable grey next to equally drab brown houses that added to the impression of misery, poverty and depression. As she passed a community centre, Robyn recognised the name of the street. She was almost at her destination. In front of them, an old man trundled along the road on a mobility scooter, blanket across his knees, woollen hat pulled low over his head. She didn't blast her horn at him. The pavement was broken, uneven and so full of holes he would tumble down one if he used it.

She passed a fish and chip shop and searched for a parking space. Number 143 was sandwiched between a house with large grey false stone walls that might have been popular in the seventies but looked hideous in 2017, and a red brick house with a plastic white door and window frames. The doorbell was answered by a diminutive woman whose head seemed disproportionately large, an impression created by the sizeable Velcro rollers in her hair. She narrowed her eyes with their lengthy, dark eyelashes coated in black mascara, and pursed her crimson-red lips. 'Yes?'

'We're looking for Mr Vincent Miller. Is he at home?'

The woman nodded; her hair rollers bounced on her head.

'I'm DI Robyn Carter. This is PC Anna Shamash. Could I come in for a moment?' Robyn and Anna held out warrant cards for the woman, who appeared to deflate. 'It's about Carrie, isn't it?' she said, her voice barely above a whisper.

'Please can we come in and talk?'

'What's the stupid cow done now? He'll go off on one if she's been banged up.' She held open the door and beckoned Robyn in.

'She's always been a bloody problem. It's been so much better since she cleared off. No more arguments, no more tantrums. It's drugs, isn't it? She hung about with the wrong crowd. They get up to all sorts here: glue, E, alcohol. It was a full-time job keeping her in control. He did his best but she's headstrong. Bit like her old man. I warned Vince that she'd screw up.' The woman kept talking, her hands now patting her pockets. She pulled out a lighter and a pack of cigarettes, tapped one out and held it to her lips. 'I'm right, aren't I? She okay?'

'Are you Mrs Miller?'

The woman shook her head. 'I'm his partner. Leah.'

'Leah, could you fetch Mr Miller please?'

'Oh, yeah. Sure. He was up late last night. He's still in bed. Hang on. I'll get him.'

She disappeared, leaving the officers in the modern kitchen. The sink was full of crockery yet to be washed. A plastic red bowl bearing the name 'Tiger' was beside the sink, a small, grey piece of meat and unidentifiable scraps in it. A strong smell of garlic permeated the kitchen, making Robyn feel queasy.

'You okay?' she whispered to Anna, whose face had lost some of its colour.

'Fine. Not sure where to put myself. I feel awkward,' said Anna.

'Think about something else – Razzle, anything. Best not to focus on the moment.'

Just as Robyn was beginning to wonder if they'd be there all morning, there was a thud above her and floorboards creaking as Vince moved about the room. Eventually he appeared. Dressed in grubby jeans and a crumpled sweatshirt that hung on his skinny frame, face unshaven, grey stubble pushing through sallow skin, he gazed bleary-eyed at them. 'What's she gone and done?'

'Mr Miller, I'm DI Robyn Carter and this is PC Anna Shamash.'

'I don't care who you are. Just tell me what Carrie's got involved with and get this over with. I've only had two hours' sleep and I have to go back on shift again later. Got to drive all the way to bloody Gatwick, then Swansea and back to Birmingham, so I'm not in a "hello my name is…" mood.'

Robyn gazed at him with clear eyes that she hoped radiated the compassion she felt. 'Mr Miller, would you like to sit down for a minute?'

'No, I bloody wouldn't. Just spit it out, will you?'

Robyn didn't want to break such dreadful news with such animosity radiating from the man. 'Sir, please sit down.'

As comprehension filtered through his brain, he flopped onto the chair. Robyn spoke quietly. 'Sir, the body of a young girl, who we believe to be your daughter Carrie, was discovered today. I'm really so sorry to give you this awful news.'

The woman let out a small cry and folded against the kitchen drawers. 'No! It can't be her.'

Vince straightened his shoulders and gave an imperceptible shake of his head. He cleared his throat, tried to speak, cleared it again, the aggression he had initially displayed now drained from him. He appeared to shrink before Robyn's eyes. 'How can you be sure it's her?'

'Mr Miller, it is Carrie. She was identified using her dental records.'

Leah groaned. 'Oh, God!'

Anna crossed over to her. 'Would you like me to make you a cup of tea or anything?'

Leah shook her head. Vince didn't move. His eyes flittered from the table to the bowl, to the cooker and back. 'How?'

'We believe she was murdered, sir. I'm so sorry.'

'You're sorry,' he said. '*You're* sorry.' He spat the first word. 'No, you're not. She's no one important to you. She's just a body. But not to me.' His face contorted and his hands began to shake as if they had a life of their own. 'She's my little girl. She's everything to me! I don't believe you. It isn't her. I'm going to bloody well ring her and prove you're wrong. There's a mix-up. It isn't her. It can't be.' He stabbed at the keys on his phone and held it to his ear, repeated the action and then gave up.

'Where did you find her?' he asked.

'Rugeley. Her body was discovered in a self-storage unit there.'

'When?'

'Yesterday. We came here as soon as we'd identified her.'

His voice trembled. 'How? How did she die? Tell me. I want to know.'

Robyn hesitated before replying. 'We believe she was attacked with a knife.'

He nodded, digesting the news, then spoke very softly. 'What are you going to do about this?'

'Everything we can, Mr Miller.'

As if a magician had waved a wand over him, his emotions changed. Aggression replaced the sorrow. 'If you don't find out who did this, I will, and then you'll have to take me in. If I ever get my hands on him, I'm going to smash him to a bloody pulp.'

CHAPTER EIGHT

Amber no longer knew if it was day or night. She didn't know how long she had been lying on the mattress. The bucket in the corner of the room stank of urine and excrement. He had left it there for her and at first she had refused to use it, but eventually she had needed to and had crouched over the plastic pot, sobbing and hoping he wasn't watching her.

The hospital gown didn't afford any warmth, so she had tucked herself under the sheet on the bed to try to keep off the cool air that wafted against her spine. He was crazy and he was going to kill her. She had cried so many tears she had none left, her face now a dried mess of mucus. Eventually she had dozed for a while and dreamt of home; of being snuggled under her goose-feather filled duvet with its scent of summer flowers, a fabric conditioner her mum used in every wash. She woke with a start. There was no smell of summer flowers, only the foul stink in the corner of the room. She would like to cover the bucket up but she had felt about the room and knew it by heart, and there was nothing she could use.

To her left was the locked door. If she continued along the wall for three paces, there was an oak desk that she couldn't lift. She had fumbled about searching for drawers in it, hoping to use them as weapons, but they'd been removed. There was nothing apart from dust that got into the creases of her hands, raw from scrabbling around on the floor, trying to feel her way. Turning left again, and side-stepping seven paces, she would come across the stinking bucket, taking care not to kick it each time. Left again would take her past the mirror where she had seen what he had done to her ruined face, and back to the bed. The room was a prison. She whimpered quietly. No one could hear her. She had pounded on the door for ages, calling and screaming, but no one had come.

She sat up, feet on the floor, stilling her hammering heart. There had to be a way out. It couldn't be a sealed room. If it were sealed, no air could get in. There had to be a vent for the air. She stood and once more felt her way to the door, hands moving up and down, hunting for a boarded-up window or anything that would give her hope.

A shuffle. A rattling of metal. He'd returned. Hopes of escape perished as she heard the lock click. She shrank onto the bed, winding the sheet around her. The door sprang open and shut immediately. He was wearing a cycling helmet with a bright light mounted on it, its beam darting around the room like a giant imprisoned firefly. It blinded her when she tried to look at him. She gave up and looked away.

'Amber,' he called softly, in a voice so like her mother's. She felt a sob rise in her throat. She would never see her mother again.

'Oh, Amber. Come out, come out, wherever you are.'

Now he was whispering in a sinister fashion. It was to frighten her further. Fear was replaced by irritation.

'I'm not hiding. I'm on the bed.'

'I know.'

In that instant, she decided she wasn't going to show any more fear. He could screw himself.

'My parents will be looking for me. My father is very influential. He's got friends in high places, including the police force. They'll have most of the force out hunting for me and you won't get away with this.'

He sucked his teeth. A glimmer of hope rose in her chest. He was thinking about what she'd said. 'And if I let you go, you promise not to tell anyone about me?'

She felt her spirits lift. 'No. I won't tell a soul, I promise. I'll say I got lost in the woods or I crashed out at a friend's house.'

He digested her words. She wriggled on the bed, trying to get comfortable. The flesh on her head was raw and stinging badly, and her limbs felt so weak, like she'd aged overnight. Still she waited. She wanted to see her dad and mum again so badly it hurt. She would never be so stupid again. If he gave her the chance to make amends, she would. She'd be the perfect daughter. His silence offered hope. Then came soft giggles that turned into loud, cruel laughter..

'Good try, Amber, but your mummy and daddy are away for a week. They caught the plane to Faro. Don't you remember? You stayed at home all alone, a grown-up girl who didn't need anyone to watch over her.'

'They'll be worried that I haven't contacted them. They'll have come home to see what's happened,' she said, a sob sticking in her throat.

'I don't think so.' Material rustled and suddenly a mobile lit up. She knew it was hers. She recognised the screensaver showing her and her best friend, Sam, sticking out their tongues, breasts straining in tight tops, colourful earrings dangling and eyes shining. They were laughing. They'd been to the pub and lied about their ages, drinking until closing time, and then on the way back to Sam's house they'd posed for the selfie. She barely recognised the pretty girl in the picture. She touched her sensitive forehead, fingertips grazing the wound, and winced. She wasn't pretty any more.

'Hi, Mum, glad you're having a fabby time. Don't worry about anything. It's all good here. Love you. Amber.' The whispered voice mocked her.

'Hi, Mum. I remembered to put the bin out. Don't fuss. Have fun. Love, Amber.' He sniggered again.

'See, Mummy and Daddy think you're being a good little girl. Now, let's look through these photos and decide which one we like best. Which one do you think?'

She hated the way he whispered everything. Was this to frighten her further? She was preparing to tell him to stop it when he suddenly dropped down beside her on the bed. It gave a little under their combined weight. He was so close she felt heat emanating from his body and the smell that always accompanied him. Before, his scent had seemed so sensual, a musky smell that had excited her. Now it made her want to gag. She edged away, but he gripped her wrist as he thumbed through the photograph collection on her mobile. Each picture made her heart ache further. She would give anything to be that girl in the photographs again.

'I don't like any of these. They're too false. Like you're trying too hard. Look how tarty you are in them.' He stood up. She thought he might be leaving again but instead he trained his torch beam on her, leaving her blinking in the light. 'Come on, Amber, say cheese.'

CHAPTER NINE

Florence Hallows shook her thick hair back and pouted, angling the mobile so it made her breasts look bigger and her waist narrower, and then clicked. She then sat on her bed and checked the photos she had taken. She didn't like any of them. Other girls on the website looked so seductive, their pouting lips made them look sexy. She, however, looked more like a frog blowing a raspberry. She tossed the mobile on the bed and dropped to her knees in front of a chest of drawers. In the bottom drawer she felt for the package secreted under her knickers, the one she had been carrying when Robyn had spotted her. When she'd asked what was in the bag, she'd reddened. There was no way she could've explained it away. The tissue rustled between her fingers as she withdrew it.

She rose and checked the door was locked. The last thing she needed was her mother rolling in as she sometimes did, for no apparent reason other than to 'chat' to her daughter and pretend she was interested in her life. She certainly wouldn't approve of her daughter's plan, but mums never did. Everyone online moaned about his or her parents. Florence thought she fared better than most, given that her parents treated her like an adult, and spent lots of time at the stables with their horses, leaving Florence to pretty much amuse herself. She often got exasperated by her mother's attempts to be 'cool' and ask Florence endless questions about her life, however, even though she didn't really understand a teenager's world.

Her mum had no idea what it was like to be young. She'd caught Florence watching the reality show *The Only Way is Essex* and made comments that it didn't seem real and it certainly wasn't like that 'in her day'. Florence ignored her. The people on the show were real, not actors – glamorous, beautiful girls with gorgeous boyfriends. She watched all the reality shows. Her favourite was *Ex on the Beach*. What she'd give to have a perfect body like the girls on that show. She was ready for a boyfriend. She looked and acted much older than other girls her age. The problem was that there was no way she'd find a boyfriend among the dorks in her class. They were so juvenile they made her want to throw up. Now and again, she'd hang around the stables, in the hope of there being some male riders. So far, those she'd spotted hadn't been her type. The boys Florence fancied were older and would never date someone her age, even if she did have nice boobs.

Florence laid the package on the bed and teased out the garments inside, feeling the delicate lace that could so easily rip. Did she dare? She lifted the red bra and held it against her body, then dropped it back on the bed, shimmied out of her jeans and undergarments and slipped on the bra and matching hipster short set. She adopted various poses in front of the mirror, leaning forward, finger on lips, then arms above her head, followed by hands on hips, one leg on a chair, and decided she would brave it.

She set the smartphone camera onto its timer setting, placed it on top of the drawers, then, lying on her front on the bed, hands propping her chin, legs crossed behind her, and with pouting lips, she stared at the mobile, waiting for it to take the photograph. She slid across the bed and examined the picture and grinned. It gave the impression she was five years older. She decided she could easily pass for eighteen. There was a hint of breast and a lot of bare legs that appeared to be longer and shapelier than they actually were. It was spot on. She would use this picture. She wriggled out of the underwear, folding it back into the paper and hiding it in the drawer, dressed again and thumbed the phone.

Florence had learnt about the app by accident. Walking over to the science block, she had overheard senior girls discussing it. One of them, Kylie Walker, had been telling the others how she had met a bloke on it who was drop-dead gorgeous and who was going to meet her at the weekend. Florence hung behind them to hear more, and once she discovered the app's name, Fox or Dog, she checked it out for herself. It was easy to join up, even though it was for over eighteens. Fox or Dog was a dating website with an app that was free to use and ensured those who signed up only 'talked to' and met users in their area, covering a radius of twenty miles. At first she'd thought she'd never get away with joining up, but seeing photographs of girls she knew from school who were only a year or two older than her, Florence decided she'd post her first picture. This was her chance to find someone like Pete Wicks from *TOWIE*.

There were rules. Those who used the application had to have a user name, declare they were over eighteen and post their profile photo. Other users would then mark that photo with a fox or a dog emoji depending on how they rated them. Should two people rate each other 'foxy', they could message each other privately. It all looked so exciting to Florence. The only downside was if you got labelled a dog, and users left negative comments on your profile, but Florence wasn't worried about that. The picture she was putting up was the best she had taken and she knew she looked good in it. She checked the time on her phone. It was coming up for eight. She had just enough time to remove her make-up and get ready for school. She'd skip breakfast. Her mum was cleaning the yard and her dad had gone off early. No one would notice. She studied the photograph again and smiled.

She'd chosen her user name already. She'd decided on 'Kitten', which, to her mind, sounded innocent and playful. She uploaded the photograph to her new profile and pressed the accept button. She watched as it appeared on her screen and then blew it a kiss for luck. Maybe this would be her chance to find romance.

CHAPTER TEN

Vince Miller lifted his head from his hands. The whiskers on his unshaven chin were damp with tears.

'I should have called her,' he said softly. Leah put her arm around his shoulders.

'You weren't to know,' she whispered, her face serious. She looked towards Robyn. 'Carrie was independent. She made it quite clear she was done with us. She wouldn't have answered even if we had rung her.'

Vince pushed her arm off roughly. 'Don't say that, Leah.' His voice rose. 'We were to blame. She was probably waiting for me to call. She'd never have left home if I hadn't been so bloody pig-headed.'

Leah stood. 'I'm going outside for a fag. I need to take it all in.'

Vince ignored her. 'It was my fault,' he repeated.

Leah sighed. 'It wasn't his fault. Carrie could be single-minded when she wanted to be,' she said before shutting the door quietly behind her.

Robyn waited for Vince to speak again. He pushed himself up using the arms of the chair and walked to the window where he picked up a china cat from the ledge and rubbed a thumb over it.

'We had a massive row the day she walked out. It was stupid really. She'd been needling Leah all evening. They never saw eye to eye. It was difficult for Carrie after her mum died. It was hard for me too, but I had to be strong for Carrie, and we got by. We did okay really, considering the hours I work. I looked after her and she looked after me. She did the washing and ironing and housework. She'd even make a meal for me when I worked the late shift. We did all sorts of things on my days off. We'd go shopping or watch some daft film on television and eat takeaways.' He rubbed the ornament again before replacing it on the ledge. Outside, two boys raced past the drive, legs a blur. For a moment, he was lost in thought. 'We were really close for a while.'

Robyn gave an encouraging smile. 'When did you lose your wife, Mr Miller?'

He drew a breath. 'Four years ago. Sofia had a stroke. She was at work – she worked at a bakery – and keeled over. By the time the ambulance came, it was too late. She was only forty years old. Even now I still can't believe it happened.'

'A terrible shock for you both,' said Robyn.

'Carrie was in bits to start with but she's a strong girl.' He stopped, remembering his daughter had been murdered. His voice cracked. 'I wish I hadn't been so hard on her that night. She wasn't really a bad kid. It wasn't the first time she'd gone off on one, but I should've contacted her, tried to talk her round. You must think I'm a lousy father.'

Robyn shook her head. 'Not at all. Parenting isn't easy.'

He sniffed back more tears. 'You're not wrong. I managed okay to start with. Losing Sofia brought us closer. I think Carrie was scared she'd lose me too. It took time for her to adjust, but she did. We both did. I thought she was coping, then suddenly she began to change. If I'm honest, it was about the time I met Leah. Carrie started hanging out with wrong'uns at school. She got caught smoking and drinking. The trouble was she always looked older than she was. That was thanks to Sofia's genes. She was from Spain and Carrie got her looks. Sofia was really beautiful. I've got pictures of her.' He plodded to a set of drawers, opened the top one and extracted a framed picture. He passed it to Robyn who could immediately see the likeness in Carrie – she had the same striking cheekbones, large eyes and honeyed skin.

'Leah doesn't like it on display. Not nice having a photograph of the ex-wife staring at you. Carrie had loads of rows about that too. She'd pull out that photo and leave it on the shelf and then Leah would move it back into the drawer. It was an ongoing battle. I hated listening to those two screaming at each other. I love them both, but some days it was too much. Carrie was always complaining and whining about Leah and vice versa.' His shoulders sagged again. 'Maybe if I hadn't met Leah this wouldn't have happened.'

'Did they row often?' Robyn asked.

'Regularly. It got worse last year, and Carrie was a nightmare at times,' he said. 'This wasn't the first time she walked out. She usually came back after a few days. It was nearly always about Leah.'

'It was just verbal arguments though?' Robyn watched his reactions carefully.

'Mouthing off, mostly. One time Carrie threw a plate at Leah but it missed. I heard the smash and went through to find out what was going on, but neither would tell me what had happened.'

'You don't think Leah would do anything to hurt Carrie, do you?'

He shook his head. 'Never. She'd never have harmed her. Don't even go there,' he said, waggling a finger at Robyn.

'No, Mr Miller. I wasn't implying that. I was trying to get an idea of why Carrie left home.'

He took a deep breath, returned to the armchair and dropped into it. 'It was stupid. I'd had a really bad week at work. I'd been on nights, and I'd not slept all day because the pair of them had been yelling and banging doors. I had to drive to Newcastle that night so I wasn't in the best of moods. Carrie was smoking and I had a go at her. I never liked her smoking. Then she said she was going out with some boy I'd never heard of.

'I got a bit heavy-handed and said something about her not going out dressed like a tart. We had a right stand-off.' Tears sprang to his eyes. 'She told me I didn't care about her, and that I thought more about Leah than her, and that I'd never loved Sofia. That if I had, I'd never have let Leah move in. Then she laughed at me. Said I had no idea of what she got up to, and smoking was nothing compared to what else she did. I was furious by now and told her that as long as she lived under my roof she'd behave properly and she'd be more civil to Leah. That was it. She gave me a look that froze my blood. "I shan't be living under your roof any more. I've already made other plans. You can keep your bloody roof and your whore," she said.

'Leah came in and that made matters worse. I ended up telling Carrie to sling her hook until she could learn to keep a civil tongue in her head. She was like a wild cat with claws out, hissing and snarling at Leah. I'd had enough. I was sick to death of the fighting. I couldn't keep the peace any more.'

'But surely, once things had calmed down, you would have wanted to contact her and make sure she was safe?'

He shook his head and tears trickled down his cheeks. 'I almost did on a couple of occasions, but Leah thought Carrie would return when she was ready, like she had before. She'd heard Carrie was still living in the area with a friend who'd been in the same class at school, so I thought it was smarter to wait for her to come round. Fact was, it was much better without Carrie and Leah at each other's throats all day. I didn't want to go back to the cat-fighting. It was easier to let it lie. Can you understand that?'

Robyn let out a soft sigh. 'You must have felt torn between them.'

'I was. I love them both, but Carrie was so difficult to handle. I couldn't bear the thought of Leah leaving me over Carrie. After Sofia died... I didn't want to face another loss like that.' He stopped and choked on a sob. 'But now I've lost my Carrie.' He lowered his head. His shoulders shook as he sobbed quietly. Leah reappeared and dropped down beside him, pulling him towards her and comforting him. Robyn backed away to the window to give the couple some space.

'Could I visit Carrie's old room, please?' Robyn looked at Leah whose eyes were swollen and red.

'Her name's on the door,' she said, quietly.

Robyn left Anna with the couple and climbed the stairs. Carrie's room overlooked the road and was large enough to house a single bed; a cream faux-leather chair with a purple pillow; a recess that acted as a wardrobe, covered by a screen of shimmering, silver fabric; and a white table, cluttered with make-up, shampoo bottles and discarded hair products. The walls were off-white and bore a collage of black and white photographs, a mixture of various high-heeled shoes and hearts – stones and clouds in the shape of hearts, coffee cups with hearts drawn in the foam, and hearts sketched in the sand. She had hung heart-shaped fairy lights above her bed. On it was a purple duvet, clean and ironed, waiting for Carrie to return.

The window sill was filled with boxes in the shape of hearts of all sizes. Robyn picked up the smallest box made of cardboard and opened it. The hooped earrings inside it were cheap; the gilt had lifted on one of them, revealing tarnished metal, but the heart-shaped crystal ones sparkled in the light. The other boxes held various items – nail varnish in outrageous colours, fake nails, hair accessories, a key ring with her name on it, a small, porcelain black cat. Behind the silver curtain hung several outfits: jumpers and T-shirts folded and stashed on shelves, a couple of pairs of shoes and a pair of boots. Either Carrie didn't like the outfits she'd left behind or she'd intended returning.

Robyn's suspicions grew. A photograph of Carrie with her mother rested on the window ledge. If Carrie had really left for good, she'd have taken this picture along with the crystal earrings. She searched in the chest of drawers, pulling open the top one. It was crammed with T-shirts and nightdresses and socks, not arranged as tidily as the clothes behind the curtain. Robyn lifted them out and spied something shining at the back of the drawer. It was a packet of unused condoms. Further investigation revealed a half-smoked packet of cigarettes and a disposable lighter along with a blue velvet box. She lifted the lid, her eyes resting on a necklace made of silver bearing the name Carrie. She returned the clothes, heart heavy. A small cough made her turn around. Leah was staring at her.

'She left because of me, you know?' Leah moved into the bedroom. 'I told Vince I wanted to talk to you. I've left him with your colleague. She seems nice. She's making him a cup of tea.'

Robyn shut the drawer and faced the woman, face still blotchy from crying.

'Would you like to chat downstairs?' she asked.

Leah walked to the window and looked outside. 'No. Here's fine.' She picked up the photograph of Carrie with her mother and studied it. 'I wanted to chuck all her stuff out. Vince told me to leave it alone because she'd come back. That's why the room looks like this. I kept the room clean and tidy, because that's what he wanted, all the while hoping she'd stay away for ever. And now she will. I got my wish and I feel bloody awful about it. I really disliked her. She crawled under my skin and pushed all my buttons, and I wanted to slap her so hard some days. I never did though.'

She faced Robyn. 'She hated me from the day I moved in. She made it clear no one was going to replace her mother and no one was going to get between her and her dad. But I did. Vince and I fell head over heels in love. He believed Carrie would come round eventually, but I knew she wouldn't.'

Leah flopped onto the bed. It was a moment before she spoke again. 'She drove me crazy with her attitude. It was worse when she was with that butch friend of hers – Jade – she's a nasty piece of work too.'

Leah looked at Robyn and shook her head. 'It was a war zone all the time.'

'What happened the night she left, Leah?' Robyn waited by the drawers for Leah to explain.

'She'd been a pain all afternoon, sat in the sitting room, telly on full blast and staring at her bloody mobile phone all the time. I asked her to turn it off because I had a migraine coming. I get them when I'm stressed. She ignored me, so I marched over to it and turned it off. We had a screaming match. She maintained she was watching it, and I said she couldn't have been because she'd been glued to her bloody phone, messaging her stupid friends like she always does. She said at least she had friends and she was going out. She stormed upstairs, which was normal behaviour for her. I went into the kitchen to make a cup of tea.

'What with the row and my headache, I was in such a state I got disorientated and bashed my face on a cupboard I'd left open. It left quite a bruise.' She rubbed at an imaginary mark on her cheekbone. 'That was the final straw. Vince was upstairs, trying to get some sleep before work but I went into our bedroom, pulled out a suitcase from the wardrobe, threw it open on the bed beside him, and started filling it with clothes. Believe me, I'm not proud of my actions but I was desperate. He spotted the bruise and asked me what was going on. I told him Carrie and me had argued and I'd had enough of her. I was leaving. You should have seen his face. He looked so... broken. "I'll talk to her," he said.

'He got the full waterworks from me. I knew he couldn't stand tears. I acted up big time. "It's her or me. Either she begins to show me some respect, or I leave," I said. Vince went to talk to her. The rest he told you.'

A large tear ran down her face. 'He'll always blame himself, won't he? He'll think this is down to him. But it wasn't. I manipulated the situation and caused that final row between them. I *wanted* him to throw her out. I prevented him from phoning her too. I told him I'd heard Carrie was fine and living with her mate Jade, even though I'd heard a rumour she'd moved out.' She lifted her head, eyes red-rimmed and damp. 'All this time, I've been hoping and wishing Carrie would find a new life and never come back. And now she never will.'

CHAPTER ELEVEN

Robyn and Anna left Vince Miller and Leah with a family liaison officer and headed to the storage unit at Rugeley to speak to the owner, Dev Khan. As they approached the Towers Business Park, an eerie blue cloud hid the cooling towers from view, leaving only their tops visible, like huge grey volcanoes rising from some ancient misty valley.

'My mum got a leaflet in the post about this self-storage place about a month ago,' said Anna. 'She kept it on the kitchen worktop for a few days and I made some joke to my dad about it. Asked him if Mum was thinking of depositing anything I should know about.' Anna's father was an ex-policeman and had worked in London. 'He laughed and said, "Only some gold bullion we couldn't find space for in the house." He's such a tease.'

Robyn smiled. Anna was trying to keep it light-hearted but Robyn was wondering why the owner of the self-storage warehouse had not been suspicious about the trunk and why he had sounded offhand on the phone when she'd spoken to him. She hoped he'd be more forthcoming in the flesh.

Dev Khan was waiting outside the warehouse for them, sitting in his van, door open, eyes glued to his smartphone. He pushed it into the pocket of his long, black woollen coat and greeted them. With his collar turned up against the cold and a simple blue scarf wrapped around his neck, dark jeans and shining shoes, he looked like the sharp entrepreneur he was. He punched in the code to the first bay door and waited as it whirred into action. 'I hate this time of the year,' he commented. 'I was hoping to go abroad for a couple of weeks. There's not usually much going on here in January and I could do with some sunshine. But it's been crazily busy since we did a big promo on the place. Did a massive leaflet delivery programme. Cost a fortune, but it was worth it. Nearly all the units are let out in this and all the other warehouses. Great for business, but not for time off in the sunshine.' His strong accent gave away his Mancunian roots, something that was substantiated when Robyn asked how many warehouses he owned.

'Almost fifty. We started in our hometown, Manchester, and we moved into Staffordshire and the Midlands two years ago. It's grown like crazy. It's surprising how many people need extra space. We can cater for all sizes from small boxes, personal stuff – bills, private documents, that sort of thing – to cars, if anyone wants. We've even got a couple of Lamborghinis up in Manchester.'

He flicked on the overhead lights and the corridor in front of them illuminated, revealing shuttered units, left and right. 'DI Shearer said to keep the area empty. Any idea when we can let folk have access to these units again?'

Robyn was taken aback by his attitude. A girl had been found dead in one of his units and he was only interested in re-letting it. 'It shouldn't be much longer. PC Shamash and I would like to look at the unit in question again. Forensics have finished work, and once we've taken a look that should be it. I understand the unit was let to a woman, a Mrs Joanne Hutchinson.'

He nodded energetically. 'That's right. It was before just Christmas. I happened to be here the day she enquired about it. I don't normally show people around but she asked to see a couple of units and I was free.' He shrugged. 'She was in her late thirties, blonde hair, about your height and very slim. She wore pale-blue jeans, a dark-blue leather jacket and a matching headband. I thought she looked rather attractive. She explained she was going through a messy divorce and wanted to store a few bits and pieces of furniture that she didn't want her husband to have – antiques that'd been in her family for years. It was a straightforward arrangement. She paid upfront for three months' rent to allow her time to get moved into her new house. She paid cash because she didn't want her old man to find out where she'd hidden the furniture and valuables.' He caught the look on Robyn's face and explained, 'It happens more often than you think. We see all sorts of strange things in this business. I wasn't here when she deposited her gear but Frank was. Frank's our sort of security guy and keeps an eye on the place. We have CCTV cameras but Frank is here daytimes in case folk need a hand moving their stuff, and to ensure there's a presence about the place.'

'Did she leave you her contact details?' asked Robyn.

Khan flushed. 'She did, and in light of what the police uncovered today, I followed them up only to discover both her telephone number and address were false. I hold my hands up to this. I ought to have run a stricter check on her but I was in a rush that day and she seemed genuinely nice. I had no reason to suspect her of anything peculiar. Her story was plausible and she paid me the money for three months so I didn't think she'd do a runner.' He shrugged.

Anna wrote in her notebook. 'Mr Khan, when Mrs Hutchinson arrived, did you happen to notice her car?'

'No, I was talking to someone in the warehouse when she came inside. I think it was Karl – he's been renting number forty-three since I opened this place. I can give you his number.'

Robyn kept pace with him as he strode down the corridor, stopping outside unit 127. He turned towards her. 'No one's been in since the forensic people left. Look, I'm sorry. I've never had a dead body left in my units before. I'm dreading the media getting wind of it. This is really bad for business.'

'It's worse for the victim's family,' said Robyn, icily.

He bit his lip. 'You're right. I'm being disrespectful. I don't mean to be. I'm an entrepreneur and my businesses are my life. I've been focused on building them up since I was seventeen. They're pretty much all I have. And so I may be coming across as callous. I can assure you, I'm not. This girl's death is terrible. I'm not very good at emotional stuff, that's all. Forgive me.'

She gave a curt nod of her head. 'Could I ask if you keep the CCTV footage?'

'We do.'

'Is there any possibility you'd have footage of Mrs Joanne Hutchinson?'

'I don't know the answer to that. We've got a box that records twenty-four hours a day but erases footage after twenty-eight days. She was here on December eighteenth. I'll ask Frank which day she came in with the trunk, and you're welcome to have the downloaded CCTV footage for the last twenty-eight days. She might have come in again and not been seen by staff.'

He left the women, the heels of his brogues echoing on the concrete floor as he marched back to the exit. The unit was open, cordoned off with yellow tape. Robyn ducked under it and stood at the entrance.

Anna joined her. 'The light wasn't working this morning. It was only a loose fitting. We got it back on for forensics. They checked the entire unit but there were no prints, not even partials.'

Robyn surveyed the room and paced it out. It was about forty square metres in total. It seemed quite a large space for one trunk. She surmised Joanne Hutchinson had not wanted to draw too much attention to herself, and renting a space too small might have done just that and indeed negated the story about storing pieces of furniture and valuables that she'd told Dev Khan.

The trunk stood open in the corner, the smell of the contents still evident. Robyn knelt beside it. 'It seems much longer than a standard storage trunk.'

'We measured it,' Anna replied. She extracted a notebook and read. 'It's 170 centimetres in length, and 80 centimetres high and wide.'

Robyn cocked her head. 'It does seem suspiciously large to me. It might have been custom built. I'd say 170 centimetres is about five foot six. I wonder how tall the victim was. Did she fill it completely?'

'She was turned slightly on her side and there was a sheet tucked in under her feet but yes, she filled the space.'

'I wonder if it was made especially to accommodate her.' Robyn stared at the trunk, lips pursed. 'Okay, I've seen enough. Let's catch up with Mr Khan, and then I'd like to interview the man who helped Joanne Hutchinson in with this trunk, and check out that chap Karl who rents unit forty-three in case he saw her vehicle.'

Back at the yard Khan was talking to a burly man on the loading bay. He waved them over. 'This is Frank. He'll be able to give you what you need. As I suspected, Mrs Hutchinson booked the unit on December eighteenth, so unfortunately we won't have any footage of that day. She moved her belongings in two days later so we might have caught her on camera that day. He looked at his BlackBerry. 'Today's the seventeenth of January, and she moved the trunk here exactly twenty-eight days ago, so we should still have that day's footage recorded. Frank will download it for you, and this is the number for the man who rents unit forty-three, Karl London. If there isn't anything else, I really have to get going.'

'You've been most helpful.'

'My pleasure. Let me know when I can rent out the unit again.' His mobile buzzed and he smiled an apology at the women. He strode away, phone glued to his ear again, and talking non-stop, he slipped into his car and drove off.

Frank was in his fifties – tall, skinny with an unshaven face and hooded eyes. 'This is a dreadful business. It's given me a right case of the jitters. I actually carried that trunk in and I'd no idea what it contained. I feel so responsible. That poor girl.'

'You're not to blame, sir. Can you tell us some more about the woman who dropped it off?'

'I wasn't around when she came the first time but I remember when she brought in that trunk. She called through to me. Said she needed a hand and "would I mind awfully" helping her out. She had a right posh accent. I was in the warehouse fixing a door shutter that had stuck. I went to help. The trunk was on the van and I tugged at it but it was quite long for me to lift on my own. I asked her to grab one end, but she said she couldn't because she'd pulled her back. As it happened, there was a bloke walking past the yard. I shouted him over and he gave me a hand.'

'Can you describe this man?'

Frank threw Robyn a look of incredulity. 'He was a bloke in a beanie hat, coat and trousers. I didn't pay a lot of attention to him because she was busy fussing about telling us not to drop the trunk and all. He came across, took the other end and helped me get it off the van. Mrs Hutchinson said it had to stay flat as it had valuables in it, so we took an end each and carried it into the warehouse for her, put it in her unit, and then he cleared off. I don't remember much about him. I was concentrating on the trunk and not bashing it against the walls.'

'The man didn't say where he was going?'

'No. We didn't really talk at all.'

'Would you recognise him if you saw him again?'

'I suppose so.'

'And where was Mrs Hutchinson when you offloaded the trunk?'

'She hung about by the entrance.'

'Didn't she check up on her trunk after you put it in the unit?'

'No. She asked me to lock the unit up and give her the key. She had to hurry back and return the van she'd hired.'

'Was that unusual?'

'We see all types here. She was no stranger than many of the folk who deposit their belongings. I got the impression she was in a hurry, that's all. She was polite, which is more than most here. She was scared her husband would find out where she'd put the trunk and pawn or sell the contents to feed his gambling habit. If I'd thought for one moment that it contained a body…' He shivered and shoved his hands into his pockets.

'You didn't happen to notice the registration plate on the van she was driving?'

Frank shook his head. 'The back door was open when I came outside, and I was focused on the trunk. Maybe the bloke in the beanie hat saw it, but I didn't.'

'Anna, would you mind talking to Frank about the CCTV footage? I want to wander about.'

She left her junior officer conducting the rest of the interview and studied the cameras on the premises. If Frank was correct, Mrs Hutchinson had positioned herself so she would remain undetected by the cameras. Joanne Hutchinson had pulled off a daring feat, but why had she brought the body of a young woman into this warehouse? Did she live close to it? And was she aware of what was in the trunk? They really needed to find the woman in blue.

CHAPTER TWELVE

It had been the same response at every house – surly faces peering through cracks in the door. 'No, mate, didn't see anything.'

Ross had knocked at every door in Gallow Street the day before, and was now returning to try those houses where no one had answered. His job required patience and people skills – both of which Ross had in abundance.

He rapped on a brown door and waited. No one answered. He moved off to try the next house. As he did, he was sure he spotted a movement of curtains at the downstairs window. He was considering knocking again, when he spotted Lauren. Dressed in tight jeans, Ugg boots and wearing a faux-fur coat, she emerged from a shop and stood for a moment, head down, studying her mobile.

'Hi, Lauren,' he called. She looked up, glared at him for a minute, then raised a reluctant hand in recognition. He crossed the road.

'You asking around about Princess?' she said.

'Yes, I've tried all the houses in your road and those in the neighbouring streets. This is my second attempt to talk to those that weren't in last time I called. I can't get the couple over there to answer the door.'

She gave a small smile. 'They'll be high. They usually are. I spoke to Roxanna who lives there with her boyfriend. She's okay when she's not off her face. They didn't see nuffin'.'

'Cheers. Saves me hammering on their door. They might think I'm on a drugs bust.'

He grinned, watching as she scurried down the road. As she disappeared from sight, he heard a cough. He turned around. It was a tall girl with blue lipstick and a matching streak in her hair. 'You've been banging on our door. What d'ya want?'

'Are you Roxanna?'

'Yeah. Did Lauren tell you my name? I saw you talking to her.'

'Yes, it's about her mum's dog.'

'Princess, yeah.'

'I'm trying to find out who took her.'

'Well it wasn't me.' The girl folded her arms across her chest and stared at Ross. 'And I told Lauren I haven't seen it.'

Ross shook his head. 'You misunderstand. I'm trying to find out if you spotted anyone you didn't recognise on the street, looking shifty, hanging about Mrs Carlisle's house, that sort of thing, at about half nine Monday morning.'

Roxanna relaxed a little and shifted position. 'I'm not sure what time it was, but I went to the shop cos we'd run out of milk. I walked past their place. I didn't see anyone with Princess.' She sucked on her teeth. 'There was a delivery van in the road, and the driver was at the back of the van with the door open.'

'Can you describe him at all?'

She shook her head. 'He had his back to me. He was shoving in a large box. Average build, I suppose. He had a baseball cap, dark trousers. Can't tell you any more than that.'

'Did you happen to notice which delivery company it was?'

'Yeah. It was a local one, Anytime Delivery. I've seen them about.'

'That might be useful. Maybe the driver saw someone.'

'Yeah.' She surveyed him through heavily made-up eyes. 'So, is that it?'

'Thanks. Yes.'

'Reggie, my man, said you had cop written all over you.'

'But you still came and spoke to me.'

'I had a bet on with him. I said you sold insurance. I suppose I owe him ten quid now.'

'I'm not a police officer these days. I'm a private investigator, so it looks like your ten quid is safe. You could tell him I was a insurance salesman though if you fancied.'

She grinned and ambled away, and Ross scratched his ear thoughtfully. Why would a delivery driver be putting a box *into* his van? He mused over the possibilities. There was an outside chance Princess had climbed into the van while the door was open, and then jumped out at the next destination and got lost. If nothing else, the delivery driver might have seen somebody hanging about Susanne Carlisle's house. It was worth following up. Ross believed if you followed enough leads, you eventually got a result. He strode back to his car, feeling more optimistic about tracking down the missing canine.

CHAPTER THIRTEEN

Robyn tapped the whiteboard. Attached to it was a photograph of the trunk and a photograph of the girl in plastic wrapping, Carrie Miller. Robyn had written the name of her father, Vincent Miller, above it, along with the name of his girlfriend, Leah Fall. She spoke to Anna and Mitz, the only members of her team she had been allocated for the investigation.

'The girlfriend, Leah, wasn't Carrie's greatest fan, but since Carrie had moved out and, to all intents and purposes, was no longer in their lives, I can't see why she would want the girl dead, unless of course Carrie had decided to move back home and Leah couldn't face that prospect. I'm not convinced she's capable or guilty of murder. She doesn't fit the description of Joanne Hutchinson and has a solid alibi for both the eighteenth and twentieth of December when she was at work. However, we can't assume anything at this stage, so Mitz, continue to run checks on both of them. And gather as much information about Mr Miller's life as you can, whether he has debts, offended anyone, rowed with anybody down the pub, that sort of thing, in case this was some sort of revenge attack.' She cocked her head from side to side, indicating it was a long shot but needed to be followed up.

Robyn was extremely good at reading people. Davies, who himself was highly trained in interrogation skills, had always admired her ability to see through people and know instinctively when they were lying. Leah had bared her soul. She had disliked

Carrie yet Robyn felt this was of no consequence, and as for Vince Miller, she knew he'd never harm his daughter. However, Robyn's investigations had often taken her in unexpected directions and provided unexpected clues. This approach might also yield results, so she'd pursue it, even though she was convinced neither party had harmed Carrie.

She wrote 'Jade North' on her board. 'This is one of Carrie's close friends. I'd like to talk to her. She might be able to shed some light on Carrie and her movements.

To one side she wrote the name Karl London in red ink. 'Karl rents unit forty-three at the self-storage warehouse. He might have seen Joanne Hutchinson, or the car she was driving on the eighteenth of December, which, as we now know, was the day she went to the self-storage warehouse, spoke to Dev Khan and paid upfront for a unit. As yet, we've not been able to get in touch with Mr London. His mobile is going to answerphone.'

In capital letters she wrote 'Joanne Hutchinson', putting her name at the very centre of the board. 'This is the woman we are most urgently seeking. We ran the name through our database and checked all the women with that name. None live in the vicinity, and of those closest to Rugeley, none match her description. The woman left fake contact details at the self-storage warehouse, so we can assume her name is an alias, leaving us with only her physical description. Both Dev Khan and Frank Cummings describe her as in her thirties, blonde, slim, about five foot ten, and well-spoken. Khan said she was "attractive" and Cummings confirmed she was a nice-looking woman "well made-up like she was an actress or model or air stewardess". It's not much to go on, so we need to find either someone else who noticed her or her car, and that includes the stranger who helped offload the trunk from a white van. Anna, how far did you get with the CCTV footage from the warehouse?'

Anna raked a hand through her hair. 'I've bee
thoroughly for the twentieth of December, which w
brought in the trunk, and can't spot her on it. I have ____ a few
seconds of Frank carrying the trunk down a corridor, but no sign
of our mysterious woman.'

Mitz made a clicking sound of irritation.

Anna heaved a sigh. 'I've contacted all van rental companies in
the area for that day. None have records of a Joanne Hutchinson.
I've emailed them the description of the woman, but so far there's
been no positive identification.'

'Try companies outside the area next.' She tapped the pen against
the board, leaving small red dots in a circle. Robyn wondered how
the trunk had got onto the van if it required two people to offload
it. Could she have an accomplice? She voiced her opinion.

'Yes, unless she cajoled another innocent party into loading it
for her.' Mitz shrugged.

'Possibly. Damn, this is frustrating. Okay, let's keep putting up
what we have.' Robyn wrote down the name Frank Cummings and
drew a line between his name and Joanne Hutchinson's, then drew
a question mark. 'I'm going to throw this idea out there for you.
What if either Dev or Frank were in on it? They're the only people
so far to have seen his woman. They might have been accomplices
or even fabricated her existence.' Robyn also thought it convenient
that Dev Khan hadn't checked Joanne's details and had taken her
cash in advance. She added his name to the board and explained
her reasoning.

Mitz piped up, 'Mr Khan gave DI Shearer the pass key code to
get into the warehouse yesterday, but he didn't know which units
we were going to search. If he had, I wonder, would that trunk
still have been there?'

Robyn tipped a nod at him. 'Indeed, and the same applies to
Frank Cummings.'

Anna shook her head. 'You saw him, guv. Frank was badly shaken by it. His hands were shaking a lot of the time he was speaking to us. He's got a sixteen-year-old daughter and was horrified he'd carried a trunk containing the body of a dead girl. We spoke about it while he was downloading the CCTV footage and, judging by his reaction, I don't believe he had any connection to the killing.'

Robyn tended to side with her colleague on this. 'Fair enough. Also, Dev Khan's an intelligent man. It's highly unlikely he'd hide a dead body in one of his own self-storage units and risk it being uncovered. If we can't find this mysterious woman, then we'll have to talk to both him and Frank again. Any luck tracking down the Good Samaritan who helped Frank?'

Anna thumbed through some paperwork. 'There's a shot of him from the footage as he vacated the warehouse, so I'm going to take a still of his face around the Towers Business Park and see if anyone can identify him.' She held up a grainy image of a man, head down in a beanie hat, wearing a Puffa jacket and large work boots.

Robyn waved her pen in small circles as if conducting an orchestra. 'That's hopeful.' She pointed at the board once more. 'To sum up, we've got one main suspect at the moment, Joanne Hutchinson. We're proceeding cautiously with Mr Khan and Mr Cummings, who are the witnesses who spoke to her. We need to locate a mystery man, our "Good Samaritan", who assisted Frank with offloading the trunk for further information. We're waiting to hear from Karl London to learn if he saw and can identify Joanne Hutchinson's vehicle and confirm her existence. I'm eliminating Mr Miller and his girlfriend for the moment, but we'll run background checks as discussed. Any other thoughts?'

They all studied the whiteboard. Robyn favoured the technique of writing everything down as if they were pieces of a puzzle, and encouraged her team to add ideas, suspects, or anything they felt might assist the inquiry.

'Anna, the trunk?'

Anna checked the list in her notebook. 'I'm still searching for companies that make bespoke trunks. Our trunk is definitely an unusual size and will have been made to order. I'm also looking into companies that sell large polythene plastic bags.'

'I had a thought about that,' Mitz interjected. 'My sofa came protected by a large polythene bag very similar to the one we found Carrie wrapped in.' Mitz had recently moved into the garage annexe at his parents' house that had been occupied by his grandma until her death. 'Could it have come off some new furniture?'

'You could be on to something there, Mitz. I'm not sure how to use that information yet but I'm sure it will be useful.' She wrote the words 'bag' and 'furniture covering?' and stood back from the board.

Robyn squared her shoulders and drew a breath. Carrie Miller left home on the twenty-eighth of July 2016. She wasn't reported missing and turned up dead in a custom-made trunk six months later. That troubled her. She pointed back to Jade's name, then spoke quietly, 'And here's the thing that bothers me most – why didn't somebody report Carrie Miller missing or voice concerns to her father? I can understand why her father didn't suspect anything was afoot, because after a massive falling-out he firmly believed she was alive and living locally, thanks to the duplicity of his partner, Leah, but her friends? Wouldn't they have wondered where she was and spoken to Vince or Leah about it? What about this so-called best friend, Jade North? Surely she'd have suspected something had happened to Carrie. I want to check all of Carrie's friends using social media and all that malarkey. Track down as many as you can from her old school and find out why they didn't think it peculiar she'd stopped communicating with them.'

Anna made another note in her book and circled it. Robyn tapped at the board again. 'This is too confusing a picture at the moment. We have to break it down into manageable chunks and work out why no one missed Carrie Miller in the six months she was in that trunk. Let's get cracking. Mitz, start with Mr Miller. Anna, find me some names of her friends. I think it's time we got some answers so we can begin to piece together our puzzle.'

CHAPTER FOURTEEN

Christine Hallows was clattering about in the kitchen when Florence got home from school and attempted to rush to her bedroom to plug in her phone charger. Her phone had died during maths and she needed to check Fox or Dog and see if any boys had decided she was foxy. She'd tried to log on throughout the day, but every time she got out her phone, her best friend Amélie would appear. She didn't want Amélie to discover the app. It wasn't that she'd disapprove, but Amélie was everything Florence would like to be. She knew she was the teeniest bit jealous of her best friend's looks and brains. The last thing she wanted was for Amélie to find out about the app and post a picture of herself. It would be sure to get hundreds of foxy emojis and admirers. Florence always played second fiddle to her friend, and for now she wanted to keep this to herself.

Her mother called out to her, halting her as she bounded onto the first stair. Her shoulders sagged as she entered the kitchen filled with the pungent aroma of garlic. Her mother stood by the cooker, cooling a tablespoon of casserole by blowing on it.

'Florrie, do you think this needs more pepper?'

In her usual attire of grubby jodhpurs and jumper, with her hair held back by a headband and face clean of make-up, her mother had a ruddy, healthy complexion and rosy cheeks. Florence always thought she would look even nicer if she wore make-up, but Christine Hallows wasn't a woman who spent a lot of time on personal grooming. She was comfortable as she was. She passed another spoon to Florence, who sniffed at it.

'Mum, I don't think it matters about the pepper. You've over-dosed on garlic.'

'I'm sure I stuck to the recipe,' Christine said, wiping her hands on her thighs and putting on a pair of reading glasses. 'Blast! You're right. I put in an entire garlic head. It says a clove of garlic in the recipe. Oh well, garlic's good for your heart.'

'It's also great at making your breath stink. I might pass on this. No one will sit next to me in class tomorrow.'

Christine pushed her glasses back onto her forehead. 'I'll make you something else.'

'You're okay. I'll sort out something.'

'If you're sure?'

Florence was quite used to getting her own food, partly because her parents' business meant they got in at all hours, and partly through choice. Her mother always insisted on doling out enormous portions and Florence struggled with her weight as it was.

Florence fidgeted, desperate to check Fox or Dog. 'I'm not too hungry. I ate a lot of lunch.'

'Well, if you're sure… there's plenty of cheese in the fridge, and cold meats if you get peckish.'

Her mother caught sight of someone in the yard and waved. 'It's the farrier. Have to shoot off. King Harold the Third lost a shoe this morning. Help yourself to the casserole if you change your mind. See you later.' She blew her daughter a kiss and bustled away, leaving Florence to her own devices.

Florence rocketed up the stairs, threw open the door to her bedroom and fell onto her bed. Tugging at the charging lead, she linked up her mobile. She had three messages from Amélie about going to the cinema on Thursday with her and Robyn. It seemed Robyn was going to come to the house to collect her, a fact that irritated her. She'd hoped to catch the bus and meet them at the cinema. Only little kids got collected and dropped off.

Florence thumbed the dating app and landed on her profile page. She scrolled below her photo and gasped. She had twenty dog emojis beneath it. They came from both girls and boys. She hadn't expected people to judge her so quickly. Her heart, heavy as lead, sank in her chest, and if it hadn't been for the three fox emojis she might have shut off the app. The first was from a boy she recognised called Baz. He was in the year above her at school. He'd decided on the name 'Killer' and looked pretty cool in his picture, but she knew that in real life he had awful acne and smelt like he could do with a good wash. The other kids often laughed about it behind his back. The second wasn't her type. He looked big and sporty and overconfident with a cheesy grin that showed off over-whitened teeth. The last, however, looked perfect. He was called 'Hunter' and described himself as *Looking for that perfect someone who is cute and makes me laugh.*

She studied his photograph. He was good-looking, with dark hair gelled into a fashionable quiff, a wide smile and sparkling blue eyes. She squirmed in delight. All she had to do was comment on his photograph, add the foxy emoji and then they could chat. She nibbled at her lower lip as she wondered what to put to engage him further, typing then erasing her words several times. At last she settled on: *If cute is freckles and a snub nose, then I could be your perfect foxy choice. I'm a joker, and if my jokes don't make you laugh then I'll tickle your toes until you do.* She hesitated. The last bit was lame. She thought about the perfect girls on *The Only Way is Essex* and deleted it, leaving only the first sentence, hoping it would encourage him to find out more about her. She hesitated. She'd never dare to be so forward in real life if she was facing Hunter, but this was somehow easier. She felt much more confident. She pressed 'send' and watched the comment, along with a fox emoji, appear under his picture.

She scrolled back to her other two admirers and was about to give the first, Baz, a thumbs-down emoji, before noticing someone had commented under his profile: *You'd do better, you loser, if you used soap from time to time.* She read through the other comments, most of which were about Baz's hygiene. She felt bad for him. He was quite a nice boy apart from being a little smelly. The comments here were mean and she didn't want to add to the boy's misery. She decided not to put either emoji – dog or fox. She looked back at her own profile. The doubts and upset of seeing the dog emojis were replaced by the euphoria of having a great-looking guy admiring her. She shrugged. Maybe the comments under Baz's profile would actually help him improve his hygiene. She relaxed onto her bed, wondering what to say to Hunter when they went into the virtual chat room together. It was such a buzz knowing someone fancied you.

CHAPTER FIFTEEN

Tiny drums beat in her temples. Every time she swallowed, her throat felt as if it were covered with sores. Amber Dalton was aware he was in the room but she was too weak to even care. In the last few hours she'd been sick, had terrible stomach cramps and now was overcome with this weakness. She was convinced she was dying.

'Drink. You must be thirsty,' he hissed. His voice reminded her of the snake in the film The Jungle Book.

She tried to speak but managed only a feeble huff. He meandered over, the light from his torch burning her eyes, and passed her a plastic bottle of orange juice. She lifted an arm that weighed a ton. She could barely grasp the bottle. She placed the rim to her parched lips and sipped. The sweet juice slid down her throat, lubricating it. She drank more greedily, glugged it until she was sucking air, then handed it back.

'Better?'

She nodded. She had no idea why he was keeping her alive. He had offered her no food for some time and the juice was the first liquid she had drunk in hours. He sank onto the bed, his phone in hand. It lit up, a blue light in the dark.

'I wanted to show you something. It will help explain why you are here. I bet you have no idea, have you?'

The creepy whispering didn't scare Amber any more. She shook her head. Her spirit was crushed. She still harboured a tiny hope that if she did as he bade, he might let her go.

'Look at this.' He showed her a photograph. In that instant, she understood. She shook her head which was now so heavy she could barely control it.

'I'm sorry. I didn't mean to…'

'But you did, all the same. You didn't care about the consequences.'

'I… it…'

'Now you know why you're here. Consequences, Amber. There are always consequences.'

The orange juice she had drunk churned in her stomach. She hadn't any strength to make it to the bucket. She rolled on her side and threw up onto the floor, with huge retches that made her muscles ache with the effort. Acid ripped the lining of her throat and made it burn further.

His voice now oozed fake concern. 'Oh, Amber, you poor girl. You appear to have drunk something rather nasty. Look how ill it's making you. Just for the record, you'll soon be dead. It was the juice. It contained ethylene glycol. Antifreeze. I was going to use a botulinum toxin, the same stuff that vain people use to keep their youthful looks. Seemed pretty appropriate to use it on you, but it proved too difficult to get hold of. You've been consuming antifreeze in drinks ever since you arrived. Little by little, without knowing it. The poison works slowly, depending on the measure. I gave you small measures until just now. I wanted you to suffer first. I wanted you to be afraid and bewildered. I've enjoyed watching your spirit break a little more each day. I wanted you to understand.' He gave a high-pitched squeal of laughter that chilled her to her core. 'Now I've shown you the error of your ways, it's time for you to depart. I'm so glad you managed to stay alive long enough to comprehend the situation. Goodbye, Amber. Give my love to Carrie Miller.'

CHAPTER SIXTEEN

It was turning into a long day, Robyn mused. Only eight hours ago she'd discovered the identity of the girl in the trunk. Since then she'd interviewed several people, including Carrie's father and his partner, spoken to the owner of the warehouse, held a team meeting and was now en route to Derby for the second time that day, to talk to the head teacher of Fairline Academy, the school that up untill June 2016 Carrie had attended.

During the journey, Robyn had pondered the facts she had accumulated since 8 a.m. She needed to learn everything she could about Carrie Miller from ex-teachers and friends, and fathom out the connection to Joanne Hutchinson. Neither Vince nor Leah had heard of Mrs Hutchinson and didn't recognise the description of her. Robyn was more convinced than ever the woman had used an alias, but who had hated Carrie enough to kill her, or had it been an accident? Or a random act of violence? And was this woman an accomplice or their perp?

Robyn pulled up by the entrance and waited as a few stragglers, a group of four boys, strolled up the road in the direction of the bus stop, ties already removed and bags tossed carelessly over their shoulders.

Fairline Academy was a far cry from Robyn's own grammar school, where she had attended classes of only eighteen to twenty pupils. She couldn't imagine attending such a large school, or academy as it was called, educating over seven hundred pupils in its numerous classrooms. Robyn had quietly enjoyed her education,

much of which had been spent at a small junior school on the edge
of a village. Even after she progressed to senior school, she hadn't
experienced any classroom difficulties or dramas. There'd been
the usual cliques of trendy girls that had rejected her, but Robyn
hadn't minded about that, and instead had hung out with the more
athletic individuals who, like her, were participants in many of the
school sports teams.

Kevin Winters, the head teacher, greeted her with a weary shrug
and a limp, damp, handshake. Robyn resisted the urge to wipe her
palm on her skirt. 'It's been a hectic week,' he said by way of explanation. He sat in his chair, back stiff, hands flat on the table. 'My
secretary has neglected to tell me why we are meeting. Has one of
our pupils got into trouble?' His small black eyes bored into Robyn's.

'I'm here about Carrie Miller.'

Mr Winters tipped his head back for a moment, then sighed. 'As
much as I'd like to, I don't know all the pupils at Fairline Academy.
However I always remember those who stand out from the crowd,
whether that be for a good or bad reason. Miss Miller is in the latter
category. She came before me on a couple of disciplinary matters.
She was abusive to one of the members of staff last year, and was
caught on several occasions with a group suspected of solvent abuse.
We couldn't find any solid evidence but they were suspended for
a week during last term. She was an arrogant young lady, bright
but lazy, and notoriously argumentative. She sat GCSEs last year
and got very low grades. She could have done much better if she'd
set her mind to it. Now, tell me why you're here. She's no longer
one of our pupils. She left last summer term. I hope she hasn't got
into more serious trouble.'

Robyn shook her head. It struck her that if Mr Winters could
recall all this about Carrie, he ought to remember also that she
had rather significant extenuating circumstances. She hoped he'd
handled her with some compassion when she'd appeared before

him. 'I'm truly sorry to inform you that Carrie's body was found yesterday.'

Mr Winters blinked a few times, and then sniffed in a matter-of-fact way. 'That is dreadful news. I may not have found her the most amenable of young ladies but I am nevertheless very sad to hear this.'

'I hoped you could give me an idea of who her friends were. I would like to speak to them.'

His head bobbed up and down eagerly. 'Now, let me see, Jade North and Harriet Cornwell spring to mind. Also, you should speak to Maneesh Shah, her form master. He's your best bet. He might still be around here somewhere. I'll give him a quick call.' He flicked open his mobile, scrolled through a list of numbers and rang one. After a while, he tutted and shook his head. 'Of course, it's his football night. He runs an after-school club at the local grounds. I don't have access to the pupils' addresses, especially ex-pupils. You'll have to wait until my secretary gets in tomorrow.'

'I'll ring first thing.'

Mr Winters looked past her, eyelids flickering. 'I think Miss North now lives in Mickleover. Jade was Carrie's closest friend. They were often in trouble together. Wherever Carrie went, Jade followed.' His head swayed side to side in slow rhythmical movements, like a large pink pendulum. 'There are so many external influences on these young people these days. It's difficult to guide them, let alone educate them.' He lifted his hands from the table, leaving two sweaty imprints, and stood to see Robyn out. 'I'm sorry about Carrie. Such a huge waste of a life.'

Robyn rang Mitz, requesting more information about the girls. Within minutes he returned the call.

'Jade North was picked up for brawling in Derby three months ago. Attacked another girl after a night out. The local police were called. According to the charge sheet she was let off with a caution. The family is also known to the police. The parents were reported for noise nuisance and antisocial behaviour. Jade left Fairline Academy in mid-April last year, and is now working part-time at a petrol station in Derby.'

Robyn wasn't far from Mickleover, and since it was only coming up for four thirty, she decided to pay Jade North a visit. Earlier, she'd asked Vince Miller if she might break the news of Carrie's death to Jade rather than him. She'd wanted to gauge the girl's reaction. He'd been glad of it.

Why hadn't Jade become suspicious about Carrie's disappearance? Was she involved in her murder? As she organised her thoughts, she punched the address into her satnav and headed to Mickleover – once a colliery, but now a large development of affordable housing – to see if Jade could throw any light on Carrie's disappearance.

Jade North's jaw moved up and down in lazy rhythm as she chewed on gum, and with arms folded, one hand brandishing a cigarette, she scowled at Robyn.

'I only get ten minutes for my break. I don't want to waste them talking to the likes of you.'

'I need your help, Jade. It's about Carrie Miller.'

The young woman took a long draw on her cigarette, releasing the smoke slowly. It curled above her hair, a mixture of dark roots and cheap home dye, and disappeared into the grey sky. She leant against the brick wall. 'What about her?'

'Have you heard from her recently? You were good friends at Fairline Academy.'

'School was school. It's different now. We ain't there no more.'

Robyn nodded and adopted a relaxed pose to put the girl at ease, leaning against the wall with her. Her hip was throbbing. Driving had made it ache like crazy.

'I understand. You can lose track of friends, especially when you move away from an area.'

Jade sniffed and dragged on her cigarette again.

'So, not a text or anything?'

'Nothing.' Jade looked away, breaking eye contact with Robyn. It was clear she wasn't telling the truth.

Robyn nodded and spoke in gentle tones. 'Jade, you and Carrie were good friends. I don't believe you wouldn't have stayed in touch. Did you fall out?'

Jade shook her head. 'No. I have to go back to work.'

Robyn decided to change tack. Jade was not going to volunteer any information. She put out her arm, a friendly gesture. 'I'm very sorry to tell you, we found Carrie's body yesterday morning.'

The colour drained from the girl's face. Her hand holding the cigarette began to tremble, and eventually she hung her head to hide the tears that were forming.

'I'm truly sorry.'

Jade seemed to recover, lifting her head in a swift movement and cocking it to one side. 'Where did you find her?'

'Rugeley.'

'Then it can't be Carrie. She's in Spain. She sent me texts. She met a bloke and they fell in love and ran off to the south of Spain. She told me.' Jade's voice rose.

Robyn put a hand on the girl's shoulder. 'Do you want me to contact anyone? I'll ask your boss to let you take the rest of the day off. This has been a terrible shock.'

Jade's face was a mask of contorted confusion. 'It can't be Carrie. Look. She bloody well left us all and ran away with Ben.' She pulled at her pocket and withdrew a smartphone. She stabbed at the screen and handed it to Robyn. There were months of Facebook messages in the conversation, an entire archive of conversation between the two girls; those from Carrie describing life in Spain and the relationship with her new man. It was all to remain a secret – only Jade knew about Ben. His family was rich and would be horrified to find out he'd bolted with a girl instead of continuing his studies at university. He was sure his folks would set a private investigator onto them.

'Did you ever meet Ben?' Robyn asked.

Jade took a last drag and stubbed her cigarette out against the wall. 'She met him online. I never actually saw him. She kept their relationship secret from us all. I suppose she didn't want him to be put off by her family.' She sniffed. 'I was put out she never brought him round to visit. Maybe she thought I'd put him off too. Anyway, her old man must have found out about Ben and they had a blazing row. Carrie walked out, once and for all. She's never seen eye-to-eye with Leah so it was no surprise. I told her to come round to mine the night she phoned me to say she'd had a massive row and walked out, but she said she was going to stay with Ben. Next thing, she was off to Spain. Didn't say goodbye. Jumped on a flight with him, and money from his trust fund, and headed to the sunshine.'

Robyn tapped the phone. 'Jade, I have to take this, for evidence.'

'Why? Carrie's alive and living in Spain.' She pointed at the phone. 'You can read the messages. That body you found isn't Carrie's.' Her voice was shrill. Robyn held onto the phone. 'It can't be.'

'There's no doubt it was Carrie we found. I'm very sorry, Jade. Come inside and we'll explain to your boss. I'm going to take you to the station so we can write this all down and then we'll get someone to take you home.'

Jade's eyes opened wide. 'No,' she whispered.

Robyn led the bewildered girl away, her mind whirring. The girls had been messaging each other since the twenty-eighth of July 2016 when Carrie left home, right up until the twentieth of December, the day Joanne Hutchinson had taken a trunk, containing the body of Carrie Miller, believed by then to have been dead for several months, into the self-storage unit at Rugeley.

CHAPTER SEVENTEEN

The offices of Anytime Delivery were located only three miles away from Gallow Street. The reception was unmanned. Ross pressed the buzzer on the desk and heard a distant noise somewhere in the adjacent warehouse. At last the door opened and a man in his late forties, dressed in grubby overalls, appeared. The room filled with the smell of grease.

'Sorry, mate. I was fixing one of the vans. Couldn't leave the nut half on. Had to finish the job and there's only me in today. Perks of being the boss, eh?'

'Not a problem.' He placed his private investigator's licence on the counter. 'I'm after some information. One of your drivers was delivering in Gallow Street on Monday. I'd like a few words with him.'

'What about?'

Ross gave a sheepish shrug, attempting to charm the man. 'A lost dog.'

'A dog?'

'I get all sorts of jobs like this. I've been asked to search for a missing pig before now.'

The man guffawed. Ross continued, 'I'm hoping your driver might be able to tell me something useful. Maybe he saw the mutt running up the road or even someone dragging it away. The owner's really upset. Dog means everything to her and her kids.' He left it there. The man's face had softened.

The man wiped his dirty brown hands on an equally filthy cloth, then fired up the computer. 'Gallow Street, Monday.' He clicked the mouse and sucked his teeth. 'I don't want to be giving out personal details to any old Tom, Dick or Harry.'

'Or Ross.' Ross's eyes crinkled as he grinned. 'I'm getting desperate and I want to be able to tell the owner I tried. It's much more than an ordinary pooch. It's one of those dogs that helps people with illnesses.' He raised his eyebrows in a pleading fashion.

'I know what you mean. Like one of them dogs that knows when a person is about to have a seizure. I saw a television programme about one. Marvellous, it was. Oh, all right.' The man picked up Ross's licence and read it. 'Private investigator, eh?'

Ross smiled. 'It's not all it's cracked up to be.'

The man nodded and clicked at the mouse again.

'Okay, Gary Sessions was in that area yesterday. He made a drop in Gallow Street.'

'Any chance I could talk to Gary?'

'He went to Buxton earlier. You should get him on his mobile, although the signal is lousy around there. I'll give you his number.'

Ross pocketed the number. 'Cheers. I'll try him.'

'No probs. Better get back to this broken van. Can't have one of the fleet out of action for long.' His mobile rang out. 'Yeah, sure. Let me check.' He wandered out the back leaving Ross alone. Ross leant across the desk to peer at the screen, which was still illuminated, and smiled. On it was a list of delivery drivers, with their addresses and contact details. Ross noted Gary's home address and then left. His satnav showed that Gary Sessions only lived half a mile away.

CHAPTER EIGHTEEN

'Last night I had a dream I was Indian speed-dating. All the girls had brought their parents. It was less of a dream and more of a nightmare.' Mitz raised his paper cup of tea and grinned amiably at his colleagues sitting in the office. He was the only single, eligible bachelor in the station. Robyn was constantly surprised by this fact. The only black mark against him as far as relationship material went was his dedication to his job. Hence he was in the station on his day off.

Robyn, who'd been feeling frustrated by the case, smiled. He had that effect on people. Mitz slid into his seat and instantly began typing. Robyn spun around in her chair and faced the whiteboard, then spun to her left and stared blankly at the window that today let in little light. Heavy clouds filled the sky and did nothing to lift her mood. She stood, straightened her leg to ease the ache in her hip and walked to the window, where she moved the slatted blinds and peered out onto the car park below. A squad car was departing. She watched it slide out into the busy street and turned back. Matt, David and Mitz were at their desks, separated by dividers to afford some privacy. The light-blue walls were bare apart from a noticeboard. Cupboards lined part of the back wall where the coffee machine had pride of place. Next to them, Anna was working silently on a computer. It was a sensible, functional space.

Matt Higham had his feet up on his desk. He tilted his head back and yawned widely. 'My mother-in-law is proper scary. Ever since Poppy arrived, she's around every five minutes telling us how to look after the kid. "Don't do this. Do that. Make sure Poppy's wearing a vest. You should use proper nappies, not these disposable ones." Life was much quieter before Poppy.'

'You think you have problems. You should meet mine. I think she was a velociraptor in another life,' mumbled David. 'What's your mum like?' he asked Anna.

'Overbearing, grumpy and can't abide fools. Much like me. Now, leave me alone. Unlike some of you, I have work to do.'

'Somebody got out of bed the wrong side.'

Anna continued typing and growled, 'Button it, David.'

David turned his attention to the contact list he was examining. Robyn returned to her notes. She had contacted Carrie's mobile phone provider and ascertained that the last voice call made from the phone was on the twenty-eighth of July, the night she left home. The killer must have been using her phone to text Jade. He or she might even have been using it to update Carrie's Facebook status. There had definitely been texts sent, but no calls.

Anna had accessed Carrie's Facebook account and security settings and explained how they could work out the account holder's locations from it. 'If a device logs onto a network other than its usual one, the location will show up in the settings, although they tend to be approximate.'

The messages that were posted until December twentieth had all been sent from Derby, leaving Robyn to surmise that either Carrie or her phone had stayed in that area. Anna was now going through Carrie's Facebook account to see if any more messages had been sent to other friends. She spoke as she typed. 'I might be out on a limb here, but could Jade North have anything to do with this?'

Robyn pondered the possibility. 'I'm going to add her to our list, Anna. She seemed genuinely distressed yesterday afternoon when I told her about Carrie, but you're right about her living in Derby.' She added Jade's name to the board and thought about the girl with the badly dyed hair. She'd broken down eventually. Inconsolable with grief, her manager had driven her home. It was unlikely Jade was involved in Carrie's death, but Robyn couldn't ignore the fact she was the only person to have been in apparent contact with Carrie, and she lived in Derby. A door slammed in the distance and a familiar voice could be heard as Shearer approached her office. Matt sat up in his chair in anticipation, like a dog expecting its master.

Shearer marched in, phone clamped to one ear, left arm waving like an agitated conductor. 'This is your last chance. Get this wrong and I'll make sure I bang you up overnight with the meanest cellmate I can find.' Robyn glanced in his direction. Shearer was wearing a smart black suit and a striped tie, his patent leather shoes shining.

He ended the call with a curt 'Okay' and spoke directly to Matt. 'Our not-so-helpful Freddie the snitch reckons one of the dealers we've been chasing after is drinking in the Barley Mow at Milford. He says the bloke's been there fifteen minutes or so. Apparently, he's in jeans, dark-blue jacket and a BMW baseball cap. Get over there. I don't think Freddie would dare to give us false info again.'

Matt and David leapt to their feet as one and hastened out of the office.

'I'll bloody murder that snitch if he's stringing us along. I swear he's involved with this whole drug thing. He's laughing at us. I'm sick of following up false leads.'

Robyn looked over at him. 'You seem somewhat overdressed for midweek, or police work, Tom.'

He picked at a speck of dust on his lapel and flicked it away. 'Got to go to a funeral.'

'Oh, sorry to hear that.'

'Old schoolmate, Vaughn. We hadn't seen each other for years, then after my divorce we got in touch online.'

Robyn's eyebrows arched, two perfect semicircles. 'You're on Facebook?'

His nostrils flared as he snorted. 'You're kidding. No way. That's not for me. I joined the Old Friends of Sandwell website. Vaughn saw my name on it and contacted me. We were best friends in those days. He was head prefect in our house in the sixth form.'

Anna's head shot up from her screen. 'Sandwell. You went to Sandwell?'

'And what's so strange about that? Can't a copper have a private education?'

'No, it wasn't that. Just recently come across it.'

Shearer shrugged. 'Spent some of my best days there. That was before life, work and divorce. This is my old school tie. I kept it to remind me that life wasn't always shit.' He held the green and grey tie gently between his fingers and gazed mournfully at it. 'Best go. Funeral's at twelve.'

Robyn felt a wave of sadness for the man. He wasn't the easiest person to get along with, but he'd suffered more than his fair share of disappointments. 'You want to grab a drink later after work? I'm off shift at seven,' she asked, aware of his powder-blue eyes studying her for a second.

Then he blinked. 'Why not? I'll come by the office.' His mouth opened as if he wished to say more, then shut, and with a nod he turned and left.

Anna looked across at Robyn who held a finger up. 'I felt sorry for him, okay?'

'Whatever you say, boss.'

'I've had a thought, based on what Shearer said – can you check Carrie's school website, Fairline Academy, to see if they also have an online club for ex-pupils?'

'Sure. I've been through her Facebook profile. She posted a message on her wall the day after she left home.' Robyn rose to better see Anna's screen.

'It says, "I'm sick of all the negativity on Facebook and the stupid comments, so I'm giving it up. I'm not posting again here. I'll let you all get on with your asinine comments and ridiculous posts. Don't bother messaging me. I won't reply. I'm moving on from here. It's time for me to start a new life and leave this one behind." She sounds really cheesed off.'

The word 'asinine' didn't ring true to Robyn. That wasn't language a teenager used, and certainly not one who'd up until then communicated using mainly emojis and text-speak. She'd posted all sorts of comments about celebrities, television shows she'd watched, and about how life was unfair. *Tell me about it*, Robyn thought. She'd uploaded endless selfies – pouting, thoughtful, tongue out – as well as pictures of fashionable shoes she lusted after, a heart-shaped tattoo she was thinking of having done, and lots of cordiform objects she'd come across. Robyn thought back to the girl's bedroom. Carrie wasn't as tough as she liked to convey.

Robyn studied the face of the pretty girl, arm around her friend Jade – a young woman brimming with confidence. Jade, even with her coloured hair, appeared dull by comparison, although seemingly content to be in the company of the girl with shining amber eyes, full lips and womanly curves. Carrie was more than pretty. The way she held her head up as if to challenge anyone looking at her added to her striking Mediterranean looks. Robyn felt an ache in her heart. The killer had destroyed this beautiful creature, a girl in her teens. The perp had let her friends think she was being a bit of a dick and neglecting them, when all the time she was hidden away, wrapped in a dense plastic sheet. A pulse quickened in Robyn's temple. This murderer was not going to slip away from her. She would hunt them down and ensure justice for Carrie and her family.

'Let me have a quick look.' Robyn slipped into the seat Anna vacated, and speed-read through the posts for 2016. Carrie was a typical teenager when it came to Facebook and had almost six hundred friends, but until the last message she had written nothing to indicate she had been irritated by anyone on the site. Robyn scrolled back further and found a few posts about school and how lame it was. There was no mention of a boyfriend. Robyn stood up again, allowing Anna to reclaim her seat.

Robyn tapped the screen. 'Print the page off and I'll look at it again. If the murderer wrote it, it says quite a lot about him or her. He or she is not a fan of Facebook users and whatever they post. Is this a clue? Did he or she take umbrage at something Carrie wrote? Go back through all her posts and see if there's anything else at all that might help us. Did she direct-message any friends other than Jade after she left home? Surely somebody who uses Facebook regularly would message lots of friends?'

Anna shook her head. 'You'd think so, yet she only messaged three other girls. There's Harriet Cornwell who's an ex-Fairline Academy pupil; Siobhan Connors, she works at the Tesco supermarket in Uttoxeter; and the last is Amber Dalton, a schoolgirl at Sandwell. Hence my surprise when Shearer mentioned the place. I'd just been googling it.'

'What a coincidence. What did those messages say?'

'Here.' Anna handed a printout and Robyn read them:

From Carrie Miller to Harriet Cornwell: *I've had enough of my old life. I'm starting a new one so I won't be around any more. I've met a really nice bloke and I'm moving on.*

From Carrie Miller to Amber Dalton: *You sound a lot like me. I hope we meet sometime soon.*

From Carrie Miller to Siobhan Connors: *You sound a lot like me. I hope we meet sometime soon.*

They sounded stilted and strange to her ears. Not only were the last two messages identical, but none of them were as conversational as the messages sent to Jade North. Robyn was more certain than ever the killer had sent them. 'When were they sent?'

'A few days after she disappeared – the second of August,' said Anna.

'And nothing after that?'

Anna shook her head.

'It's most odd that Carrie only sent messages to these four. It only makes some sort of sense if we assume the killer sent the messages. Then we're still left with the question why. Mitz, how are you getting on?' Robyn asked.

Mitz twisted around in his chair. 'Still running background checks on Mr Miller and his partner. I've found nothing suspicious so far. Got a call from the van driver, Karl London, who was at the self-storage warehouse the same day as Joanne Hutchinson. He's coming in this afternoon to be interviewed.'

'I'll leave you to do the interview, if that's okay. Anna, contact details for those girls, please, and talk to them immediately.' She checked the list she had left on a desk of leads to follow up. 'Anyone tracked down or talked to Carrie's form teacher, Maneesh Shah?'

Anna looked up momentarily from her screen. 'I rang him this morning. He said Carrie had underused potential. She was one of the class rebels, uncontrollable some days.'

'So, Carrie was a wild child with a penchant for trouble.' Robyn stared out of the window. Outside, a dark grey curtain of cloud had formed, making the day seem even more morbid. She rubbed her hip absent-mindedly. It didn't hurt as much as earlier but it was a sign that she wasn't getting any younger.

'I might talk to Mr Shah in person and see if he can come up with anything more.' Robyn voiced her thoughts to no one in particular.

Mitz looked up at her and grinned. 'Don't be late back for your hot date with DI Shearer.'

Robyn made a growling noise. 'If it were anyone else but you, I'd tell them to—'

'Boss!' Anna's urgent tone stopped Robyn in mid-sentence. 'There's a misper out on one of our girls. Her parents reported her missing just over a week ago, on the eighth.'

'Who?'

'Amber Dalton, our Sandwell girl.'

CHAPTER NINETEEN

Florence sat on the toilet seat in the cubicle and thumbed her screen. Hunter had messaged her and wanted to chat at three in the afternoon, during one of his work breaks. She hadn't wanted to let on she was still at school, and couldn't talk to him, nor had she wanted to put him off in case he didn't invite her again, so she'd pleaded a stomach ache during an art lesson and told Miss Cousins she had 'women's troubles and cramps'. Miss Cousins was too timid to question the lie and excused the girl. She didn't feel such a fraud as she hadn't been able to eat any lunch, thanks to the anticipation of chatting with Hunter. What if he thought she was too stupid, or figured out she was only thirteen? She had managed to look convincing on her profile photo with the help of make-up, but it was another matter when talking to someone who was a fair bit older than herself.

She had almost reached the toilets when she bumped into Mr Chambers. Elliot Chambers was the newest teacher to join Delia Marsh School, having arrived this academic year from university. Every girl in her class, including Amélie, was in love with him. He was in his early twenties, with dark, mournful eyes; clean-shaven and debonair, with a curling thatch of hair, he had a look of Harry Styles from One Direction. Mr Chambers taught English and drama and had already made a big impact on his pupils, being enthusiastic, cooler than the other teachers, and interested in those he taught.

'Hi, Florence. You okay? Shouldn't you be in lessons?'

'Yes, sir. Art.' She wasn't sure if she could blag it with Mr Chambers. He knew all about acting. 'Just going to the toilet.' She couldn't tell him any more.

'Sure. Don't let me hold you up. You'll be wanting to get back quickly. Art's very much your subject, isn't it?'

'Yes.' She stared ahead then down at her feet, unsure of where to look. Her heart thudded against her ribcage. She didn't want to be late for Hunter.

'Miss Cousins showed me around the art studio, and there were several of your paintings on the wall.' He smiled at her. If she wasn't so keen to speak to Hunter, she'd have enjoyed chatting to him. Not many people, let alone good-looking men, praised her.

'Well, can't put it off. I have marking to do,' he said, moving away and leaving her with a wide smile that almost made her knees go weak. Florence hurried to the toilets, locked herself in a cubicle and dropped onto the seat.

She brushed her hair back from her shoulders, took a deep breath and opened the Fox or Dog app. Hunter's photo was up, showing he was online. Florence typed.

> *Kitten: Hi Hunter.*

> *Hunter: Hey Kitten! You made it.*

> *Kitten: I managed to get a few minutes off. Hope I'm not needed back in the office.*

> *Hunter: What do you do?*

Florence had anticipated this question.

> *Kitten: Secretary for a small business.*

It was best to keep it vague. She didn't want him to try and track her down. She wasn't even sure how far she wanted the relationship to go. For now, she was happy to have an online relationship with someone who wouldn't see the real Florence, the podgy teenager who wasn't very good at academic work, wasn't great at sports and spent most of her free time daydreaming or reading.

Hunter: I guess you have to spend hours at a computer.

Kitten: Yeah. It's okay. I sometimes get sent abroad to conferences. Last year, I was sent to a meeting in Barcelona and got booked into a five-star hotel.

Florence wondered if that sounded grown up or just like she was bragging.

Kitten: That sort of thing doesn't happen very often though. Most of the time, I'm stuck in the office.

That sounded better. The stale smell of the toilets was beginning to get to her. She ought to have rushed to the park instead and sat on a bench.

Hunter: Wow. Barcelona. Lucky you. No such fun for me. I'm a computer programmer. It sounds impressive, but I spend too much time in a room with complete geeks. One of the blokes is a right weirdo.

Florence giggled and sent a laughing emoji.

Hunter: You like Star Wars films?

Kitten: They're okay.

Hunter: Please don't tell me you're into chick flicks.

Florence shifted on the toilet seat. Her bum was getting numb. She liked romantic comedies yet she'd sound too girlie if she admitted it. Luckily, with her parents fully occupied with the stables most of the day, she had ample opportunity to watch anything she fancied. Her mum trusted her to 'be sensible'. Her parents both treated her the same as the stable girls, who were all seventeen or older.

Kitten: I love horror. The Final Destination films were great.

Hunter: They were ace. Pretty gory in parts. Loved the Saw series. You watched those?

Florence hadn't, but she had an idea of what they were about.

Kitten: They were brilliant. I jumped a few times during them.

Hunter: So, you don't mind being scared.

Kitten: Not much scares me. Besides, they're only films. It's all about acting and make-up. I quite like the thrill though. Sometimes it's good to be scared.

Florence thought she sounded quite cool. Hunter seemed to think so too and sent a thumbs-up emoji.

Hunter: I like strong women. Not scared of spiders then?

Kitten: No.

This was a complete lie. Florence detested the creatures, but she wasn't going to confess that to Hunter. The conversation batted backwards and forwards, and too soon for Florence, was at an end.

Hunter: Fancy chatting again?

Florence breathed a sigh of relief. He liked her. The corners of her mouth twitched.

Hunter: I'll catch you again soon. I'm not going to be about until Thursday evening though. I've got a work project to complete for a client.

Florence waited a minute so as not to appear too keen, then remembered she was supposed to be going to the cinema after school on Thursday. She ought to be back by eight or eight thirty. She'd make sure of it.

Kitten: Okay. Maybe talk to you then.

Outside the cubicle she heard the sound of voices. The door to the toilets opened with a squeak. She kept silent.

Hunter: I'll look forward to it.

She signed out and stared at her phone for a moment. She no longer felt like a thirteen-year-old, or a plain Jane. Florence Hallows had a boyfriend.

CHAPTER TWENTY

DCI Neil Forge of the Derbyshire Police beckoned Robyn into his office. He bore the look of a man who'd seen enough horrors to last a lifetime – thick lines etched into his forehead and, between his eyebrows, deep furrows that had intensified over the years. At six foot seven, he filled the chair and the room. 'Have a seat, DI Carter. I'll cut to the chase. The technicians have examined Amber Dalton's laptop. We were hopeful of extracting something useful from her computer – after all, teenagers today seem to bare their souls online. Amber, however, is an exception, and uses her laptop solely for schoolwork.' He bent over a pile of papers and extracted several sheets, passing them to Robyn. Amber had spent considerable time searching for information on First World War poetry, economics and various authors, including Shakespeare and Milton.

He spoke again. 'There's nothing there to raise any alarm bells. It's the sort of browsing history you'd expect from a diligent student. The technicians also looked for deleted browsing history, cookies or hidden files, but again came up with nothing. She's only had the laptop since Christmas – it was a present from her parents. Essays, some notes, and that's pretty much it.

'We gained access to her social media accounts which she usually accesses via her mobile. She hasn't posted any pictures on Instagram since New Year's Eve, when she put up a photo of some fireworks and wished everyone a "mega 2017". Again, on her Facebook page she hasn't posted anything since the day her parents left for

Portugal on the second of January. She appears to have got fed up with using it. Her last message was this one.' He passed the sheet to Robyn who read:

> *Fed up with Facebook. Too much hypocrisy here. Going to give it up for a while. Maybe for ever. I'll leave it to those who want to whinge and be critical.*

Robyn felt the hairs rise on the nape of her neck. The language and tone was very similar to that in the message Carrie supposedly posted on her Facebook wall. The coincidence was too great to ignore. She hoped she wasn't right, because if she was, then Amber Dalton's life was at risk. She had to talk to her parents and she needed to locate Siobhan Connors, the other girl who'd received a direct message from Carrie's phone.

'Could you pull up her page on the screen for me?' Robyn asked.

'Sure, hang on a moment.' Amber Dalton's profile page appeared on the screen. Amber in black and white, large eyes focused on a spot in the distance, arms tucked around her long legs, sitting on a brick wall in front of a tall block of 1960s flats. The wall had been decorated with graffiti: 'Life Sucks'. Amber, with a sombre expression and wearing a lace top with billowing sleeves, tight jeans and Ugg boots, could have been advertising a fashion brand. She exuded sadness and beauty, as if she found life too much to endure.

'Did Amber message anyone on Facebook privately?'

'No activity at all.'

Robyn rubbed her sore hip absent-mindedly. Carrie had sent private messages to Siobhan Connors and Amber, saying she hoped to meet them soon. Amber, however, hadn't sent anything on Facebook or by text.

'So none of her friends have tried to contact her?' she said.

'You can see from the comments on her Facebook wall that several have asked what was up with her.'

He scrolled down the page. 'Quite a few tell her to take some time out, or leave hearts on her page, and that they're "here for you if you want to talk". This one asks, "What's up, you mardy cow? Having another downer? Call me." It's from one of her friends from Sandwell, Samantha Dancer. Although Sandwell's a boarding school, Amber's a day pupil there. That means she stays until nine each day. She has a room in the same boarding house as Samantha, who's a full-time boarder, so they see quite a lot of each other. We spoke to Samantha who told us it was quite normal for all of them to get a bit depressed from time to time. Amber's no different to any of them, although, according to one or two of them, it isn't like her to throw a complete wobbly. Samantha put it down to the pressure of schoolwork. Amber's desperate to get into Oxford or Cambridge and has been working flat out. Samantha suspects her parents have been putting pressure on her and wondered if it had all got too much for Amber so she'd run away. She left voicemail messages on Amber's phone but didn't get a reply. At the time, she was busy herself with studying, so she assumed Amber was really knuckling down to work. It was only once term began again that she realised Amber was missing.

'We interviewed all Amber's friends at Sandwell, not that she has many. In recent months she's chosen studies over friendships. They corroborated what we surmised – Amber Dalton is a bright, attractive girl who put studies first.'

'Have you had any leads from the public since the television appeal?'

'The usual. People phoning in saying they've spotted her all over the country – you know how it is. It uses up so many resources trying to establish how many of these leads are plausible.'

'Nothing from any of the neighbours?'

'They didn't even know she was at home. It's an estate of six houses, all spread out. Each has its own driveway and gates. They are all "private" people.' He sniffed in disapproval.

'Relatives?'

'There's only a grandmother in Wales. No uncles, aunts. Amber isn't with her grandmother. If she has run away, no one can work out why, other than pressure of schoolwork. Her parents say they often tell her to take time off studying. They maintain she isn't struggling with her studies at all, that she's a perfect daughter – no arguments or fallouts – and a happy, content teenager.'

'Boyfriend?'

'She went out with a lad in the same year as her for a while, but she dumped him in April last year, so she could focus on her GCSEs.'

'Have you a name for him?'

'Justin Bolt.'

Robyn noted it down along with the boy's address. DCI Forge sat back. 'I'm holding out little hope of her coming back unharmed. It's been two weeks. Her parents are convinced she's been abducted. It's most unlikely she would have run away. We've had units out all over the area but there's no sign of her.'

'And what about traces on her mobile?'

'It was last used on the seventh – that was the day before her parents returned. A transmitter at Derby picked up the phone's signal. It's been switched off since then and we've been unable to get a trace on it.'

Once again, a mobile phone had been used in the Derby area. Is that where the killer lived, or had Amber used her phone that day? Robyn made a mental note. Any information at this stage was relevant.

'I know it's irregular, but do you think I could chat to her parents?' she asked.

'It *is* irregular, but they'd do anything to help. They're both what you'd call upright citizens. He's an economist and she's involved with various charities. It's awful to see them going through this.

They're devoted to Amber. They have this blinkered faith in our ability to find her. I wish we could give them some good news.'

A sour taste rose in Robyn's throat. The message posted on Amber's Facebook wall had confirmed her fears and there was little doubt in her mind Amber and Carrie's disappearances were connected. With no word from Amber and her phone switched off, Robyn's fear was that the girl might no longer be alive. With that thought, she phoned the office and asked Anna to get in contact with Siobhan Connors.

CHAPTER TWENTY-ONE

Robyn drove back towards Uttoxeter. The Daltons lived en route in the village of Tutbury, best known for its ruined medieval castle. As she passed the fortifications, she thought carefully about what to say to them. She didn't want to worry them unduly, but she had to work fast and find out what she could if she were to stand any chance of finding Amber alive.

Bianca Dalton, a diminutive woman with clear, porcelain skin and deep ebony eyes, was holding up better than her husband was. Mr Dalton, tall and stooped with sparse, feather-like white hair and round metal-framed glasses that gave him the appearance of a professor, looked haunted. His eyes widened at the sight of Robyn. 'Is she…?'

'No, Charles. She's not been found yet. This is DI Carter of Staffordshire Police. She has some questions about one of Amber's friends. She telephoned earlier. I said she could come around.' Mrs Dalton's accent was charming, with a singsong lilt.

'Are you sure this is okay? I don't want to intrude.'

'Of course it is okay. We want to help if we can. It's good to focus on other matters. Since we landed back home, we haven't dared to go out in case the house phone rings and it's Amber, or in case she returns and we're not here to welcome her back.'

Mrs Dalton guided her husband by the elbow to a large armchair where he sat, dazed. She turned to Robyn. 'Charles blames himself.

We should have insisted she came with us to Portugal, but no, we let her stay here on her own. Amber said she had coursework to do and didn't want to get behind. How many girls that age would turn down sunshine by a pool to study? Would you like some tea, Inspector?'

'No, thank you. I don't want to impose.'

'Not an imposition at all. I'd just brewed a pot before you arrived.'

'Only if you're sure. White, no sugar, please.'

'It makes me feel useful.' The cup trembled on the saucer, a repetitive chinking. Mrs Dalton replaced it on the table. 'Who am I kidding? I don't feel useful. I'm just waiting, biding my time, praying, hoping. I can't bear this not knowing.'

'Now now, Bianca,' said her husband, coming out of his reverie. 'You mustn't give up. We have to stay strong. For when Amber comes home.' His voice trailed to a whimper.

Robyn couldn't upset him. He was at breaking point. Amber had been reported missing eleven days earlier, and no one was any the wiser as to her whereabouts. Robyn felt uncomfortable wheedling information from them when they were so obviously distressed. She ought to have arranged to meet the liaison officer assigned to the case at the house. 'Look, I'll chat to the officer in charge of Amber's disappearance again. I can't pester you at this time.'

'Has Amber's friend gone missing too?' Bianca Dalton stared at Robyn, suddenly grasping the situation. 'No, don't answer that. I want to carry on believing Amber is safe and will come home. I don't want to know what's happened to this other girl. Ask your questions and we'll help if we can.'

'Is the name Carrie Miller familiar to you?'

Bianca shrugged and looked to her husband, his brow wrinkled in thought. 'No, I can't say I've ever heard Amber mention her. Is she one of Amber's friends from Sandwell?'

Robyn shook her head. 'No. We're unsure of how they know each other. It might only be through social media.'

Charles shook his head again. 'Amber's never mentioned her, and she certainly hasn't visited the house. Amber hasn't invited anyone round for a long time. She decided her studies were to take priority. The school has high hopes for her.'

Robyn followed his eyes to a framed photograph of his daughter, in which she could almost have been mistaken for a model, with pale skin like her mother's, large eyes framed with long eyelashes, a perfectly straight nose and full lips; she was a young version of Sophie Marceau.

'When did you first realise Amber had disappeared?'

'It wasn't until we returned from holiday, on the eighth of January. That was twelve days ago,' she said, her chest rising. She regained control and continued. 'She'd been texting us every day while we were away, so we believed everything was fine. I reminded her to put the rubbish bins out and she said she had. When we got back home, the house was locked, food I'd left her was still in the fridge, and the bins hadn't been emptied. We called the police immediately. Inspector Forge believes she left home shortly after we caught our plane.' Bianca inhaled deeply. 'We checked with all her friends and with my mother. Amber wasn't with any of them. The police did a door-to-door enquiry and no one had seen her. We waited to hear from her again, but there were no more texts and no phone calls. The last we heard from her was a text she sent the day before we got home, telling us to have fun on our last day.' Bianca's eyes filled.

'Inspector Forge advised us to make an appeal on television which we did two days ago, on Saturday night. So far, we haven't heard anything. The police say they're following up leads. It's as if she's vanished from the face of the earth. I wish to goodness I'd insisted she'd come with us. She could have done her coursework at the villa. She told me not to fuss when I asked if she'd be okay alone.'

Bianca shook her head. 'She's such a good girl. I know parents say that all the time, but Amber really is. She's perfect. I couldn't wish for a better daughter.'

'The police will do whatever they can to find her.' Robyn couldn't bear to look at Bianca, now hopeful again. 'Could I please see Amber's room?'

Bianca's face clouded. 'I don't see how it will help, but okay. Don't touch anything. I want to keep it as it is for her. For when she returns.'

Charles stood to accompany Robyn, appearing to regain control of his emotions. 'I'll accompany you upstairs. Bianca, could you get some more tea, sweetheart?' His wife obliged.

Charles led Robyn through the oak-panelled hall and up thick-carpeted stairs. 'She's putting on a brave face. It will kill her if anything's happened to Amber. She's our world.' He stopped and turned to face Robyn. 'The officers who came to help us through this time, I think they believe she's dead. But out there, somewhere, is my girl. She's got backbone. She's got spirit. She'll return to us,' he said, and repeated it as if to convince himself. Then he continued upstairs. Robyn followed him, concerned about the prickling feeling that crawled up her spine. Amber had been in contact with her parents by text while they were abroad. Jade North had received messages supposedly from Carrie long after she'd been murdered. Robyn couldn't shake the idea that the perpetrator was sending the messages, and that Amber Dalton was in the hands of a killer.

CHAPTER TWENTY-TWO

Robyn's thoughts cascaded as she drove back to the station. She feared she was dealing with a serial killer; that they were only at the beginning of a killing spree. How many more victims would there be? Her other concern was that there was insufficient evidence to convince DCI Flint or his superiors. With only one body, it was unlikely he'd take her seriously. Her superiors were not always accommodating of her instincts. Louisa Mulholland had been, but now she was gone it was going to be more difficult to convince them she was correct.

She wished she could talk to Davies about it all. He'd always been the person who'd believed in her implicitly. The pain of his loss hit her in her chest. She'd never get over it.

'Davies, what do I do?' she asked, knowing there'd be nothing but silence.

She rubbed the back of her neck. A dull ache had begun in the base of her skull. She'd forgotten to eat again and was suffering a sugar dip. If Davies were still alive he'd have probably phoned her to remind her to eat too...

'Come and sit down. I've made a sandwich. Get it down you.' Davies leans across, his gentle eyes on her. 'You're doing yourself no good by not eating.'

Robyn picks up the ciabatta roll; lettuce and tomato are packed around slices of Leerdammer cheese, a food flag of green, red and yellow. Her stomach gurgles. Davies laughs. 'See. Your body's telling you it's starving.'

'I didn't have time to eat,' she says, biting into the floury bread and savouring the sweet cherry tomatoes he has added, knowing they're her favourites.

He's looking as dapper as ever, in a white shirt and jeans. His face is clean-shaven, his dark hair is swept back in a casual style that manages to fall somewhere between stylish and unkempt, and his eyes twinkle as he watches her shove the sandwich into her mouth.

'Nonsense. You can't run on empty. I understand cases can completely absorb you, but you mustn't neglect your body. It's your machine, and the brain needs nutrition. I want a full report that you've been eating while I'm away. If I come back to a skeleton you know what will happen,' he says with a wide grin. 'I'll force feed you all sorts of horrible, fattening, greasy dishes of food until you beg for mercy. Case or not, promise me you'll look after yourself while I'm away.'

She nods. Davies is often involved in cases far more demanding than her own. He never talks about them. As a military intelligence officer, he's not allowed to discuss his operations. She only knows about his job because of a chance meeting at the police station, when he was called in to interview a suspect picked up for possessing bomb-making equipment. She spotted the serious-faced Davies being led to an interview room, and noting only his smart appearance, she had gone about her own business. One of her colleagues let on that the stranger at the station, hustled in by the superintendent himself, was an officer from the Intelligence Corps. Later she had met him in the corridor by the ancient coffee machine. In spite of her cajoling it with kind words, thumping it and finally cursing, it had not given her the coffee she desperately required. Davies, amused, had proposed they go to the café nearby. Chat had turned into a date and that date had led to another.

In Davies, she'd met her soulmate. He was wise beyond his forty years, calm and patient. He had coaxed her out of her protective shell and into his arms. Her well-being was always of concern to him, as Robyn was notorious for burying herself in work. His own took him away frequently. To the world, he was a consultant for a technology company specialising in microchips – a job that was dull and required him to travel often. No one, other than Robyn and his ex-wife Brigitte, knew the true nature of his occupation. Neither would divulge the truth. The truth would put Davies in danger.

'Eat up,' Davies says. 'You're looking peaky.'

'It's only work. You know what it's like when I get bogged down with a case.'

Davies sits beside her, caresses her face, then leans in to kiss her. 'Then maybe you should give it up and consider a new life as a mother.'

Her heart hammers. There is nothing she would love more. Their wedding is planned for the following year and a child would complete her happiness. She gazes into his eyes, her body filled with a warmth and love for this man. She nods, a small smile creeping across her face. He lifts her hands. Kisses the back of them.

She shook her head, dispelling the memories. Davies was no longer here to make sure she didn't neglect herself. He'd died in Morocco, and taken with him her love and any hope for future happiness.

It was just before seven when Robyn returned to the station. Tom Shearer was waiting in her office, top button undone. Streaks of silver in his dark-brown hair caught the light as he bent his head to study his shoes. 'Thought you'd stood me up,' he said.

She grabbed at her desk drawer and rummaged for a couple of aspirins. She threw them back and dry-swallowed. Shearer observed her actions.

'We can cancel if you want,' he said.

'Wouldn't let a colleague down. Besides, I could do with a drink.'

They left the station, crossed the road and walked through the pub car park.

Shearer pushed open the pub door. Voices rushed out to greet them. In one corner was a group of officers, part of Shearer's team. David Marker looked over and raised a hand. Robyn acknowledged the wave. 'Do you want to join them?'

'I'd prefer a drink by the bar. I've been shut in with that lot all afternoon. I don't think they'd enjoy my company again so soon. I wasn't in the best of moods. Our suspect wasn't very forthcoming, so I've had him banged up for the night to see if he'll cooperate in the morning. He's being tight-lipped at the minute but I'll work my magic on him.' Robyn observed the steely look in his eyes. She fished about for her purse.

'What do you fancy?'

'On me.'

'I invited you.'

'Stop being Miss Hard-Arse. I'll get these. Don't think I wasn't grateful you invited me out. I'd have only come in here alone and got completely ratted, and then probably pissed off my colleagues over there even more. At least this way, I'll manage to stay moderately sober. I wouldn't want to lose face in front of a fellow DI.'

'Go on, then.' She shoved her purse back in her bag and drew out a stool. 'I could do with picking your brains.'

'You're welcome to the few grey cells I have left,' he growled, signalling at the bartender. 'Two bottles of Stella. That okay with you?' he asked.

'Sure. Fine.'

They clinked bottles. She noticed his chewed fingernails and the ripped piece of skin on his thumbnail. Davies had always had clean, neat fingernails, square and filed regularly.

'To absent friends,' he said. He took a long swig from the bottle.

She blinked and the vision of Davies departed. 'To absent friends.'

He took several noisy gulps and plonked the bottle on the bar with a clunk. 'That was welcome. What a crap day. Makes you think about your own mortality. Here I am in my forties, divorced, a son that barely acknowledges me, and absorbed completely by my work. I sat in that church today at Vaughn's memorial service and wondered what it would've been like if I hadn't signed up for the force. Would I be working for some other company and going home to the wife, holidays in the Algarve, children who actually weren't embarrassed by me? Then I studied the faces of the men around me, who were lads back in the day, with hopes and expectations, and saw the light had gone out in their eyes. They were no better off than me. Tied up with mortgages, anxieties, pressures and probably with blocked arteries or stress-related illnesses they don't yet know they have. I guess I'm happier doing this, in spite of knowing that there are some genuinely sick fucks in society. It gets you like that, doesn't it? I have days when I want to scream to the rafters but then I use that energy, redirect it towards solving crimes and trying to make the world a better place.'

Robyn nodded. Shearer had never spoken like this before. He was ordinarily sarcastic or brusque, to the point where she thought he had no compassion at all. 'I get it.' She tipped her own bottle back. Shearer watched her.

'We're two of a kind,' he said. 'Look at us. In a local bar after work with nowhere to go, no one to spend time with, and nothing to do other than dwell on what we have or haven't accomplished this day.'

She replaced the bottle on the bar. 'We accomplish plenty. This is more of a vocation than a job, and it isn't for everyone. You soon discover that when you sign up. And as for life outside – well, isn't it overrated? I bet those men thought your life was far more exciting than theirs. The grass always seems greener…'

He nodded in agreement. 'Fair point. I'm being maudlin because of today. Vaughn was a great bloke. He wasn't like the rest of us. He was the boffin of the house. Always had his head in a book. Helped me out time after time with maths. He was singled out early on for greater things. Went to Cambridge and got a first-class honours degree, then took a masters in philosophy.'

'I take it you didn't find studying as easy.'

He barked a short laugh. 'I was one of the bad lads. Skived lessons when I could. I was more into sport. There were times in the house when Vaughn needed looking after. I was his bodyguard, if you like, and in return he helped me out academically. I might have handed in one or two essays that I didn't actually write myself.'

'Bullying? You had to protect him from bullies?'

'It wasn't proper bullying. It was a tradition. The younger boys suffered a little at the hands of the older boys. The seniors often came into our dorms and tipped us out of bed, forced us under cold showers, hid our shoes, that sort of thing. I was tall and a bit rougher than them. Came from a council estate. One night, they bed-ended me so I fell on the floor, tangled up in the duvet, and they threw another lad into a bath filled with, well, I'll leave it to your imagination. They stripped Vaughn, started wrapping him up with duct tape. I went ballistic, managed to crumple the ringleader's nose. After that it became calmer. The following year, Vaughn and me shared a room. The older boys never dared bother us.' He drained his bottle. 'Another?'

'Why not? I'm not driving. I'm headed back to go through some files. Derbyshire lot are looking into a missing girl, and I think it might be linked to my case. She's a Sandwell girl. As it happens, also an Oxbridge candidate.'

Shearer opened his mouth to say something, closed it again and signalled for the barman. Robyn checked her mobile while the barman flipped the tops from two more bottles. Shearer turned to her. 'Talk to her houseparent. She'll know the girl better than anyone.'

'It's really Derbyshire's case. I'm still working out what happened to Carrie.'

'I'd talk to her anyway.' He said something to the barman, who returned with a couple of bags. 'Here,' said Shearer pushing a bag of nuts in her direction. 'If you're going to work through the night, you'll need some sustenance. Can't have you fading away.'

Robyn cocked her head. 'Careful, Tom. You're beginning to sound like a regular nice guy.'

He threw back his head. 'No chance. I'll be back on my very usual nasty form tomorrow. Make the most of it.'

After a second drink with Shearer, Robyn returned to her office where she read through a statement made by Karl London, the man who rented unit 43 and who'd been at the self-storage warehouse on the eighteenth, the day Joanne Hutchinson had rented unit 127.

London hadn't noticed any vehicles. He'd been too busy clearing out some stock from his own unit and had backed his truck right up to the doors, blocking any view of the outside. He recalled seeing Joanne Hutchinson and confirmed she was an attractive woman, dressed in blue with matching headband, who looked 'tasty' and spoke 'posh'.

Although there had now been three different sightings of Joanne Hutchinson, Robyn had flirted with the possibility that the woman didn't exist at all and that Dev Khan or Frank Cummings, or even both of them, had concocted the story and coerced London into confirming it. Khan was friendly with Karl London so it was a possibility. She was still puzzled by the fact Joanne Hutchinson hadn't appeared on any CCTV footage, which was difficult for anyone to avoid She'd written 'Is Joanne Hutchinson a set-up by Khan?' on a bright green Post-it note and pondered some more on that theory. Davies had introduced her to the use of Post-its. He'd found her puzzling over files, scrawling on A4 paper...

Robyn lets out a long groan and stretches. 'This is hopeless.'

Davies looks across, turns off the late news he'd been watching and wanders over to her. The delicious smell of pine-scented body wash clings to his skin, and she has the desire to stop working and kiss him. He leans over her shoulder and studies her scribbles. 'No offence, but you'd do better if you clarified your thought process,' he says. Robyn grunts.

'It's okay for you. You have a phenomenally logical brain. I have to do things my way, which means organised chaos. I get there in the end.'

He gives her a wide smile. 'I know you do. I have supreme confidence in your abilities. However, here's a little trick I picked up that helps me.'

He bends down and reaches into the brown satchel that accompanies him on all missions and pulls out a pad of multicoloured Post-it notes.

'Here we go. Write down an idea or two, not more, on one of these. Choose different colours, so if you are writing about one person, keep your ideas on yellow notes, for example. If you're looking at another suspect or a different idea, change the colour. Lay them out in front of you on the table or the floor. Change the order around if you need to, but treat it like a huge puzzle. If you think about each idea, you'll gradually pull together the whole picture. You'll find it helps.' He places the notes in front of her, drops a kiss on her head.

She stopped thinking about the case for a while and instead thought about the man she still loved. It had been almost two years since the ambush in Morocco. She ought to be able to move on, exist without him, not think about him every day, or maybe even find somebody else to care about. As it was, she couldn't. She was stuck in a time warp, held back by memories and love for a man who couldn't hold her or love her back. She'd undergone psychoanalysis before rejoining the force. The therapist who'd worked with her had told her it would take time for her to heal. 'How long?' she'd asked. He'd given her a sad smile and no reply.

She gave up on her Post-it notes around 1 a.m. and caught up with the files left on her desk while she'd been visiting the Daltons. Anna had interviewed Harriet Cornwell, one of the girls Carrie had messaged on Facebook. She'd expressed little concern over her disappearance, being too preoccupied with her newborn baby to fret over an old schoolmate who'd run off with a boyfriend. Anna's report was detailed and she'd emailed a recording of the interview for Robyn to listen to. Robyn sank back into her chair and pressed the start button. She approved of the way Anna gently coaxed the information from the reluctant girl. Initially Harriet resisted the questioning, before eventually giving way to Anna's persistence:

Anna: Were you not concerned about Carrie in any way?

Harriet: Carrie always knew her own mind. She could be a bolshie bitch when she felt like it, and she'd often go off on one about her dad and his girlfriend, and then storm off. She did it all the time when we went on a night out. I gave up going after her.

One time, she walked all the way home from Derby to Uttoxeter at two in the morning. Anything could have happened to her but she didn't care. She turned up the next day, full of remorse and with a bottle of wine for me. She was like that – one minute all high and happy, the next, flat. I sort of understood. Her mum died when she was a kid, and she didn't get along with her dad and Leah. Carrie walked out a couple of times before; the last was January last year. She hung out with friends in Nottingham. When I read the stuff on Facebook and got the texts, I just thought she was having another tantrum.

Anna: Who were these friends she hung out with?

Harriet: No idea. She didn't talk about them afterwards. I don't think they were really friends, as such. They were probably some lads she got off with at a club. She wasn't fussy, if you know what I mean.

Anna: She's had casual relationships, then?

Harriet: Yeah. She doesn't like to get serious. If you want my opinion, she may have had the looks and everything, and was into everything, but inside, she was scared of getting involved properly with someone. She dumped a few guys at school. She never had to try to get a fella, but she never kept them neither.

Anna: When you say into everything, what do you mean?

Harriet: She was adventurous.

Anna: Did she take drugs?

Harriet: Now and again. Only light stuff – the odd E, that sort of thing. She smoked weed too but never nothing too heavy. She wasn't a druggie, if that's what you want to know.

Anna: And after you received the message telling you about the new boyfriend, did you try to contact Carrie?

Harriet: Yeah. I phoned her a few times. It always went to answerphone. Left a message about the baby. I thought she'd like to know he'd been born, but she didn't return the call or even send a card. I thought she was a right cow for ignoring me and probably jealous, so I didn't bother with her any more. I called her a bitch. How could I? She wasn't, was she? She couldn't answer me because she was dead.

Robyn checked her watch. It was almost three but she didn't feel tired. Her mind was restless. She had to solve this puzzle. Carrie was cavalier in her attitude towards men. Had she met someone, tried to dump them and been murdered? If so, where did Amber Dalton fit in? And did Siobhan Connors also fit in or was Robyn going off-piste with that suggestion?

She stood, stretched, and ambled towards the whiteboard. She had two possible victims. One had been murdered in July or August 2016 and taken to the self-storage unit on the twentieth of December 2016; the other had disappeared sometime before the eighth of January 2017. One had attended an academy in Derby while the other was at a private school in Sandwell in Derbyshire.

The only connection Robyn could come up with was that both attended schools in Derbyshire. She jotted this down on a Post-it note in her hand and stuck it on the board. She considered the relevance of both girls' phones being used in the Derby area before writing 'mobile – Derby' on a note and adding it to her board, now a multicoloured collage. Robyn paced her office floor, convinced there was something she was missing.

She tried to connect the girls in other ways. She wrote down 'attractive' and 'only a few close friends'. She stared at the notes before sticking them on the whiteboard. She couldn't detect any connection between these facts. With a heavy sigh, she removed the notes from the board and read through the rest of Anna's paperwork.

Unable to speak in person to Siobhan Connors, the other girl who'd received a message from Carrie, Anna had left an answerphone message on her mobile. She'd also contacted the supervisor at the supermarket where Siobhan worked, who'd confirmed she'd taken compassionate leave. It was a dead end until they could talk to her. *Siobhan was out of contact.* Robyn listened to the accelerated beat of her heart. Had she really taken compassionate leave or was she now also in the hands of the killer? Anna had added an address – a rented flat in Uttoxeter that Siobhan shared with her boyfriend. Robyn wrote out the three girls' names and studied it. Derby, Sandwell, Uttoxeter. The girls moved in completely different circles. They didn't attend the same school or work together. What was the connection? It had to be the Internet. The trio were on Facebook, yet weren't 'friends'. Anna had explained that messages could be sent to people even if they weren't friends on Facebook. While Carrie was friends with Jade and Harriet on the site, she was not friends with either Amber or Siobhan. So why the strange message about meeting up with them? She read the message Carrie had supposedly sent once more: *You sound a lot like me. I hope we meet sometime soon.*

Robyn shook her head. It wasn't coming together for her. She drew out the photograph of Siobhan Connors from the file. Like the other young women, she was striking in her appearance, with large, olive-green eyes, ebony skin and dark brown hair styled expertly in a sharp, graded bob cut that enhanced her elfin features. She was older than the other two and in a steady relationship. She noted the man's name – Adam Josephs. She'd arrange for someone to speak to them both.

She yawned. It was now almost six thirty. A door banged. The station was coming to life. It was three days since Carrie had been found. Robyn had to find her killer. There was no time to waste, especially if he intended to murder again.

CHAPTER TWENTY-THREE

Ross had been watching the property for a couple of days and was convinced he'd found Princess. Gary Sessions was not best pleased at having his lunch interrupted.

'What d'ya want? I'm trying to get some grub before I go back to work,' he snarled. Somewhere inside the house a dog barked.

'I'm sorry, sir,' said Ross, wafting his investigator's licence. 'I have reason to believe you have a dog stolen from a property in Gallow Street.'

'Naff off. Dog's mine.' Gary Sessions stood at five foot five, with coal black eyes, a shaved head and a thick neck decorated with a tattoo of a large skull. 'Bought it, didn't I?'

'In that case, we don't have a problem, and when you prove that, I'll be on my way.'

'I got it from a breeder.' The man scowled at Ross.

'Then you'll have paperwork to show that, sir.'

'Who the fuck are you, anyway? You could be some hustler after my dog. Why don't you just fuck off?' Gary shoved at the front door and scowled again as it bounced against Ross's heavy-duty boot.

'I'll call the police if you don't clear off,' he shouted, spittle flying from his mouth. Ross maintained a level voice.

'That would be fine too, sir. Why not give them a call? Then we can settle this argument.' Inside, the dog howled, a melancholy wail.

'I've had enough of this nonsense. Get off my property.'

'You maintain the animal inside is yours?'

'Yes, it fucking is. Now for the last time, get lost or I'll give you a battering you won't forget.'

Gary Sessions's neck went red as he breathed out noisily, reminding Ross of a bull about to charge.

'The dog I'm searching for has a microchip which will identify it and the real owner.'

For a second, Gary Sessions seemed perplexed. He blinked several times. A voice rose behind him.

'Gary, you muppet. Bloody animal's been chipped.' A woman appeared behind Gary. She'd been in hearing distance the entire time. She was about the same size as Gary, with short, cropped hair and a stud in her nose. 'Who are you?'

Ross held up his licence again. 'Private investigator, madam. You must be Mrs Sessions.'

'It doesn't matter who the fuck I am. Gary found the mutt wandering the streets. We thought it had been abandoned, didn't we, Gary?'

Gary turned his head sharply, caught the look in his wife's eyes and nodded repeatedly. 'Yeah, it was outside. Looked hungry. I whistled for it to come to me. We like dogs so we thought we'd look after it for a bit, like.'

'And it didn't have a collar?'

'No, mate. That's why we didn't know where it had come from.' Gary's eyes narrowed.

'And you didn't check with the police to see if the dog was missing, or take it to the vet to see if it had an identification chip?'

'Look, I told you the dog was wandering about outside. We took it in. Good citizens, like. We fed it and looked after it. Not had time to find out what careless bastard lost it.'

'Shut up, Gary.' His wife pushed ahead of him, her body filling the doorway, thick arms folded across her chest. 'Gary's telling the truth. What are you after? Are you one of them reward seekers, cos if there's a reward, we want it. We found the animal and we're not handing it over to you so you can collect money from the owners.'

Ross shook his head. 'There's no reward money. The owner is as skint as can be. She's a single mum.'

'Then how come she's hired a private detective?' Her eyebrows rose.

'I'm working the case for free. She's devastated. I couldn't bear to see anyone that unhappy. Her dog is everything to her but she can't afford to pay to get it back. Now, can I take the dog, please, or do I have to involve the police? I'm quite happy to ring them and explain the situation.'

'Oh, for pity's sake, take the fucking animal. It shits everywhere and whines all the time. But don't you say nothing to the cops. We found it outside, like I told you. Legit, like.'

'Of course, Mrs Sessions.'

Ross waited patiently while Gary fetched the creature, dragging it to the door. A piece of rope hung around its neck. 'See, like I said, no collar.'

'Hello, Princess,' said Ross. The dog looked up at him. Its tail thumped once against the doorframe. 'Time to take you home.'

CHAPTER TWENTY-FOUR

DAY FOUR – THURSDAY 19 JANUARY

Mitz leaned forward into his computer screen as if it might yield the answers to all the questions that puzzled him. His face bore a faint trace of stubble, unusual for a man who took enormous pride in his appearance and never came on duty without pressed shirts and accompanied by a pleasant smell of deodorant, body spray or aftershave.

Robyn wasn't feeling quite as wholesome, with the effects of working all night and the frustration of making little progress. In spite of all their efforts, they'd not got closer to finding the woman in blue, nor tracked down Siobhan Connors, and Amber Dalton was still missing. They'd interviewed Carrie's ex-school friends and neighbours and got no more useful information, and to cap it all, Robyn had a meeting with DCI Flint.

Flint waved his hand for her to sit down. The report she'd written was laid out on the desk. He rested his hands on it and spoke, his voice ponderous.

'I've read through your concerns and given them due consideration.'

She waited for the inevitable 'but' she sensed was coming.

'But we have little reason to believe that Amber Dalton's disappearance is in any way connected to Carrie Miller's. He held up a finger as her mouth opened to protest. She closed it again.

'Your reasoning that there is some connection due to a message sent on Facebook has some validity, but insufficient for it to warrant investigating.' Again she began to protest. Flint quietened her with a look. 'I've spoken to DCI Forge, who's investigating the girl's disappearance. They now suspect Amber Dalton has run away. Further interviews with her friends have led them to believe she was under considerable pressure from her parents to do well at school and pass the Oxbridge exams. Amber told one of her friends that she'd never live up to her parents' expectations and some days she felt like "doing a bunk". In fact, she told the same person, she'd fantasised about running away. In light of this, they're looking into that possibility.'

'Which friend spoke to the police? I understood she was the model student.'

'It's irrelevant who gave them that information. Derbyshire Police is handling Amber Dalton's disappearance. She's not our responsibility. However, Carrie Miller is. Unless you can provide more concrete evidence than a message on Facebook, I can't allow you to use resources and go off on a wild-goose chase.'

'Sir, I must protest—' she began.

He cut her off by raising his hand. 'Noted. What progress have you made in the Carrie Miller case? Have you located the woman who deposited the trunk?'

'We're still looking into it, sir.'

'No suspects yet?'

She shook her head.

'And you spent yesterday afternoon talking to Amber's parents?'

'I had good reason to believe the cases were connected,' she said, head up, defiance in her eyes.

'I'm sure you did.'

His voice suggested she had been wasting her time and not concentrating on Carrie Miller.

'Sir, you read my report. I believe these cases are connected and I'm concerned we have a potential serial killer on our hands here. Amber Dalton and also Siobhan Connors might be in danger, and I think we should act on that.'

'I understand your concerns but unfortunately there's insufficient evidence to support them. Give me more and I'll be more accommodating.' He raised his hands, open-palmed, a resigned gesture. 'For now, concentrate on Carrie Miller. The clock is ticking, DI Carter. I want this Joanna Hutchinson found, and I mean soon.'

Her watch read 2.50 p.m. and she blinked her eyes, gritty from lack of sleep. She'd have to give Flint more evidence or a suspect. Her instincts rarely let her down, and she was convinced Amber and Siobhan were in danger. She needed to think. She would take a few hours off and relax her mind. Davies had taught her that too: that by not thinking about the very thing that was troubling her, she could actually look at it more clearly. She checked her watch. She'd slip out and take the girls to the cinema. That might help her.

She heard Sergeant Matt Higham's infectious laugh, an explosion of sound and then clattering as boots tramped down the corridor. He thumped the door to the office. 'Okay to join you, guv?'

'Thought you were working on Shearer's team.'

'Nailed the bastards. Freddie the snitch was right about the man in the pub. Don't know what DI Shearer said to him, but he coughed up all the information we needed to make an arrest. Bagged ourselves four criminals and a wardrobe stuffed with goodies – a massive stash of heroin and pills. Shearer's like the proverbial dog with two tails. He's with DCI Flint. No doubt getting a pat on the head. He told us to "bugger off back to DI Carter." He also said, "Ask her why she's still here looking like a panda that's gone several rounds with a boxing champion and lost when, according to the rota, she's supposed to be off duty."'

'Charming as ever, then.' Robyn was pleased for Tom. His tenacity had paid off. Sounded like they'd both been up all night. 'Good thing you're back. We've a few leads to chase up on. Mitz, give these two heroes, Matt and David, some names to check out. Pass David the dimensions for that trunk and set him to work on that. Matt, once Mitz has given you the details, go back to the self-storage warehouse and find the man who helped Frank Cummings offload the trunk. He might work in the area or have been visiting one of the other premises there. Anna has a CCTV photo of him.'

'So, it isn't your day off?' Matt Higham grinned at her.

'It is, but I'm only taking a few hours out. I'll be back later.'

Matt grinned. 'Is that to check up on us?'

'Right, because as soon as I'm out of here, you'll be swanning about drinking coffee and scoffing the office supply of custard creams. The tin has only just been refilled.'

He batted his eyelashes. 'I can't help it. I'm addicted to them. They make the best dunkers.'

Don't talk rubbish,' Mitz said. 'You can't get a better dunking biscuit than a Rich Tea.'

Robyn retrieved her keys from under the file she'd been reading. 'Please tell me you're going to get on to proper police work and not spend the afternoon debating which biscuit is the best for dunking.'

'Course, guv. There's no debate. Custard creams win every time.'

She shook her head in mock despair. This lot were worse than children when they were having what she called a 'silly moment'. At least she had a good-natured team. For that she was very thankful. 'Bye, bye, kiddies. Behave yourselves or I'll have to ask DI Shearer to come and sit with you.'

She shut the door and checked her watch. Time for a quick shower, and then to collect Amélie and Florence. She couldn't let them down again. She'd been promising to take them out to the cinema for ages. It was probably a blessing she didn't have children of her own. She'd never be able to fulfil both functions at the same time – a detective and a mother. A familiar pang rose in her chest. It would have been nice to have been given the opportunity.

CHAPTER TWENTY-FIVE

Florence could barely contain her excitement. Hunter was due to chat to her, but before that she had to go to the cinema with Amélie and Robyn.

Ordinarily she'd have been really pleased to go to the cinema, but today she didn't want to go. She wanted to think up answers to Hunter's possible questions and prepare for her boyfriend. That's how she now viewed him.

Hunter had changed everything even though they'd only chatted the once. Before Hunter, she'd been a silly teenager, angst-ridden and desperate to be liked. Amélie was everything she wasn't. Not that Florence begrudged her friend being so attractive and clever. But the fact remained that she was Amélie's less attractive sidekick. She was the frumpy, boring one who couldn't answer questions during science and had no idea how to do fractions, while Amélie found everything so easy. If Amélie had been vain and started getting all bitchy, like many of the others, Florence would have dropped her, but she was simply a nice, quiet, clever, composed girl who put her friend first. Florence couldn't ignore that fact.

The year before, Florence had chased after an older boy, thinking he was interested in her. It had transpired the only reason he'd talked to her was because he was interested in Amélie. She'd felt so stupid. Anyway, now she had a boy who was interested in her and her alone.

She checked her appearance again. She'd spent ages brushing on thick eyebrows. Her real, pale-ginger eyebrows were almost non-existent. These ones were awesome and she looked at least three years older. She may only be going out to the cinema, but she wanted to look as good as she could. She flopped onto her fluffy pillow and sighed. No matter how much make-up she put on, there was no getting away from her age. She was going to have to tell Hunter the truth, or near-truth. He was expecting someone over eighteen. She examined her fluorescent-pink nails. She'd stuck the false nails over her own chewed nails and one was already lifting. She searched for the nail glue and attempted to squeeze some under it, hoping it would stay in place. She would tell Hunter she was sixteen. That wasn't too far from her real age, after all.

She looked around her large bedroom. It was really a bedroom/ studio. On one side was a proper easel, and on it a portrait of Sampson the Third, one of her parents' priciest horses. He was a magnificent specimen, and Florence had spent several days attempting to capture his majesty and the sparkling intelligence in his eyes. Here she had a perfect view of the stables below. The stables and the horses were what she enjoyed painting most. Her mother and father worked full tilt. The horses were groomed, trained, raced and looked after almost twenty-four seven, and when the pair weren't actively working with the animals, they were abroad, seeking new horses they could train, or on the racing circuit.

Florence had ridden as a child, but a tumble from a mare had left her determined never to mount a horse again, in spite of entreaties from her folks. She worked in the stables for a while, helping out the stable girls, but she developed a severe allergy to the straw and hay and sneezed incessantly every time she cleaned them out. In the end, taking pity on her daughter, Christine admitted the equestrian life was not for Florence. For the most part she distanced herself from it all, and along with it, her parents. Content to stay inside and paint or draw, Florence had never had any problems or concerns until the previous year when, without warning, her body had developed and she found herself torn between remaining a child and wanting to experiment at being a young woman.

Her mother was downstairs, bustling about in the sitting room with the vacuum cleaner. She was expecting a potential buyer for two of the horses. Her mother wasn't big on housework, and it was best to stay out of the way during cleaning frenzies. If Florence went downstairs, she'd likely be asked to help. A small voice spoke up, saying the real reason was she didn't want her mum to see her until it was too late to ask her remove her make-up and change her unsuitable clothes. She tugged at the top. It covered her expanding chest but left her stomach on display. Florence hadn't been eating much the last couple of weeks and her normally pudgy belly was much flatter.

Her mobile lit up. It was Amélie: *On our way. See you in ten minutes.*

She hesitated. She didn't really want to watch the film. She could still call it off and say she felt sick. She thumbed the keypad, then hesitated. She'd still be home in time to talk to Hunter. She'd have to make sure Robyn didn't come in for a chat with her mum or she'd be stuck with Amélie when she should be online. She'd think of some excuse at the cinema.

Downstairs, Christine was cleaning with gusto. She gave her daughter a smile and turned the machine off. 'Almost finished. You look…' she pursed her lips, searching for the right words, 'very grown up.'

She knew her mother disapproved, but that was tough luck as far as Florence was concerned. It was her body and she'd do whatever she liked. Christine gave her the same look she gave her favourite horses, head to one side. 'You know, you don't have to race towards becoming older. It'll happen naturally and quickly enough. You've done your make-up very well but you look even nicer without it.'

Florence snorted and hunched her shoulders, making her tiny sparkly top cover some of her midriff. There it was, the maternal way of disapproving. What did her mother know about make-up or clothes? She always looked like she'd slept in a barn. 'I'm thirteen,' she mumbled, knowing she was going to lose the argument before it began.

'Thirteen going on twenty. I know, sweetheart.'

Florence cringed. Her mum always called her sweetheart when she wanted to manipulate her. This time it wouldn't work. She was standing her ground and she was not removing any make-up.

Christine moved towards her and examined her. 'Sweetie, you're going to the cinema with Amélie, not a nightclub.' Seeing the dark look on her daughter's face, she changed tack. 'You are a beautiful girl. You don't need to wear all that warpaint.' She paused, offering a smile, but was met with sullen silence.

Florence crossed her arms and dug her chin into her neck. 'It's not warpaint. Just because you don't like to dress up doesn't mean I shouldn't.' She bit her tongue. She hadn't meant to say that. It was unfair. All she knew was she wanted to get away from her mother before she suspected there was a boy in her life.

Christine sighed. 'I think it's time for a talk.'

'I know all about sex, so don't bother.'

The conversation was halted by the blast of Robyn's car horn. Christine appealed to her daughter one last time. 'When you get home, let's chat.'

'Whatever,' said Florence, moving towards the door, relieved to escape. As soon as she shut the door, she felt a pang of guilt. Her mum was only trying to be nice to her. She'd say sorry later.

CHAPTER TWENTY-SIX

Ross found a parking space outside the shop in Gallow Street. The dog spent the journey on the passenger seat, staring out of the window, tongue out, panting lightly. Ross had been convinced it was smiling and chatted to it as if it were human.

'Yes, you're home. No pulling me over in the rush to get back to your mum.' Princess stood, eager to get out. A steady thump, thump, thump of her tail against the car seat.

'Come on, pooch, let's go make your owner very happy.'

Princess bounced out of the car and stood beside him while he fumbled with the lock, one hand loosely holding the length of rope around the dog's neck.

'You're most obedient, aren't you?' Ross patted the animal. It nosed him affectionately.

'Ohmigosh!' The shriek made him jump. Lauren raced towards him, fell to her knees, covered the excited dog's face with kisses. 'You found her. You bloody well found her. You're a friggin' awesome detective.'

Ross shrugged. 'I got lucky.'

Lauren stood up. In her heels she was five inches taller than Ross. She beamed at him. 'Mum's gonna be made up. Can I take her?'

'Sure.' Ross handed the rope to Lauren.

'Where was she?'

'Some delivery driver had her. Claimed he found her wandering about lost. I figured it was best to get Princess away from him than argue the toss. It's not worth involving the police. I think he'd hoped there would be a reward and he'd claim it. This sort of thing happens a fair bit.'

Princess strained at the lead, tail up, eager to get home.

'I didn't think you'd find her, you know?' Princess sniffed at a brown paper bag bearing the logo of a fast food outlet, now discarded on the pavement. 'Do you look for missing people too?'

'I have done, why?'

'I think one of my mates has gone missing.'

'Think?'

'I'm not sure. Her name's Siobhan Connors. She split up from her boyfriend a couple of weeks ago, and we were supposed to meet up for a drink – a girl's night out – to help her get over it. She didn't show. I texted her and got a strange message back saying she was sorry but she'd met a new fella on the Internet and had gone away with him. It seemed really weird. Surely she'd have told me about him beforehand?'

'What about her parents? Have you spoken to them?'

'I don't have their numbers. They both live in Ireland but they're with different partners now. They split up when Siobhan was little and she doesn't have anything much to do with them. She came over on her own when she was seventeen and met Adam. It became serious and they moved in together. I met her at a nightclub in Derby. We ordered exactly the same drink. Got chatting after that and then got pissed on vodka shots and danced the night away. She crashed out at our place. Adam was proper annoyed. They had one of those hot and cold relationships. You know, lots of fighting and shouting and then lots of making up.'

'Does Adam have any idea where she is?'

'I phoned him. Said he didn't give a shit where she was or who she was with. He'd had enough of her moods. I called her manager, Lucy, at work too. She said Siobhan had taken compassionate leave, whatever that is. She sounded right narked that Siobhan had taken off without letting them know in advance.'

'Have you considered reporting her missing?'

Lauren made a 'pfft' noise. 'I'd look a right idiot, telling the coppers I think she's missing. She texted me two days ago.' She lifted her phone and read:

'"Hi Lauren. Having great time. New bloke is awesome. Won't be back for a while. X"'

'Sounds like she's decided to buzz off for a while. She might even have been seeing this new chap while with Adam.'

Lauren shook her head. 'Nah. It's always "Adam this" and "Adam that". She never mentioned anyone else.'

'If you've received a text from her, why are you concerned?'

Lauren gazed at him with large eyes. 'It just doesn't sound like her. None of this sounds like her. I know it sounds silly but I've got a feeling something's happened.'

'Call her.'

'I have called. I'm not stupid. It always goes to answerphone, and that's odd too. It's like she's avoiding me.'

'You're probably concerned about nothing, but I'll look into it.'

'Would you? I'm actually beginning to worry about the silly bitch. Fancy going off like that with someone you hardly know off the Internet. It seems mental. I can't believe she wouldn't have told me.'

Lauren put her phone away. She pulled gently at the rope. Princess trotted beside her, towards number forty.

'This is the best thing that's happened all week. Can't wait to see Mum's face.'

CHAPTER TWENTY-SEVEN

Robyn glanced at the teenager in the back seat, thumbing her mobile phone, and then at Amélie, who merely shrugged. The girls made an odd couple: Florence was chubby, shy, with patches of freckles on her pale skin, and bushy, ginger-blonde hair that never looked tamed; and Amélie was dark-haired, willowy, confident and intelligent, with a beauty that was beginning to bloom.

Robyn was happy to have Florence join them. In her opinion, the girl was lacking in self-confidence. Today, the Florence that clambered into the back seat of the VW Golf was a different one to normal. Robyn waved at Christine, who stood by the door watching the car drive away and gave a tight smile. Florence, however, after saying hello, immediately pawed at her mobile phone and didn't notice her mother.

Amélie, sitting beside Robyn, didn't seem to find the fact her friend was heavily made-up, inappropriately dressed for a cold January afternoon and wearing bright pink lipstick that did nothing for her complexion, peculiar. Florence stabbed at her phone and cursed under her breath.

'You okay?' Amélie turned to face her.

'Nail's broken off.' Florence held up the pink falsie.

'Put it in your purse or pocket. You can stick it back on later. You can't wear them to school tomorrow anyway. One of the teachers will only make you take them off.'

Florence scowled. 'I know that. I just wanted to try them out tonight,' she replied.

Amélie shrugged.

Robyn caught the look on Florence's face and waved a hand devoid of any varnish. Her nails were short and in need of attention. 'Do you think I should get mine done?'

'I've got a nail file with me, if you'd like me to tidy them up.' Florence pulled an emery board from her purse.

'Brilliant. A meal, a film and a manicure.' Robyn grinned at Florence, who returned the smile. The tension had disappeared.

The film couldn't end soon enough for Florence. She'd said she needed the toilet and escaped twice, checking on her phone to see if Hunter was active on Fox or Dog. She found she was checking other girls' pages more frequently, hoping he wasn't looking them up too. Today, she found another five dog emojis under her photo, and a girl called Sex Muffin had posted:

Kitten, I think you've Photoshopped your photo. Fess up!

Florence flushed crimson. She checked Sex Muffin out, and to her dismay recognised her from school. She was one of the final-year students. There was a chance the girl actually knew her. When she returned to her own profile, another girl had joined the conversation:

Sex Muffin, you cud be right. ROFL at way she's pouting.
Kitten, you're not a bloody supermodel. LOL

Florence's lip trembled. Why were they being so horrible to her? She answered:

Don't be so bitchy.

Her hands shook as she typed. She was conscious that she wasn't skinny like most of the girls in her class, or beautiful, but it was horrible to read the comments. She definitely didn't want Hunter to spot them. He might go off her. There was a sudden rapping on the toilet door. She sat up with a jolt. Robyn was outside.

'Florence, are you feeling all right?'

Florence flushed the chain, stuffed the phone into her back pocket and came out, a sheepish look on her face. 'Sorry, Robyn. I think I've got a bit of a stomach bug.'

Robyn nodded but her eyes narrowed. Florence squirmed. It was impossible to lie to the woman. 'I'm feeling okay now.' She washed her hands and followed Robyn back into the cinema, her mind on Fox or Dog and worries that Hunter would not chat to her later.

'Look, I know I'm not one of your schoolmates, but you can talk to me, you know?'

Florence considered her words. She couldn't tell Robyn about Hunter. It would get straight back to her mother.

'No, it's nothing, really. I've got stomach cramps, that's all.' Florence wished she'd let it drop.

'If you ever need to chat just ring me.'

Florence nodded. 'Thanks. I will.' She was thankful when Robyn finally moved off back to the film. Just for good measure, she clutched her stomach as she slipped back into her seat.

Robyn's mind wasn't on the film. She'd been thinking about the missing girls until Florence had got up and squeezed past her, smiling apologetically. The first time, she'd paid little heed, but it was clear from Florence's restlessness that she was also thinking about something else. She'd waited outside the toilet door the second time Florence had disappeared, suspicious of Florence's excuse. She was certain Florence had been on her phone in the cubicle. Whatever she was doing had been so important that she'd made up a poor excuse to leave a film she'd wanted to see, to hide out in the toilets. The secrecy bothered Robyn. She ought to mention it to Christine, and then she recalled the troubled look on the woman's face as she drove off earlier.

She'd tried speaking to her again when both of them had waited while Amélie went to the toilet after the film. She'd tried chatting about subjects she knew interested Florence, and then about school and asking how things were going, but she got nowhere. Florence wasn't giving any clues as to what was wrong. Robyn felt thwarted and annoyed with herself for not being able to gain the girl's confidence. Perhaps Christine already suspected something was up.

Florence stuck to the stomach bug story and sat in the back of the car holding her belly to make it seem more credible, occasionally screwing up her face as if in pain when Robyn caught her eye in the rear-view mirror. Once they reached her house, she thanked them.

'Make sure you take something for that stomach ache,' said Robyn, hoping Florence would pick up on her tone and understand that she'd not put up a convincing performance. Florence mumbled something about an early night and bolted from the car before they could follow her into the house.

The trip to the cinema left Robyn puzzling over Florence. When she asked Amélie about it she said she thought there might be a boy involved, although Florence had not mentioned one. That made sense to Robyn. Undoubtedly, a relationship was causing the girl to behave quite differently. Soon Amélie would change too and maybe her relationship with Robyn would shift. Robyn recalled becoming secretive as she went through puberty. She no doubt caused her own mother some grief from time to time. It was tough coming to terms with no longer being a child and entering a world where you wanted to be considered a grown-up but were not quite ready for it.

'So, what did you think of Bob?' Robyn asked once they'd dropped the subject of Florence.

'Amazing. You know how much I like cats. Grandma's cat, Pipette, is so beautiful. I keep asking Mum if we can get a cat. I'd really love to own one but Richard is allergic to the fur. He sneezes like mad when we go to Grandma's. He said he didn't mind if we got one, but Mum isn't so sure. I'll have to keep asking, won't I?' The corners of her mouth lifted in a wide smile so like her father's.

'Dad would have loved a cat too. I remember him reading a story to me about a cat called Mog, who helped some kittens and then went to heaven.' She let out a small sigh. 'Do you think there's a heaven, Robyn?'

Robyn was surprised when she mentioned Davies. She hadn't spoken about him in a long while. She was taken aback by the question. It had come out of the blue.

'I think there's more to life than we understand,' she replied. 'We aren't capable of comprehending what the universe is truly about.'

Amélie gave the answer some thought, then faced Robyn. 'Thanks.'

'What for?'

'For not treating me like a little kid. I'm not sure where Dad is or what heaven is supposed to be, but I'd like to think he's somewhere in the universe, watching and smiling at us.'

Robyn lifted her hand from the steering wheel and took Amélie's in her own. She wished Davies could see what a wonderful daughter he had, and her heart ached for the girl beside her who was, like her, still struggling with her loss.

With Amélie back home too, she returned to the office and spent several hours going back through her notes, trying to make sense of the case. She rewrote the list of possible suspects. She circled Dev Khan's name and considered the possibility of him being in cahoots with Frank Cummings and Karl London. Could he possibly have hidden Carrie in the trunk? It seemed too unlikely. She shut her eyes and considered that possibility again before reading through information Mitz had left her.

Vincent Miller, an HGV driver employed by the same company for the last twelve years, had no criminal record. A statement from the company described him as a reliable employee with a willingness to work overtime. There were no reports of violence, and at this stage, nothing to indicate he was connected to the murder of his daughter.

She sighed and ploughed on. Somebody had killed Carrie. She stared at the photograph on the whiteboard and wondered what sort of person would murder a young girl. It fell to her to fathom out who could commit such a crime.

CHAPTER TWENTY-EIGHT

DAY FIVE – FRIDAY 20 JANUARY

Robyn arrived at the station just after ten on Friday morning. Sleep had finally overtaken her in the early hours and she'd slept through her alarm. DCI Flint stood in her office talking to Mitz. He handed her a report, his face a grave mask. 'Amber Dalton,' he said, simply.

Robyn's heart dropped to her stomach. 'Oh, no.' She glanced at the first page. The body of Amber Dalton had been found on Cannock Chase. She'd been wrapped in a plastic bag and hidden under a pile of leaves, near a path by the woods.

'I'm afraid so. Derbyshire Police have identified her. I've requested all relevant information be sent over to you to ascertain any connection between her murder and that of Carrie Miller.'

Robyn sank into her chair, ran her hands through her hair and closed her eyes. Two beautiful young women with their lives in front of them had been spirited away, murdered and dumped, wrapped in large plastic rubbish bags. She thought about the anxious parents, putting on brave faces, who'd been hoping their precious child would return. Robyn wasn't sure she could continue, her heart felt so heavy, but then she had a vision of Amélie and her determination rose once more to the surface. She had to uncover the murderer before the killer targeted any other girls.

'Mitz, while I'm going through the paperwork, will you talk to her friends, especially…' She rummaged through a stack of notes on her desk, each headed with a name. 'Samantha Dancer,' she continued, softly. 'I'm looking for any connections between Amber and Carrie. Ask the tech boys to go back through Amber's laptop. I understand nothing was flagged up last time it was checked but she *must* have visited some website that would give us a clue. And can somebody talk to Amber's ex-boyfriend, Justin Bolt?'

'Roger that, boss.'

Anna appeared at the door, her face grey and grim. 'Just heard Amber Dalton's been found.'

Mitz nodded. Robyn handed Anna the top sheet of paper in the report without looking up. The phone rang, interrupting her reading. 'DI Carter.' She knew who it was instantly. The small cough before she began speaking. The damn woman was like a ferret up a trouser leg. How had she got hold of this so quickly? Amy Walters was a local journalist who had, after getting a scoop on the Lichfield Leopard case in November 2016, been promoted to senior journalist. 'Amy, it's a no comment from me.'

'Don't hang up. I might be able to help you.'

Robyn tucked the phone under her chin while lifting the crime scene photograph of Amber to the light. Amber Dalton had been mutilated, her face a bloodied mess, eyes open and glassy. A large piece of skin had been cut away from her forehead, leaving a jagged rectangle of magenta flesh on display. The girl was dressed in a plain hospital gown, and had been wrapped in a polythene bag. Cause of death was not yet confirmed, but forensics had ascertained she'd been dead for over a week and her body had been moved the day before. *While I was at the cinema with Amélie and Florence?*

'How? How can *you* help?'

Robyn wanted to concentrate on the facts, and at the moment the removal of the rectangle of skin was troubling her. Amy Walters was the last person she wanted to deal with, yet on this occasion she would make an exception. Robyn wanted to catch the monster who'd taken this girl's life so much she would enlist the help of the wretched, conniving journalist who had almost blown her last murder inquiry by not sharing information.

'I have a witness who believes they've seen something relevant to the Carrie Miller case.'

'Who? Why didn't they come forward and tell the police?'

'They want to remain anonymous.'

'For crying out loud, Amy. You know how it works. If they are withholding valuable information from the police I can get them brought in and questioned.'

'I doubt it. Meet me in half an hour at the Wyevale Garden Centre at Wolseley Bridge.'

'I'm really up to my eyes here.'

'It'll be worth it.'

'If you're messing me about…'

'I'm not. See you in half an hour.'

Robyn slammed the receiver down. Amber's sightless eyes stared up at her. 'Sodding hell.'

Mitz looked across and Robyn shook her head. She rarely swore. She was the queen of controlling her emotions. This time though, she knew she looked as if she could do more than swear. Two girls were dead. She needed to ask Harry McKenzie to take another look at Carrie's forehead, and to find Siobhan Connors. Instead, she was off to have a cup of tea with a slimy reporter. She straightened her shoulders and, without another word, she picked up the photograph of Amber Dalton and placed it on the board next to Carrie Miller's. Then she stomped out of the office.

The garden centre stood next to the canal. At this time of the morning there were only a few visitors. A blue BMW pulled into the adjacent space. Amy Walters emerged wearing a fashionable black cape over a checked black and red skirt, teamed with thick tights and high-heeled ankle boots. Robyn had never seen her without the large canvas bag slung over her right shoulder. She got out of her own car and faced her.

'I've not got time for stupid games, Amy.'

Amy's eyes narrowed. 'Neither have I.'

'Where's this witness, then?'

'What's in it for me?' Amy smirked.

Robyn felt heat rise up her neck. 'How about you behave like a responsible citizen for once? I'm investigating a serious crime. If you don't have anything that will help, shove off. And don't you dare print any of this conversation or so help me…'

Amy raised both hands in surrender. 'It's all off the record. I want to help. I also want a crumb – something, anything at all you can give me. Come on, Robyn. I don't want to have to use unreliable sources for this. It's sensitive. It's about a murdered girl. I'm not going to sensationalise that, am I?'

'Give me what you've got first.'

Amy's lips twitched. 'And you'll let me have an exclusive after the case like you did with the Lichfield Leopard last year?'

'If your witness is reliable and provides me with a lead, I'll consider it. That's all I'm prepared to say at this point. I got into trouble last time for speaking to you.'

'It's not for the newspaper. Some of it will be. I'm writing a book about murderers – what makes them tick, that sort of thing. I want to get some details on the case. I won't reveal anything came from you. I'll have to dig deeper if you don't assist and that might mean upsetting some of the victims' families. Deal?'

Robyn glared at the woman, almost tasting the disgust she felt. Amy was hard-nosed. She would ask anyone and everyone if it meant a good story. Better it came from Robyn than have Carrie's friends and families hounded by the career-driven Amy Walters. 'Witness first.'

Amy shrugged. 'Okay. Follow me.'

They strolled into the garden centre, past the trays of plants and into the tearoom, one side containing a children's play area, the other filled with painted tables and chairs, and a long food counter. It was empty apart from one table. In the far corner sat a woman, hands wrapped around a bone china mug. Amy ordered two coffees.

The woman in the corner looked up when the women were almost upon her, eyes searching behind them, moving continuously from side to side, like a caged animal. 'She alone?' Her voice was distinctly Eastern European. Amy nodded, pulled out a chair and slid onto it.

'This is DI Carter. You can tell her what you told me.'

The woman's head wobbled from side to side. 'No one saw you come here?'

Amy drew up a chair and spoke softly. 'Nobody saw us. Now, Ivanka, you must tell DI Carter what you saw.'

Ivanka was in her late fifties, with sharp features, dark-haired and shapeless in her woollen coat. 'Okay.' There was a lengthy silence. Robyn sat back, ensuring she did not crowd the woman. Amy kept a steady eye on Ivanka.

'I was on way to work. I saw a white van at warehouse.'

Robyn waited.

'I saw this white van and in back of van was big box, no, not big *box*, it was big chest for travelling. I saw man trying to lift this chest. He not able to. He called to man walking by. This man, he helped pick up chest and they carry into warehouse. I went to work. I did not think anything funny about this. Then, on Monday last, I was again going on shift and I saw many police. I walked past and I saw police carrying this same chest. At work, everyone was saying there was a body in the warehouse and I thought, this trunk had body in it.'

Robyn felt a sudden rush. Ivanka had been at the self-storage warehouse the day Joanne Hutchinson had delivered the trunk containing Carrie Miller's body. She had seen Frank, together with the man who had assisted him in offloading the trunk, and probably had a good look at Joanne Hutchinson.

'Is good information.' The woman stood up, pulled her coat around her.

Amy shook her head. 'Not so fast, Ivanka. DI Carter needs to ask a couple of questions first.' She smiled at Robyn.

'Ivanka, this is very useful information. You saw the two men who carried in the trunk?'

Ivanka nodded.

'And did you see a woman with them?'

Ivanka nodded again. 'She was a skinny lady, yellow-white hair. She had jeans and a blue leather jacket, very expensive, I think. I liked her shoes. She had boots with high heels. Very high heels.'

Robyn nodded and smiled in encouragement. 'Did you see the registration of the van. The number plate?'

'No. It was white van and had orange box with white lettering. Two letters, I think, maybe three.'

'Anything else?'

'Man who help with trunk, he went to get pills.'

'Pills?'

Amy chimed in. 'Ivanka means he went to the place that produces and sells vitamin pills – Vitamed. It's on Towers Business Park.'

Robyn pulled out her mobile and sent a message to Mitz to arrange for somebody to check it out. The sooner they found the stranger, the better.

'Will you come into the station and help us further, Ivanka?'

The woman's head shook violently. 'No. I not go.' She shrank into her coat.

'It would only be to write down everything. Maybe try and help you remember more?'

Ivanka stood abruptly. 'No. No more questions. I tell you everything. I must go now.'

Robyn rose to prevent her from leaving, but Amy placed a hand on her arm and shook her head. She sat again. Ivanka shoved her hands into the pockets of her coat, hunched her shoulders and looked at Amy.

Amy gave her a smile. 'Don't worry. You did the right thing.'

Ivanka nodded, tight-lipped. 'You keep your promise.'

'You know I will.'

Without another word, Ivanka shuffled away. Amy sat back with a small grin on her face. Robyn began to feel needled.

'Why wouldn't Ivanka speak to the police and tell us this without all the cloak and dagger stuff?'

Amy leant on her elbows and spoke quietly. 'She can't. She's in a witness protection programme. She turned evidence against her violent husband some years ago. He shot his business associate and was sentenced to life. She's terrified he'll find out where she is and send someone to deal with her.'

'She still didn't tell us much.'

'She told me more than you. I recorded that interview with her. I wanted you to meet her first, before I played it to you. There's more on it. Not a lot, but some more.'

'How come she chose to speak to you and not the police? Members of the public, especially those who are in hiding, don't normally seek out journalists for this sort of thing.'

Amy crossed her legs. 'When I was ten years old, my mum and dad split up and my mum had to take on a full-time job in Exeter to pay the mortgage. That meant she could no longer collect me from school, so she employed a woman to fetch me, make my dinner and sit and play with me until she got home. The lady who looked after me didn't have any children of her own and was like a mother to me.'

Robyn's eyebrows rose. 'Ivanka?'

'She wasn't Ivanka then. I can honestly say I love that lady. I wouldn't want to jeopardise her new life. She works as a chef in the pub at the Towers Business Park. I went in there for a works event and spotted her. She didn't recognise me, and when I actually got to talk to her, she swore me to secrecy. She was frantic when she learnt who I was – that someone from her past had found her. A few days ago she called the newspaper and asked for me, personally. She didn't want to compromise her new identity by talking to anyone else.' Amy uncrossed her legs and leant forward again. 'I've handed over the information I have. Now you must agree to let me cover this story.'

Robyn shifted uncomfortably. Her hip grumbled. 'Okay. But not yet. There's too much sensitive information and I want to keep it from the public for now. I can't have this woman being alerted.'

'Fair enough. I'll email you my full interview with Ivanka. I've heard a rumour the body in the trunk was of a young girl, wrapped in plastic.'

'I can't tell you any more for now.'

Amy gave a curt nod. 'I'll only report any facts for now. I want the whole story soon, though, DI Carter. I don't want anyone to get in ahead of me. You understand. Big stories sell newspapers.'

Robyn drained her coffee and stood to leave. Amy was closer to the truth than she realised. This was big. If Carrie and Amber's murders were related then Robyn quite probably had a serial killer to unearth.

CHAPTER TWENTY-NINE

Robyn bustled into the office, threw off her coat and called for a meeting. They shifted the chairs to face her. David Marker rustled a family bag of Maltesers and offered it to Robyn, who refused.

'We've got a witness, who can't be named because she's in a police protection programme, who spotted Joanne Hutchinson at the self-storage warehouse on the twentieth of December.'

'That's good, because I was beginning to wonder if Joanne actually existed,' said Matt. 'I was starting to believe Dev Khan, Frank Cummings and Karl London had conspired to murder Carrie Miller and fabricated this woman.'

Robyn gave a tight smile. 'Me too, Matt. However, we're going to continue searching for her because now this person claims to have seen her and a white van with white lettering inside an orange box. She believes she saw two or three letters. Matt, go through every van hire establishment that has orange and white logos on the side of their vehicles. I know Anna's already contacted hire companies, but we must have missed it. Maybe it's a vehicle Joanne borrowed rather than rented. Check out local firms and talk to any that have orange and white designs on their vans. The witness thinks the unknown helper who lent a hand with the trunk went to a company called Vitamed. If we can find him, he might also be able to tell us more about Joanne Hutchinson. Matt, you already tried Vitamed, didn't you?'

'I spoke to the girl on the desk. Didn't recognise him at all. Told me most of the customers were regulars and she hadn't seen him.'

Anna waved a large black and white image. 'We managed to clear the CCTV still up a bit so he's more visible. Want me to take it and try again?'

'Whichever one of you has a free moment first.' Robyn paused. 'Here's a conundrum for you to work out. Our witness revealed that the woman in blue, calling herself Joanne Hutchinson, wore high-heeled boots on the day she went to the self-storage unit to deliver the trunk. Frank Cummings said Joanne couldn't help offload the trunk that day because she had pulled her back. Surely, if you have a bad back, you wear flatter shoes? I've had trouble with my hip recently and I couldn't stick on a pair of stilettos and prance about in them for love nor money.'

David sniggered. 'Sorry, guv. The thought of you prancing anywhere made me chuckle, especially in stilettos. They don't really go with the uniformed officer look.'

'Indeed not.' She gave a brief smile. 'Why would Joanne Hutchinson wear high heels to a self-storage warehouse? And wouldn't the heels interfere with her driving?'

'Maybe she fabricated the bad back purely to avoid CCTV cameras, or leaving any fingerprints on the trunk.' David flicked a chocolate into his mouth.

Robyn nodded. 'Possibly so.'

'Or, she's used to driving vans. Plenty of women have jobs delivering goods in vans or lorries these days. Maybe she prefers to drive in high heels. My wife manages okay in hers.' Matt shrugged and gave a boyish grin.

Robyn rubbed her chin. 'You're right, Matt. I overthought that one. She could simply have had a pair of flats that she changed into for driving. I don't mind admitting I'm flummoxed. And now we have a second victim, another young woman who received a Facebook message from Carrie Miller and who, like Carrie, also disappeared.' She pointed to Amber Dalton's photograph – 'Amber

Dalton, sixteen years old, a bright, enthusiastic student at Sandwell, a private school in Derbyshire. Never been in trouble that we know about. No boyfriend. Diligent – responsible, even. Parents leave her to go away for a few days. She refuses to accompany them, citing coursework as the excuse. While they're away, she sends them text messages and answers theirs, and it's only on their return they discover she's disappeared from home and alert the police.' She tapped the photograph. 'Derbyshire Police carried out a full search of the area and found nothing to indicate where Amber might have been. There were no witnesses whatsoever. Her parents are not considered to be suspects.

'Amber died approximately a week to ten days ago. Death between January eighth and January thirteenth. Forensics concluded she'd been transported sometime in the early hours of Friday the twentieth. They also believe that examination of tissue and the state of decomposition suggest she'd been kept in cold storage for a few days, prior to being buried. I don't need to remind you Carrie's body was also frozen at some point, and that concerns me. We're quite probably looking for one and the same killer. Amber was found in a shallow grave, covered with leaves and bracken on Cannock Chase where it adjoins Penkridge Park Road.' She indicated a red cross on a map, showing the location of the discovery.

Matt Higham held up his biro. 'It strikes me that this conceal-ment wasn't as well thought out as the first. What I mean is, Joanne Hutchinson went to a great deal of trouble to rent a self-storage unit, put Carrie's body in a trunk and then hide it from sight in a locked unit, which would not have been opened had we not been on a hunt for drugs. Carrie could have been in there months, or even years. There wasn't the same planning involved in hiding Amber's body. Her body wasn't buried in a deep grave, for one thing, and the location is right on the edge of the woods near a path, where there's a good chance of it being discovered by a passer-by.'

'Valid point. What might that indicate?'

Matt pondered the question, rubbing his bald head. David swallowed a chocolate and spoke. 'She's getting sloppy? She couldn't carry Amber's body too far?'

Mitz fiddled with a paper cup. 'If she had an accomplice, they could have carried her further, so maybe it proves she was working alone. Or, possibly, she didn't have as much time to organise the disposal of Amber's body.'

'Or she's getting cocky,' added Matt. 'She might have grown in confidence. Got a bigger ego. It happens sometimes. A criminal gets away with a crime and then makes mistakes afterwards by not being as meticulous in their planning, or she wanted Amber to be found.'

Anna leant forward, elbows on her desk. 'How about if she had to move quickly because she thought we were on to her?'

Robyn chewed at her lip. 'Yep, these are all valid hypotheses. If only somebody had seen suspicious activity near where Amber's body was uncovered. The car park near the Birches Valley Forest Centre closes at dusk so Joanne, or whoever did this, must have parked a vehicle along the road and transported her body from it, to the forest area. We might have to ask the public for help in this. David, do a door-to-door along Penkridge Park Road.' She added the word Facebook to the board. Under it, she wrote Amber Dalton, Carrie Miller and Siobhan Connors. 'These girls are connected, not only by a message on Facebook, but also in some other way. I'm going over to talk to Siobhan's boyfriend, Adam Josephs. Siobhan's taken compassionate leave from work and I want to track her down.'

David crumpled up the empty packet. 'Think she's involved in the murders?'

'I really don't know at this stage. We could do with Amber and Carrie's mobile phones to trace the history of websites they visited or apps they used. That'd help us hugely. Unfortunately, we don't have them. I'm hoping Siobhan can throw some light on all of this.

But considering the circumstances of her disappearance are much the same as Amber and Carrie's, my hopes aren't high.' She tossed the board marker pen onto her desk. 'Mitz, did you have any luck with Amber's ex-boyfriend?'

'News hasn't yet reached the school that Amber's body's been found, so I asked the headmaster if I could talk to a couple of pupils in connection with her disappearance. He was most cooperative. The boyfriend's a sixth-former called Justin Bolt. According to him, Amber and he weren't that serious a couple. She decided to knuckle down to work instead of fooling about with him. He said Amber could be a bit "up herself" sometimes, so he wasn't upset when she dumped him. He said he'd have split up with her anyway because he'd been embarrassed by her. She'd been a queen bitch to a girl, Shannon Right, also in the same house as her.

'There was an inter-house music competition. Amber and three others had been chosen to represent her house, Chapel, and they were the favourites to win it. Amber took the contest very seriously, and when they lost she blamed Shannon, calling the girl a "right retard". As it happens, Shannon Right has Asperger's syndrome and broke down in tears. Amber refused to apologise and flounced off. Justin felt "a bit shit" afterwards but Amber wouldn't back down. He claimed that was a side to her he hadn't seen before.'

'Interesting. Amber wasn't as perfect as we've been led to believe. Is Shannon Right still there?' asked Robyn.

Mitz ran a finger down his notes. 'She left Sandwell after taking GCSEs. Lives in Lichfield with her parents. She claimed she didn't have much to do with Amber at school. She admitted there were the popular girls in the house – tight cliques – and girls who kept under the radar. Shannon was one of the latter. Amber hung out with the trendies. She also said Amber was okay if she wasn't with the others, but when she was with the crowd, she showed off and could be cruel.'

'Wait a minute. Carrie was described in similar terms.' Anna rifled through the sheets of paper on her desk. 'Her form master Maneesh Shah at Fairline Academy said she was one of a gang of girls notorious for picking on others in the class – those girls considered to be less "with it". He'd reprimanded Carrie and Jade for bullying in the past. They picked on one of the other girls in the class during a form period and reduced her to tears.'

'That's interesting. Two girls, both of whom could be catty to others. That could be significant.' Robyn wrote 'bullies?' on the board. 'Who's Amber's houseparent?'

'Deborah Hampton. Thirty-six years old. Married to Dan and has two children. Been houseparent for three years.'

'Anna, arrange for me to interview her at the boarding house later today, and then call Jade North, Carrie's friend. Get her back here in the station. I'd like to know a little more about this.'

CHAPTER THIRTY

'Siobhan, can you hear me?'

Siobhan Connors fought to respond but couldn't. Her tongue wouldn't work. In fact, no part of her body would listen to the commands her brain was yelling. She needed to get out of this prison cell. At least, she thought it was a prison cell. It smelt horrible – of bleach and stale sweat. A light coming from the top of a helmet that he wore on his head shone into her face, making her eyes screw up. His face loomed in front of hers and he grinned widely at her. A shriek of terror rose from her chest but couldn't escape her mouth. It had been stuffed with material that tickled the back of her throat and made her want to gag.

'Don't struggle. I'll release you in a minute. It'll be all right. I only wanted to make you understand why you're here.' He put a finger to his full lips. She thought she understood what he wanted and tried to nod. She couldn't. Instead she made a noise that emerged as a muffled groan. He continued talking in a low whisper, his words slow and deliberate.

'Good girl. I've been through the photos on your mobile. I hope you don't mind. This one is fabulous. You could be on the cover of a magazine.' He turned the phone to reveal a picture of Siobhan posing in a bikini, full breasts straining against the gossamer-thin golden top. The thong bikini bottom showed off perfectly rounded buttocks, golden brown from several visits to the suntan lounge before the holiday with Adam. It had been a great trip with endless sunshine and heavy drinking in Ayia Napa. Adam had snapped that photo on the first day. Later that day, drunk on rum and happiness, she'd put

the photograph up on Facebook so everyone could see the sexy, wild, carefree Siobhan – the same Siobhan who was lucky to be in such a close and happy relationship.

Her mind gave up the memories. She wasn't in Cyprus or on a beach. She was on a bed. No, it wasn't a bed. It wasn't wide or soft enough to be a bed. It was a table like the ones used in beauty salons for massages. The man in front of her shook his head then hissed, 'It's a bit saucy, eh? It shows a lot of flesh, and yet you put this one up on your Facebook wall for anyone who cared to look. You wanted men to see you in that microscopic piece of material and to fantasise about you being their girlfriend. And no doubt you wanted to show all your girlfriends that you look so much better than they do naked. Make them feel insecure and wish they could look like Siobhan Connors. It must be amazing to be as stunning as you. I see over a hundred people "liked" that photo, and what about this one?' He thumbed through the gallery, stopping at a picture of Siobhan naked in front of a mirror. 'I adore this one. I didn't find this slutty photo on Facebook. I expect they'd have blocked it. Did you share it privately?' He put out his tongue and then slowly licked the screen.

She blinked away tears of anger and fear. She would not give in to this freak. Whatever he did to her, she'd remember and make him pay. She'd get Adam to sort him out. Adam would break his neck. She might have left him, but he knew it wasn't really over. He'd still do anything for her. Her mind whirred. The guy obviously wanted to have sex. He was positively salivating. Siobhan had met men like him before, desperate to shag her but scared of her. He was probably into S & M, given they were in some sort of dungeon and she was tied to the bed. She could cope with that too. Adam had tied her up once and smacked her arse until she couldn't sit down for a week. It was all too kinky for her, but she could put up with it if it meant her freedom. She'd let him have his way, be all demure and then, when he let her go, make sure she kneed him good and hard in the nuts so he'd never be able to do it again.

He gazed at the photo. 'You're quite something, Siobhan,' he said, his voice soft and charming. 'You must have so many doting men who want to caress your beautiful body, love you and pleasure you.' He smiled at her. She cringed. 'Pleasure you' sounded weird and old-fashioned. This guy had to be a virgin. A weirdo virgin.

'Would you like me to pleasure you?' He threw his head back, the light from the helmet casting shadows on the ceiling above, and laughed an unnatural high-pitched laugh. Then, in one swift movement, he dropped his body onto hers, bearing his weight on his arms. The headlight blinded her completely, forcing her to shut her eyes. Ice ran through her veins. This wasn't some weirdo into sexual fantasies. He wasn't the faintest bit aroused by her. Thoughts bounced about in her head. She became acutely aware that she was no longer in her own clothes. The fabric she now wore was coarse and her legs were bare. She was in terrible danger.

She tried to twist away but he pushed her head down with a strong arm. She couldn't break free from the straps that bound her to the bed. She bucked, trying to free herself. He made tut-tut noises. 'You have to stay still for this next part.' With that, he lifted himself from her and she opened her eyes, wishing immediately that she hadn't.

'This is going to hurt,' he said in a high-pitched, sing-song voice, caressing the handle of a large knife. 'Words can hurt, you know?' Her pupils dilated to large discs of black. She was unable to shut her eyes, transfixed by the knife blade in front of her.

'What do you imagine I'm going to do? You have no idea, have you? I'm not going to kill you... yet.' She could barely hear his words for the drumming of blood in her ears. His tongue flickered out, like a snake's, and holding it between his lips in concentration, like a child writing, he scratched the blade into her forehead. At first she felt nothing; then, a blaze of white heat as warm liquid trickled down her head and into her eyes, and she screamed.

CHAPTER THIRTY-ONE

'I can't thank you enough.' Susanne Carlisle was on her knees hugging the dog. 'You don't know what this means to me.'

Ross had a good idea. The shriek at seeing her dog had almost deafened him and he hadn't been hugged so enthusiastically in a long time. Brandon watched the proceedings with vague boredom, a scruffy, hand-me-down Buzz Lightyear in one hand.

'I'm never going to let 'er out of my sight again.' She checked the dog for injuries. 'Where's 'er collar?'

'The man who found her said it had come off.'

'I don't think so. It were a good 'un. Proper leather. Found 'er? Where was she?'

'Only a few miles away. I don't believe she wandered off. She'd been taken, for certain. I reckon it was one of those scams to try and get you to put up a reward for her return, and when you did, he'd have returned the dog and claimed it.'

'The git. Have you reported 'im?'

'I'll be letting the police know about him, don't you worry. Any dogs disappear again and he'll be getting a visit from the boys in blue.'

'I'd thought about a reward too. Lauren was going to get an advance on 'er salary and offer it up. In't she lovely?'

Lauren shrugged. 'It'd have been worth it to get her back.'

'She's a good kid. Don't know what I'd do without 'er. Be a mess.'

Lauren huffed. 'Don't be soft.'

Brandon picked up an equally tatty, plastic cowboy. 'Bang, bang, bang.' He beamed at Ross who grinned back. Brandon dropped down from his chair and wandered over on sturdy legs.

'Is that Woody?' Ross sat on his haunches to chat to the boy, who passed the cowboy to him. The dog trotted over to join them.

'P'incess,' Brandon said.

'That's right, Brandon. It's Princess, and she's not going away again.'

Ross handed back the plastic toy and earned a wonderful, open smile. Susanne spoke.

'Okay, you play with Lauren. I must settle up with Mr Cunningham.'

As she went to fetch the money, Ross took in the close-knit family: Lauren tickling her brother's stomach, making him gurgle in delight; and Susanne, who blew her daughter a kiss when she thought no one was watching. He noted the neat, clean home, short of material possessions but filled with love.

'I don't want payment,' he said.

'But we agreed. I have the money. It's our emergency money, and this was an emergency. You brought Princess back. It's worth every penny. I bet you 'ave bills to pay too. Can't do it all for free.'

Ross shrugged. 'True, but call it my Boy Scout good deed. It didn't take me long to track her down, and it's sufficient payment to see you look so happy. Sorry, that sounded corny.'

Lauren pulled a face. 'Yeah, like out of some soppy film.'

A look of puzzlement clouded Susanne's face. 'But why? It's your job. You found her 'n' I should pay you for that. It don't make no sense. I don't want no charity, neither. I might not be rich, but I ain't no charity case.'

'I don't want money from you, but there is one thing you can help me out with. Tell me where I can find a dog like Princess.'

Susanne's mouth lifted. 'You want a Staffie?'

'Yes. I've been thinking about getting a dog, and I think one like her would suit me.'

Lauren called over. 'I know where there's one. I saw a photo of it on the Dogs Trust website. I'll give them a ring. My mate works there.'

'I'm still paying you, and that's that.' Susanne ferreted through her purse and extracted some notes. She held them out to Ross, waving them. 'Take it. I 'ave me pride.'

Ross hesitated and took the money. 'Tell you what. I'll look for Siobhan in exchange for Lauren's help with a dog. How's that?'

Lauren nodded. 'That'd be really cool.'

Brandon swooshed his spaceman contentedly through the air, Susanne dropped beside him and Princess plopped down on her feet. The picture was one of contentment. Ross and Jeanette would have liked children of their own. Ross sighed. You didn't always get what you wanted in this life.

He sauntered from the house and mused: he and Jeanette might not have kids, but they could certainly shower some of the pent-up affection they both had on a worthy, loyal animal.

CHAPTER THIRTY-TWO

Robyn readjusted her Post-it notes on her desk. She wanted to speak to Adam Josephs and find out more about Siobhan, but she had a meeting with Amber's houseparent in an hour or so. She'd try and do it afterwards if there was time. She also wanted to find out if there'd been any progress on the van Joanne Hutchinson had used. She left a note for David, who'd been looking into it.

'Getting anywhere?' Shearer looked wrecked. His tie was hanging loosely around his neck and his shirt looked like he'd slept in it for several days.

Robyn shook her head. 'It's been five days since we found Carrie Miller and all I have are dead ends. I keep coming across pieces to this puzzle and then realise I've selected the wrong bits and it doesn't fit together.'

'Did you have a thing about jigsaws as a kid?'

'If you're going to be obstructive you can bugger off. I've got more than enough on my plate.'

'Now now, that's no way to talk to a concerned colleague.' He gave her a weak smile and held out a brown paper bag. 'Bet you skipped lunch.'

The corners of her mouth twitched. 'How did you guess?'

'You're irritable. Probably due to lack of sugar,' he quipped.

'Funny man.' She opened it and peered inside. Shearer had chosen a salad, yogurt and a flapjack.

'Crumbs, Tom. This is a first. Why are you being so nice to me?'

'Don't get used to it. I happened to be in the café grabbing a sandwich for lunch, and it crossed my mind that you'd put yourself out to be nice to me and go out for a drink. Thought I'd return the favour. But that's it. We're quits. I can go back to being caustic and impossible to work with.'

'Ah, the Tom Shearer we all love to detest.'

'I'm going away for a few days. Flint is sending me on second-ment to Newcastle. They require my expertise. Thought I'd see how you were getting on before I disappeared.'

'I'm pulling my hair out. I've got all my team out interviewing people and I don't feel I'm making big enough steps. In fact, I was just on my way out to interview someone in Uttoxeter. It's one of the most complicated cases I've tackled, and I've got DCI Flint breathing down my neck every two minutes wanting to know if we have anything.'

'You'd better get that food down you. You'll need all your brain power.' He checked his watch. 'Got to go. Good luck. And eat it all up.' He lifted a hand and departed.

Robyn stuffed a couple of mouthfuls of the salad in. She hadn't thought about food until it had been presented to her. The lemon dressing on the salad was her favourite and for a minute she savoured the crisp, sweet lettuce and pieces of sweetcorn. Her phone buzzed. It was Mitz.

'Found our stranger. I took the CCTV photo capture of him back to Towers Business Park and struck lucky this time. He's called Luke Sanderson. He's not one of Vitamed's regular customers. He was served by one of the staff, a young lad, who's normally out the back helping on the production line. When Matt passed the photo around, the kid wasn't in. I've interviewed Luke. He's not got anything new to add except he was called over by Frank Cummings to help manoeuvre the trunk, and Joanne Hutchinson kept yelling to keep it straight and level because of the valuables in it. He thought it was glass or something, because the trunk didn't weigh too much. It was awkward to offload and manoeuvre it down the corridor into the unit. He didn't pay much attention to the woman. He did, however, say she had a right posh accent and noticed when she waved her hands at them she was wearing leopard print gloves.'

Robyn groaned. 'No fingerprints in any van, even if we do locate it, then?'

'It'd have been wiped clean anyhow. She's meticulous.'

'I can live in hope, Mitz. We're not getting any lucky breaks.'

'We're eliminating suspects, and in the end that'll narrow the field down.'

'Unless we run out of suspects.'

'This isn't like you, boss. You're always upbeat. You taught me to try every angle and never give up.'

Robyn sighed. 'You're bang on with that. I put my mood down to lack of sleep and food, and an irritating pulled ligament.'

'Want me to bring you back a sandwich?'

'Tom Shearer's already brought me in some food.'

'DI Shearer? Really?'

'I can tell by your voice that you're reading too much into that statement.'

'I'm a sentimentalist, guv.'

'Concentrate on your own love life first.'

'I am. Got a hot date later tonight.'

'In that case, you can tell us all about it tomorrow. If you're done there, call it a day, Mitz. Everyone here is out and I'm going to interview Amber's houseparent. Go get ready for tonight.'

'Cheers, boss.'

Robyn ended the call. She shovelled some more salad into her mouth and put the yoghurt and flapjack in her bag for later. She turned to look at the whiteboard. It was a mess of names and suggestions. She drew a line through the word 'Good Samaritan' – another lead crossed off. It still left her with too many questions, and no closer to unveiling the woman who called herself Joanne Hutchinson.

Deborah Hampton was fresh-faced and appeared much younger than her thirty-six years. Chapel boarding house with its sixth-form extension, and home to seventy-five girls, was set in extensive gardens that exuded calm and contentment. Deborah welcomed Robyn into the house and their private kitchen, a happy, chaotic mess created by two young boys painting at the table. The boys, dressed in oversized shirts that appeared to have belonged to a grown-up at some stage, were so engrossed in splodging bright colours onto huge pieces of paper they didn't notice the police-woman.

'Sorry about the mess. Dan normally has the kids, but Fridays he helps out at the art centre.'

'I won't keep you long.'

'Take as long as you want. The girls are still in lessons, so I won't be needed until they come in and we have tea.'

'You eat with the girls?'

'Yes, every house has its own dining room and chef. Poor Charles and Bianca. This is going to break them.' She looked off into the distance, fighting back tears. 'It's dreadful. Just awful. Some of the girls have been in shock about her disappearance. When term began and Amber went missing, it was bad enough, but the staff were told about her death at lunchtime, and I don't know what to expect from the girls. The headmaster intends breaking the news to the entire school later at a special service in the church. Poor Amber.' She paused, drew in a breath, and continued. 'As you know, she didn't board here but she was very much part of this house, as are all day pupils. They have their own study accommodation so that they are able to make Chapel a "home from home". Amber's is untouched, although the police went through everything when she first disappeared.'

One of the boys knocked over a jam jar of murky water, and a large mucky stain spread out on the tablecloth. Deborah moved at speed, mopped the mess up with paper towels and refilled the jar almost in one movement.

'You've got quick reflexes.'

'It's practice.' She stood over the paintings, making appreciative noises, then approached Robyn once more. 'How rude of me. I ought to have asked you if I could get you anything. I'm a bit… numb, I suppose.'

'Thank you, but no. It's a very difficult time for you. Actually, I wanted to ask about Amber's relationships with the other girls in the house. Did she get along with the other girls? I understand there was an incident after a music contest?'

Deborah collected her thoughts. 'It was some time ago. The inter-house music competition is a big event for us, and we were in with a good chance. We had some talented musicians and singers. Amber was one of those, and she was put in charge of the harmony section. Although the girls sang really well, they were beaten into second place. Amber took the result badly. She blamed Shannon and accused her of singing off key. She was extremely rude to her.'

'I heard that was the case.'

'Shannon wasn't one of the most confident girls in the house and it had taken a lot of persuasion to get her to participate, so you can imagine the effect it had on her. She shut herself in her room and threatened to slash her wrists. We talked her out and she spent a few days in the sick bay with matron. Amber managed to turn the entire event around to make it seem Shannon was at fault. She fell out with a few of the girls after that. I think some of them sided with Shannon and decided Amber was becoming too self-absorbed. I spoke to her about it but she wouldn't climb down. In her defence, many pupils take the contest seriously. If they're ever up against another house, their house comes first, regardless of petty grievances between its inhabitants – like a fiercely loyal family.'

'So this was a one-off incident?'

'I'm finding it difficult to talk about a girl whose body has just been found,' she whispered so her children couldn't hear. The older boy was beginning to fidget about, prodding his brother. 'Mummy, Leo spat paint at my picture.'

'Okay, Kyle. Why don't you put on a *Peppa Pig* DVD and watch it with Leo? I'll only be a few minutes.'

There was a scramble as the boys tumbled down from chairs and disappeared from sight. Deborah turned to Robyn. 'By and large I liked Amber. She was a bright young lady. She was polite, energetic and keen to work. Her teachers always spoke highly of her academic performance and her parents are one of the nicest couples we have at the school. They're supportive of all our events. I really don't want to speak ill of her. However, there were a few occasions when she wasn't as perfect as she made out. I have a feeling Amber was involved in some of our "incidents".'

'Such as?'

'One of the girls smuggled in alcohol and several of them were caught in a bedsit, drunk. Amber wasn't caught drinking, but she wore this smug expression when she was being questioned – a holier-than-thou look that I felt was hiding the truth. Then there was a more serious incident when a group of boys discovered a teacher's password and got into his email account. Two of the boys were expelled over it, another suspended for confessing, but there were rumours two girls were also involved. We suspected Amber was one but she denied it.' She shook her head at the memory.

'Every month, a different senior girl watches over the junior members while they do their prep. It reached my ears that Amber had threatened to hit them for not working quietly enough while she was trying to do research on the computer. Again, she denied it. When I talked to the junior girls about it, they clammed up. I always thought they'd been forced to keep quiet; the looks they threw Amber in the dining room, the quiet grumbles – it added up, but I couldn't prove it. That's all I can say. It's mostly conjecture, and Amber is a shining example of what we can produce here at Sandwell – a truly gifted girl.' Her eyes moistened. 'It doesn't matter if she made mistakes or was out of order sometimes. Most of them have their moments. She'd have changed, and grown and been a successful woman. Now…'

Deborah pulled at her sleeve, regained control. 'Now she's been denied that. We're a happy family here at Chapel House, DI Carter. Dan and I feel privileged to be the girls' "parents". We share in our family's success, help them get over failures, and care for them. Today we've lost a dear member of it. It'll take a long time to get over this.'

'I understand. Would it be okay for me to take a quick look at her study before the girls return from lessons?'

'Yes, actually that might be best. It's going to be chaos. They'll have been told by now about the meeting at six and rumours will be flying. It'd be better if they didn't spot you here before then. Feel free to have a quick look about though.' Deborah gave Robyn directions, then grabbed some tissues from a box on the kitchen worktop and blew her nose, before wiping her reddening eyes. 'Can't let the girls down,' she said. 'We'll have to be there for them.'

Robyn gave her a smile of encouragement. 'They'll be fine. They've got masses of support here, from you and each other.'

Robyn left Deborah and wandered into the house itself. There was a clattering coming from the kitchen. She peered into the dining room – three rows of benches and tables. The walls were filled with wooden boards containing the names of girls who'd won scholarships dating back to 2002 when the house opened. Various gleaming trophies, including a large polished silver cup for the inter-house hockey competition, stood on a large shelf.

She opened the door to the common room, where the juniors did their prep. The room was in fact a pleasant, light sitting room, filled with comfy chairs in various colours, large cushions and beanbags pushed to one side to make space for six desks and chairs. A modern pine bookcase containing numerous paperback novels and housing a workstation for an Apple Mac computer filled an entire wall. A large bay window overlooked the garden with its neat lawn and borders.

Robyn headed to Amber's landing. Paintings adorned the walls leading upstairs. Robyn thought fleetingly of Florence, who was artistically gifted, and even at thirteen, showed talent equal to that displayed on these walls. The house smelt of deodorant, perfume and shower gel. The communal showers were near Amber's room, one of several along the carpeted corridor. Robyn peered into the first room where shoes, trainers and hockey boots were higgledy-piggledy on the floor, and A4 files were tossed onto the bed covered with a bright-yellow duvet. A photo taken outside the building of a group of friends beaming at the camera stood on the chest of drawers. A large fluffy bear sat on a chair, and pictures of various celebrities, cut from magazines, combined to form a collage on the wall. It clearly belonged to a boarder.

Amber's room was stark by comparison. Notes about deadlines and essay titles were attached to a corkboard with brightly coloured pins. Course books and A4 files stood to attention on shelves, and her desk was completely clear apart from a desk-tidy tub stuffed with pens and pencils.

Robyn stared at the corkboard. Amber had listed her deadlines for coursework. Two essays were due to be handed in on the day term began again, the ninth of January. Her story about remaining at home to complete her work while her parents went abroad appeared to be true. Robyn picked up one of the files marked 'English' and read through the work. Amber's handwriting was clear and neat, not scrawled like Robyn's own. She flicked through the notes, marvelling at the girl's insight into some of the poetry she was studying.

She picked up a copy of *The War Poems of Wilfred Owen*. The book opened at one with which she was familiar, 'Dulce et Decorum est'. The final line in the poem meant, 'Sweet and fitting it is to die for one's country.' For a second she again thought of Davies, who had died for his country. He'd given his life, and yet no one really knew what good he had accomplished over the years he'd been an intelligence officer, nor how much safer the country was because of him and others like him. She shut the book firmly. His death was not in vain. Without people like Davies, the world would be in worse turmoil.

As she turned to leave, she spotted a folded piece of paper on the floor. It had slipped from the book. She recognised Amber's perfect handwriting. She'd written three names: Orion, Horus and Wōden, and encircled them with hearts, each with curling tails. It made no sense for the paper to be in the book. Robyn decided to take it with her. It was probably nothing important, but as Mitz had reminded her, she should explore all avenues.

CHAPTER THIRTY-THREE

Amélie was getting on Florence Hallows's nerves. She was such a goody two-shoes. She'd come top in Friday's spelling competition and hadn't shut up about it all day. Ordinarily, Florence would have been pleased, but today she was feeling mean, and not at all impressed. Amélie was brilliant at everything. She had an amazing memory and she always got As in her schoolwork.

Florence was extra annoyed because she'd tried hard to memorise all the spellings. She'd spent hours learning them and thought, for once, she'd do well. Mr Chambers had set the test and she'd wanted to impress him. He was one of the best teachers they had, the youngest and the most interesting. He often broke off from teaching to discuss the latest hot drama on television, or celebrity gossip, or just listen to the pupils gripe. He encouraged them to voice their opinions in debates or on paper, and she wanted to show how much she enjoyed being taught by him, by doing well. Ever since he'd shown an interest in her paintings, she'd worked harder in English, even though she found it difficult to remember what a verb, an adjective and a noun were, let alone understand the difference between colons and semicolons.

Amélie liked him too and that served to irritate Florence further. She'd been wittering on about him since they'd left class and headed to the school library. 'He's got the dreamiest eyes, and he looks at you like you're the most important pupil in the class.'

Florence snorted. 'You should write romance novels. You make him sound like some drippy hero in a book.'

'That's a good idea. Maybe I should ask Mr Chambers about it.'

'Pur-lease. I'm only joking. Will you shut up about him?'

'Why?'

'Because I'm up to here with you droning on about how wonderful you think Mr Chambers is. He's a teacher. That's it. He teaches us English. He's no different to Mrs Donaldson or Mr Roberts.'

'Yes he is. He isn't as old as them. He's into all sorts of films and music and stuff we like. Mr Donaldson wouldn't have a clue who Rag'n'Bone Man, or One Direction, or Ed Sheeran was.' Amélie laughed. 'Besides, I think you secretly like him too.'

Florence's shoulders hunched. 'Shut up.'

Amélie waved her hands in front of her face, fanning her cheeks and giggled. 'Yes, you do. I can see it in your face. You *do* fancy him. Besides, I've seen you staring at him when he's reading aloud. Florence fancies Mr Chambers!' she sang.

Florence's neck went bright red. 'Keep your voice down. You sound like a stupid little kid. I don't fancy him. He's ancient anyway.'

Amélie giggled again. 'No, he isn't. He's only in his early twenties.'

'That makes him at least ten years older than us.'

'That's not too old. Plenty of older men go for younger women. When he's in his thirties, we'll be in our twenties. Loads of men and women that age get together.'

'I can't believe we're having this conversation. Are you crazy? He's a teacher. He's not interested in thirteen-year-olds.'

'You're very grown up for thirteen. You've got boobs and you looked so much older when we went to the cinema, with your make-up and false nails. Oh, that's it!' She pulled a face, a round 'oh' of her lips. 'You're trying to look grown up for Mr Chambers. That's why you've started wearing make-up to school. I know you're wearing mascara, I can tell. And a bit of lip gloss.' Amélie giggled.

Florence thought about Hunter and flushed again. She was trying to pull off being older, but not for any teacher. She'd been practising her new look in case she ever had to talk on Skype or meet Hunter. Amélie was making her feel rotten now, mocking her, which only made her more bad-tempered.

'Shut up, Amélie. I mean it.'

At last Amélie picked up on her friend's sour mood and dropped the silliness. She attempted to slip her arm through Florence's and found it clamped to her side. 'I'm only messing with you, Florence. It's not serious. Everyone likes him. He's a really nice teacher.'

'Well, I don't.'

'Because you did badly at the test?'

'No. Because he creeps me out. He's always smiling and being so friendly to everyone. It's not normal for a teacher to behave like that. You all treat him like he's some pop star. He loves it. All that attention.'

'Now *you're* being stupid. He doesn't. He's just… nice. You're annoyed with him because of the test.'

Florence marched off, leaving Amélie to scurry after her. 'Florence, wait!'

'Get lost, Amélie. I'm fed up hanging about with you. I'm sick of you putting me down all the time. I'll never be like you. Everyone laughs at me because I'm your friend. Clever, pretty Amélie and her thick, ugly friend.'

'Florence, stop! I don't put you down! I never have. And no one thinks that about you. Florence, please. I was only joking with you. You know I don't mean it.'

Florence ignored the protests, her mind foggy. She turned by the door of the library. 'You don't struggle like I do with school stuff and I don't want it rubbed in every time you do well. I tried hard today for that test and I came bottom. You didn't even ask how I did in it. You assumed I did rubbish as always. Do you know how that makes me feel? Do you know what it's like to come last in the class? No. You don't.'

'I didn't know you came bottom. Oh, Florence, I'm dead sorry. I was so excited about coming top. I had no idea—'

'Try thinking about other people sometimes, Amélie. We're not all perfect like you. Now piss off. I don't want to be your friend.' She slammed the library door in her friend's face and stomped off, furious that the one person who should understand how she felt didn't know her at all.

CHAPTER THIRTY-FOUR

Siobhan lay on the mattress that smelt slightly of urine, and sobbed. The lunatic holding her prisoner had left the room, taking with him the only light. Dried blood had hardened like a clay mask on her face, tightening the skin, stretching it and making her forehead hurt like mad. It had bled copiously, but he hadn't moved to mop up the blood, leering at her as he carved into her skin.

She shifted uncomfortably. She needed painkillers urgently. Her throat was bone dry from the material that had been rammed into it to prevent her from calling out. He had removed it after she passed out with pain. She had no clear idea of how long she'd been unconscious, vaguely recalling him humming as he removed the restraints and lifted her from the table. She'd blacked out again and come around on the bed, not daring to move in case he heard her and returned to inflict more pain.

If only she hadn't rowed with Adam and accused him of shagging a co-worker. She knew in her heart he wouldn't have been unfaithful to her. She shouldn't have broken up with him. The relationship was a bit turbulent, but Adam understood she was volatile. That's what had attracted him. She was feisty. They were good together. When she got out, she'd tell him how much she loved him. She'd never shout at him again.

A sharp smarting in her head made her wince. Oh God, she really needed some painkillers. She screwed her eyes up tightly and concentrated on thoughts of Adam. If she hadn't had a complete freak out on him and thrown him out of their flat, he'd be out searching for her. Maybe he was anyway. Maybe he'd returned like he usually did after a falling-out, and discovered her missing. It was likely. He always came back. He was probably at the flat now, a bunch of flowers in his hand, calling for her. He'd know something was up and check with Lucy, her manager at Tesco. He'd find she hadn't come to work and would become anxious. He'd call the police. He'd find her. Everyone would be looking for her. Adam would make sure of it.

'Please, Adam. Look for me,' she whimpered. 'Please come and find me.'

The sound of a key in the door made her choke on her words, and she was overcome by uncontrollable shivering. She pulled her knees to her chest, wrapped her arms around them, and tried to curl into the tightest ball.

'Tsk, Siobhan. You're behaving like a baby. Pull yourself together. I've brought you some painkillers. Your head must be throbbing.'

The soft murmuring made her shudder. It was mocking and cruel. She raised wet eyes.

'Oh, yuck. You look a mess. Better wipe off some of that manky blood.' The torchlight shone onto a bowl he put on the bed next to her. A grubby facecloth floated in the water. He passed her two tablets and a bottle of water 'Take those first. It'll help with the pain.'

She uncurled and held out a shaking hand for the pills and took them without question.

'Face,' he hissed, pointing at the cloth. 'The water's warm.'

Siobhan wrung out the facecloth and rubbed a cheek with it. The blood was caked on and needed to be dampened before she could lift it. Her head was too tender to wipe. She pressed the cloth several times against it, wincing as she touched it. After a few dabs she returned the cloth to the plastic bowl. The water was rust-brown with her blood.

'You could try saying thank you.'

'Thanks,' she mumbled.

'You're welcome, Siobhan. You look a little better. Unfortunately, not as good as you used to look. What a pity. No more strutting your stuff. You're one of the ordinary ones – no, not even ordinary. You're one of the misfits now.' He cackled.

'Time for a photo.' He pulled out her smartphone. 'Now, how shall we do this? Want to pose on the bed, or stand up?'

Siobhan pulled her knees into her chest again.

'Come, come. You love taking photographs of yourself. Don't be shy. Phone's filled with them.'

'No, don't,' she whispered.

'No, don't,' he repeated in a girlish voice, then more loudly, 'Siobhan, pose for the camera or I'll come over there and break your arms.'

Siobhan's eyes filled again and she began to snuffle. 'Please,' she begged. 'Please stop this.'

'Stop what, Siobhan? I'm not doing anything. I've given you pain-killers, water and a cloth. I'm going to take your photo. That's really nice of me, isn't it? You love having your photograph taken. Look at all these super piccies you have on your mobile.'

'Stop tormenting me.'

He laughed loudly. 'Tormenting, that's the key word. You know all about tormenting. I haven't finished tormenting you yet. Now smile or I'll smash your face to a pulp.'

Siobhan stared out with huge eyes into the darkness and forced her lips into a stretch. The shaking had begun again. She clenched her knees and kept her head raised. There was a flash of light as the picture was taken.

'Good. I think that's okay. Hmm. What do you reckon?' He lifted the screen to her face. Siobhan gulped back a sob and stammered, 'Let me go. Please. What more do you want? You've ruined my face. You've ruined my life. I don't know what to say to you to let me go. Please, please...'

'Shut up! I can't bear needy, whining, whinge-bags. I thought you were one of the strong ones. I thought you'd battle this out with me, resist, shout and scream and put up a decent fight. You're so full of yourself and yet now you're acting like a little, wussy, girlie-wirlie.' He sang the words, his voice rising in pitch.

Siobhan sucked in air. 'Please…' A noise rose from deep within her body and the room was filled with loud blubbing. He thrust the mobile back into a pocket and held his hands over his ears.

'Shut up! Have some dignity.'

Siobhan wrestled to take control, until eventually the cries became dull sobs.

'Dear, oh dear. I'm going to have to dispatch you sooner than I hoped. You're not going to be as much fun as I'd anticipated.' He paced around the room.

Siobhan struggled to speak. 'Please. I'll get money or whatever you want. Just tell me what you want.'

With two quick strides, he dropped down beside her on the bed. 'But you're already giving me what I want. What I want is for you to suffer. You see, Siobhan, I had rather hoped to string you along for a while. Keep you here another day or two. Taunt you with false hopes. Convince you I was going to free you. Tease you by telling you Adam and the police were searching for you. That people cared about you enough to look for you.' He sniggered, making little tee-hee-hee noises that confused her.

'The reality is, no one gives a damn about you. Adam has no idea you've disappeared. And your work colleagues couldn't care less where you are. No one knows you're even missing.'

Siobhan could barely hear for the thumping in her chest. The fear had mounted to such a level she thought she would die. He turned his head this way and that, studying her and, all the while, grinning at her in a demented fashion until her eyes burned and she wanted to scream.

'What do you want from me?'

He pulled out the phone again, thumbed the screen and showed it to Siobhan, handing it to her.

'*Comprehension. Dismay. Regret. I want you to understand.*'

'*But I don't,*' said Siobhan. '*I don't get it. Please. Let me go. I haven't done anything.*'

He let out a lengthy hiss that chilled her. '*But you have. Think, Siobhan. Think. Look. Look and understand.*'

She shook her head manically. '*This is crazy. You're completely mad.*'

'*Crazy? You have no idea, have you? You self-obsessed cow.*'

'*I haven't… done… anything… wrong,*' she repeated, her voice wobbling with fear.

He snatched back the phone and marched to the far end of the room. She gulped as the light turned once more onto her, causing her eyes to squint, then close. She heard him approach and mutter, '*Siobhan, I've decided your time is up. I've become decidedly bored of you.*'

With those words, he produced a plastic bag from out of nowhere, dragged it over her head and held it tight around her neck while she thrashed, hands tearing at his. Her legs kicked out but didn't connect with him. She flailed for only a few minutes before her body went limp and her hands fluttered and dropped, unable to fight any more.

CHAPTER THIRTY-FIVE

It was quiet in the office with only the tapping of keyboards and the odd stifled yawn from Matt Higham. It was five o'clock and pitch dark outside. Cars rumbled down the road as people anxious to start their weekend left offices and headed home. The day had seemed to go on for a week. Robyn read through all the findings from her team and absent-mindedly rubbed her hip. She really ought to get it massaged at the gym.

'Coffee, guv?' Anna's eyes were sunken and her face pasty.

'Thanks.' Robyn scrolled through the search engine pages. Amber's note lay in front of her. There was too much information online to get any clarity. Orion, a man with a bow, was the god of hunting in Greek mythology, and the constellation was named after him. Horus, an Egyptian god, was portrayed as a man's body with a falcon's head, and like Orion he was also a god of hunting. The third name was yielding pages and pages of information that had to be sifted through. Anna placed a cup filled with dark liquid on Robyn's desk.

'Cheers. Anna, do you know anything about mythology?'

'Studied it a little way back. Why?'

'Orion, Horus, Wōden. Amber wrote these names down on a piece of paper.' She passed the note to Anna.

'Sorry, can't help you. I only recognise Orion and I can't remember what he was a god of.'

Robyn stared back at the computer. 'Hunting. The first two names are gods of hunting. Oh, hang on, I have something interesting here.' She read the page and eased back in her chair, shifting to get comfortable. 'Wōden is the Anglo-Saxon equivalent of the Norse god Odin. If this website is correct, he was the leader of a band of predatory warriors. I figure that makes him a hunter too.'

'It seems that way. What's the significance?'

'I don't know yet. Amber might have enjoyed fact-finding, but drawing hearts with curling tails around the names is curious.'

'They look like doodles. I do that sort of thing when I'm on the phone sometimes. I doodle triangles that interlink, or anchors. No idea why.'

Robyn looked at the paper again. 'I suppose she could have been talking to someone on the phone and doodling at the same time. Amber studied English and economics, not mythology, yet she's jotted down the names of three gods all associated with hunting. It's out of place, and that makes me suspicious.'

She took a sip of her coffee and wrinkled her face. 'I must get that machine looked at. That's way too strong. It's dumped an entire jar into that cup.'

'It's probably been tampered with, in a dastardly attempt to keep us operating on full power.' Matt grinned. 'I better get a cup. I need all the caffeine I can get.'

'Take mine. I can't drink it. I'll be far too hyper.'

David Marker tapped lightly on the office door. 'Guv, Jade North is here.'

Robyn rose. 'Any volunteers want to assist me?'

'I'll come. I'm getting nowhere here.' Anna shoved her chair under her desk. 'I've counted the custard creams, Matt.'

'It isn't me who's nicking them,' he said, hands up in protest.

'Whatever. They've been counted, so be warned,' she replied her face deadpan.

Jade North looked more upset and bewildered than the last time she'd been interviewed.

Robyn spoke as she eased onto her seat. 'Hi, Jade. Thanks for coming in.'

'When can we hold Carrie's funeral service? I can't get nothing out of Mr Miller. He doesn't want to talk about it. Taken to drinking down the Hounds. Leah looks like shit too. I went to see them. She says he's off his face most of the time and not been into work since you found Carrie.'

'I'm sorry to hear that.' She took in a breath and let it out gently. 'We really would have liked to let Carrie come home, but because it's an open case we've not been able to release her as quickly as we'd like. We'll do our best to make sure it isn't for much longer.'

Jade pouted like a petulant child. 'I think that's stupid. We need her back, you know? To say goodbye properly.'

Robyn nodded to diffuse the anger building in Jade. 'I understand. Try and be patient with us for a little longer. And I'll ask a bereavement officer to visit Mr Miller and talk things through with him.'

Jade relaxed a little. 'Yeah. Might be good.'

'Jade, if you don't mind, I wanted to ask you about your schooldays with Carrie. You were her best friend.'

A smile played on Jade's lips. 'Besties, yeah. We were. Did most stuff together. She was such a laugh. I'll never have another mate like her.'

'She seemed to be a popular girl.'

Jade's cheeks dimpled at the memories. 'It was cos she was always up for a challenge and was so adult. She always had the trendiest clothes and hairstyles, and even when the teachers told her to take the coloured extensions out of hair, or remove the studs in her ears or nose, she wouldn't. She'd stand up to them. I think that's why she was so popular. She was rebellious. Most of us wanted to be more like her, cos she didn't give a shit about the teachers, lessons or exams. She was just Carrie. She got away with things too cos she

looked so much older. If there was a concert on in Derby, she'd blag
tickets and get us in. She only had to bat her eyes at the bouncer
on the door and we'd get in.'

'Did she have sex with these men?'

Jade clamped her mouth shut.

'I'm only trying to work out who might have harmed her, Jade.
I'm not judging who she was. She was your best friend. Help me
find her killer. Did she have sex with any of the bouncers?'

Jade shifted in her chair and twiddled at a bracelet on her
wrist. 'She wasn't a slag. There was a bloke on the door at Stardust
nightclub who let us in a couple of times. She went round the back
with him. Gave him a blowjob.'

'You don't happen to know this man's name, do you?'

'Logan. Don't know his surname. He told Carrie he was married.'

Anna wrote down the name of the bouncer and the nightclub
and threw Jade an encouraging smile.

'And can you describe him?'

'Big, huge shoulders, big hands. Carrie said he had a giant
boner too, said it was like trying to suck on a giant cucumber and
she had to stretch her mouth to get it in. She pulled a face like
this.' Jade pulled at her lips, widening her mouth comically. 'She
said she nearly choked to death on it. And she almost made me
wet myself laughing.' She paused, eyes dewy with tears. 'He wasn't
bad-looking, had a shaved head, and a tattoo down his arms, one
of those tribal tattoos, of a deer with horns. He showed it to us.
Carrie loved it. Wanted one like it. I think she'd have had it done
too when she had enough money.'

Robyn threw Anna a look. 'That's very helpful. Thank you. Were
there any more men in her life?'

'She didn't want serious relationships. Liked being a free agent
going with whoever she fancied when she felt like it. She'd not had
a bloke for a while. That's why I was surprised when she suddenly

found this new fella and buzzed off with him without telling me first. We always shared secrets. I figured she'd finally fallen for someone. She told me so.' Jade bit her lip to stop the tears.

Robyn didn't contradict her. Jade had to come to terms with Carrie's death in her own way. She'd eventually accept that there had been no boyfriend. 'I wanted to ask you about an incident last year, at Fairline Academy. Mr Shah, your form teacher, said he had to reprimand you both for bullying another girl in the class.'

'I don't see how that's got anything to do with Carrie being killed.'

'Like I said, Jade, we're looking into anything that might be relevant.'

'It was only a bit of fun. The silly cow got lippy with us. Made some comment about Carrie's hair. Carrie told her to button it or we'd shave her head and make her sorry for opening her gob. She backed down. Carrie didn't take criticism from anyone. It's like that at school.'

'And you had her back, didn't you, Jade?'

'Yeah. She was my mate. She'd have done the same for me.'

'Did Carrie often threaten girls?'

Furrows appeared on Jade's forehead. 'She stuck up for herself and sometimes that meant keeping silly tarts in their places. That's all. No one messed with Carrie or me.'

They chatted about life at Fairline Academy and Carrie for a little while longer. Jade seemed to appreciate being able to talk about her friend. Eventually she left, escorted by Anna. Robyn stared into space, thoughts ticking over, and jumped up in one swift movement when Anna came back in. 'Get this Logan checked out. The man has a hunting tattoo and I wonder if there's any connection between that and Amber's note with the names of hunting gods. Somebody at Stardust nightclub will know where he lives. We must also track down Siobhan Connors. I'll phone her boyfriend Adam Josephs after I've spoken to Harry McKenzie again. The killer removed a piece of skin from Amber's forehead. I wonder if Carrie's head was cut too.'

Anna vacated the interview room, leaving Robyn to reflect on Jade's words. School could be tough for many pupils, and there appeared to be definite pecking orders at Fairline Academy. To get to the top of that order, Carrie had intimidated others and maintained a rebellious streak to attract hangers-on like Jade. Jade was clearly in awe of the girl. The way she had spoken about her had been almost with reverence. Robyn wondered if the real Carrie was actually a bully or going through the motions for self-preservation. She picked up her notepad and left the room, shutting the door behind her. As she turned to leave a familiar face beamed at her.

'Ross. What are you doing here?'

'Sorry to bother you. I might have a missing person. Thought I should report it.'

'Relatives not gone through the usual channels?'

'They didn't know she was missing. They last heard from her at Christmas. She moved away from home in Ireland some time ago, and doesn't keep in touch. Her friend Lauren raised the alarm. I spoke to the girl's boyfriend, Adam Josephs, who claims they split up a couple of weeks ago after a blazing row. He hasn't heard from her since that day. The only person to have had any contact with her is Lauren. She received what she thought was a weird text message, about her friend running off with a new man, thought it was fishy and asked me to look into it. I've done all the checks and I think there's good reason to suspect she has disappeared. Thought I'd run it past you first and see if you thought I should make it official.'

Robyn felt a tightening in her stomach and the lemon dressing she'd had earlier suddenly became acidic in her throat.

She held her breath. Carrie had also messaged her friend Jade to say she'd met a man and gone away with him. This was beginning to sound ominous.

'The girl's called Siobhan. Siobhan Connors.'

'Oh, crap.'

Ross looked up in surprise. 'This is serious, isn't it?'

Robyn swallowed to clear the acid she could still taste. 'Could be. Can you ask her friend Lauren to come in and talk to me?'

'She might be a little reluctant. I don't think she has much time for our police force.'

'I'll go to her, then.' She checked her watch. 'It's almost six. Will you come with me? Might help if she already knows you.'

'Sure. Come on. I'll call her first to make sure she's in.'

'You drive. I have to talk to Mitz before we go. Where are we headed?'

'Gallow Street, Derby.'

Ross led the way to the car, Robyn behind him punching numbers into her phone, her yogurt and flapjack now completely forgotten.

CHAPTER THIRTY-SIX

Lauren sat on the floor next to the kitchen table with Brandon, brightly coloured bricks between their outstretched legs.

'So, if you don't mind talking to Robyn, she'll be able to look into Siobhan's disappearance for you.'

Lauren cast a look at Robyn and nodded. 'She's really gone missing, hasn't she?'

'We're not certain but you've given us enough cause for concern.'

The back door opened with a whack and an excited Staffordshire bull terrier entered, dragging its owner, Susanne. 'Oh, sorry, love. Didn't know we 'ad guests. I'd have come home quicker. Hi, Ross.'

Princess snuffled at the guests then plonked down next to Brandon, tongue out, content to be part of the proceedings.

'So what's up? Why're you here?'

Robyn spoke up. 'Siobhan Connors.'

Susanne snorted. 'She's a fiery one. She's probably deliberately gone off to wind everyone up. I told Lauren that after she asked Ross to check it out. I didn't like 'er wasting 'is time.'

'She's not like that,' said Lauren, standing and folding her arms.

'She's exactly like that. I've made my feelings clear about that madam in the past. She's wild, to say the least, and I'm not that keen on her. Still, you're not a kid, and you can make friends with 'oever you want. I'm not the best person when it comes to judgement of character. Made me own mistakes often enough.'

'Is it okay if I chat to Lauren somewhere quiet?' Robyn asked Susanne

'Course. Want to use the sitting room? I'll fix the little'un some dinner.'

Robyn, Ross and Lauren moved through to the sitting room, stylishly furnished and dominated by a dark grey corner sofa on which bright-yellow plumped cushions stood to attention.

'Could you go back through what you told Ross, please, Lauren? It might help us work out what's happened to Siobhan.'

Lauren gazed at her with clear grey eyes. 'Siobhan's been with Adam for over a year. They live in Uttoxeter. A couple of weeks ago, they split up and we arranged a girls' night out to cheer her up. She was well up for it, and we arranged to meet for a few drinks and then go on to the nightclub where we first met. I turned up at Derby railway station but she didn't. I thought at first she might have missed her train and then I got pissed off cos she hadn't let me know, so I rang her. She didn't pick up. I sent a text asking where the hell she was and that I was freezing me tits off waiting for her at the station. I got one back almost straight away saying she was sorry, she'd forgotten about the meet-up. She'd found a new bloke and they'd been shagging non-stop. I rang her again, and again it went to answerphone. I was majorly cheesed off with her by now and went home. I didn't bother about her after that. It wasn't that she'd not turned up, it was that she never told me about this boyfriend. She usually told me everything. And it was well odd that she'd even got involved with him. She'd been going on about Adam before that and how they'd get back together. She was just keeping him waiting a bit. I thought she really loved him. And then I got a message a few days ago saying she was going away with this new bloke. I rang her and got the answerphone again. I tried Adam but he'd no idea where she was, and said he didn't care anyway. I rang Tesco and her manager said Siobhan had gone to Ireland to stay with her family, which I knew wouldn't be true. She doesn't even like talking about them, so I went round her flat but she weren't in, and her neighbours had no idea where she was. I'd have rung her mum or dad if I'd known their numbers, but I don't and nor did Adam. It didn't seem right her going off like that so I asked Ross to find her.'

'Which day had you arranged to meet Siobhan?'

'Last Friday. Friday the thirteenth. I waited at Derby station for 'er train. It was due in at half seven.'

'And she texted you after you sent your message?'

'Yeah, but like I said, she didn't pick up the phone and speak to me when I rang her straight after I got it. That's odd, isn't it?'

'You received the second text two days ago, on Wednesday the eighteenth?'

Lauren nodded and passed the mobile to Robyn who read out, '"Hi Lauren. Having great time. New bloke is awesome. Won't be back for a while."' She paused. 'Do you think Siobhan might be winding you up, as your mum put it?'

'No, and I don't believe she'd go off with another fella. And, I don't think she'd pretend to either. She loves Adam. I know she does. That's why I think something has happened to her. This doesn't sound like her at all.'

'How did you meet her?'

'At a nightclub in Derby. We met at the bar. Ended up sharing a bottle or two of wine and crashing at my house.'

Robyn nodded and continued making notes. 'And that was where you were going again on the thirteenth?'

'They've got a good DJ on Fridays, and it's half-price drinks until nine.'

Robyn suddenly realised she knew the answer to her next question. 'Which nightclub was it?'

'Stardust.'

CHAPTER THIRTY-SEVEN

DAY SIX – SATURDAY 21 JANUARY

Robyn had held an emergency meeting with her team at 6 a.m. Siobhan's name had been added to the whiteboard and she'd explained what she'd learnt from Lauren. She'd then driven to Uttoxeter at seven o'clock and spoken to Lucy, Siobhan's manager, who'd confirmed Siobhan had an unblemished record of attendance, so when she'd phoned in tears, saying she had to take time off on compassionate grounds, Lucy hadn't hesitated to agree.

Robyn made notes as Lucy answered her questions.

'You last heard from Siobhan a week ago?'

'It was last Saturday morning – the fourteenth – I was about to go on shift and Siobhan rang me. At first I thought she had a cold, because her voice sounded rough, and then I realised she was crying. I asked her if everything was okay and if I could assist in any way, but she said it wasn't anything I could help with. She needed to go to Ireland for a couple of weeks. There was a family crisis – something to do with her mum and dad – that she couldn't discuss, and she asked if she could take compassionate leave. I told her of course she could.'

Robyn already knew that the Connors family weren't experiencing any problems. Earlier that morning Mitz had spoken to both parents, who'd confirmed what they'd told Ross: they hadn't heard from Siobhan. Mr Connors, now living with his second wife, hadn't heard from Siobhan since Christmas, and her mother had last spoken to her on New Year's Day.

Neither of them had any idea where their daughter might be, but following Ross's call, said they'd checked with other members of the family in case she'd turned up. They showed little concern about her sudden disappearance. Her father had declared Siobhan was a free spirit who did whatever she fancied without thought to others. Robyn gathered they weren't a close-knit family. Siobhan's only anchor appeared to be Adam.

'Does Siobhan have any friends at Tesco?'

Lucy shook her head. 'Siobhan isn't close to anyone here, but that's not unusual. There are full- and part-timers of all ages. As you can see it's a twenty-four seven store so we're all on different shift patterns and spread about all over the store, taking different meal breaks; it's not a place for hanging about chatting or making new friends. You manage a few words with each other and that's about it. The customers seem to like her. I think it's her Irish accent. She comes in on time, does her job well, and leaves the minute her shift is over. She usually spends break times outside with a cigarette, on her mobile. Is everything okay? Is she all right?

'I hope so,' said Robyn. 'We're checking up to make sure she is where she says she is.'

'You've got me worried now. I'll give her a ring when I clock off.'

Robyn gave a small shake of the head. 'I don't think you'll find she'll pick up, but if she does, let me know straight away.'

She left Lucy and headed directly to Hamilton Road, a short drive away, where Siobhan's ground-floor flat was in a surprisingly smart residence with a cream and brown brick frontage and wide parking spaces allocated to each flat. Adam Josephs was waiting outside the block, cigarette between his nicotine-stained fingers. He greeted Robyn, ground his cigarette underfoot and rubbed a hand across his stubbled face. He tried to suppress a yawn. 'Sorry,

I'm not on form. I'm working nights at the moment – ten till six,' he said, 'so I've not had any sleep yet. After you called, I couldn't help but wonder if Siobhan is okay. She might be a prize bitch at times, but I hope nothing's happened to her.'

He unlocked the main entrance and turned left, stood in front of the flat and hesitated. 'I've not been back here since she kicked me out a couple of weeks ago. I took my gear and left. I forgot I still had the key to the flat. It was with my car keys. I nearly turned and shoved it through the letter box but I didn't want her to try and talk me round. Every time we row and she chucks me out, I say sorry and we patch it up. I wasn't going to this time. I'd had enough of Siobhan's tantrums.'

The door opened to a reasonable-sized sitting room. A three-seater, cream, faux-leather sofa was pushed against the far wall, and standing on a red rug was a wooden coffee table.

Robyn wandered into the kitchen, which was untidy by comparison, with piles of crumpled garments stacked on a chair, and cluttered kitchen worktops. A large wine glass with a blue glitter exterior and silver interior, and emblazoned with a diamante letter 'S' was on the small round table squeezed into one corner. Robyn donned plastic gloves, picked up the glass and sniffed, the sour, vinegary smell making her stomach churn and reminding her she hadn't eaten any breakfast.

'I bought her that glass. It's what they called a diamanté dazzler. She saw one like it on *Big Brother* and loved it. She went on and on about it. I bought it for her for at Christmas.' Adam's heavy eyebrows lowered and creases formed between his eyes. 'Maybe she's staying over with friends. She might be having the mother of all parties and be out of her head. I wouldn't put it past her. She's done that before, especially when she's pissed off with me.'

'Adam, would you mind waiting outside? I might want to take prints. I'll check the rest of the place on my own.'

Adam stared at the glass as if it might divulge the whereabouts of his ex-girlfriend. 'You don't think something horrible's happened to her, do you?'

'I don't know, Adam. It's a precaution at this stage.'

Once he'd gone, Robyn headed for the bedroom where a silver skirt, black strappy top and a pair of skyscraper-heeled shoes had been tossed on the bed in a jumbled pile, along with a blue jumpsuit and a stretchy jersey dress – outfits that Siobhan had chosen not to wear. The scene suggested somebody had been preparing to go out – a bath towel thrown onto a stool next to the dressing table, hair straighteners resting on a stand, hairdryer on the floor, make-up and brushes lined up on a dressing table and several pairs of earrings that had probably not matched her outfit, discarded. Robyn closed her eyes to assimilate the information. Could Siobhan have been packing to go away? Robyn opened the wardrobe and alighted upon a small red suitcase on the top shelf. Unless Siobhan owned two cases it was unlikely she'd suddenly gone off. This scenario smacked more of preparing to go out for the night rather than away. Outside, Adam, sitting on a low wall, smoking, confirmed he'd taken the only other suitcase.

Back inside, Robyn rooted about for a handbag, keys, purse or mobile phone, but none were to be found. Everything pointed to the fact Siobhan had gone out for the night, but where had she gone and why had she not returned by now? As she shut the door to the flat, Robyn's gut told her Siobhan was most likely in the hands of the murderer.

Judging by the way he glowered at her, DCI Flint wasn't in the best of moods.

'So, Miss Connors upped and left following a break-up with her long-term boyfriend?' He sniffed several times as if he had a cold, a habit Robyn found infuriating. 'She called her supervisor, explained she wanted compassionate leave, and told a friend she was going away with a new boyfriend. This is not unusual behaviour. According to Mr Josephs, Miss Connors has left on several occasions, usually after disagreements, only to return several days later. Her neighbours have witnessed arguments, raised voices through walls and slamming doors in the past.'

'Yes, guv. But we shouldn't rule out the possibility of her being snatched because of her past actions. Carrie Miller also stormed off on a few occasions.' Robyn waited while he picked up the statement made by Adam Josephs and studied it again. Robyn knew what it said. She'd been present when they'd taken it.

'I'm not convinced this woman has any bearing on your case. As far as I can tell, Miss Connors is a few years older than our victims, is or was in a relationship, and held down a steady job. Her employers believe she is trustworthy and have no reason to disbelieve her story that she's gone back home to Ireland. It seems logical to me that she might do just that if she were upset enough about her boyfriend leaving her. She doesn't necessarily have to be staying with her parents. Remind me again of her parents' reaction to the news she'd gone off?'

Robyn inwardly cursed the man. 'They weren't overly concerned, but they haven't seen her in a while and don't know much about her life.'

'And how many of her friends and work colleagues are worried about her?'

'One, sir.'

'And as we've established she's gone off before, hasn't she? According to Adam Josephs' statement, she'd "go off in a right huff every time we had a major row. One time, she went to Derby and didn't come home all weekend. She liked to make me sweat it out." Miss Connors could well be deliberately hiding out, hoping to cause anxiety.'

'She hasn't taken a suitcase and her clothes and make-up are scattered on the bed as if she was preparing to go out.'

'Or, go away for a few days, DI Carter. She could have been rummaging for outfits to take away, put the clothes and items she needed into a small holdall, or even a plastic bag.'

Robyn refused to give in. 'I think there are sufficient similarities between her disappearance and that of Amber and Carrie to be concerned. She's not answering her mobile and she's sent a text to a friend saying she's with a new boyfriend, just like Carrie did.'

'Did she name the boyfriend? Was it the same name as used by Carrie?'

'No, sir.'

'I understand you believe there are similarities. However, she might have made up the story about a new man solely to antagonise Mr Josephs.' That thought had crossed Robyn's mind but she'd discounted it. Flint tapped the statement.

'The fact she received a Facebook message identical to the one Amber received is a concern, but until we have more evidence that she's actually missing, and hasn't gone off for a few days' holiday to get over splitting up with her boyfriend, or isn't deliberately trying to "make him sweat", we can't jump to conclusions.' He sniffed again. 'I want you to concentrate on finding the person or persons responsible for the deaths of Amber Dalton and Carrie Miller. That is your priority. For the moment, I want you to deploy all your resources on that. Carrie Miller was found six days ago. Are we clear?'

Robyn nodded. Flint wasn't going to be swayed. She'd do as he suggested but she wasn't going to let Siobhan Connors be the killer's third victim.

'We're interviewing Logan Crompton in the next half-hour, sir.'

'You think he's our man?'

He's the only person we've been able to link to the two girls. I'll keep you informed, sir.'

He replied with a curt nod.

She dialled Ross as soon as she left Flint's office. 'Ross, you'll keep looking for her, won't you?'

'You bet,' was all he said. She could hear the determination in his voice. Ross believed in her, and for now that was enough.

She strode outside and breathed in the cold air. Louisa Mulholland would have let her pursue her enquiries. Louisa hadn't always agreed with Robyn's methods, but she'd rarely doubted her instincts. Maybe she should look at transferring to Yorkshire. Flint was never going to warm to her and she couldn't be stifled like this. She thought she could hear Davies's voice, 'Do what *you* believe is right.' He'd always told her that. He'd trusted her instincts too. Flint needed proof they were dealing with somebody who could strike again and Robyn knew his next victim was going to be Siobhan. She'd get the proof she needed to convince Flint of that. She dialled another number.

'Harry, can you examine Carrie Miller for me again? Concentrate on her forehead. I want to know if any flesh might have been cut away from it.' She snapped off her phone. Now she'd deal with the bouncer at the nightclub. She was not going to let another girl die.

CHAPTER THIRTY-EIGHT

Mitz shoved his head around the door. 'He's here.'

'Good. Have you set up the recording equipment?'

'All done. I'll meet you in interview room two.'

Robyn pushed back her chair. She was eager to speak to Logan Crompton, the bouncer at Stardust nightclub.

Anna was going through pages and pages of Facebook posts, hunting for anything that would give them a clue as to why and how Carrie, Amber and now Siobhan were connected.

'Still no luck,' she said, as Robyn rose to interview Logan.

'Stick at it, Anna. I have confidence that if there's anything important there, you'll spot it. While you're scrolling through, check out Stardust nightclub and see if any of them mention it.'

Logan Crompton filled the plastic chair he sat on, beefy arms folded, thighs rubbing against each other. He wore the uniform of a biker: boots, jeans, a knotted neckerchief around his throat, T-shirt over which he sported a leather gilet. A heavy leather jacket hung on the back of his chair. His head turned as Robyn entered the room.

'Finally, I can find out what this is all about,' he said, hazel eyes boring into hers. 'Whatever it is, it's a mistake. I haven't done anything.'

His voice was soft, and in spite of his gruff exterior, his face was smooth and clean-shaven – a pleasant face with arched eyebrows that looked quizzically at her.

'I'm sorry about this, Mr Crompton. We have to ask you a few questions.'

He shrugged. 'Do I need a lawyer?'

'That's up to you, sir, but at the moment, you've not been charged with anything. This is merely to ascertain information relating to our enquiries.'

'Which means what, exactly?'

Robyn gave him a short smile. 'Would you mind if we record this?'

He waved an arm at her. 'Go ahead. I haven't committed any crime, so why not. Now, what's this all about?'

Mitz spoke clearly: 'Interview with Mr Logan Crompton begins at eleven twenty a.m. Officers present: Sergeant Mitz Patel and DI Robyn Carter.'

'Mr Crompton, are you currently employed at Stardust nightclub in Derby?'

'Yes. I work there Friday and Saturday nights. I'm actually a landscape gardener by trade, but at weekends I'm on the door at the nightclub, especially this time of the year. Not many gardening jobs about.'

'How long have you worked at the nightclub?'

Logan sat back. 'I suppose two years, on and off.'

'Do you recognise this girl?'

Robyn pushed a photograph of Carrie Miller towards the man who swallowed and shifted in his chair. 'Yes.'

'Where have you seen her?'

'She came to the nightclub a few times.'

Mitz spoke up. 'DI Carter has just shown Mr Compton a photograph of Carrie Miller.'

'How well did you know this girl, Carrie Miller?'

'Not very well. She and her mate turned up at the club one Friday and asked to be let in. They didn't have any ID. It wasn't too busy in there that night, so I let them in.'

'Did you not suspect they might have been underage?'

'No. Not at all. They certainly looked old enough to come in. They said they'd forgotten their ID. I wouldn't have let her in if I'd thought she was underage. Was she?'

Robyn ignored his question, her eyes never leaving his face. 'Mr Crompton, did you, in return for allowing her entry into the nightclub, ever have sex with Miss Miller?'

Logan spluttered, his eyes bulged in their sockets and his face went pink. 'No. Absolutely not. I wouldn't. Is that what she told you? The lying cow. Believe me, I didn't.'

'Did you accept sexual favours of any description from Miss Miller?'

A deep blue vein pulsed in his temple. 'No. What do you mean "sexual favours"? I didn't touch her.'

Robyn ignored his protests of innocence, continuing with her rapid-fire questions. 'Did you allow Miss Miller to perform sexual acts on your person?'

'You're kidding me? She's making this all up. I want a lawyer brought in, and we'll put an end to this. She'll tell the truth then.'

'And what is the truth, Mr Crompton?'

'She threw herself at me. I was having a cigarette at the back of the nightclub and she came outside. She was all over me. I had to push her away. She asked me if I thought she was attractive and I said yes, she was. I only told her that to get rid of her. She was tipsy and I didn't want any histrionics from her.'

'So you took advantage of the fact she was drunk?'

'No! No way. I told her she should find her friend and go home.'

'And how did she respond?'

Logan flushed crimson red and swallowed again. 'She reached up and tried to put her arms around my neck but I pushed her off. Then she just dropped to her knees, reached for my flies and pulled down the zip.'

He cricked his neck from side to side. 'Whatever she told you is a lie. I didn't let her do anything.'

'You're telling me an attractive young woman flirts with you, then in a dark alley behind the nightclub offers herself to you, and you did nothing?'

Logan looked at his hands, and finally looked up. 'I told her to go home. I told her I was married.'

'But, according to our records, you aren't married.'

He shook his head. 'I figured she'd buzz off if she thought I was married.'

'Mr Compton, did Miss Miller perform fellatio on you?'

'Am I being charged with raping her?'

'No, Mr Compton. I asked you a question.'

'She didn't.'

'I'm afraid we have good reason to believe she did. And that you accepted it as reward for allowing her into the nightclub.'

His voice rose once more. 'I didn't. I mean *she* didn't perform fellatio on me. I told you what really happened. I honestly thought she was eighteen and she'd forgotten her ID. Have you seen her? She looks at least eighteen. What's going on here?'

'Please calm down, Mr Compton. There are only a few more questions. Look at this picture for me and tell me if you recognise the girl.'

Robyn pushed forward the photograph of Amber Dalton. He shook his head, eyes wide. 'No. I haven't seen her. I don't know her.'

'Mr Compton has been shown a photograph of Amber Dalton.'

'And how about this young woman?' Robyn revealed the photograph of Siobhan Connors. The man let out a groan.

'She comes to the nightclub. Irish girl. I haven't had sex with her either. She's never forgotten her ID to my knowledge. Please, what is this about?'

'Mr Compton, do you have a tattoo of a deer on your arm?'

Deep creases appeared in his smooth brow. 'Yes.'

'Have you any other tattoos?'

'I've got a bow and arrow on my wrist,' he said, lifting his left arm and revealing a neat black tattoo, 'and an eagle from my right shoulder, all the way down my back. Why?'

'Do you hunt, Mr Compton?'

'These are the weirdest questions. What have they got to do with anything?'

'Answer the question, please. The sooner we get through these, the sooner we can move on.'

'I shoot birds, pigeons and rabbits with an air rifle. Now and again. My father taught me to shoot when I was young. He's a farmer.'

'What's the significance of these tattoos, then?'

'No significance. I watch a lot of nature documentaries and am quite taken with both species. They're beautiful, powerful creatures. I decided I wanted to have them tattooed on my body. There's no law against that, is there? Am I helping you with your enquiries or are you looking to charge me, because I'm getting uncomfortable here and I don't understand why you're asking me these questions.'

Robyn maintained her steely gaze. 'You're assisting us, sir. Does the name Orion mean anything to you?'

'It's a star, isn't it?'

'Horus?'

'What? Are you taking the mickey? I don't know who she is.'

'Wōden?'

'Is that even English?'

Robyn gave a small huff in acknowledgement, sat back and crossed her legs. 'Have you met or had dealings with a woman called Joanne Hutchinson?'

Logan shook his head slowly, trying to keep up with the questions. 'Not a name I've come across. What does she look like?'

'She's in her thirties, blonde hair, slim, speaks very well.'

He shrugged. 'Can't say she rings any bells. Is she saying I've tried it on with her too?' He studied his hands once more and sighed again.

'Thank you. Mr Compton, I'd like to ask you again about Siobhan Connors. Did you ever communicate with her?'

'I spoke to her on a couple of occasions. She used to say hi.'

'Nothing more?'

'She asked me for a cigarette one time. She was supposed to have given up smoking but couldn't manage without a nicotine fix. We chatted about how hard it was to give up.'

'Did she make any sexual advances to you?'

He placed his forearms on the table, held his hands out and shook his head. 'No, she went inside the nightclub. I didn't see her again. I haven't seen her for a while. Last time, she was with a brunette. Both dolled up and worse for wear. Not seen them for a while.'

'Were you working at the nightclub on Friday the thirteenth?'

'Last Friday I was off with that stomach bug that's been doing the rounds.'

'You didn't go to Stardust nightclub that night?'

'No, as I said, I was sick. Started puking on Friday morning. Was totally wiped out until Sunday afternoon.'

'Did anybody visit you during this time? Anybody who can corroborate this?'

He sighed, long and noisily. 'Are you going to explain why I'm here? These questions are beginning to get tiring. And do I need a lawyer? Are you charging me with anything?'

'We're pretty much done, Mr Compton. And thank you for your cooperation. I want to go back to earlier when you denied having sex with Carrie Miller. I'm afraid we have strong reason to suspect that she did indeed, perform sexual acts with you. Have you anything you'd like to add to your earlier statement?'

'For the last time, nothing happened.' His nostrils flared as he spoke. 'She unzipped my flies before I realised what she was up to, and tried to get to my pecker. I pushed her away. She fell onto her backside and swore at me. I pulled up my zip, lifted her onto her feet and told her I was getting a taxi for her. She kicked me in the shin and swore again. Said she could get her own taxi. She didn't come back after that.'

'Thank you.' Robyn nodded.

Logan let out a groan. 'I wish I'd never let her into the damn nightclub. She's making it all up. Fetch her in. I don't know why she's accusing me of this. Nothing happened. I swear on my life.'

'You weren't flattered, aroused in any way?'

Another lengthy sigh escaped his nostrils. 'I wasn't at all interested in her, or any of the girls who come to the club.' He placed his hands in his lap. 'I'm gay. I have a boyfriend and we've been in a steady relationship for almost a year. He'll vouch that I was sick on Friday. He'll also tell you that I wouldn't have attacked any of these women. You've got the wrong man. So whatever Miss Miller has told you is an out and out lie. Now, if you want to charge me with molestation or rape or whatever, then please allow me my phone call – one of my neighbours is a lawyer and I'd like to ring him.'

CHAPTER THIRTY-NINE

Florence curled into a ball on her bed and hugged a large soft teddy bear. Tears dampened its head. *What was the matter with her?* She'd rowed with her best friend and told her to piss off. She was torn between ringing her to say sorry and still fuming. If she apologised, Amélie would certainly forgive her, but it would be the same old thing when they got back to school on Monday. Florence would, at some point in the day, be overcome with jealousy and hate Amélie for little reason other than she was a better person.

Florence despised her body. No matter how little she ate, she still looked fat compared to the leggy Amélie with her perfectly skinny body and shining dark hair, and no matter how much effort she put into learning, she was still one of the thickest in the class.

She didn't fancy Mr Chambers. She liked him, but that was different, so why had she got so prickly when Amélie was teasing her? It was down to Hunter. Hunter was almost the same age as Mr Chambers. Florence had been kidding herself when she thought she could have a boyfriend like him. He was way too old for her. Even with her make-up and her grown-up outfits, she was still only thirteen and she'd been living in a fairy tale believing she could be his girlfriend.

Up until today, Florence had been harbouring fantasies about meeting Hunter in real life, holding his hand, sitting on a park bench and perhaps kissing. She wasn't even sure how to go about that. She'd researched online but nothing prepared you for proper kissing. The reality was she simply had no idea how to act like an adult and, if he wanted to do more than kiss her, maybe touch her boobs… the thought thrilled and frightened her.

She was going to have to finish it with him and tell him today that she couldn't meet him. She'd make up an excuse about how she was moving away for her job. Then she wouldn't use the app again. It was pointless when you were only thirteen. She would have to wait. Tomorrow she'd be ugly, boring, stupid Florence without anyone to make her feel better about herself. She hugged the bear into her chest and sobbed angry tears. When she was spent, she washed her face and stared out of the window. Below, her mother was barking instructions at a new rider who sat high in her saddle, nervously clutching the reins. *Too tight*, Florence thought. The girl needed to relax. Her mother's strident voice probably didn't help. Christine Hallows was not a quiet woman.

Florence had deliberately turned her mobile off after school on Friday and now she saw Amélie had called three times and sent six text messages. She deleted them all without reading them. She needed a break from Amélie. They'd been friends for too long and now Florence felt stifled by her. She'd be okay on her own. A reminder popped up. It was time to talk to Hunter. She positioned herself comfortably on the bed, pillow propping her back, and opened the Fox or Dog app. There were a couple of dog emojis and somebody had asked if she had spots. *They were freckles.* One girl calling herself LaBelle18, had been crude about Florence's ginger hair. Florence had felt so indignant she'd retaliated and left a rude response.

At least I don't look like a pig with a moustache.

She regretted it as soon as she'd posted the comment, but it was too late to remove it. LaBelle18 deserved it, she reasoned. She checked her profile picture once more. She didn't look as grown up or as beautiful as she first thought. It was now obvious she was a little girl pretending to be a big one. She was nothing more than the fraud others had accused her of being. She chewed on her lip. Hunter was online and free to chat. She inhaled deeply and set her profile to online. Hunter greeted her:

Hunter: Hey. How's it going?

Kitten: Okay.

Hunter: Sure it is?

Kitten: Not had a good day. Feeling a bit low. There are some horrid comments about me on my profile page.

Hunter: Ignore them all. You're beautiful. They're from girls who're jealous, that's all. You're here with me now. That should make you feel better.

She smiled. It was nice to talk to Hunter. He was always so positive and easy to chat to. The heaviness in her chest wouldn't go away. She needed to tell him the truth or break up with him. She began to type.

Kitten: I have to tell you something.

Hunter: Before you say anything, I've really loved talking to you. You're the funniest, nicest and the sweetest person I've met on this site. The other girls are nothing compared to you. You've made me laugh and I really like you. I'd like to meet up with you.

Kitten: I can't.

Hunter: Oh no. You've found out, haven't you?

Kitten: Found out about what?

Hunter: That I'm not really at work and in my twenties.

Kitten: You're not?

Hunter: I thought you'd found out and that's why you didn't want to meet me. I look a lot older than I am. I'm sure we could still hit it off. There can't be too much difference in our ages.

Kitten: How old are you?

There was a pause. Florence waited, heart thudding against her ribs.

Hunter: I'm only sixteen. Actually I'll be sixteen in May. I understand if you don't want to meet me now. I'm very adult for my age. Don't give up on us because I'm too young for you.

Florence began to giggle – loud, uncontrollable giggles.

Kitten: Oh dear. I have to admit I lied too. I don't work in an office or travel. I'm not nineteen.

Hunter: NO!

Kitten: I'll be fourteen in November.

Hunter: OMG! We're both still at school. I thought you were way older, looking at your picture. We blagged each other? That's hilarious. Would you still like to meet me, even though I've fibbed about everything?

Kitten: Would you still like to meet me?

Hunter: Deffo. I'd love to meet you. All that stuff I said about you is true. You're lovely.

Florence went pink.

Kitten: Where shall we meet? I live very near to Uttoxeter.

Hunter: I'm at school at Sandwell. We have sports on Wednesday but if we're not involved in a match, we can have the afternoon off and go to Derby. I can catch a train from there to Uttoxeter. You could bunk off lessons early and meet me or after you finish. What time's best?

Her pulse quickened. The school wasn't far from the railway station. She could walk there after classes, and it was art on Wednesdays, so she could sneak away earlier if she tried. The art teacher wouldn't mind, given Florence was such a good pupil. It wouldn't take long to reach Uttoxeter station.

Kitten: I could meet you at Uttoxeter railway station at about three fifteen.

Hunter: That's a good idea. I'll be waiting. Are you sure you really want to meet me?

Kitten: Sure.

Hunter: Can't wait to actually see you. You and me are going to have such a laugh together. I have to go now. Got loads of homework to do and I have some really strict teachers. One is patrolling the studies now and we're not supposed to have phones while working so I'd better turn it off.

She grinned again.

Kitten: I understand. See you on Wednesday.

Hunter sent a smiling emoji and a kiss and disappeared offline. Florence sat back against her pillow, an enormous smile on her face. She no longer felt dispirited. She had a real boyfriend.

CHAPTER FORTY

Robyn leant back in her chair, eyes closed. Compton had seemed genuine, and she was convinced he hadn't had any relations with Carrie Miller. Mitz had come to the same conclusions. She opened her eyes. 'He was our only suspect. I haven't even got enough grounds to search his house or check his electronic equipment, and the flipping boyfriend was adamant Logan was too sick on Friday to move, so he couldn't possibly have snatched Siobhan Connors.' She threw the file onto her desk where it landed with a hefty thump, and rubbed the base of her neck.

She checked her notes, reading through dates to seek some pattern or significance, but nothing made sense. On Monday the sixteenth of January, Carrie Miller had been found in the self-storage warehouse, six months after she went missing. Her last Facebook message to Jade North had been sent on the twentieth of December 2016. Had she been alive until that date? The pathologist's report had put her death sometime between late July and mid-August, so it was not likely. Amber Dalton had gone missing sometime after the second of January, her last message was sent on the seventh of January, and her body was discovered thirteen days later, on Friday the twentieth of January. It had been ascertained that she'd been murdered sometime between the seventh and thirteenth. Meanwhile, Siobhan Connors had disappeared on Friday the thirteenth of January. She had last sent a message on Wednesday the eighteenth of January. Where had she been kept hidden during that time, and had she made contact with Amber? And more importantly, was she still alive? Robyn could decipher no pattern that made any sense. Carrie's body was found in Rugeley, and Amber's on Cannock Chase. Where, oh where, was Siobhan? Was she even being held captive? She searched through her files for the forensic pathologist reports. She needed to establish some pattern. She opened the file and read.

Carrie Miller's throat had been slit and she had bled to death. There was tissue evidence that indicated her body had, at some stage, been frozen. She wondered how Harry McKenzie was getting on and if he could confirm that a rectangular piece of flesh had also been removed from Carrie's head.

Amber Dalton had been poisoned, although until the full toxicology report arrived, the exact poison was unknown. So far, post-mortem findings showed the girl's lungs had been congested, her trachea had contained blood, and her stomach walls had been inflamed. Tissue damage indicated she too had been kept in cold storage. Both had suffered cruel and horrific endings to their young lives.

The phone rang. Matt Higham was on the end of the line. 'Guv, I'm calling from a B&Q store. I came in to buy some wallpaper, and at the checkout there was a bloke with a load of plasterboard. I made some comment about hoping he had a very big car to fit it in, and he told me that it was okay because the store lets you rent a van by the hour. I checked it out, and you can rent vans for as long as you want. The vehicles bear a B&Q logo and an additional Hertz logo in yellow but the older vans on the fleet have the original logo which is white lettering inside an orange square.'

'Oh, you top man,' said Robyn, suddenly lifted again. 'That could be what we're looking for. We'll get onto it. Enjoy your day off and don't overdo the wallpapering.'

She turned to Anna. 'Can you email all the B&Q DIY stores in Staffordshire, and the hire company they're teamed up with, to find out who leased vans on the nineteenth and twentieth of December last year, and particularly any women?'

It was too much to hope that Joanne Hutchinson had rented a vehicle from the company using the same alias, but stranger things had happened. Robyn pulled up a map of B&Q stores in the area and decided she ought to check those in the neighbouring county of Derbyshire as well, especially given that Carrie was from Derby. She sighed as the map filled with the locations of stores. It was going to be another long job.

Mitz was working at his desk when his email alert pinged. 'Got something too, boss.' His eyes sparkled. 'I've had a response from a company in Manchester that makes bespoke travel trunks. They confirmed that one fitting the dimensions of the trunk we discovered was paid for and delivered to an address in Manchester. They have no name or invoice, because whoever bought it paid by cash, but you'll never guess who owns the property they delivered to. It's only Mr Dev Khan, the owner of the self-storage unit at Rugeley.'

The team paused as they all waited for instructions. Robyn strode to the window, her pulse once again racing. They might have lost one suspect but now they had two new pointers. At last, things were beginning to move. It was unthinkable that Dev Khan would murder a girl and leave her body in one of his own units. It defied logic. Or maybe that's what he wanted them to believe. It could be a double bluff. Either way, he owed them an explanation. A trunk matching the description of the one they'd found had been delivered to one of his properties. It might be no more than a coincidence, but Robyn didn't much like coincidences. She'd find out what he had to say for himself.

She watched raindrops slide down the windowpane as she considered her choices. She could telephone him and ask him about the trunk or she could ask him to come to the station. She made the decision in a flash. 'Bring him in for questioning, Mitz.' The faces of Carrie and Amber swam in front of her. Robyn blinked back a tear. She'd avenge these girls. She'd make sure Mr Khan didn't leave until she'd squeezed every bit of information out of him. She wouldn't let them down.

CHAPTER FORTY-ONE

The call came shortly after Mitz had left for Manchester. Amy Walters sounded aggrieved.

'I kept my part of the deal and yet someone has leaked information to a rival paper.'

Robyn drew herself up in her chair. She didn't need this. Not now. Not when they had hot leads and a suspect coming in.

'Which paper?'

'*Derby Times*. Victoria Kenilworth's written a piece in today's edition about missing schoolgirl Amber Dalton.'

Robyn tapped into her computer and found the *Derby Times* website. Sure enough the piece was headline news, with a picture of Amber's parents emerging from a funeral home, Bianca's face ashen but hauntingly beautiful and Charles, zombified, an arm around his wife's shoulders. The headline read: 'Was Amber Murdered by a Schoolgirl Stalker?'

'Is it true?' Amy's voice whined like an irritating mosquito.

'Let me read it first.' Robyn scanned the article:

Staff and pupils were in deep shock following the discovery of a body believed to be that of Amber Dalton (16).

Amber, a student at the £30,000 a year, fee-paying school, was considered one of the brightest stars of her year.

Her father Charles Dalton (52) and mother Bianca (46) were unavailable for comment. Neighbours said the couple are in shock following the discovery of a body on Cannock Chase earlier this week. Derbyshire Police have been searching for Amber since January 8th when she was reported missing from the Daltons' £850,000 mansion in Tutbury where she had been staying while her parents were on holiday in the Algarve.

'Bianca and Charles are devoted parents and Amber is one of the politest girls I've ever met,' said Mr Wilfred Jones (67) a neighbour.

Today, Sandwell School was in mourning for Amber, a high-flying Oxbridge hopeful. Samantha Dancer (17) one of Amber's closest friends told us, 'I can't believe she's gone. I keep expecting to see her at her desk. She was so clever and so beautiful.'

Tributes have been appearing on social media websites including one that reads, 'RIP Amber. May you continue to shine brightly in heaven.'

The last paragraph bothered her the most.

There is further concern that Amber Dalton's disappearance is connected to that of Derby schoolgirl Carrie Miller, an ex-pupil of Fairline Academy, whose body was also discovered earlier this month, and begs the question: is there a schoolgirl stalker out there?

A small muscle flexed in Robyn's jaw. 'It hasn't come from here. We're keeping information to a bare minimum.'

'Are you denying there's a connection between the murders?'

'I'm saying "no comment". Ask Victoria Kenilworth where she got her information.'

'She's not exactly on speaking terms with me. Victoria is somewhat overzealous about her vocation and refuses to discuss her stories. Of course she won't divulge her sources. In short, she's a sneaky mare.'

Robyn bit her tongue. As far as she could tell, Victoria was no worse than Amy. Amy would sell her soul for a good story. And this article, which should have focused on how heinous this crime was and garnered sympathy for the grieving parents, chose instead to highlight the Daltons' wealth, and even dared to hint that their absence was somehow to blame for their daughter's disappearance. Robyn ached for them and hoped they had not read the piece. They had been advised not to speak to the press and now would need further guidance on how to deal with the public's reaction. Journalists were parasites, preying on emotions and fears, and fuelling the public's demand for sensationalism. Amy huffed into the earpiece.

'Well, is there a connection between the girls?'

'I can't tell you that.'

'You can't or you won't?'

'I can't. We really don't know. It's as simple as that. And when I do get that information, I refuse to compromise this investigation by leaking it to you or anyone else. You know how I operate. I made a promise. You'll get your story.'

'Have you got a suspect yet?'

'No further comment, Amy. Go and pester Victoria. She might be able to satiate your uncontrollable thirst for a story.'

Robyn dropped the phone onto her desk. She could do without the likes of Amy Walters and Victoria Kenilworth. The media had a role to play and could be useful, but stories like this helped no one. She read it through once more. There was a photo of Samantha Dancer, Amber's friend, laying a red rose outside Chapel House.

'Anything yet?' she asked Anna.

'Amber's Facebook wall is filling up with messages, so I keep losing my place, but I think I might have something here. There's a section that shows pages she's liked. There are all sorts of films, celebrities and internet games, fashion pages and there's this.' She pointed out a page with a jolly header of a cartoon fox and a dog. It's a dating app for over eighteens called Fox or Dog. I cross-referenced the sites with Carrie Miller's Facebook page and she also liked the Fox or Dog Facebook page. Mind you, they also liked lots of the same pages so it might mean nothing.'

Robyn wrote down the name of the app on one of her Post-its. 'Can you find out if other girls liked the Fox or Dog Facebook page?'

'Who did you have in mind?'

'Any of the girls we've come across during this investigation.'

'I can. It'll be quicker to ask Jade North and Samantha Dancer, rather than me trying to get into their accounts. I'll phone them.'

'Do that first, then check out Siobhan Connors's.'

Finally, the case had momentum. She felt she was actually getting somewhere. The face of Siobhan Connors stared out at her from the whiteboard. Robyn only could hope she would be in time to save her.

CHAPTER FORTY-TWO

Dev Khan, dapper in a bright-blue suit that hugged his frame, an immaculately clean shirt open at the neck revealing a subtle gold chain, and dark nubuck shoes with bright-blue laces completing his ensemble, was surprisingly charming. Robyn had fully intended to launch into the interview by asking him a barrage of questions and found herself disarmed.

'Good afternoon, DI Carter. I understand you have some questions for me about some properties I own in Manchester. Could you not have rung me about them? I'm a busy man. Like you, I have to work weekends.' He dropped his BlackBerry and leather-encased smartphone on the table to make his point.

'I'm aware of that, and thank you for coming here.'

'I didn't have much choice, did I? Sergeant Patel hunted me down.' He nodded in the direction of Mitz who stood beside the door.

'Interesting choice of the word "hunted",' she said.

His left eyebrow arched quizzically. 'Not really. According to my secretary, Sergeant Patel's been tracking my movements. It was a good job he caught me when he did. I was on my way to Milton Keynes to look at a site for a new storage warehouse.'

'Mr Khan, how many properties do you own in Manchester?'

'We have fifteen houses in our property portfolio, all of them in and around Manchester. My brother and I have a property company that's separate to the storage units.'

'Is 13 Edgar Street one of the properties you still own?'

'It is.'

'Do you live in it?'

Dev's white teeth gleamed as he chuckled. 'No chance. It's not my idea of a dream house. I let it out to students. All the properties are student lets. It's within walking distance of many of the university buildings, and rooms are spacious. I removed it from the university's list a couple of years ago as I was getting fed up vetting students who I thought would be suitable, and now it gets let out via word of mouth and I only take students known to and recommended by someone already renting.'

'How many students live in it?'

'It's a three-bedroomed house, so three. It's one of our best houses, so it's only let out to students in their final year. Hopefully, by then, they've got over the all-night party phase.'

'Can you tell me who rented it last year, between September 2015 and June 2016?'

'Dominic Granger. His cousin had rented it the year before.'

'Is Dominic still living in Manchester?'

'No idea. I don't stay in touch with any of them.' He snorted and rolled his eyes.

'You say three students rented it. Who were the other two?'

Dev's mobile glowed blue, interrupting proceedings. 'Can I take a quick look at my message? I think it might be important.'

'We're in the middle of an interview.'

'I'd like to remind you I came here voluntarily. I'm here to assist the police. I could have refused to come along and gone to my meeting instead.' His demeanour remained relaxed although his eyes glittered.

'Mr Khan, the names of the other two students, please.'

He huffed. 'Let me check my emails. I might still have their details.' He thumbed his BlackBerry and looked up after a couple of minutes. 'Stephen Robinson and Phil Eastwood.'

'I expect you have their contact details. It's customary for landlords to have such records.'

Dev gave a dry cough. 'I have one slight confession in that department. While I have the details of those individuals because they signed agreements prior to renting, and all paid a refundable deposit of £600, Stephen Robinson did not in fact, take up the room. I think he failed his exams and didn't return for his final year. His room was let out to another of their friends. The boys didn't tell me the tenant had changed until they'd vacated the property and Dominic confessed.'

'Did Dominic divulge the name of the third occupant?'

'It didn't crop up. Dominic was loading up his car and keen to get off when I saw him. I was checking the place for damages. I signed off on his rental agreement and we shook hands, wished each other well. That's it.'

Robyn pursed her lips. 'I'll need all the contact details you have, if you don't mind.'

'I don't have them on my email. I'll have them scanned and sent over to you. My secretary should still be there. Is it okay if I ring her?'

Robyn waved a hand in agreement. Dev lifted his smartphone and read his text. His thumbs flew over the screen as he replied to his message, then called a number, requested the information and, returning the phone to the table, asked, 'Is that everything, DI Carter?'

'I'm somewhat concerned, Mr Khan, that you have no details for the third student who rented your house. I'd like to remind you that you didn't take down Joanne Hutchinson's details correctly either.' Robyn sat back, arms folded.

'I accept it was lapse, DI Carter. Some days, I'm simply too busy to deal with everything and some things slip through the net. Neither of these slip-ups are offences, and I've been as helpful as possible.' The man was smooth, articulate and irritating.

'Could your brother not have dealt with interviewing students? You and he share the property portfolio.'

Dev shook his head with a smile. 'He's wrapped up at the convenience stores. They're scattered about the country. He's even busier than me. I spend more time in Manchester than him, so it was my responsibility to deal with the houses.' Robyn gave a slight shrug, a sign Mitz recognised as his cue to join them at the table and speak.

'Mr Khan, a trunk was ordered and delivered to 13 Edgar Street. Did you order it?'

'Why would I do that? No, I did not.' He studied Mitz for a moment. 'I get it. It's about the trunk at the self-storage warehouse, isn't it? I can categorically say I did not buy, borrow or order a trunk and have it delivered to that house, or anywhere, for that matter. I'd have to be off my head to order a trunk for a dead body to a house I own – and to hide anything, especially a body, in one of my own warehouses. And, I can assure you, I'm not off my head.' His voice took on an icy edge.

'Did you ever come across a trunk on a visit to the house?'

'If I had, I'd have mentioned it. I didn't come across any trunk until the day that poor girl's body was discovered. Happy now?'

'You must admit, sir, it's a coincidence that a trunk was delivered to one of your houses, and a trunk exactly like it was found at one of your self-storage facilities,' said Mitz, unperturbed by the stony look Dev was giving him. He continued his line of questioning.

'We've yet to locate Mrs Hutchinson, and given you are one of only a few people to have seen her, I wondered if you could tell us any more about her?'

'No. I've already told you everything. I'd recognise her immediately if I met her again, but I can tell you no more, given she supplied a false address and name.' He held up a finger. 'There was one thing. She mentioned receiving a leaflet about the self-storage

warehouse. That's how she found us. I forgot about that. Those
leaflets go out all over Staffordshire. We use the post office to deliver
them, so she could have been from anywhere in Staffordshire.'

Mitz made a note. 'Thank you, sir.'

'As I said a moment ago, I'd have to be off my head to hide a
trunk, a body, or drugs, in one of my own units. It's pure coincidence that a trunk similar to that one was delivered to one of my
houses. I've got forty-eight warehouses, fifteen properties, twenty
convenience stores and any number of other little businesses. I
have connections to half the people living in this area one way or
another. And coincidences do happen. Can we be clear on that
matter or do I have to involve a lawyer?'

Mitz shook his head. 'That won't be necessary. And again for
the records, can you account for your movements on Friday the
thirteenth?'

Dev huffed. 'Give me a moment.' He reached for his BlackBerry,
head bent to read his agenda. 'I was in Manchester for a site meeting
at ten, visited the Bradford self-storage in the afternoon and held
interviews for the position of a security officer. I finished at six,
drove back home, went to the gym, trained for two hours, returned
home, answered some emails then went to bed.'

'And you have witnesses who saw you at the gym?'

Dev nodded an affirmation.

'Can I ask when you were last at the Rugeley warehouse?'

'That would be the last time we spoke, Officer Patel. I haven't
been in this area since then. I've been up to my eyeballs in work. My
secretary will have my exact movements and appointments since then,
should you need them. Have we finished? I really would like to get
to Milton Keynes this afternoon. It's getting pretty late in the day.'

Robyn had no grounds for keeping him at the station so she
pushed back her chair and extended a hand. 'We appreciate your
help, Mr Khan. Thank you for giving up your valuable time.'

Dev rose as well. He gathered his phones and took her hand. A sardonic smile played across his lips. 'My pleasure. Next time you want me, DI Carter, don't send the good sergeant to hunt me down, just give me a buzz.'

Robyn flopped back into her seat. It was, as Mr Khan had just pointed out, getting late. Her team was exhausted and there was not a lot more they could achieve by staying behind. Once Dev had left the room, she spoke. 'You and Anna should go home. We'll tackle this better when we're rested. You're both off tomorrow, aren't you?'

Mitz nodded. 'I don't mind coming in, boss. I want to catch this perp.'

Robyn threw him a smile. 'I know you do. We all do. Take time out and approach it with fresh eyes on Monday. Matt and Dave are in tomorrow. We'll handle it.'

'Okay, guv. Let me know if you need me.' She waved at him to leave. Staring into space, she brooded over her decision to send Mitz to fetch Khan, and acknowledged it had been over the top. The irritation in Khan's glittering dark eyes had been unmistakable – a look of scorn mingled with annoyance. The evidence they'd had against him had been flimsy. She propped her head up with one hand. Her zeal to charge someone for the murders would endanger Siobhan's life if she didn't exercise more caution. If Khan had been their perp and was keeping Siobhan captive, angering him might have caused him to act hastily and harm her. She yawned and rubbed at the ache in her neck. She needed some time off too. She had hardly slept since the discovery of Carrie Miller's body.

Anna knocked on the door.

'Sorry, guv. It's a no-go for Fox or Dog. I spoke to Samantha Dancer and Jade North. Neither has heard of the app. Carrie and Amber didn't mention it to them. I looked through Siobhan's Facebook account too and she hasn't liked the Fox or Dog Facebook page. I cross-referenced all the pages that the girls liked and it's an eclectic mix from beauty product pages to games apps. As I said before, they liked quite a few of the same pages. I don't think the fact two of them liked one dating app page is as hopeful as we first thought.'

Robyn shook her head. 'Bother. It seemed promising. Any other pages that look hopeful?'

'Nothing that stands out. Jade said it was quite normal to click on the like button randomly for these pages. They pop up in your Facebook feed and you can like them purely because they look interesting. She said Carrie didn't need to use any dating app. She was popular enough.'

'That's true. She has a point. Okay. Thanks for going through all that. I'll see you on Monday. Have a good day off.'

After Anna shut the door again, Robyn stood up from the hard chair. She'd head back to the office and leave a list of tasks for David and Matt. She'd try and relax tomorrow. Her body could certainly do with a rest.

CHAPTER FORTY-THREE

DAY SEVEN – SUNDAY 22 JANUARY

Amélie's text to Robyn said she wanted to chat urgently. Robyn had only just got home from a morning at the gym. The tension in her skull had risen to such proportions overnight she had deemed it necessary to train solidly for three hours. It had felt good to be back in control of her body. The hip flexor that had been injured was feeling stronger, and Robyn put the discomfort in her legs down to lack of use rather than any damage. It had been a tough few days and she'd missed her regular training. The endorphins she got from pushing her body had been the medicine she'd required.

Mindful her jeans were hanging on her hips, she tipped a handful of nuts and raisins into her mouth before ringing. Amélie picked up at once.

'Hey, what's up?'

'Mum says it's nothing, but it isn't. I've fallen out with Florence.'

'And have you tried to make it up?'

'She refuses to talk to me. I've left messages and phoned but she isn't answering them.'

'Didn't you have a similar situation last year when Florence fell out with you over a boy?'

'This is different. It happened so quickly. On Friday we were talking about a teacher, Mr Chambers, and she got really snarky with me. I was being a bit silly and messing about, saying she fancied him, but when I said sorry, she blew up at me. And she swore at me. She never swears. She said I always thought about myself and that she was fed up being my friend. She said she was sick of me acting the clever one and her being the stupid one. She gave me such a horrible look. Like she hated me.'

'So was this fallout over a teacher, or because she thinks she's less intelligent than you?'

Amélie's words were garbled and incomprehensible. Robyn listened patiently as the girl attempted to voice her concerns.

'I came top in an English test and I didn't know but Florence came bottom in it. She was upset about and I didn't have any idea, which makes me a bad friend, doesn't it?'

'Your mum's right about this. You and Florence have been best friends since for ever. Florence will get over it. You'll soon be friends again.'

'No, we won't. She really hates me. Will you speak to Florence for me? She isn't answering my calls and Mum will only say no if I ask her to ring. Can you tell her I'm sorry?'

Robyn pulled a face. She had no idea what to say to either girl. This all seemed so trivial but she couldn't bear to hear Amélie so upset.

'How about I drop by Delia Marsh tomorrow afternoon to collect you instead of you catching the school bus, and *accidentally* bump into Florence? I could pretend I don't know what's happened between you two, and offer her a lift home as well. And then, we'll take it from there.'

'That'd be great. We've got geography last lesson on a Monday. The classroom's in the main building. If you wait near the entrance, I'll come out after Florence, then that'll give you time to talk to her. Convince her to speak to me.' She sounded more hopeful.

'Sure. We'll do it that way. See you tomorrow. If I can't make it, I'll call you and you can catch the bus as normal.'

'Thanks, Robyn. You're the best.'

Robyn smiled at the mobile. Amélie was the closest she had to her own daughter. If parenting meant helping to mend a little girl's heart, then she'd do it. Florence had certainly changed recently, physically and in her attitude. Surely she couldn't be jealous of her friend? Robyn thought back to the charade at the cinema when Florence pretended to be sick to hide in the toilet and use her phone. A love interest must be at the heart of this matter. She would have to try and get Florence to open up.

The phone bleeped with another message. This time it came from Tom Shearer and simply said, *Don't forget to eat.* She tipped the remainder of the nuts into her mouth and chewed thoughtfully.

She rearranged her Post-it notes and stared at them. She had the names of three young women lined up in front of her. On luminous orange paper were her suspects; on blue, places they lived; and on pink, the locations where Amber and Carrie had been discovered. She dragged up a map of the area on her computer and studied it closely, trying to see the connection, but it continued to evade her. The phone buzzed again and broke her concentration. The irritating voice at the other end made her roll her eyes.

'I'm not complaining this time. Mr and Mrs Dalton were interviewed on BBC Radio Derby this morning and I fully intend to interview them myself later today. I thought I'd be generous and give you the heads-up.'

'Amy, I can't stop you, but exercise caution.'

'I wanted to get your take on it for exactly that reason. Mrs Dalton told the radio listeners that she believed a serial killer had murdered Amber and warned parents to keep an eye on their daughters.'

Robyn let out a loud tut of exasperation. 'That's exactly what I didn't want to get out. Parents everywhere will go mad with worry. Can you do any damage limitation on that?'

Amy was quiet for a minute. 'What are you suggesting? It's a big story and I don't think we should dumb it down. As callous as it sounds, serial killer stories sell papers. You'll have to go on record if you want the article to be more neutral in tone.'

'Curse you, Amy. There's no other way, is there?' She rubbed at both her temples with one hand. 'You'll have to talk to the press team at the station about this. I'm not going to be able to comment.'

'Is that it?'

'I'm afraid so.'

'Off the record, do you think there's a possibility that one person murdered both these girls?'

'No comment.' Robyn willed Amy to hang up.

'Do you want to know what I think? I think you *are* searching for one person in connection with the murders, and I hope I'm wrong. A lunatic hunting down schoolgirls is a terrifying picture. I won't be able to keep a lid on it, especially now Mrs Dalton has voiced her concerns on air. I won't sensationalise my article, but you're going to have to work quickly. The press will be breathing down your neck, and for a change it won't be me leading the charge.'

Amy disconnected and Robyn let out a hefty sigh. She really didn't need media involvement. She rang the station to let them know what she'd told Amy. Her mobile rang. She feared it would be Flint, but it was Harry McKenzie. He confirmed her fears.

'Robyn, it appears your supposition was correct. I've examined Miss Miller's head again, especially the ragged edges of the flesh on her skull which was fairly badly decomposed. On closer examination, after I scraped it away and pulled off the flakes that remained, straight lines, consistent with cuts made by a sharp knife, were visible in the layers below the epidermis. There were also some scratches on Carrie's Miller's skull that weren't obvious from the X-rays I took. It appears you could be correct, and skin was cut away from Carrie's forehead, and if I'm not mistaken, it's in a shape of a rectangle.'

Her phone vibrated as she spoke, alerting her to the fact her superior was after her. She ended the call with Harry and dialled Flint's number.

'We need to talk,' was all he said. She sighed and picked up her car keys.

Flint was in the foulest of moods. A red flush had crept up his throat and spilled onto his cheeks.

'So, who put the Daltons up to this?' he barked as soon as she sat down.

'I understand the Daltons took it upon themselves and contacted the radio station. I spoke to the radio presenter on my way here. They were fearful that other young girls might go missing and wanted only to make people more vigilant.'

'I don't need to tell you that we can't have the public panicking over a serial killer. The press will have an absolute field day with this.'

'I agree, sir.'

'I'll have to consider addressing the public.' He spoke more to himself than Robyn. 'It's a complete mess. Have you got anything we can use to reassure the public?'

'I'm afraid not. In fact, I've spoken to Harry McKenzie in the last half an hour and I'm now sure we are dealing with a serial killer.'

He groaned loudly, throwing his head back against the headrest. 'Go on,' he moaned.

She told him about the piece of skin missing from Amber's head and how there were cuts and scratches that indicated a piece was also removed from Carrie's forehead. She added the information about both bodies being frozen and reiterated her concerns.

'I think we're going to have to come clean. This sort of thing can't be kept from the public. I'll arrange a press conference for tomorrow. It would help if you had another suspect to bring in.'

'We're working hard on it. We're looking into every possible avenue, and we'll find the person responsible.'

He sat motionless for a moment then nodded. 'I'm going to talk to the press team. See how best to handle this. I might like you to team up with Tom Shearer on this. We'll need a result quickly.'

'With all due respect, sir, there's been a lot of information to process and people to speak to since this investigation began. I had limited assistance at the outset, and I believe since then we've covered many angles, eliminated suspects and are making progress. We're dealing with somebody who is devious – clever enough to avoid CCTV footage, use aliases and snatch young women without being spotted. I'm sure we'll find that piece of evidence we need. I shall personally make sure we do, and in the quickest possible time. Giving me more officers who need to be brought up to speed when I have an efficient team will only hinder my progress. I'd like you to leave me to handle it my way.'

His jaw muscles clenched and unclenched. He studied her as she sat straight-backed, facing him.

'Okay.'

'Thank you, sir.'

'Find this person, DI Carter. And quickly, before I change my mind.'

David and Matt were in the office. Both looked fatigued.

'Didn't expect you in, boss,' said Matt.

'Things are heating up, Matt. We've got to work faster.' She told them about the most recent developments.

'Find those students who rented Dev Khan's house, will you? Pull them in to help with enquiries. David, we need to locate Siobhan Connors. Tell me when you have something.'

She slid behind her desk where she once more rearranged her Post-its: Carrie first, then next to her name, Amber, and under that, Siobhan. Carrie had sent Siobhan the same message she'd sent Amber, *You sound a lot like me. I hope we meet sometime soon.* If the killer had sent that message, Siobhan was in real danger. Robyn pondered the actual meaning of the message. Perhaps the sender intended them all to meet in death.

She couldn't focus on the task. There were too many loose ends that she couldn't tie up. Davies would have known how to tackle it. Post-it notes weren't enough. How she missed him. He would have let her fire off all sorts of ideas and helped her pick her way through them. She needed him more than ever. This was the most confounding case, and she had no one who could help her reach the right conclusions. She'd pulled in suspects only to discover they had no connection to it. She'd raced around interviewing people and had no real results, and all the while the killer was out there.

With a heavy sigh, she snatched up the autopsy reports from her desk. She had a job to do. The young women whose names were on Post-it notes needed her, and she had a murderer to find.

CHAPTER FORTY-FOUR

Delia Marsh School in Uttoxeter was on a large site consisting of over twenty buildings. Robyn watched the main entrance for signs of movement.

Florence and Amélie had been at the school for eighteen months now and were in Year 8. Amélie was relishing the challenges provided by the school and the vast array of subjects. Robyn had noticed subtle changes in her – a shift in her focus, the way she acted. She was growing up fast, as was Florence, and Florence was the reason Robyn was standing near the school entrance on a freezing cold January afternoon, instead of sitting in her office where she ought to be.

Matt had found out where the students who rented Dev Khan's house were now living, and she'd dispatched Mitz to talk to them. The other members of her team were occupied with various other tasks that she desperately hoped would finally pinpoint a suspect and, more importantly, the location of Siobhan Connors.

She cupped her hands and blew into them. A loud buzzer sounded, marking the end of the school day. Gradually the building spewed out pupils, and Robyn soon spotted Florence with her mane of hair tied back from her face. She called to her. Florence, clutching a schoolbag to her chest, didn't respond.

'Florence.' Robyn moved position until she was in the girl's line of sight and before she reached the gate.

'Oh, hey. What are you doing here?' Her voice was taut.

'Came to collect Amélie.'

Florence didn't seem to know what to say, or where to look. Pupils brushed past them, eager to mount coaches and leave for the day. 'Look, why don't I drop you off too? Save catching the bus.'

Florence's hair bounced as she shook her head. 'It's okay. I don't mind the bus.'

'My car's more comfy and you'll get home quicker.' Robyn regretted the words. She was handling it incorrectly. Years of experience as an investigator in the police force and she couldn't even chat to a thirteen-year-old girl. She sighed. 'Truth is, Amélie asked me to speak to you.'

Florence squeezed her bag more tightly.

'She's so upset about what happened. It seems such a silly reason to fall out.'

A muscle in her jaw pulsed. 'What did she tell you?'

'She was being silly. Made a daft comment about you fancying a teacher and that she was a rotten friend for not thinking about your feelings.'

Florence's chin jutted out. 'Robyn, this is between Amélie and me. She shouldn't have brought you into it. It shows what a kid she still is. She can't deal with it herself.'

'To be fair to her, she has tried. She says you refuse to take her calls.'

'Whatever. I don't want to hang about with her any more. That's all. There's nothing more to be said.'

'But Florence, why?'

'Because it's time for me to become my own person. Not Amélie's shadow. It's difficult enough being me without being best friends with someone like her. I need space. I need to find out what I'm like on my own. What it's like to be *me*. Get it?'

Robyn didn't wholly understand, but there was no denying that Florence was not going to back down on the subject. 'I get it, but do you have to cut her off like this? She's been your friend for six years. That's a lot of friendship to turn your back on. If you spoke to her about this, she'd give you space and just see you now and again. That's better than cutting her off altogether.'

Florence's eyelids flickered. 'I've made up my mind. It's time for us both to make new friends.' The words sounded rehearsed. 'I have to catch my bus now. Tell Amélie I'm sorry.'

'You should tell her yourself. You see her every day. This is making her really miserable, Florence.'

'Then she'll understand how I feel a lot of the time.'

She gave Robyn a sad look, skirted around her and got onto a bus opposite the gate. Amélie exited behind a straggling group of teens. She spotted Robyn and made for her. Robyn put an arm around her shoulder and together they headed for the car.

CHAPTER FORTY-FIVE

It was after seven when Robyn got back to her house. As always, the place seemed so empty. It would be so different if someone was sharing it with her. Thoughts drifted back to Davies. Even when he was absent, she'd felt his presence. The pillow would smell of his aftershave, and somehow the house had felt more homely, more alive. How she missed him.

She ought to get a cat. Then at least there'd be someone to share her life with and to care about. That's what she needed. Shearer had been right. They were two of a kind. Work was the only thing that kept them both motivated. She stared at the ceramic egg-timer Davies had bought her. He'd liked his eggs boiled for exactly three minutes. The timer had been a joke present after she'd overcooked them one morning. She'd not use it since his death. She picked it up and wiped the dust from it with her sleeve, then prepared a meal and sat at the kitchen table, simultaneously eating and reading through her reports.

She ran the possibilities through her mind. Both Carrie and Amber were or had been at schools in Derby. The bodies of both girls had been frozen before being removed and hidden elsewhere. And it seemed the murderer had collected a piece of skin from both girls. Had Joanne Hutchinson killed them both, and if so, why? Robyn stuck a fork into her salad. She needed more than this. She only had fragments of clues and still numerous ends to tidy up.

Her phone buzzed on the table.

'Jade North has just rung the office again.' Anna spoke with a slightly tremulous voice. 'She has something for us.'

Robyn's fork clattered onto the plate.

'After I spoke to her about the Fox or Dog Facebook page she began thinking about Carrie and she's remembered something that might help. She was a bit upset she didn't think of it before. The night Carrie called her to say she was leaving home, Jade heard a Tannoy announcement that caused Carrie to stop speaking for a moment. She believes Carrie was calling from a railway station. Do you think it could've been Derby station?'

'Can we get any CCTV footage from there for that night? It was some time ago.'

'I've already requested it. I've also received the list of calls made from Carrie's mobile provider and can find out exactly what time she made that call to Jade. I can then work out which trains were at the station or due out at around that time. That is, if she caught any of them, and wasn't waiting for a later one.'

'It's worth the exercise. If there's any footage of her at the station, that'd be perfect. I'll organise for somebody to take her photograph to the station and see if anyone can remember her being there. It's a long shot, but it's all we can do at this stage.'

This was yet another piece of information that would only take more time to follow up. It might also lead to a dead end. She thought for a minute. Carrie might have caught a train from Derby station. A spark of a thought.

'Amber lived in Tutbury, didn't she? Is there a railway station near her house?'

Robyn held her breath while Anna clicked her computer mouse several times.

'There's a small station at Tutbury and Hatton. There's no ticket office and no waiting room or facilities. It's on the Crewe to Derby railway line and offers an hourly service. It takes about eighteen minutes to get to Derby. And,' Anna said with some satisfaction, 'it's only a ten-minute walk away from the Daltons' house.'

'I'm assuming Derbyshire Police looked at the possibility that she'd caught a train when they were looking into her disappearance.'

'They did, and she wasn't seen at Tutbury and Hatton station.'

'I might be going off at a tangent here. Okay, thanks, Anna. I'll see you in the morning.'

Robyn retrieved her fork and, carrying her bowl to the sink, dropped it in. She was overthinking this case. She leant against the kitchen unit and stared into space. Somehow, the station seemed relevant. She opened her laptop and checked the stations along the route from Derby to Crewe. There were eight in all. The first stop was Tutbury and Hatton. The second was Uttoxeter.

Carrie, Amber and Siobhan were linked not only online, but by that railway line.

CHAPTER FORTY-SIX

DAY NINE – TUESDAY 24 JANUARY

The following morning brought some more news. Matt Higham had a list of people who'd rented vans from the DIY stores in the area.

'There are seventeen women on this list, not one of them called Joanne. Can't somebody, somewhere give me a break!'

'You didn't expect it to be that easy, did you, Matt? Joanne will have used another alias.'

'No, guv. Sorry. I'm a bit tetchy because Poppy spent all night screaming, and Mrs Higham made me get up to feed and change her.'

'Mrs Higham, is it? You must be in a bad mood.'

A sigh, like an old-fashioned kettle, escaped his lips. 'Damn right I am. This is the third night in a row I haven't slept. It's torture.'

'How about volunteering to do a night shift here and kipping in one of the interview rooms?'

'You have no idea how tempting that sounds.' He punched at his keyboard, huffed, punched some more. 'I've put them through the database and there are seven who could pass for the woman. I'm going to speak to them.'

'Good thinking, Matt.'

Mitz wandered in, a Tupperware box in his hand. 'My mother's been cooking. She sent these in for us.' He opened the box to reveal sticky, deep-fried dough balls, covered in sugar. 'She got carried away making *gulab jamun*.' He passed the box to David, closest to the door.

'What are they?' David dipped his hand into the box and pulled one out, bit into it and chewed, all the while making appreciative noises.

'Sweet milk dumplings. Mum adds a secret ingredient and they're the best.'

David swallowed and waved the remaining piece in his hand. 'These are delicious.'

'Guv?'

'Thanks.' Robyn unglued a dough ball from another. They were very sweet and moreish.

'Your mum's the best.'

Mitz's mother was well known for sending in titbits for the team. She'd even drop in occasionally with meals for them if they were working late, claiming she had cooked too much. She was the perfect matriarch.

'What's the occasion? Surely she hasn't made these just for us.'

Mitz grinned. 'She heard I'd got a second date and got overexcited. Thought she'd celebrate by making them.'

'A second date. Wow! Now, that's worth celebrating. So, what's this woman like?' Matt licked his fingers.

'Very nice.'

'That's it?' said Matt. 'Come on. There's more. You always have something else to tell us. Your dates always go wrong.'

'This one didn't, and that's all I'm saying for now.'

Matt waved a pencil at his colleague. 'You're going to have to cough up more information, or I'll be forced to put you in a cell for the night.'

Mitz threw back his head and laughed.

David reached for the box again. Matt tsk-tsked. 'You ought to save a couple of those for Anna. Besides, if you have any more sugar you'll get too hyper, and I don't want you bouncing about all over the place when we interview these ladies.'

Robyn snorted. David Marker was the least likely person in the universe to get hyper. He acknowledged Matt with a pained expression.

'Where is Anna?'

Robyn wiped her slightly sticky fingers on her skirt. 'She went to Derby station. Trying to track Carrie Miller's movements the day she left her dad's house. Jade North thinks Carrie called her from Derby station.'

'That's hopeful, then. Just need to work out where the heck she went to by train. Is it me, or is this one of the worst cases we've had?' Matt rubbed at his chin.

'It's tricky but I have faith in you all.' Robyn meant it. She was fortunate to have such a dedicated team.

Matt huffed. 'Glad someone has. I keep looking at that board and wondering where it's all taking us.'

Robyn knew what he meant. The board now bore the photographs of three girls. They still hadn't tracked down Joanne Hutchinson, but thanks to confirmation of all his movements, Dev Khan had been eliminated as a suspect. Frank Cummings could account for his movements for the week Amber disappeared – he'd been at his daughter's in Scotland. Robyn was now convinced neither he nor Dev were involved. There wasn't much left to go on. Names had been struck through as alibis had been established, and no one could yet fathom a motive for the deaths. 'No luck at Cannock Chase, Mitz?'

Mitz shook his head. 'No vehicles were spotted. I'm going back to the car park later today to try again.'

Robyn stood and stretched. 'David, you've been looking for the three lads who rented Dev Khan's house. Any joy?'

David gave a cough to clear his throat. 'I couldn't get hold of Dominic Granger so I spoke to his parents. Dominic's currently in Australia but he's on board a catamaran, not backpacking as we thought. He'll probably be out of contact for the next three to four days. Stephen Robinson's joined the army. He's on an exercise at the moment and can't be reached until tomorrow night. And Phil Eastwood's taken up acting. He's rehearsing for a new show in Birmingham. His phone's been off all day so I rang the box office and now I'm waiting for him to get back to me.'

'Which theatre is he at? I'll go and chat to him myself. I don't want to wait all day for him to call.'

Mitz scribbled down the address. 'I feel a bit like Matt. It's like we're all pedalling like crazy but none of us are getting anywhere.' He replaced the lid on the Tupperware box and slid it onto Anna's desk.

Robyn swivelled in her chair to better study the board. The team was becoming demoralised. She had to find some way of keeping them motivated. They had to get a breakthrough soon.

CHAPTER FORTY-SEVEN

Phil Eastwood wiped beads of sweat from his forehead on a damp cloth and faced Robyn. The rest of the dance troupe was still rehearsing moves for the *Bat Out of Hell* show, bass notes vibrating through the floorboards.

'It's not the acting career I expected,' he said, nodding in the direction of the group now gyrating furiously to one of Meatloaf's tracks. 'Still, it keeps the wolf from the door. This is a vast improvement on last month; I was trussed up in a turkey outfit, handing out leaflets for a frozen food store, making gobbling noises.'

Robyn watched the group, who leapt about the stage in an orchestrated frenzy, until someone from the shadows of the auditorium barked an instruction at them and they came to a stop while he changed aspects of the routine. Phil moved away, grabbed a bottle of water from out of a plastic bag, and lowered his voice. 'Best not be long.'

'Sure, I wanted to ask you about your housemates at university. You shared with Dominic and were going to share with Stephen Robinson, but he dropped out.'

He chugged his water and returned the bottle to the bag, along with the cloth. 'Stupid idiot didn't revise enough. He'd been going out with a medical student and spent too much time working on biology exercises, if you get my drift. Then he flunked the retakes over the summer. He phoned to tell us only a couple of weeks before term began again. Dominic and I were so pissed off with him. We'd wangled this house, a really good one at that. There aren't many decent places to share, certainly not places for only three students. We visited a few and they were manky or too expensive, or miles away from the town centre, and then Dominic's cousin put in a good word for us with Mr Khan and bingo! We were all thrilled, and then Stephen buggered up the plan by getting chucked out of uni.'

'So you found someone else to take up Stephen's place.'

'Uh-huh. I knew a guy on the same English and drama course – Elliot… Elliot Chambers. He'd tried to get off campus too but he couldn't find anyone to share with. He turned out to be the perfect housemate but a bit weird. He kept his room freakishly neat and even cleaned the whole place on his free days, and he could cook. Used to make a mean curry. Spent nearly all the time holed up in his room. Hardly ever saw him.'

Robyn gave him a smile of encouragement.

'As soon as he completed his last exam he packed up his stuff and left, without a word! I don't know where he is now. I tried ringing him but the number he gave us doesn't work any more. Dominic's gone travelling and I rarely hear from him either. He's one of those gung-ho types. Loves adventure and the outdoors. I can't imagine him ever taking up a nine-to-five job.'

Robyn nodded. 'Do you recall seeing a large trunk in Elliot's room or in the house, or maybe you were there when it was delivered?'

His cocked his head. 'No. I rarely went into Elliot's room. He was one of those private sorts – you know, would open the door to talk but not let you inside. The final term, he wouldn't even answer if you knocked on his door. Dominic and I used to laugh about that; joked he had loads of naked women hiding in there with him. As long as he paid the rent, we weren't that bothered. It's not like we were best mates.'

'Is there anything else you can tell me about your housemates?'

'We were pretty dull by comparison to some students. Got on with our work. Didn't get up to much mischief. Somebody told me Elliot is a teacher now. I forget who. He went back to his hometown. Where did he live? Place with a racecourse? Uttoxeter. That's it.'

Robyn's heart missed a beat. Elliot Chambers. Hadn't Amélie mentioned a teacher called Mr Chambers? Could it be the same man?

Phil was still talking. 'That surprised me. He was an exceptionally talented actor, much better than me. Mind you, the money is probably better in teaching and there's the job security. I live from hand to mouth, taking on all sorts of roles.' He grinned again and wiped his fringe away from his face. 'We performed together in a modern-dress production of Oscar Wilde's *The Importance of Being Earnest* at the end of our second year. I've got a photograph of us on my mobile. Hang on.'

He rummaged in the plastic bag, pulled out a phone, and once it had turned on he flicked through the pictures. 'That's us.' Phil held up a picture of a cast of nine. Phil wore a sharp suit and beamed merrily at the camera, arm around an attractive girl.

Robyn scanned the faces. 'Which one's Elliot?'

Phil gave a triumphant grin. 'I knew you wouldn't guess. There.' He pointed at the woman standing behind him wearing a sleeveless dress. 'That's Elliot. He played snooty Lady Bracknell. Doesn't he look amazing? No one believed he was really a man. Most convincing Lady Bracknell ever.'

CHAPTER FORTY-EIGHT

'Get me everything you can on Elliot Chambers.' Robyn kept her foot to the floor as she drove back up the M6 toll road, trying not to exceed the speed limit but desperate to get back to Stafford. Traffic was light for a Tuesday at 5 p.m. and the temptation to push the Golf to ninety was great.

She could hear the smile in Mitz's voice. 'Anna's got CCTV footage. She's going through it at the moment.'

'Good. Ask Matt and David to return to the station. I want to run something past you all. I'll be back in about thirty minutes.'

'You're not speeding, guv?'

'As if.' She gave a slight smile. Suddenly things were shaping up. She might even have got the breakthrough she'd been hoping for. Elliot Chambers could well be a suspect. She had enough information to bring him in for questioning, but she was concerned that if he were holding Siobhan captive and suddenly thought they were on to him, he might harm her. They needed to plan their strategy. Siobhan's life was not to be put in danger. Robyn did not want another girl harmed. She dialled Amélie. The girl sounded pleased to hear from her.

'Hey. Just wondered if you were okay and wanted to see if you and Florence had made up?'

Amélie's voice changed. 'No. She sat next to Ingrid today. She's ignoring me.'

'She'll come around. Don't worry. It was over something silly, wasn't it? Did you tell me it was over a teacher?'

'It was so dumb. Yes, I accused her of fancying Mr Chambers. He's pretty fit. He teaches us English and drama. What should I do? Try and talk to her?'

'Leave her for a little longer. Trust in your friendship. She needs to calm down a bit and realise it was silly to fall out over such an unimportant thing. Okay, I have to go. I wanted to see if you were okay.'

'Yeah. Thanks, Robyn. You've cheered me up a bit.'

Robyn drove on. She had to uncover everything possible about this man. Not only did they have reason to suspect him of involvement in the disappearance and murder of Carrie and Amber, but he was dangerously close to those she cared about.

The office was bustling when she finally got in. Anna, in one corner of the room, was glued to a screen, scanning every possible detail of the CCTV footage, hand poised over the mouse to halt and rewind. Mitz scrutinised his computer screen. As Robyn entered the room he waved a sheet at her. 'Elliot Chambers, twenty-three years old, took up a position at Delia Marsh School, Uttoxeter in September last year.'

Robyn felt another pang of anxiety similar to the one she'd had when speaking to Amélie about the man. She urged Mitz to continue. She couldn't afford to sidestep the real issue here. Was Chambers their perp?

'He studied at Manchester University and graduated in June last year with a BA in English and drama. No convictions. Driving licence but no car registered in his name. Father, Thomas David Chambers, died January 2006. Mother, Cheryl Denise Chambers, aged forty-five, currently unemployed and receiving sickness benefit. Chambers rents a flat in Derby Road, Uttoxeter, which is very close to the school. His mother lives just outside the town in Field Lane, at The Oaks.'

'Okay, okay, okay. Let's think this through.' She held up a finger. 'Firstly, we believe Elliot Chambers took delivery of a trunk, identical to the one that contained the body of Carrie Miller.' She held up the second finger. 'Secondly, Chambers has had acting experience. Mitz, did you print off the attachment with Phil Eastwood's email?'

Yes, guv.' Mitz passed out photocopies of the picture.

'Chambers is the woman in the yellow dress.' A small sound of surprise escaped Matt's lips. Robyn allowed them enough time to digest this piece of information before speaking. 'Is it only me who thinks he might, just might, have disguised himself as a woman to take on that unit in Rugeley?' She paused and looked at her officers.

'He looks remarkably like a woman.'

'I asked his housemate Phil about the part, and apparently Lady Bracknell is portrayed as very plummy. He said Chambers was excellent at mimicking upper-class folk. Our witnesses said Joanne spoke with a posh accent.'

Matt nodded. 'Could be him. He's slim, tall and good-looking in this photograph. He could be the evasive Joanne Hutchinson.'

'Do we agree it's a plausible assumption to make?'

There were nods of agreement. 'Finally, and I am going out on a limb again with this idea, Chambers's flat is close to the railway station, and I can't help but wonder if both Amber and Carrie caught trains and ended up there. I'm almost certain Siobhan went to Uttoxeter station to catch a train to Derby.' She strode to the window and observed the dark clouds scudding across the sky. 'Chambers lives in Derby Road. Mitz, how far away is that flat from the railway station?'

'On foot? Sixteen minutes. It's less than a mile.'

'So it's conceivable he could have met any of those girls at or near the station, and then taken them back to his flat. Or they could have made their way to his flat?'

David continued to scratch at his ear. 'But no one spotted them disembarking from a train or walking towards the flat.'

Anna joined in. 'Uttoxeter station only has two platforms. There's no ticket hall and there are only two trains per hour. Someone could have been waiting for the girls in the car park and driven them away from Uttoxeter. Or the girls might have exited the station on foot, cut across the car park at Dovefields Retail Park, and joined Derby Road without being noticed. People are coming and going all the time at these places.'

Robyn's lips twitched as she pondered. 'Chambers may have moved to his flat simply because it's near Delia Marsh school, but my instincts are telling me to delve further.' She folded her arms. 'I want him checked out but I don't want to spook him. If he has abducted Siobhan and clams up, we might never find her. It's been twelve days since she disappeared. Siobhan isn't a high-priority case for missing persons. She's almost nineteen years old and there is a belief that she's taken off for a while, after the break-up of her relationship. However, I'm concerned that she's fallen victim to our suspect. The careless disposal of Amber's body leads me to suspect he might kill Siobhan if he feels the net is tightening around him. This is tricky. I want to haul his arse in here and question him, yet that could be the wrong move. Without concrete evidence he could slip away, and who knows who his next victim might be.'

Anna looked across, eyebrows furrowed. 'I hate to say it, but Siobhan could already be dead.'

Robyn nodded gravely. 'I really want you to be wrong, Anna. The message that Carrie supposedly sent her on Facebook, "I hope we meet sometime soon", is niggling at me. Matt, check all the van hire establishments again, but this time ask if Elliot Chambers rented one. If that's a no-go, gather information on all Chambers's associates or friends in case any of them hired a vehicle on his behalf. Let's check that route from the station to the flat. David, head off to Dovefields Retail Park with the photographs of Amber, Carrie and Siobhan. See if anyone saw any of the girls wandering around alone or with someone.' She glanced at her watch. She could reach Uttoxeter by seven if she left soon. 'Any information on Chambers's family might be useful too.' She looked at Mitz. He acknowledged the look and began searching.

Robyn marched over to the whiteboard and added Elliot Chambers's name. What was the connection between him, Carrie, Amber and Siobhan? She stared at the board as if it might yield the answer. The girls came from different areas, were different ages and weren't even friends on Facebook. Only the message sent by Carrie connected them. She slipped into her seat and brought up Amber's Facebook page. She hadn't friended anyone called Elliot Chambers. Could he have used an alias? She carefully scrolled through each of Amber's friends, scrutinising the faces. None were Elliot. After forty minutes she sat back, none the wiser. Mitz had been more successful.

'I've got more information on his family, although there's not a lot. His father worked for a large dairy farm until he passed away. His mother, Cheryl, was a self-employed make-up artist, working on local theatre productions until last year when she stopped work and began to draw sickness benefit. Their daughter, Charlotte May Chambers, committed suicide on the third of March 2016. She'd only just turned fifteen.'

The sound of a siren approaching the station broke the heavy silence that fell.

A frown scudded across Robyn's brow. 'Chambers's sister killed herself?'

Anna interrupted the conversation. 'Got her! I've got Carrie.'

Both Robyn and Mitz raced to Anna's desk and huddled in front of the screen. Anna had it paused on a grainy image of Carrie Miller, a large black bag over her shoulder, clearing the ticket turnstile.

'Run it.' Robyn held her breath as they watched the girl pass through to the station platforms.

'It's definitely her. Any other images?'

Anna nodded, eyes wide. 'Here.' She fast-forwarded the footage until she came to the section she wanted. They all could see her clearly. Carrie Miller was squatting on her black bag, phone to her ear.

'That's definitely her.' Robyn felt her heart hammer. 'Which platform is that, Anna?'

'Platform 2B. And, according to the timetable, Carrie was waiting for the train to Crewe.'

'The train that stops at Uttoxeter.'

CHAPTER FORTY-NINE

'I think you need to act on this. Get Chambers in and interview him.'

DCI Flint's face was cherry red, as if he'd been boiled in a pot. No sooner had Robyn entered the station than she had been summoned to his office.

'Sir, I can't risk Chambers becoming spooked. If Siobhan Connors is being held captive, we could put her life in jeopardy.'

'That's guesswork. Miss Connors could be anywhere. We've discussed this before, and while I understand your concern, there's insufficient evidence to suggest she's involved in this case.'

Robyn felt her neck crick, a sign of tension. Flint wasn't making this easy for her. 'I've amassed a huge amount of information—'

'And used a large number of resources chasing around.'

'With the greatest of respect, sir, we're talking about the deaths of two girls here, and possibly a third if we don't handle this correctly.'

Flint's dark eyes bored into her. 'I understand you hauled in Mr Khan for questioning.'

'He came voluntarily.'

'That's not quite how I heard it. I understand Sergeant Patel was dispatched to chase him down and bring him in, when he could easily have been contacted by telephone.'

'Sir, at the time we had reason to believe he was connected to the murder of Carrie Miller. I deemed it appropriate to send Mitz to Manchester. I didn't want Mr Khan to suddenly decide to vanish.'

'And you brought in Mr Logan Compton, a bouncer at the Stardust Nightclub. Yet you're unwilling to bring in Mr Chambers. Can you explain that logic?'

'I was wrong.' Robyn looked her superior in the eye. 'I acted hastily, and had either of those men been connected to the case, I could have endangered Siobhan. I've given this considerable thought since then, and I want to make sure I have an airtight case against Chambers. I can't afford for him to slip away. He's at work today, so I doubt he suspects we're on to him. I only need a little time, sir.'

Flint returned her steady gaze and pulled his chin in. After a moment, he spoke. 'I've a different way of handling things to DCI Mulholland. There are procedures to follow, as you well know, and sending officers willy-nilly all over the country is a waste of their time and our resources. Likewise, dragging in innocent citizens on a whim.'

'I believed I had call to question them.'

'I'd still like you to bring in Mr Chambers for questioning.'

Robyn drew in a breath. 'If he's involved in the disappearance and murder of these girls, he could well have also abducted Siobhan Connors. We need more concrete evidence before we interview him. So far, all we know is a trunk was ordered to his university address. It might or might not be the trunk we found at Rugeley containing Carrie Miller's body.

'Sir, we're dealing with a perp devious enough to hide Carrie's body for several months, hire a self-storage unit without rousing any suspicion, disguise himself as a woman and abduct three women without being spotted. We simply don't have enough evidence against Elliot Chambers. I daren't risk calling him in or searching his flat on the off chance we get something. If he knows we're on to him, he could well murder Siobhan. That is, if he hasn't already.'

Flint studied the back of a podgy hand, mottled with brown spots. 'Okay. I can't say I'm happy about this but I'm going to trust you on it. Your reputation for getting results is formidable, and I'll give you the opportunity to prove me wrong. One chance. That's all.'

'Thank you, sir.'

'You have DCI Mulholland to thank. She told me you were one of her outstanding officers. For the moment, I'll let you do it your way. I have yet to draw my own conclusions.'

Robyn shut the door to DCI Flint's office behind her and exhaled noisily.

'Missed me, then?'

Tom Shearer seemed to materialise from nowhere.

'You back already? It only seems five minutes since you went to Newcastle.'

'Case resolved. I'm back. Got a shedload of paperwork to get through.' Shearer looked world-weary. 'Any progress?'

'Might have, at last. Flint isn't too pleased with me. We're not getting results fast enough and I'm burning through resources.'

Shearer looked vaguely amused. 'He's a bit intense at times. Probably getting pressure from the super.'

'Pressure. We're all under pressure.' With a wave of her hand, she bounded down the corridor and into the office. 'Come on, Mitz. Let's go talk to Mrs Chambers.'

Large puddles reflecting the ink-black sky stretched across Field Lane. The squad car had drenched hedgerows as they drove from Uttoxeter to The Oaks. The grey house, named after the trees that once surrounded it, now stood in little more than a plot of overgrown grass and weeds. The trees had long since been felled. The entire house wore a mantle of neglect and sorrow, as if it had seen too much tragedy. It stood next to several outbuildings, each in a similar state of disrepair. The door to the first had fallen off, leaving two large rusting hinges. A dark-blue Vauxhall Zafira was parked inside it, a disabled user badge propped up on the dashboard.

Mitz joined Robyn who rapped against the front door. It creaked open and Cheryl Chambers, clinging to walking sticks, peered at them, greying hair hanging straight and uncombed. As she escorted them through a cold hallway to a sitting room, she admitted the place had seen better days.

'I ought to move but somehow I can't.' Cheryl eased herself from her sticks into an automatic recliner chair in front of a television and beckoned for them to sit.

'I hope you don't mind us visiting you.'

'You wanted to ask about Charlotte. After you phoned, I wondered if I'd be able to talk about it again. I keep trying to bury the pain of her loss. It never eases.'

Robyn nodded. 'I understand. I'm looking into the disappearance of another girl and wondered if you could tell me anything that might help.'

'A girl's disappeared?'

'Siobhan Connors?'

'I've never heard of her. Lotty never mentioned her. Is she one of Lotty's friends?'

'I honestly don't know. Did Charlotte have many friends?'

She shook her head sadly. 'No, she kept herself to herself. She was quite timid. Not outgoing at all. It's been ten months. I still can't believe it happened. Some days, I wake up feeling happy because I've forgotten that she's gone, and then it hits me and I can't think for the pain of it. She's gone. She'll never come back. I failed her. We all failed her.'

'Can you tell me a little about her?'

Cheryl winced as she settled back into her chair, struggling to find a comfortable position.

Losing Charlotte had taken its toll on the woman. She looked older than her years, with deep creases in her forehead. She cleared her throat and spoke. 'Lotty was my walking miracle. She was born with a life-threatening condition that meant she spent the first twenty months of her life in hospital.' Tears sprang to Cheryl's eyes and she dabbed at them with a tissue pulled from a sleeve. 'One of her lungs was too small. It was touch and go as to whether she would live. She endured endless operations as a baby. Twenty-five, I think it was – twenty-five operations on that fragile, tiny body. There were complications and she had to have a tracheostomy. She lived with a tube in her throat, and another – a gastrostomy – in her stomach. That's how she was fed for years. Without those tubes, Lotty would certainly have died.' She gave a small sigh.

'She was such a fighter, and eventually her lungs became strong enough for her to breathe without the tube. That was an incredible day. It was a sign she was going to get better and that we wouldn't lose her after all those years of thinking she could be taken from us at any moment. She was still very weak and susceptible to illnesses, and although she missed a lot of schooling, she succeeded – she succeeded in surviving. I was so proud of my girl. When she was eight, the doctors removed the gastrostomy and she was able to lead a normal life at last, although the whole ordeal left her smaller, frailer and weaker than other girls her age. She kept surprising us though. My brave Lotty.' Her voice caught in her throat. 'Sorry, I can't go on.'

'Can I get you a drink of water or anything?'

Cheryl shook her head, wet tears on her cheeks glistened. 'I'll be okay in a minute.' She dabbed at her eyes. 'She was so full of joy and love. She'd fought for survival all her life, and then she gave up. Why? Why would she do that?'

Robyn had no answers. One sunny afternoon in March, Charlotte had sat on her bed, placed a plastic bag over her head, tied a cord around it in a double knot, and suffocated herself. Mitz had read the autopsy report to her during the journey to Uttoxeter.

'I have the note she left. The police officers that came took it away at first. I asked for it to be returned. It's in the drawer.' She indicated a table. Robyn rose and opened it. The note lay at the top. Written on floral paper in large looped handwriting was Charlotte's last message. It read:

> *I'm sorry, Mum. I can't bear my life any more. I feel like I'm drowning in a sea of hatred. I hope Dad will be waiting for me when I get to the next life, and it's easier than this one. I love you. I love Elliot. I'm so sorry I couldn't be stronger.*

Robyn could almost feel the woman's sorrow. 'You obviously had no idea she felt this way.'

'No, and I blame myself every waking hour of every day. I didn't notice anything unusual. She was a bit withdrawn and spent a lot of time in her room online. I put it down to being a teenager. Elliot was the same at that age and he came out of it, so I figured that Lotty would come through this phase, just like him. We were exceptionally close until she hit fourteen and then she began to pull away from me. Girls that age are feeling their way into adulthood. Nowadays I ask myself over and over: if I'd not been so sick, would she have involved me more in her life? Was I somehow to blame?'

'Was she close to Elliot?'

'There's almost an eight-year age difference between them. By the time she was able to come home, Elliot was ten. At first he wasn't interested in having a baby sister, especially a sick baby sister, one who took up all our time. Tom and I were always at the hospital in the early days and Elliot's life was incredibly disrupted, but he was a good kid. After Tom died, in 2006, Elliot adopted a greater role in looking out for her. It was like he needed to do something to block the upset of losing his father, so he gave Lotty all his attention. He'd feed her or play with her, take her to the park, read to her. I even found him half asleep in her room one night when she had a cold. He was curled up on a chair by her bed. I asked him what he was doing there and he replied he was making sure she didn't die in the night.' Her cheeks dimpled slightly at the poignant memory.

'He was very fond of her. Even after he left home for university, he'd come home and visit us and sit with Lotty in her room, listening to music or chatting.' Cheryl swallowed hard. 'He had a week's study leave just before his final examinations and he wanted to spend it at home. Lotty had been in her room all afternoon. She told me she had an art project to complete. Art was her favourite subject and she excelled in it. She wasn't too good at other subjects. All those years missing school sort of caught up with her and she struggled. Not at art though. She was top of the class in that.' She paused, looking ahead, lost in memories. 'I left her alone. She didn't like to be disturbed when she was drawing or painting. Elliot had been studying here in the lounge and nipped upstairs to tell her tea was almost ready. I don't think I'll ever forget the noise he made when he found her. It was like listening to a wild animal. I hobbled up the stairs, all the while thinking, *hurry, hurry*.'

She blinked away the tears. 'It was too late. The rest you know. She'd taken her own life, and to this day I don't know why.'

Robyn reached to touch the woman's hand. Cheryl continued. 'I don't know if this girl you mentioned was a friend of Lotty's, but I hope you find her. It's a dreadful thing to lose a child.'

'Does Elliot still live with you?' Robyn asked, even though she knew the answer.

Cheryl shook her head. 'He moved into town. I think he found it a strain coming back here to live, what with Lotty gone – the memories of that day. You understand. After we buried her he returned to university. "Mum, I don't know what else to do," he said. "I have to go back. I have to carry on for us both." He managed to continue with his studies in spite of the pain he was going through. He did well too. Got a good degree and a job offer immediately afterwards. Such a brave boy. I'm so proud of him. I had two brave kids.

'I'd been struggling with my health before all of this, but I became very ill after Lotty passed away and now, as you can see, I have trouble walking and some days I can't move for pain. The doctors have diagnosed fibromyalgia. I don't know what'll happen to me. I take each day as it comes. I can't expect Elliot to become my carer. He visits once a month, sometimes more often, and he's not far away if I need him.'

'So he spent last summer here at The Oaks?'

Cheryl's face screwed up and she eyed Robyn suspiciously. 'Yes. He returned in June last year. Why?'

'No reason. Sometimes graduates work over summer, just to pay back student debt.'

Cheryl frowned again. 'No. He worked around the house and helped me with cleaning and cooking. He's a good cook.' She stopped talking and pointed above a table. 'That's Lotty.'

The shelf held photographs of the Chambers family: of Cheryl and Tom with broad smiles on their faces next to two pigs staring through bars at the camera; of the whole family in wellington boots outside the grey house; of a young Elliot in shorts; of an older Elliot with his arm around his sister. Robyn lifted the frame containing the picture of a shy girl in school uniform – a school photograph. The girl looked awkward, frail and so young. Robyn wished she could help Mrs Chambers and return her daughter to her. But she couldn't, and now she might even be taking away another child from this woman who'd done nothing to deserve it. Robyn hoped she was wrong and that Elliot Chambers was not connected in any way to the case. It would break this woman's heart all over again if he was.

CHAPTER FIFTY

Robyn glanced around the office. Matt and David had been called out to an incident in Stafford and Anna was with the technicians, going through Amber's laptop one more time. Mitz was working through the list of van hire companies to see if Elliot Chambers had hired one. The visit to Mrs Chambers had unsettled Robyn.

There had been an inquest into Charlotte's suicide. It appeared she had not been very popular at school, having failed to become part of any particular circle of friends. Her illness and time off school had left her struggling to forge relationships with girls who had known each other for years.

Her mother testified that Charlotte didn't own a smartphone or a computer – her own income wasn't sufficient to pay for 'luxury items'. The girl was indeed a loner, and hadn't been a member of any social networks. Robyn was now driven to uncover further information on Elliot, yet torn between wanting the man to be guilty and hoping he wasn't.

There was nothing to indicate he was anything other than a young teacher who lived alone. He had no past convictions and had never been in trouble with the police. She set out her Post-it notes on a spare desk. She put Carrie, Amber and Siobhan's names in a line, and under them the note bearing the name Stardust Nightclub, another with Facebook and a third with Uttoxeter railway station. Only Carrie and Siobhan had been to the nightclub, so that couldn't be the link. She moved it to one side, leaving Uttoxeter railway station and Facebook.

Her thoughts were interrupted by a phone call from Amélie.

'Hey. You okay?'

'I'm fine but I'm worried about Florence.'

Robyn resisted the urge to sigh. 'I'm sure she'll come around in time. She's struggling with coming to terms with growing up. Give her the space she thinks she needs.'

'No, it's not that. She didn't catch the school bus home as usual and she left the art lesson early. I tried calling her to see if she was okay, but she didn't pick up. I figured she had a dentist appointment or something but I was chatting to Grace online and she said she spotted Florence walking down the road and dressed up like she was going to a rave. Grace almost didn't recognise her. She must have sneaked out of art to get ready. What do you think?'

Robyn sighed. 'Which road?'

'The main street.'

Florence could have been headed to any of the coffee houses along that road, or any of the shops. Robyn had picked her up from that same road only a few days earlier. She shook her head. It didn't sound ominous. 'She's possibly gone shopping or she's meeting a lad and she wants to keep it under wraps. It's Wednesday afternoon. Highly unlikely she's going to a rave.'

'I wondered if someone should tell Mrs Hallows. What if Florence is running away?'

'I shouldn't think Florence is running away. She'd have taken a bag with her if that were the case. If Florence is meeting a boy and her mum finds out thanks to you, she's definitely not going to want to be friends with you. Friends keep secrets, don't they?'

There was silence as Amélie digested this information.

'Her mum might even know Florence is in town.'

'I suppose so. Thanks. I'll let it drop. I don't want to make things worse between us.'

She hung up. Robyn wrestled with her conscience. Florence was beginning to behave in an increasingly concerning manner.

Christine Hallows had always let her daughter have a freedom that many would disapprove of, and to date, Florence had exhibited nothing to worry about. What if Amélie's suspicions were well-founded and Florence had started hanging about with older kids, a bad crowd into drugs? They came across many instances of drug taking among the young in their line of work. She ought to speak to Christine. The world was a dangerous place, and there were so many challenges for teenagers.

She thought about ringing the woman, then reasoned Florence wouldn't be too pleased to find out somebody had snitched on her and she might behave more secretively in the future. It was so tricky knowing how to handle teenagers. She was at risk of becoming frustrated by them, wishing they'd just sort it out. But Amélie had been through so much, and it was no surprise she was scared at the thought of losing her best friend.

Her shoulders rose and dropped. She would keep out of this. She had more pressing matters to attend to. She stared again at the report on Charlotte's death. She couldn't deal with teenage angst, but she could help Siobhan Connors.

Discovering the footage of Carrie at Derby Station had been useful. At least they could now establish she had been heading towards Crewe on the twenty-eighth of July. But had she returned to Derby soon afterwards, then been abducted? The messages she supposedly sent Jade had been sent from the Derby area. No, the messages had been sent by the perp. He or she had sent them from Derby. Could Elliot Chambers have sent messages from Derby when he lived and worked in Uttoxeter, some twenty miles away? Might he have sent them on his days off? There had to be an explanation. She'd ask Anna if it was possible to change the location on Facebook so it appeared as if messages were coming from the Derby area.

Robyn put her head in her hands. She was going around and around in circles. She had to break free from this. Her gut was telling her to pursue the station angle. It was possible all three girls had been to Uttoxeter railway station and it was, for the moment, all she had to go on. She'd return to Uttoxeter and see if she could get any further inklings or leads.

CHAPTER FIFTY-ONE

Florence felt horribly sick and dizzy. She could make no sense of what had happened. She curled into a tight ball on the mattress, willing the feeling to stop. She didn't want to throw up. She wanted to go home.

The room was pitch black and smelt so strongly of bleach it caught in the back of her throat and made her want to gag. She felt dreadful. Her head was too fuzzy to reason what was going on.

She waited for the waves of nausea to wane. Beside her was a wall. Her fingers flicked across the wallpaper. The contact helped her overcome the panic in her chest. She was in a room. At least it wasn't a coffin. She'd seen a horror film where a girl got buried alive in a coffin. The thought made her shiver. She pushed into a seated position, her bare feet dangling over the bed. Cool air brushed against the soles of her feet. Where were her shoes? She dropped an arm to the floor. Felt for them. They weren't by the bed.

She shut her eyes tightly to better fight another wave of nausea, and when she felt it recede she wriggled forward, feet touching wooden floorboards. Breathe. There would be a simple explanation. She wanted her bag and phone. She'd call her mum. Mum would know what to do. With a hand outstretched she felt for a bedside table. There was a lamp on her bedside table at home. She only had to touch the base and it would automatically light up. There was no such table here. Where was the light switch?

She had no option other than to feel her way along the wall in the hope she'd find the door and a switch or, better still, a way of getting out of the room. Her feet padded silently as she felt up and down, frightened of coming into contact with something sharp or harmful.

As her fingers found a doorframe, she heard a soft wheeze, as if someone was letting out a breath they'd held in for a long time. There it was again. Somebody was behind her. Rooted to the spot, she could no longer think. Her worst fears were about to play out. She was going to be murdered.

A ghostly orange light bounced off the wall in front of her.

'I hope you weren't thinking of leaving just yet. Turn around. Let's get a proper look at you.'

She turned slowly to face it, trying desperately to control the fear that was mounting. A figure wearing a cycling helmet topped with a bright light stood in front of her.

'What do you look like? Oh dear, oh dear, Florence. You and I need to have a serious conversation.'

CHAPTER FIFTY-TWO

Mitz and Robyn headed back to Uttoxeter and the station. The rain had stopped but now a chilly wind blew. Robyn's heart was heavy. The visit that morning to Mrs Chambers had not given her much to go on. She had so little to pin on Elliot Chambers, and no other suspects.

Mitz checked the arrival board and glanced about the station. 'Train due in two minutes.'

'Okay. Let's wait.'

Robyn wrapped her coat tightly around her and waited as the train hissed into the station. A door opened and a guard in a blue uniform dismounted, allowing the passengers off. Mitz waited until they'd disembarked then spoke to the man. 'Couldn't help but notice there are only two carriages.'

'That's normal,' replied the guard. 'Not usually very busy, although it gets busier when it's race day at Uttoxeter.'

'You do this route frequently?'

'Fairly frequently, why?'

Robyn pulled out photographs of Amber and Carrie. 'I don't suppose you've seen either of these girls on this train?'

'I don't recognise them,' he said.

Robyn held up the photograph of Amber. 'Would it help if I said this girl might have boarded the train at Tutbury and Hatton, sometime around the second of January?'

He studied the photograph again. 'No. I'd have remembered her face. She's a pretty girl, isn't she? Sorry. I can't help. We have to leave. Timetable and all that.' He climbed back into the train. The doors swished shut and the train eased away.

Robyn felt defeated. Here she was on a miserable Wednesday evening, clutching at straws. Mitz surveyed the empty car park. 'I'm not sure about this, boss.'

'Me neither. I thought we were getting close, and now…' She marched back to the squad car and threw herself into the passenger seat. She took one more look at the station as they pulled away. She couldn't shake the feeling that the station held significance. She had to trust her hunch. It was all she had.

'Am I looking at this all wrong, Mitz?'

'No, guv. We just don't know what we're supposed to be looking at.'

She stared into space as Mitz drove back towards the police station. Flint would not give her long. She had to figure out Chambers's part in this. She shut her eyes. What did they have to go on? Three girls linked by a station and a cryptic message on Facebook. Her eyes flew open. That was it. Mitz was right. She didn't know what she was looking for. She'd been focusing on Uttoxeter station. There were other avenues still to check. She thought about her bright-green Post-it note bearing the word Facebook. Amber and Carrie had both liked the Fox or Dog Facebook page. It had been a dead end, or so they had believed. She dialled the office. Anna answered.

'Anna, did you go onto the Fox or Dog website at all? No. Okay, take a look for me now.'

Mitz raised an eyebrow. 'Fox or Dog?'

'It's a sort of dating app.'

'I know it is.'

Robyn raised a hand to silence him and spoke again. 'Forget that, Anna. I'll sort it when I return.'

Mitz continued. 'I've used it. Don't tell any of the team. I only went on it a couple of times before I realised it's mostly for youngsters in their late teens or early twenties. It matches you up with people in your area. You create a profile, a little like for Tinder – a photograph and a line or two about yourself and what you're looking for in a match. The site throws up a list of the girls in your area. It's not sophisticated. It's merely a list of names and pictures and it's up to you to scroll through. If you fancy the look of them you leave them a sign – it's a fox emoji. If the feeling's mutual, you can chat through private messages.'

Robyn nodded furiously. 'What happens next?'

'I don't know. I ditched it after a week. It was too juvenile, too cruel. It invited you to insult people just based on their looks. I should have guessed from its name – Fox or Dog. If a person doesn't like the look of somebody, they leave a dog emoji. I wasn't too keen on that. I don't use anything like that now. I listened to my mum, who told me to let nature run its course.'

She glanced across. A smile played on his lips.

'Your latest date is working out, then?'

He grinned at her. 'It is. How did you guess? You should be a detective.'

The corners of her lips rose. 'Glad it's going well.'

'It's going better than well.' Mitz waggled his eyebrows.

'About time too. You've had too many disasters. Aren't you going to tell us about her?'

'Not until I know it's going to work out.'

'Fair enough. If I keep quiet about our conversation can you get me onto it?'

'Are you blackmailing me?'

She laughed. 'No. But I could do with you helping me navigate it. I want to see if either of our victims or Siobhan Connors were members.'

CHAPTER FIFTY-THREE

Nobody was in the office when they returned. 'You can use it on your phone or on your computer,' said Mitz. He scooted over to the computer and fired it up, typed in the website address and waited for his superior to join him. Robyn pulled a chair over to his. 'How do we discover profiles?'

'As I said, it works off your location.'

'Both Amber and Carrie lived in or near Derby.'

'I'll create a new profile and set it for Derby. It should throw up girls who live in that area.' The keys clattered as he typed in the necessary information. Robyn was amazed that he could set it up in a matter of minutes, and there were no security checks or ID confirmation of any kind. It returned over two hundred results. 'Ouch! That'll take a while. I'll get onto it.'

'No, it's okay. I'll take over. Can I assume from what you've told me that should our perp be meeting the girls using this app, he lives in the same area as them?'

'Within a radius of twenty miles. The app accesses your location via Google.'

'Can you work out the distance between Uttoxeter and Derby, then do the same for Sandwell?'

Mitz slid over to another desk and tapped at another terminal. 'Uttoxeter to Derby is almost twenty miles. Uttoxeter to Sandwell is sixteen miles.'

'Uttoxeter to Tutbury?'

'Ten, almost eleven miles.'

'If our suspect lived in Uttoxeter, and was using this website, he'd be able to connect with Carrie, Amber or Siobhan?'

Mitz nodded. 'Or if he lives in Derby.'

Robyn heaved a sigh. Mitz was right. Then she remembered that Dev Khan's leaflets advertising his self-storage warehouse had gone out to homes in Staffordshire, which suggested the perp had to come from that area. She hoped she wasn't wasting more time. The official search for Siobhan had been scaled down. There wasn't enough information to prove she had gone missing, and work colleagues and friends had suggested she was volatile and an attention-seeker. It was viable that Siobhan had taken herself off for a break, but Robyn couldn't let go of the message sent to Lauren. Carrie had also run off with a new man, and there were the two messages to Siobhan and Amber that read the same. Robyn trusted her instincts on this. Locating Siobhan was going to be up to Robyn, who was sure the girl was being held captive.

She scrolled through all the faces of the young women. Everyone on the website used phoney names, which meant she had to spend time clicking onto each profile, enlarging the photo and seeing if it bore any resemblance to any of the girls. Robyn was beginning to lose heart. She'd stared at sixty different faces without success. 'This would be a lot easier if we'd been able to locate their mobile phones or computers and check them for apps and login details.'

'We had Amber's laptop but there was nothing on it.'

'Oh hi, Anna. I didn't hear you come in.'

Anna waved a hand. 'You looked too busy. I sidled in. I've been going back through the girl's Facebook page and can't find anything.'

Robyn tilted back dangerously on her chair. 'Does it not strike you as strange that a sixteen-year-old would only have schoolwork items on a laptop? Surely she'd have visited websites unconnected with research. I can't believe she was so studious.'

'I gathered her parents had only recently bought the laptop. They might have been very strict about its use.'

Robyn tapped a pencil against her teeth and pondered the situation. She thought about Amélie in her bedroom, chatting on Skype even though her mother would disapprove of her being online at such a late hour. It was natural for youngsters to be rebellious or push the boundaries. She certainly had been when she was in her teens. And Florence. Florence who'd broken away from the quiet, shy, easy-going Florence and was now behaving like a fully grown teenager, engaged in regular online activity. Christine Hallows would probably have no idea that her daughter was online so often. She would talk to Christine about the episode at the cinema and voice her concerns over the fallout with Amélie. Florence could be chatting to anyone online – and it was only right to be concerned about her welfare. She made a mental note to speak to Christine.

Amber was a teenager. She must have been accessing social websites. Would she only have accessed them from her mobile phone? The fact remained there was nothing on the girl's laptop. She turned her attention back to the dating app.

Anna walked across to her desk. 'Is it okay if I clock off, guv?'

Robyn looked up. It was almost eight o'clock. 'Sure. I hadn't realised it was so late. Thanks for staying on. Mitz, you'd better go too. I don't want your mum telling me off for keeping you late.'

He laughed. 'She's used to it.'

Robyn gave a tired smile. 'Yeah. Well, I appreciate it. Thanks, guys.'

She hunched over her desk.

'Night, boss.'

'Night, both.' Robyn wandered over to the window. She ought to go home. She needed fresh perspective on this case, and sitting in the office wasn't helping. Maybe she'd go for a run. She was about to turn away when she caught a glimpse of Mitz putting an arm across Anna's shoulders as they walked away from the station. She drew back from the window and smiled.

CHAPTER FIFTY-FOUR

DAY ELEVEN – THURSDAY 26 JANUARY

Robyn walked into the office in a determined mood. She hadn't been able shake off the idea that Amber was accessing Fox or Dog from a computer. The fact the girl only used her laptop for schoolwork projects had elicited these suspicions. It didn't sit right with Robyn. Teenagers loved being connected, and although Amber could have used her mobile for that purpose, she would have used her laptop too.

The flashback had come in the early hours of the morning. Robyn remembered there had been a computer in Chapel's common room. Deborah Hampton, the houseparent, had commented on the seniors using it while keeping an eye on the junior girls doing their prep. She had also said Amber had been working on the computer when on prep duty, and had got snappy with the girls for talking.

She rummaged through papers and pulled out the note she'd found in Amber's room. The three names of gods associated with hunting – Orion, Horus, and Wōden – encircled with hearts, each with curling tails. Anna had pointed out that these were like the doodles she made when talking to somebody on the telephone. Could Amber have been chatting to her killer online during prep time? It made sense. As soon as her officers arrived she would act on this hunch.

She opened Fox or Dog and began studying each young woman's face in the hope she'd find one of the three girls there. Mitz and Anna arrived a few minutes later, Mitz throwing himself immediately behind his desk.

'Anna, can you collect a computer from Sandwell School? It's at Chapel House. I'll phone Deborah Hampton and tell her you're coming. Once you bring it back, go through the history on it. I'll give you specific dates to check, once I've spoken to Mrs Hampton. You'll be searching for the Fox or Dog website.'

'On it.' Anna picked up her hat from where she'd just placed it, and left.

Robyn continued scouring the pages. David had had no success in Uttoxeter. He'd shown the photographs of Amber, Carrie and Siobhan at every store, restaurant and pub on Dovefields Retail Park. Elliot Chambers hadn't rented a van in his own name either, so once again they were left with little to go on. David had gone to Uttoxeter again to try his luck, while Matt was currently dealing with a break-in at a scrapyard and not available to assist her. Not that there was much more they could do at the moment.

'Boss.' Mitz's voice was a mixture of anxiety and excitement. 'I think I've found Carrie Miller.'

The picture of Miss Mischief was a young woman sticking her tongue out, and the description read: *I'm up for a laugh. I don't take life seriously and love a challenge. I'm wild and know my own mind. Think you can handle me?*

There was no doubt it was Carrie Miller. Robyn's heart began to hammer. 'Good. Good. We're getting there. Can you check the profiles of all the guys who liked Carrie's profile and gave it a fox emoji? Maybe one of them is our killer.'

She dialled Deborah Hampton's number and told her to expect Anna. Deborah sounded tired and low.

'The Apple Mac? Of course. I'll unplug it now and have it ready for your officer. The girls are planting a cherry tree in the garden for Amber tomorrow after a church service. Her closest friend, Samantha Dancer, is going to say a few words and we'll say goodbye to her properly. I spoke to the Daltons. They're coming to our little service. I hope it'll help give them some closure.'

Robyn doubted they'd ever get closure. She feared they would always blame themselves for going abroad and leaving their daughter behind. She ended the call and reflected that life was unfair. She couldn't change what had happened but she could try and apprehend the person responsible.

Time raced by as Robyn and Mitz clicked through web pages. Robyn was so engrossed she didn't register the phone at first. Amy sounded petulant. 'You haven't kept me up to speed at all. I've learnt another young woman has gone missing. Is this related to your case?'

'Amy, pack it in. No comment. I'm up to my eyeballs here. Leave me to do my work. Talk to the media department. I haven't any time for this.'

'I have my work to do too.'

Robyn slammed the phone down. How did that woman know what was going on? 'Mitz, is there anything in the newspapers about Siobhan Connors?'

She continued searching the faces that had all swum into one. 'A paragraph in the *Uttoxeter Daily* that reads:

The hunt continues for Siobhan Connors (18) last seen in Uttoxeter on Friday 13th. Police are appealing for any witnesses who may have seen Miss Connors at or around 7 p.m. that evening. Miss Connors, believed to be wearing jeans and a black coat, was headed to Uttoxeter railway station when she disappeared.

'The missing persons department must have made the appeal. I expect that's where Amy read about it.'

'She on the phone?'

'She never gives up, does she?'

'Sounds like you, boss.' Mitz gave her a grin. 'I've got the list of all the men who gave Carrie's profile a foxy sign. There are loads of them. This one might interest you though. He's calling himself Hunter.'

Robyn stopped typing. Was this Chambers? Had she finally found the lead she needed? Mitz swivelled the screen around. The young man in the photograph was in his late teens or early twenties, dark-haired with a quiff and very handsome.

'Let's think this through. The killer would use a fake picture, so that photograph tells us nothing. We need to talk to the people who run Fox or Dog and find out who set up this account. They ought to be able to pinpoint their location or their IP address. Anna will know what to do.' Robyn suddenly felt drained. All this energy wasted. She needed to get out of the office and clear her head.

She strode down the corridor and outside into the cold air. She stamped her feet and marched about the car park. Anna pulled the squad car into a space near her. She dragged out the computer and tucked it under her arm.

'Got it, boss. I'll get onto this immediately.'

The young woman looked pink-cheeked, flushed with optimism. Robyn's heart sank. What if she'd got this wrong? She couldn't allow her team to become deflated. She valued them, their loyalty and trust in her. She hadn't got anywhere with the railway station theory, and what if this website theory didn't pan out? It might not unless they could get an exact location for the person calling himself Hunter. Where would she turn next after that? She looked at her watch. It was early afternoon. She hadn't got long before DCI Flint took her to task and demanded she pulled in Chambers. She ignored the growls coming from her stomach.

She had to believe her team could pull this together. In the meantime, try as she might, she couldn't think of any reason

Chambers would have had a specially made trunk delivered. Surely it was the trunk containing Carrie Miller's body. She could ask Mrs Chambers about it. Her son might have brought it back to the family home when he returned from university. The only problem was that if he found out she'd been asking about him, he might flee. What should she do? She had to close the net on Chambers. It had to be him. She slowed her beating heart. She had to ask Mrs Chambers the question. It would be a gamble if she then spoke to her son, but Robyn had no other option. She found Mrs Chamber's number and dialled. It was a while before the woman answered.

'It's DI Carter. We spoke yesterday morning. You told me Elliot came home from university and stayed with you for a while?'

'Yes. What's this about?'

'I'm not at liberty to tell you, Mrs Chambers, but we'd very much appreciate your help.'

There was a silence at the end of the phone. 'I don't understand why you're suddenly asking about Elliot. It was Charlotte who died.'

Robyn spoke smoothly, her voice friendly and calm. 'It seems an odd request, I grant you, but we're investigating another case and your help would be hugely appreciated.'

The voice at the other end of the line became colder. 'I don't see how asking about Elliot has any bearing on any case.'

'It's only a simple question, Mrs Chambers, and then I shan't pester you any more.'

Robyn waited. She hoped Cheryl Chambers wouldn't put down the phone on her. Eventually, the woman spoke. 'Okay. One question.'

'Thank you, Mrs Chambers. When Elliot returned from university, he'd have brought home all his possessions. Did he transport them in suitcases and boxes or in a trunk?'

There followed yet another silence before the slightly confused reply, 'Boxes. He had lots and lots of boxes.'

'No trunk?'

'No, I told you. He had boxes of books and kitchen equipment, all labelled. He's a very tidy person. There wasn't enough room in his old bedroom for everything so he kept them in one of the old outbuildings until he moved, then he took them with him to his new flat.'

'And how did he fetch all the boxes home, Mrs Chambers?'

'That's another question, and I don't understand why you're asking them.'

'Please bear with me. It's important.'

'He borrowed the old car. I hardly drive it these days. He couldn't travel down on a train with it all, could he? I lent him the car. It was large enough to fit everything in. It's an old Vauxhall Zafira. Used to belong to my husband.'

'Thank you very much, Mrs Chambers.'

'Elliot's not in any trouble for borrowing it, is he?'

'No, not at all. Thank you again.'

What had happened to the trunk? Had Elliot not brought it back with him or had he hidden it from his mother's sight? There simply wasn't enough to go on, yet it was all she had. For the umpteenth time that day she wondered where Siobhan Connors was being held and if she was still alive. 'Hang on,' she whispered. 'We'll find you.'

CHAPTER FIFTY-FIVE

Anna's eyes never left the screen of the Apple Mac as she spoke. 'There's oodles of history. Do we know which dates I should be searching for?'

Robyn checked her notes. 'Amber was on duty every evening in November.'

'I'll go through all the sites during prep time, shall I?' Anna manoeuvred her mouse deftly across the screen.

Robyn watched her young colleague. 'Yes, and if that doesn't yield results, search for Fox or Dog and note when it was accessed.' She wandered over to the whiteboard and added the words 'trunk' and 'Zafira', then began searching websites.

'Anyone know anything about cars?'

Mitz shrugged. 'Not really. What do you need to know?'

Robyn looked across. 'The boot capacity of a Vauxhall Zafira.'

'It'll be big, because you can fold the seats down.'

'Think it would be big enough to fit that trunk you found in?'

He nodded. 'Don't see why not. Why not google it?'

'Good idea, Mitz.' After several attempts and calculations, she had the information she needed. The trunk would be able to fit into a Vauxhall Zafira. Elliot could have transported it to The Oaks when he returned from university and hidden it. But where had he kept Carrie Miller for so long? There were too many questions still to be answered. She rubbed at her forehead and stood. 'Coffee anyone?'

Mitz gave a lengthy yawn that was cut off, leaving his mouth wide open. 'Siobhan. Siobhan Connors.'

Robyn stopped in mid stride. 'You've found her.'

Mitz pointed at the screen. 'Sexy S.'

'She's called herself Sexy S?' Robyn crossed the room to join him.

'Yes, it's her.' Mitz tilted the screen so Robyn could see more clearly.

She nodded, re-energised by this news, and her words burst out. 'Cross-check all the men who liked her profile picture with those that liked Carrie's, and start with Hunter.' She strode back to her desk, coffee forgotten.

'It's not a very friendly site,' Robyn said, scrolling down the list on her own computer. 'Some people leave snide remarks about each other. I thought it was for finding dates. I didn't register the comments at first, they're hidden below the profiles and you have to click on the comment box there to see them. One or two caught my eye. Someone called Twiglet called Angel19 "a mega dick-licking mongrel".' Whatever possessed people to behave in such a way?

'Some are followed up by "LOL". I think they're joshing each other,' said Mitz.

'I have no idea what makes youngsters tick these days,' Robyn replied with a sad shrug.

'Me neither, and I'm only just out of nappies myself,' said Mitz, earning a smile.

'How are you getting on, Anna?'

Anna's face told Robyn what she needed to hear. 'You were right. One of the girls accessed Fox or Dog every evening between seven and eight for the last week in November.'

'Was it Amber?' Robyn asked.

'I'm just checking that. Yes. It was Amber. This is her profile page.'

Amber Dalton, wide-eyed and beautiful, stared out from the screen. Robyn's breath caught in her throat. The girl was stunning.

'All these girls used this website. I have a strong feeling about this. Mitz, how're you getting on?'

'Slowly. Both Carrie and Siobhan attracted many of the same men. There are so many fox emojis under their profiles it's difficult to work out who they might have chatted to.'

'I'll help,' said Anna. 'It'll be quicker with us all on it.'

Mitz threw her a wink. She returned it along with a warm smile.

Robyn stared at her own screen with unfocused eyes. Then she stood and wrote 'dating app' on the whiteboard. A thought flittered through her mind before evaporating. She couldn't hang onto it long enough to register its significance.

CHAPTER FIFTY-SIX

PC David Marker came into the office, his hair flattened by the wind. 'It's lousy out there.'

'What do you expect? It's January,' said Anna.

'I've spent all morning freezing my nuts off at Dovefields Retail Park while you've been sitting snugly in the office.'

'We've been out too,' Mitz said.

David made a harrumphing noise and shuffled over to the coffee machine. 'I found someone who might have spotted Amber Dalton.'

'Might?' Robyn asked.

'It's a waitress. She was on duty at the Frankie & Benny's restaurant and nipped outside for a quick fag break. She thinks she saw Amber walking across the car park, looking at her mobile phone.'

Robyn leapt to her feet and picked up the black marker pen. 'Day?'

'Tuesday the third of January. She wasn't too sure about the time. Put it between seven fifteen and seven thirty.'

'What time does the train from Tutbury and Hatton get into Uttoxeter?'

'Five past seven.' David took his cup and wrapped his hands around it. 'I timed it, and it only takes ten minutes to walk up to Dovefields. I'll go back later and see if any other staff on duty that night noticed her. There's a pub, a cinema, a bowling alley and an ice-skating rink. Somebody else who works there must have seen her too.'

'Well done, David.' Robyn added this new information to a Post-it note.

David sipped his coffee. 'What's happening here?'

Robyn folded her arms. 'We've got three young women who signed up to the same dating app and who are dead or, in the case of Siobhan Connors, still missing. We think they were all involved with the same man online. Mitz found a guy using the name Hunter, and we've contacted the website owners to try and find out his real identity.'

A small squeak escaped Anna. 'I've cross-checked every person who left emojis under the girls' profiles. Hunter is the only one who left fox emojis under the profiles of all three girls, and all three of them left fox emojis under his profile. They could all have chatted with him.'

Robyn waved her black pen. 'Good. It's coming together. We have a possible suspect if only we can uncover his identity. Anna, contact the website administrators again. We must find out the real name of this man calling himself Hunter.' She looked at her watch. It was coming up to five o'clock. How much longer would she have before DCI Flint insisted she dragged in Chambers for questioning?

'Boss?' Mitz had turned around to face her. 'Who do you think this looks like?'

Robyn peered at the picture. The young girl looked frail. She looked up at the camera with a half-smile. *I'm not perfect but I've got a lot to offer. I'm looking for someone to love me simply for being me. I like nature, animals and art. I'm looking for a quiet, gentle person to be my friend.*

The words stuck in her throat. Her head swam with possibilities. 'It looks like Charlotte Chambers.'

'I thought so too. She even calls herself Likeable Lotty.'

'Has she been left a fox emoji from Hunter?'

Mitz scrolled down the page and shook his head. 'No. She's got no fox emojis. There are quite a few dog emojis. There are comments too.' He read through them, his nose wrinkling in disgust. 'This is awful. There's comment after comment about her weight, her face and even her sexuality.'

'Was she being bullied online?' Robyn leant across to read out the vile statements: '"No point you even looking for a fella. You're an ugly cow." That's really harsh. She's only a kid.' Robyn said indignantly.

Anna voiced her opinion. 'People can be cruel at times, but when they hide behind the barrier of the Internet, they're completely callous.'

Robyn read out another comment, 'This person isn't joshing: "No one cud ever fancy you. You're an absolute dog. Woof woof!" That's unnecessary.' She shook her head. 'I see Charlotte replied. She got involved in verbal fisticuffs with them. It seems to have escalated into an online fight.'

Mitz was reading through the comments too. He drew in a breath. 'Have you seen who wrote this? "Don't diss me, you silly little slag. Take a look in the mirror."'

'Sexy S. That's the name Siobhan Connors uses.'

A flash of comprehension made Robyn gasp. 'What's Amber's nickname on this site?'

Anna called out, 'Enchantress.'

'She's involved too. She called Charlotte a freak,' Mitz said.

'Okay, what's going on? How come these girls have decided to pick on Charlotte?'

'Carrie commented too. They've all criticised Charlotte.' Anna read through them all. 'They're the ones involved in the abuse. Looks like they sided with each other to call her names. These are the most recent comments. There's quite a history. I'll print it out so you can all look at it without scrolling up and down.'

The mood had changed in the office. Robyn gave a satisfied grunt. 'I think we might have found a motive. Anna, find out if anyone else other than these three made comments on her profile and track them down. They might be in danger. Mitz, make a list of everyone who left a dog emoji on Charlotte's profile.' It was looking increasingly likely that Elliot Chambers was involved in avenging his dead sister. The net was closing in on him. The printer whirred, then spat out printouts of the communications among the girls.

Robyn picked up several sheets and sat down at her desk with them, a different coloured highlighter pen for each of the girls. She selected a blue one and struck it through the first comment made by Siobhan. These girls had formed an online alliance and together they had systematically cyberbullied Charlotte Chambers. If Elliot had also uncovered this, it would give him cause to retaliate. But what had made them create an alliance? They didn't know each other.

She set up her computer so she could see all of the girls' profile pictures at the same time. It helped to see their faces as she read through their conversations. As she glanced at Siobhan's profile, she noticed for the first time that she had a star against her name. Amber's and Carrie's also had stars, whereas Charlotte's did not. It took a moment to uncover their significance. Robyn clicked on Carrie's star, which opened a new window, and a page she hadn't uncovered before. The page revealed the 'Top Ten Foxiest'. All three girls had been on what was referred to as the foxy leader board. *They were all the foxiest girls.*

Charlotte's name had no star. Beside it was a cartoon image of a dog's bone. Robyn clicked onto it. At last, it all made sense. She speed-read the conversation among the girls, highlighting passages and creating the full picture of what had happened. She spun around to face her team.

'I think I know what occurred here. There's a leader board of the most popular girls and boys on the site.'

'Is there?' said Mitz. 'How did I miss that?'

'We weren't searching for it. We were concentrating on finding out if these three girls were using the website, and if they knew Hunter. Siobhan, Amber and Carrie were all on what they call the Top Ten Foxiest. It's a chart of those members with the highest number of fox emojis each month. If they're on the leader board, they automatically get preferential positioning on the website, which in turn means new members will automatically be shown the hottest or foxiest top ten before they look for others.'

'Oh, yes. I remember being offered the chance to meet some foxy girls when I joined up,' said Mitz.

'You joined the site?' Anna gave him a quizzical look.

He blushed. 'It was a while ago. I only went on a couple of times before I decided it wasn't for me,' he said, seeing her expression. She rewarded him with a grin.

Mitz continued. 'So all this top ten stuff, it's almost like an online popularity contest? You collect fox emojis, and the more you get, the higher up the chart you go?'

Robyn nodded. 'Yes, it's like that. The site is primarily for meeting and chatting to people, but there's this additional part to it. It's a little confusing, but it seems not only must you get fox emojis to stay in the chart, but if you receive a dog emoji you are pulled down the chart or leader board, as they call it. Worse still, there's a Top Ten Doggiest. The communications between Charlotte and these three girls start in January 2015, just after Charlotte joins the site. Charlotte must have left a dog emoji under Siobhan's profile because Siobhan makes the comment, "Oi bitch. Why the dog emoji? You must be fucking blind or stupid. I didn't deserve it." Charlotte answers, "I didn't think you were attractive. That's all." Anna, can you print off copies for you and Mitz, and read through it?'

'Sure.' She beetled across to the printer, snatched the printouts as soon as they fell, and handed Mitz a copy. In unison, they hunched over the sheets and read the script. Robyn waited for them to come to the same conclusions as her, and looked back through at what she'd already seen on the screen:

Siobhan/Sexy S: Fuck you. At least you deserve the dog emoji I've given you.

Charlotte/ Likeable Lotty: I don't deserve it. You're just annoyed with me because I gave you one.

Amber/Enchantress: She gave me a dog emoji too and now I'm no longer number one on the board.

Siobhan/Sexy S: It's deliberate, Enchantress. She's well-jel of us. Not surprising. She's a skank.

Amber/Enchantress: Christ! Look at those glasses. She must be blind.

Charlotte/Likeable Lotty: I can see well enough to know that you're not attractive.

Siobhan/Sexy S: Get a life, loser. Thanks to you, I've just dropped off the leader board. Don't even know why you're here. You'll never get anyone to chat with you – you speccy cow.

Charlotte/Likeable Lotty: Leave me alone. I only did what the site said. I gave out fox and dogs emojis to people. I was being honest. It was my opinion. No one else has complained.

Carrie/Miss Mischief: You turd sandwich. I see you gave me one too. You're the only person ever to give me a dog emoji. Is it cos you resent me and the others on the top ten list? You'll never get on it, Likeable Lotty – a better name for you is Unlikeable Loser.

Amber/Enchantress: Nice one Miss Mischief. Tell the slut to get a life.

Charlotte/Likeable Lotty: I did what the site said. I gave out foxes and dogs, that's all. Why're you picking on me?

Carrie/Miss Mischief: Why're you so obsessed with us? You do know you're supposed to look at boys, you freak, not girls. You're supposed to leave emojis for boys.

Siobhan/Miss Mischief: She must love girls more than boys. Do you love girls?

Amber/Enchantress: Yeah, right. She's a pussy-lover, everyone.

Charlotte/Likeable Lotty: I'm not. I like boys. You're being a bitch. I think some girls can look nice but I don't fancy them.

Amber/Enchantress: I'm a bitch? Your mum's a bitch for having a bitch like you. Face it, you're not likeable and I bet you know deep down that everybody hates you. That's why you're here, trying to put us down.

Carrie/Miss Mischief: I bet everyone you know thinks you're a freak and talks about you behind your back.

Charlotte/Likeable Lotty: Fuck off!

Carrie/Miss Mischief: Ooh, so you know a grown-up swear word. I'm so impressed – not! You're a stupid kid with an attitude. You're playing with proper grown-ups here so be careful, you skanky, twat-loving freakball.

Amber/Enchantress: Are you having a little girlie cry now, loser?

Charlotte/Likeable Lotty: No.

Amber/Enchantress: You should be crying. If I had a face like yours, I'd cry every day.

Siobhan/Sexy S: I'm going to tell all my mates about you and soon you'll have so many dog emojis you'll be on the top ten dogs leader board.

Charlotte/Likeable Lotty: I didn't know about the boards. Don't, please. I'm sorry, okay?

Amber/Enchantress: Good idea. We'll get you top of that board.

Mitz sat back in his seat. 'Terrible,' he said.

Anna spoke up. 'It appears these girls were all keen to be in the top ten foxiest chart each week, but when Charlotte gave them dog emojis, it affected their rankings and they lost their position. They began by criticising her for her actions, and resorted to insulting her.' She flicked through the sheets. 'Then the situation becomes more charged and they encourage others on the website to give Charlotte dog emojis, until finally she is placed in the top ten dog chart.'

Robyn nodded gravely. 'It was punishment for her actions, but she saw it as an attack on her personality. As far as I can see, the later comments are more vindictive. The girls took pleasure in her dismay and, using their own popularity, attempted to keep her in that dog chart for as long as possible.'

Anna grimaced. 'This sucks. It's a place where anyone can be victimised or ridiculed.'

'Looks like our victims took the leader board and the emojis seriously.'

'But it's so petty,' said Anna. 'It's only a stupid, made-up board. It isn't important.'

'It was important to these girls. Imagine what this did to Charlotte's morale? It must have crushed her spirit. Having struggled through her ill health to be accepted at school, here she was being laughed at by three young women who didn't even know her. Teenage girls struggle with self-image, and this situation would have been enough to destroy Charlotte's, which I imagine was more fragile than most. We'll only find out the truth if we can find Siobhan Connors. She might be able to enlighten us. It's probable Charlotte took her life thanks to the events and exchanges on Fox or Dog. I think this points again to Elliot Chambers. It is looking increasingly likely he set out to avenge his sister's suicide.'

'What shall we do, guv? Bring him in?'

Robyn folded her arms and rested her chin on an open palm. 'I'm not sure. I'm very concerned about Siobhan's welfare. I don't want to spook him into harming her. Let me think about it for a moment.'

Her computer screen had timed out. She moved the mouse to bring it back to life and double clicked by accident. Instead of bringing Amber's profile back up it brought up the profile of a girl calling herself Kitten. Robyn's eyes opened wide. Wearing provocative underwear and staring innocently at the camera was Florence Hallows.

As she sat back in surprise, her phone rang. It was Christine Hallows. 'Robyn. I don't know what to do. Florence has disappeared.'

CHAPTER FIFTY-SEVEN

Christine Hallows wrung a patterned woollen hat around in her hands. 'I didn't give it a second thought. She phoned me yesterday after school and asked if it was okay if she stayed at Amélie's house for tea because they were working on a project together. I said it was fine. At about six, she sent a text message saying Brigitte had suggested she stay over rather than go home as they hadn't finished the project, and they had to hand it in this morning. I wasn't keen, but I didn't want to be the nagging mother. I'd already had a go at her about wearing make-up this week.' Her shoulders sagged at the thought.

'When did you realise she had gone missing?' Robyn wanted to spend time with Christine, coax the information out of her gently and then reassure her it would be fine, but she couldn't. If the same person who'd abducted the other girls had seized Florence, they had to act immediately. Florence had used Fox or Dog, and although she hadn't ridiculed Charlotte Chambers, it was a connection they couldn't ignore. It appeared they had greater reason to suspect Elliot; he knew and taught Florence. Christine was now at the station, facing Robyn, a cup of untouched tea in front of her on the desk.

Robyn had already spoken to Flint, his words still smarting. 'I asked you to bring in Chambers and now another girl has gone missing – one he teaches. This could have been avoided.'

'I can only apologise, sir. You trusted me to find the perp and I've been concentrating on getting sufficient evidence to convict our killer.'

His voice dropped to an icy hiss. 'This is too great a coincidence to ignore. Haul him in now and pray he hasn't hurt her.'

She should have acted on Flint's instructions. If she'd brought Chambers in, he wouldn't have been able to snatch Florence. Robyn felt awful for not getting to the bottom of things sooner, but she knew that if she'd brought him in without evidence there'd have been no hope of a conviction. She'd have had to release him and they could be in the same position, or worse. It was little comfort. Florence was missing. Officers had been dispatched to Uttoxeter to search for her. Her father, Grant, was out in his car, combing the area, unwilling to leave the hunt to the police. She hadn't shown up for lessons that day. Robyn felt sick to her stomach This was her fault. She'd been given ample reasons for concern, yet she hadn't paid heed to Amélie when she rang about her friend, hadn't challenged Florence about the episode at the cinema and hadn't voiced her concerns to Christine; nor had she alerted her to the fact Florence had bunked off early from school, and was spotted wandering around Uttoxeter on Wednesday afternoon. And on top of everything, she'd known Chambers was a suspect and that he taught at Delia Marsh. She had made a monumental error. She'd become so embroiled in the investigation she'd forgotten all about Florence, and now the girl's life was in danger. Christine's own guilt was evident from her posture. She twisted the hat around and around, squeezing it tightly.

'Oh, Robyn, what have I done? I should have rung her or checked with Brigitte to make sure she really was with Amélie, but I just believed her. She's a sensible girl. I trust her. She's never given me any reason not to.'

Robyn put a hand on her shoulder. 'Don't worry. We'll find her. I'm going to leave you with PC Marker. He'll take all the details from you. I'll talk to you later.'

Christine bit her lip. 'Thanks, Robyn.'

Robyn raced down the corridor to her office where Mitz was waiting for her. 'Chambers left the school at three thirty with a colleague who teaches maths – Joe Furnish. We don't know if he went directly home. Matt's gone to his flat and will wait outside it for instructions. I've got the search warrant you requested.'

'Thanks. I'm not happy about this but I can't see what other choices we have. DCI Flint has made it quite clear we're to arrest Chambers in connection with the disappearance of Florence Hallows and Siobhan Connors. I can't afford to let anything happen to either girl.'

Robyn shook her head in dismay. Something didn't quite add up. Why had he taken Florence? If her theory was correct, Chambers was targeting only those who'd been cruel to his sister. This seemed to suggest otherwise. Had he decided to go after other girls he met online? Anna had gone through Florence's profile on the Fox or Dog website, establishing that she too had made contact with Hunter. He'd liked her profile and she'd reciprocated. But Florence hadn't known Charlotte. Why would Chambers want to kidnap or harm her? All she knew was that she had to act fast. If Elliot Chambers, aka Hunter, had abducted Florence, there was no time to waste. He was able to spirit young women away as if by magic. The responsibility to get her home safely rested heavily on Robyn's shoulders. She needed focus.

'We're going to have to fetch Elliot Chambers in. I'm still concerned about one fact. Florence didn't leave any messages or comments on Charlotte Chambers's profile. This doesn't follow the same pattern.'

'We don't have much choice, guv,' said Mitz. 'DCI Flint has ordered us to question him.'

Robyn gave a slight nod of her head. 'Okay, let's get him.'

Matt was well hidden in Derby Street. Robyn joined him. Matt shrugged. 'He's in there. He came home about ten minutes after I pulled up, carrying a bag of shopping, and hasn't left the flat since.'

'Stay here and I'll go up with Mitz and Anna. Be ready in case he runs.'

She motioned the pair over and together they climbed the stairs.

Elliot Chambers was dressed in jeans and a sweatshirt. His eyes opened wide when he saw Robyn and Mitz at his door. He wiped his hands on a tea towel. 'How can I help you, officers?'

Robyn held up the warrant. 'I have a warrant to search your flat, Mr Chambers.'

He stood, mouth slightly agape, his boyish features contorted with confusion. 'I don't understand,' he stammered.

Robyn continued. 'Please allow us entry, sir.'

He stood to one side, letting Robyn, Mitz and Anna pass into the hallway. Mitz and Anna moved off, taking the first door on the left and disappearing from view. Elliot tilted his head. 'Why are you searching my flat?'

Robyn breathed in deeply. 'Would you mind answering a few questions, Mr Chambers?'

'What's this all this about?'

'I'd prefer to ask the questions, sir. Or, if you like, you can accompany us to the station and answer them there.'

'This is preposterous. You can't march in here and search my flat without good reason.' A high colour flooded his face.

'I'm afraid we have good reason, and a warrant that allows us.'

Elliot moved towards a door on the right and pushed it open. 'In here,' he mumbled. Before them was an open-plan kitchen-diner, filled with an aroma of Italian herbs – basil, rosemary and thyme. A pan bubbled merrily on the stove and next to it stood an empty chopping board. 'I was making my dinner,' he said.

Robyn nodded. 'Best turn off the gas for the moment. Is that a chest freezer, Mr Chambers?'

She pointed at a white freezer by the wall.

'Yes, I prepare my meals in bulk. It means I don't have to cook every night. Tonight's an exception.'

'Seems a rather large freezer for one person.'

'I cook double portions and take some to my mother. She's not very well. I like cooking,' he said.

Robyn lifted the lid and peered inside. An icy blast of air caressed her face as she looked upon several plastic containers. She closed it again. 'Sit down, sir.'

He obliged and offered her a chair at his breakfast bar. She declined. 'Mr Chambers, when did you last see Florence Hallows?'

'Florence?' His face contorted once more with confusion. 'Why?'

'I asked you a question, sir.'

Elliot raised his hand and rubbed his head. 'Yesterday. Lesson three. Why? What's happened to her?'

'Did you see her leave the school yesterday afternoon?'

Elliot shook his head. 'I usually leave after the pupils. Yesterday was no different. I went into the staffroom to pick up a pile of marking and chatted to Sue Jones, the head of English, for a while. I went home immediately afterwards, but I didn't see Florence en route or hanging around the school. Are you going to tell me what this is about?'

'In good time. Can I ask if you recognise the name Carrie Miller?'

Elliot's mouth flapped open. 'Well, yes. She's the girl they found dead in Rugeley, but she wasn't one of our pupils. I've never met her. I've only seen her picture in the newspaper.'

Robyn wrote in her notebook. She recalled Phil Eastwood's words that Elliot was a very fine actor. He was certainly exhibiting the appropriate responses for a bewildered and innocent suspect – wide eyes, confusion flickering across his furrowed brow. She decided to stick with this line of questioning for now. There'd be time to break him later. 'Amber Dalton.'

He groaned. 'She was in the papers this week too. She was at that private school in Sandwell. Again, I don't know her.' He raked a hand through his hair, his eyes pleading innocence.

'Siobhan Connors?'

He shook his head. 'I don't know her. Will you please tell me what this is about.'

Robyn heard Mitz leave one room and enter another. 'I understand you were at Manchester University last year.'

He took a breath, apparently glad of the change of topic.

'I was.'

'Where did you stay in your final year?' Her eyes didn't leave his face.

'In a house in Edgar Street.'

'Did you order and pay for a specially made travel trunk, Mr Chambers, and have it delivered to the house?'

Again, he dragged his fingers through his hair and nodded.

'Why did you buy such a large trunk?' She waited as he digested her words.

'It wasn't for me,' he blurted. 'It was for part of my drama exam. A few of us wrote a play about the escape artist, Harry Houdini. I ordered the trunk for the production. It had to be big enough for me to fit inside. I was playing Houdini, you see, and I didn't want to be too cramped. I was on stage in that trunk for over half an hour.'

Robyn's eyebrows rose. 'You ordered an expensive trunk for a production? How could you afford it?'

'I intended to sell it afterwards. I was given some money from the drama department towards it.'

Her face remained impassive. 'And you'd be able to find fellow students or university staff to corroborate this story?'

His head bobbed up and down. 'Pretty sure, although I have no idea where any of the students on my course are now.'

As Robyn had expected, he'd thought about what to tell her. He'd fabricated a plausible story about the trunk. 'Where is that trunk now, Mr Chambers?'

'It's the oddest thing. When I moved back home, I left it in one of the outbuildings at my mother's house and it disappeared. I don't know what happened – gypsies, thieves, a chancer – somebody snooping around the outbuildings saw it and stole it.'

'You didn't report it as stolen?'

He shrugged. 'It wasn't worth getting the police involved for a trunk. There was nothing valuable inside it. I had other things to concentrate on. I was preparing for my position at Delia Marsh School and was looking for somewhere else to live.'

'You left university in June last year?'

'Yes.'

'And you returned home to The Oaks where you lived for the rest of the year until you moved into your flat on the twentieth of December last year?'

He nodded and shifted in his chair.

'You didn't seek temporary employment while at home? You must have accrued some student debt.'

Elliot swallowed hard. 'I had some debt. Not too much. My salary from teaching allows me to pay it off month by month.'

'So you were effectively unemployed while living at home from June until September. What did you do while you were at home all that time, Mr Chambers?'

He looked at his feet. 'This and that. Not much. You know… I'd worked hard for my degree. I just chilled for a bit.'

'You "chilled" for three months.'

'Look, I don't see what relevance this has to anything,' he said, his fists clenching.

Mitz appeared and shook his head. He hadn't uncovered anything. She beckoned him into the kitchen where he began searching the drawers.

Robyn waited while Elliot watched her officer delving into a cupboard. 'If you tell me what you're looking for, I'll tell you where it is.'

Mitz closed the door quietly. 'That's okay, sir.'

Elliot turned back to her. 'Have you ever used the Fox or Dog app?'

'Never heard of it,' he said.

'You must have. Surely your pupils have spoken about it?'

He shook his head, shoulders drooping, as Mitz churned paperwork over in a drawer. 'Please, don't mess it all up. I can't abide mess.'

'Are you certain you haven't heard of the app, Mr Chambers?'

He nodded furiously. 'Of course I'm sure. What is it? A game?'

'It's a dating app,' Robyn said, coolly.

Elliot watched Mitz with darting eyes. 'There's got to be some mistake,' he said. 'I have no idea what this is all about.'

There was a tap at the door. Anna beckoned Robyn, who turned from Elliot. 'Wait here, Mr Chambers.'

Back outside in the hallway, Anna moved towards Elliot's bedroom.

She'd pulled out a box marked 'acting props' and removed neatly folded clothes from it. They were now on his bed.

'What have you found?' Robyn asked.

'These,' said Anna, lifting up a blue leather jacket and a blue headband.

CHAPTER FIFTY-EIGHT

Elliot, bent over in his chair in the interview room at the station, held his head in his hands. Robyn and Mitz sat down opposite him.

'Mr Chambers, can you explain why these items of clothing were found in a box at your flat?'

Robyn pushed the leather jacket and headband across the table towards him. He didn't lift his head. 'They're clothes I use for acting. Sometimes I take on female roles. It's nothing more than that.'

Robyn continued. 'Did you wear these items of clothing on the eighteenth or the twentieth of December?'

He shook his head. 'No. They've been in that box ever since I left university. I packed them away when I left. Thought I might need them one day.'

'Where were you on the twentieth of December?'

'I moved to my flat that day.'

'How did you move your possessions?'

He let out a long breath. 'I borrowed my mum's car.'

'What time would that have been?'

'I packed the car up the night before and drove to the flat first thing that morning. I was there all day.'

'All day?'

'I had to unpack everything and put it in its new place. It takes time.' He straightened his back and gave her a stony look.

Robyn ignored the look. 'Mr Chambers, where were you on the third of January?'

'Oh, for goodness' sake! I don't know. What time?'

'In the evening, at about seven o'clock.'

His raised his hands. 'Out. I was supposed to be going with a couple of friends to watch a play at the Garrick Theatre in Lichfield, but they cried off at the last minute. They'd both caught a stomach bug. I don't have a car and I didn't feel like shelling out for a taxi so I went to the CineBowl over on Dovefields Retail Park to watch a film.'

'What did you watch?'

He studied his hands for a moment. 'I watched *A Monster Calls*.'

'And what's that about?'

'A boy being bullied by classmates who escapes by going into a fantasy world.'

Robyn wriggled in her seat and drew herself up. 'That's interesting. An odd subject for a grown man.'

He shrugged. 'It's about a kid being bullied. I thought it'd help give me insight into kids' minds. There's always bullying going on in schools. There's some at ours and I wanted to help. Make a difference. I want to be really good at my job.' His voice tailed off.

'What do you think about bullies?'

'What sort of question is that? I'm a teacher. I try to educate young people to be better, to make the most of themselves. I think they can unwittingly be crueller than adults and don't understand the effect bullying can have on those they victimise. What did you expect me to say? That I approve of it? If this is about my opinions, then I should warn you I disapprove of many things, Detective Inspector Carter. Would you like me to list all the things I dislike about our world?' He slapped the table with the palm of his hand. 'This is farcical. Why are you questioning me?'

'Please calm down, Mr Chambers. I have to ask you these questions. Can you account for your movements on the night of the nineteenth and into early hours of the twentieth of January?'

He gave a helpless shrug. 'Not really. I expect I was at home watching television or marking until I went to bed. I usually turn in at about ten. I wouldn't have been up after that.'

'You didn't go out at all that evening?'

'No, I didn't.'

'When did you last borrow your mother's car?'

His shoulders rose and fell. 'I haven't used it since I moved to the flat. It's been in her garage since then, I'd imagine. She's been too ill to drive in recent months. She asked me if I wanted it, but it's not my sort of car and there's nowhere to leave it outside the flat. That road gets very busy most days.'

Robyn sniffed and cocked her head. 'I see,' she said.

The man's hands were beginning to shake. 'Please,' he whispered. 'What am I supposed to have done?'

'You said that you returned to your mother's house after you graduated and stayed there throughout the following months until you moved to your flat. You must have done more than just chill out, Mr Chambers. We're looking at almost three months. I'd like to know more about your movements at that time. Did you go out at all? Meet friends? You must have done more than sit in the house.'

'No. I didn't go out. I wasn't too well.' His words tailed away and he hung his head.

'Mr Chambers, can you tell us where you're hiding Siobhan Connors and Florence Hallows?'

His mouth opened and shut. 'I've no idea what you're talking about.'

There was a tap at the door. It was Anna. 'Guv, there's a phone call for you. Urgent.'

Robyn nodded. 'Thanks. Can you fetch Mr Chambers a drink while I'm away?'

She headed to the office. It was Ross.

'Hey, how's it going?'

'We're making progress.'

'I know I'm not supposed to interfere with police investigations, but today I was at Uttoxeter station again, asking guards and regular commuters on the Crewe to Derby train if they'd spotted Lauren's friend Siobhan on the thirteenth. While I was waiting for the train, I came across a local man working in the small garden next to the station. He's one of the volunteers who help maintain it and he happened to be in that garden on the evening of the thirteenth.'

Robyn's pulse quickened.

'He'd been to the pub and decided to pass by to check up on some young trees he'd planted. It'd been very windy the day before and he was adjusting some post straps that had loosened when he heard raised voices. He noticed a young woman being bundled into a people carrier. He thinks it was a Vauxhall. She seemed drunk, and the man inside the car had trouble hauling her inside the vehicle. My witness said the girl shouted, "Get off, you bastard." There was then a slight scuffle and she flopped into the man's arms. His comment was, "You see too much of it these days, young women drinking too much. It was only coming up for seven as well." The car drove off at speed and he thought no more about it.'

'Could your witness describe the girl?'

'The interior car light was quite dim but he caught a glimpse of her face. I showed him the photograph of Siobhan and he thought it looked a lot like her. I'm now going to call it in officially to the missing persons team. Thought you might find it useful information.'

'You bet, and thank you. Are you going to continue searching for Siobhan?'

'Are you asking me that question in an official capacity?'

'No.'

'Then yes I am. I promised Lauren and I'm a man of my word.'

*

Robyn cast her eyes over the board once more, her eyes drawn to Chambers's name. She needed as much evidence against him as she could gather. It wasn't going to be easy to get Chambers to talk, but she would, and she promised herself she'd find Siobhan and Florence before the night was over.

CHAPTER FIFTY-NINE

It was almost eight and she couldn't get anything further out of Elliot Chambers. He'd refused to talk about his movements during the months of June, July and August; had denied visiting Derby; stuck rigidly to his story about the trunk, and to his account of his whereabouts on the day Joanne Hutchinson delivered it to Rugeley and the night Amber Dalton had been spotted near Derby Road in Uttoxeter. He'd refuted any claims he'd been in his mother's car on the thirteenth, the night Siobhan Connors disappeared, but had no concrete alibi. He'd also denied driving it on the nineteenth. Moreover, he was adamant he didn't know the whereabouts of Florence or Siobhan.

Finally, Robyn had asked him about his sister. His face had crumpled as if it had been punched.

'Please, I don't want to talk about Charlotte. I *can't* talk about what happened. It's too much for me. Please don't drag it up. I can't go through it again.'

He'd begun to shake uncontrollably and tears flowed down his face. He'd become incoherent and Robyn had him taken to the cells to calm down.

She faced her team. 'I can't believe he's that good an actor. He looks completely shell-shocked. I don't know what to make of it.'

Mitz pulled a biscuit from a packet and passed it to Anna. 'I agree.'

Robyn lifted her hands; a disheartened gesture. 'We're talking about an accomplished actor who's acted many roles, including a convincing upper-class woman.'

'That part of his story's true. A lady called Veronica from the university dramatic society confirmed Elliot ordered a trunk for a production as part of his final exam work,' said Anna. 'They'd tried using an ordinary trunk, but he hadn't been able to squeeze into it.'

Robyn groaned. 'Just because he has good reason for owning it doesn't change the fact that he owns it.'

Anna shrugged, unconvinced.

'This is hopeless. Let's go through this one more time.' Robyn held up the Post-it note that read Fox or Dog. 'We have three girls, all of whom left cruel messages on Charlotte Chambers's profile page. In March last year Charlotte killed herself, leaving a note that said, "I can't bear my life any more. I feel like I'm drowning in a sea of hatred." To my mind, that suggests she found the cyberbullying too much to bear. Any comments so far?'

There were shakes of heads. She walked to the whiteboard and erased the writing on it, starting afresh. She wrote Fox or Dog and Charlotte's name, then wrote down the names of each of the three young women who'd interacted with Charlotte online. She drew connecting lines to them and Charlotte. Below this, she added Elliot's name and repeated, 'Charlotte Chambers might have committed suicide thanks to comments made by these three girls. All three appeared to have chatted to, or been in contact with, Hunter.' She wrote 'Hunter' beside Elliot's name. 'All three disappeared without trace. We can't find anything else that would link these girls. Charlotte is the only connection we have between them all, which leads us back to Elliot Chambers – a loving brother who found his sister dead in her bedroom.

'Elliot has the motive. He can't provide solid alibis for the nights that any of the girls went missing. At the time Carrie Miller disappeared he was at home "chilling". He had ample opportunity to snatch her, imprison her and murder her during this time. He maintains he was unpacking all day on the twentieth of December, the day Carrie's body was transported in a hire vehicle to a rented self-storage unit, but he has no witnesses to him being in the flat. He owns a chest freezer. That seems strange. A single man doesn't need a large chest freezer. Both Carrie Miller and Amber Dalton were kept somewhere icy cold. Could that have been a chest freezer? We'll need forensics to examine Chambers's freezer for traces of DNA or anything that might suggest it was used to hide those girls' bodies.'

'On it, boss,' said Mitz.

Robyn wrote 'station' below Elliot's name and stabbed at it with her pen.

'I can't help but feel the station is significant. Chambers lives near Uttoxeter station. Carrie Miller was seen boarding a train that passed through there. On the third of January, Amber Dalton was spotted crossing Dovefields Retail Park from the direction of this station, headed towards Derby Road, where Chambers lives. And a member of the public witnessed a young woman who looked remarkably like Siobhan Connors being bundled into a car at the station car park – a large car that could well be a Vauxhall Zafira.'

She swung around and added 'Vauxhall Zafira' next to 'station'. 'Chambers has access to his mother's car. He used it to transport boxes and his trunk back from university. He *might* have also used it in the early hours of the twentieth, in order to transport Amber Dalton's body to Cannock Chase.'

Anna put up a hand. 'I spoke to Mrs Chambers, asked if she happened to have been out in her car that evening. She said she hardly ever goes out these days because of her illness. She was even thinking of selling the car. On the nineteenth, she took some extra-strong painkillers and went to bed early because of her back. She recalled it had been very bad that day, and by the evening, she couldn't stand it any more.'

'Thanks, Anna. Elliot could have driven the car from her garage without her knowledge,' said Robyn. She rubbed at her neck. The tension headache was returning. 'I'd like another sweep along Penkridge Park Road. We couldn't find any witnesses last time, but we might have missed somebody who only walks there now and again. Yes, I'm clutching at straws. We might not be lucky, but if anybody saw a Vauxhall Zafira in the area of Cannock Chase where Amber's body was found, it'd tie that vehicle in with two of the girls. Matt, you up for that?'

'It's not far from where I live, so I'll do that. Might catch some late-evening dog walkers if I go now.'

'Thanks, Matt. Then go home afterwards.'

'Cheers, boss. If Mrs Higham suggests me doing the night feed, I'll be back here before you can say "nappy change".'

The door closed quietly as he left and Robyn wrote down 'trunk'.

'We know about the trunk. Chambers bought it for a drama production. He brought it back from university in his mother's car, and maintains it was stolen from one of the unlocked outbuildings outside her house. That's a little too convenient for my liking. What are we left with? Anything? David?'

David reached across to Matt's desk and lifted a list. 'Sorry, boss. We drew a blank searching for the hired van. There were no vans hired by either a Joanne Hutchinson or an Elliot Chambers, although there *is* a Mr Chambers on this list,' he said, studying it with a frown. 'Mr Thomas Chambers.'

Robyn spun around. 'Thomas Chambers.'

'It isn't Elliot, guv – this guy's in his late forties.'

'Show me.' Robyn stared at the sheet, then sifted through her Post-it notes and grabbed at one. 'Elliot's father was called Thomas, born in 1958 and died in January 2006. He was forty-eight years old. David, can you please escort Chambers back to the interview room.'

Once David had left the room, she spoke to Mitz and Anna. 'I have one major problem in all of this. Where does Florence fit in? She didn't have anything to do with Charlotte Chambers. The only connection I can think of is that she is a pupil at the same school where Elliot Chambers teaches. They chatted using the app. What am I missing?'

There was silence, then Anna spoke. 'Maybe Florence saw something, stumbled across Chambers behaving strangely, or found out he was Hunter, so he tried to prevent her from saying anything.'

Robyn nodded slowly as she assimilated this new idea. 'Yes. That's possible. It would certainly help explain why he's taken her. Thank you.'

Anna pulled up the website and Florence's profile picture. 'She hasn't given any boys other than Hunter a fox emoji. She's got quite a few dog emojis under her own picture, poor kid, and there are some comments about her hair, being fat and her freckles.'

Robyn moved behind her and read the taunts. Florence hadn't responded other than to ask them not to be bitchy, although she had left a barbed comment for one girl called LaBelle18. *At least I don't look like a pig with a moustache.* LaBelle18 had replied with, *Fuck you, you ginger minger.*

Anna looked up, her face suddenly anxious. 'It might seem to be petty jibes to the outsider, but these taunts could really upset a sensitive person. You don't think Florence might have taken these insults to heart, do you, like Charlotte did?'

Robyn's blood turned to ice. Surely not. Florence wouldn't have tried to kill herself, would she?

CHAPTER SIXTY

'I haven't the foggiest what you're talking about.' Elliot's face was drawn, eyes baggy and bloodshot from crying in his cell. 'I haven't done anything, I swear. I don't know any of these girls. I've never used the Fox or Dog app. Check my phone. Check my laptop. Do what you must, but I haven't spoken to these girls.'

The photographs of Amber, Carrie and Siobhan were laid out in the middle of the table, facing him. Robyn added Florence's picture and sat back to watch his reactions. Elliot let out a keening sound that filled the room as he tore at his hair. 'I haven't seen Florence since we had English yesterday. How many more times are you going to ask me?'

'You are denying renting a van in your deceased father's name?'

'Yes… yes… yes! I've never rented a van in my life.' He dropped his head into his hands.

Robyn remained composed. She scrutinised him before speaking. 'The thirteenth of January.'

'Not this again. I did *not* go out that night. I stayed inside, did some marking and watched television.'

'Isn't it odd for a young man in his early twenties to stay at home on a Friday night?'

'Not in January. It was perishingly cold. Do I have to keep repeating myself over and over? Is that what you want? I didn't go out that Friday. I can't remember what I watched. What did I watch? Oh yes! Now I remember.' His eyes lit up for a moment.

'The new comedy series of *Not Going Out* with Lee Mack started that night at nine. I watched that. That's proof I didn't go out.'

'I'm afraid that only proves you know what was on television that night.'

His head dropped again. 'I give up. What do you want me to say?'

Robyn gave a polite smile. 'The truth.'

His hands fell to the table with a thump. 'I've been telling the truth.'

'Were you aware your sister was signed up to Fox or Dog?'

Elliot's face turned grey. His eyes flashed for a second and his lips flattened into a thin line. 'I made it quite clear that I don't wish to discuss my sister.'

'Did Charlotte ever mention the app to you?' Robyn kept her eyes trained on his face. He ignored her and stared at his hands, refusing to speak again.

'Mr Chambers, did you know your sister used the Fox or Dog app?'

He would not lift up his head again. Silent tears rolled down his cheeks.

Mitz took him back to the cells and returned to the office a few minutes later. Robyn grumbled, 'He denies everything. I won't be able to charge him at this rate.'

'We'll keep tabs on him,' said Mitz. 'Make sure he doesn't leave the flat, and when he does, follow him.'

Robyn shook her head. 'Once Chambers is released, that'll be that, unless we can come up with some other reason to bring him back in. He'll be on his guard, and I doubt he'll suddenly lead us to Florence or Siobhan.'

Anna looked pensive. 'What if Chambers is telling the truth and we've got the wrong person?'

Having observed Chambers's reactions to her questioning, Robyn had similar concerns. She felt trapped – if she released him, he might kill Siobhan and Florence, and if she charged him, could the real killer still be out there? ... 'I really hope we haven't. We've got no other suspects.' The phone rang and she picked up on the second ring. 'Carter.'

'It's Matt. I've found a gentleman, Stuart Glover, who lives in Penkridge Park Road. He passed a large people carrier that was pulled over on the hard shoulder, in the early hours of Friday the twentieth. He was headed to the airport at the time. He's been away in Germany all week and didn't know about Amber Dalton. He couldn't be sure of the make of the car but he remembered some of the number plate. It ended in Sierra Golf. He remembered only because they're his initials.'

After the call she stretched, letting out a long sigh, before speaking. 'The Vauxhall Zafira belonging to Mrs Chambers. What's it registration, Mitz?'

Mitz flicked through his notebook and read it out.

Robyn tapped her long fingers together. 'The evidence is stacking up against him now. A Vauxhall Zafira with a number plate ending in the same letters as Mrs Chamber's was spotted in Penkridge Road. If I question Chambers about it, he'll only deny it. Give me a minute. I need to think about how best to handle this.' She shrugged on a coat. 'I'll be back soon.'

Outside, the cold bit into her face, sharpening her mind. She crossed the car park and paced down the road. It had to be Chambers. Everything pointed to him. She ran through the facts, the statements, and thought about Chambers's reaction to everything. He'd vehemently denied any of the accusations. He'd not changed his story. He'd been cagey about his movements in July and August and had no alibis for the dates the girls went missing. Yet it didn't feel right. Anna had voiced Robyn's concerns. She had to follow her instincts, and that was saying she had the wrong man. Why did she feel this way? The man was an actor, able to disguise himself as a female, and he owned an outfit exactly like that worn by Joanne Hutchinson. He had a chest freezer that was currently being examined for evidence of any DNA. He denied knowing any of the girls. He refused to account for his movements during the time Carrie went missing. Chambers had no alibis.

Alibis.

She stopped in her tracks. The wind whipped her hair into her face but she didn't feel it stinging into her flesh. That was it. If Chambers was a killer who could meticulously plan to drop a trunk off in a self-storage warehouse and come up with a plausible excuse as to why he owned it, why hadn't he also given himself elaborate alibis for the nights in question and for the months of July and August? It didn't stack up. There was no other evidence in the flat that he was involved in abduction or murder, and where had he hidden the pieces of flesh cut from the girls' foreheads – the trophies? They weren't in his chest freezer or his flat. Where else might he conceal them?

Robyn marched back towards the station. The wind pushed her onwards as if to urge her back to work. If Chambers wasn't a killer out to avenge his sister's death, then who else might it be? The answer came so suddenly it stopped her in her tracks. It could only be one other person.

CHAPTER SIXTY-ONE

Robyn raced along the corridor and clattered into the office, surprising her officers chatting at their desks.

'We've been looking at this all wrong. The fact that Chambers has such weak or non-existent alibis for the nights all three girls disappeared is not consistent with the careful planning of the first concealment. What I mean by that,' she said, picking up her marker pen, 'is that someone went to a lot of trouble to hide Carrie Miller's body. Our mysterious Joanne Hutchinson paid cash for her unit, avoided detection from CCTV cameras at the self-storage warehouse, hired a van but left no trace. The only thing anyone who saw her can remember is how well-spoken she was and how groomed she looked. She wore a smart leather jacket, high-heeled boots and a matching headband. What was it one witness said about her?' She checked through her notes. 'That she was "made up like an air stewardess". It struck me as odd then that a woman would dress up to drive a van and deliver a trunk to a self-storage warehouse. I now think it was deliberate.' She wrote, 'Joanne Hutchinson: overdressed, over-the-top, plummy accent.'

Anna's eyebrows knotted together in concentration. 'Are you suggesting that whoever went to all this trouble to create such a cover would have airtight alibis for the third and thirteenth of January when Amber and Siobhan went missing?'

Robyn waved her pen like a conductor. 'That's exactly what I'm suggesting. Ever since I saw the photograph of Elliot Chambers dressed as Lady Bracknell, I've believed that he disguised himself as Joanne Hutchinson, but what if Joanne Hutchinson actually was a woman?'

Mitz heaved a sigh. 'I don't get it. Am I being extra thick this evening?'

Robyn shook her head. 'Far from it. These are only theories. I could be wrong and I need your input. What if this woman were able to make herself look younger by wearing heavy make-up, a smart outfit and maybe a wig? She might even add to the distraction by speaking, as our witnesses have said, "posh".'

'I get that, but where does Hunter fit in?' said Mitz.

Robyn waved her pen again. 'I'm getting to that. We've established that anyone can put up any profile picture on Fox or Dog. No one knows who's behind the picture until they meet that person in real life. Hunter hasn't used his own photograph, I'm sure of that. We still need to confirm where the photo came from, but the tech team will surely be able to assist. It's probably taken from the Internet or a magazine, but either way, it isn't of the man calling himself Hunter. And what if Hunter isn't a man at all? A woman might be behind that profile.' She added the name Hunter and wrote 'female' beside it.

'That brings us on to why. Our theory is that Hunter has been targeting those young women who bullied Charlotte Chambers. Elliot was very close to his sister and might well have decided to seek revenge. He certainly ordered a trunk the same size as the one that contained Carrie's body, but has consistently insisted it was stolen. It *sounds* too convenient, but he hasn't wavered from that story. He believes it was stolen from an open outbuilding at The Oaks.'

Anna wriggled in her seat, head bobbing in excitement. Mitz smiled. 'I've got it. I see where's you're going with this theory.'

'Good. There are two people who were directly affected by Charlotte's death – one is Elliot; the other is Cheryl Chambers.'

Anna tilted her head. 'Mrs Chambers is too weak to have committed these crimes. She's crippled with fibromyalgia. Mitz told me she was struggling to walk. Surely Elliot must be involved as well?'

'That's what I believed too, Anna. She is unemployed and receiving sickness benefit, but we only have her word she's suffering from a debilitating illness. Unfortunately, such sensitive information won't be handed over to us without a warrant.'

'So, you think she could be faking her illness?' said Mitz.

'I do.'

'Do you really suppose she's strong enough to lift a trunk containing a body, carry Amber onto Cannock Chase, dig a grave and drop her in, alone?' Mitz asked. 'It seems unlikely. She'd need some assistance. I agree with Anna that both of them could be involved.'

'To be honest, Mitz, that's where I'm also struggling. It's a heavy trunk.'

'She might be able to haul the trunk onto the van if it was empty. That would be plausible. She might have done that, and once it was loaded, placed Carrie's body into it.' Anna said. 'That would also explain why she couldn't offload it. It was too heavy for her to manage once Carrie's body was inside it.'

'True. Good point, Anna. To my mind, Elliot's demeanour shouts "not guilty". He was in tears when he went to the cells. We know he's an actor, but he'd need incredible skills to carry off the performance he put on in that interview room. My head says he might be acting to save his bacon, but my gut says he's not our perp. If I'm wrong and he is culpable, then he's an accomplice in all of this. We need to dig deep. Pull up everything you can on Cheryl Chambers and her son, and I mean everything. We have to get this right. One or both of them must be involved in this.'

She threw herself in front of her computer, focused completely on her task. The room fell silent.

Mitz spoke first. 'I've got something from the government public records database. Cheryl Denise Chambers, born second of June 1972. Maiden name Cheryl King. Attended school in Birmingham. From 1990 to 1993 studied drama and theatre arts at the University of Birmingham. Took part in a few local productions. Moved from acting into make-up. Worked on regular productions at the Garrick Theatre in Lichfield. Involved with Stagecoach Productions in Uttoxeter. Not much else here of note. Married to Thomas David Chambers in 1994. Elliot Chambers born later that year.'

Robyn looked across. 'That's interesting, and certainly supports my theory that she could have disguised herself as a younger woman. I suspect she has access to theatrical props and make-up too, if she's been working at local theatres.'

'I've found a photograph of her from those early days,' said Mitz.

'Print it off, Mitz. Dev Khan or Frank might recognise her face from it. I've found one of her with her husband at a dairy farmers' event but her face isn't very clear in it.'

The printer clicked and spewed out the picture. Robyn studied it carefully. 'You can see Elliot's her son. They share the same nose, eyes and cheekbones.'

Flint wanted her to charge Elliot Chambers. Her instincts said Chambers wasn't the guilty party. She stared at the photograph once more. She was going out on a limb yet again. She was going to have to ignore her superior's wishes. If he didn't like it, she'd transfer to Yorkshire. It was far more important to find Florence and Siobhan.

'Either of you know if DCI Flint's still around? I need another warrant. This time for The Oaks.'

CHAPTER SIXTY-TWO

'It's gone ten. Do you think she'll be up?' Mitz pushed his hands deep into the pockets of his coat.

'She will be once I bang on the door,' whispered Robyn. Flint hadn't been keen to start with, but once she'd explained her reasoning, shown him the photographs and her latest findings, he'd made the necessary phone calls and the warrant had been issued.

They walked up the drive, keeping noise to a minimum. Anna brought up the rear with David. Robyn pointed to the outbuilding where the Vauxhall Zafira stood. 'Check out that building. If she transported Amber in that car, there might be something in there. Take a good look around.' The officers peeled off into the darkness, guided only by torch beams.

A light burned downstairs, accompanied by the sound of canned laughter. Cheryl Chambers was watching television. Robyn hammered on the door. A curtain twitched. A face appeared and disappeared as quickly

'Mrs Chambers, open the door, please. It's DI Carter.'

It was an eternity before Cheryl appeared, dressed in a faded, woollen dressing gown. She was bent over, clinging feebly to her sticks, face contorted in pain. Her voice was tremulous. 'What do you want?'

'We'd like a few words with you.'

'You can't come in. It's late. I'm not feeling very well. I've been in bed all day.'

'We have authority to enter your home,' Robyn said.

'Why? I don't understand.' Cheryl's voice wobbled.

'We have reason to believe you might have information regarding the abduction of young women and the murders of Amber Dalton and Carrie Miller.'

The woman's eyebrows shot up in alarm. 'There's been some kind of dreadful mistake. I don't know anything. I rarely go out. Look at me – I can hardly walk.'

'Can we come in for a moment, please, Mrs Chambers?' Robyn said.

'I don't have a choice, do I?' Cheryl grumbled and shuffled backwards, grimacing as she did.

More laughter came from the television. Robyn accompanied the woman to the sitting room.

'I have to sit down,' Cheryl said, struggling to get into the chair. 'The pain's been dreadful today.'

'Of course,' Robyn replied. 'Mrs Chambers, where were you Friday the thirteenth of January at about seven in the evening?'

'Here, of course. I've already told one of your colleagues that. She questioned me about my car. I don't get out much at all. I can't drive at the moment either, thanks to my back.'

'How do you manage for shopping?'

'I shop online and get it delivered,' Cheryl said.

Robyn continued, 'And you were at home on the twentieth and twenty-first of January?'

Cheryl nodded.

'We have reason to believe your vehicle was in Uttoxeter on the thirteenth and at Cannock Chase in the early hours of the twentieth of January.'

'Wasn't my car. I haven't driven it for months.' She shrugged lazily.

Robyn sighed. 'That's what I thought you'd say. The only other person who has access to the car is your son, Elliot.'

'No, I'd have known if he'd borrowed it.' Cheryl shook her head vehemently.

'You might not have heard him take it. If you were here with the television on, or were knocked out on your medication, you wouldn't have heard the car drive off.'

The chair creaked as she shifted in it. 'No, Elliot didn't take the car. He'd have told me if he wanted to borrow it. Ask him. He'll have been doing something else on each of those evenings. He'll have been out with friends.'

'We have asked him.'

'Then you'll know he had an alibi for that night.'

Robyn shook her head. 'Unfortunately, he didn't have one.'

'He must have had one. I'm sure it was about that time he was going Lichfield or somewhere to watch a play with friends. I think I remember him saying he was going out on the third.'

Robyn gave a small smile. 'That wasn't the case. We've had to bring him in as a suspect.'

Cheryl's mouth opened and shut again, eyes blinking repeatedly. 'No, he couldn't have taken the car. I keep the keys in the house. He doesn't have a door key.' She looked up at Robyn with wide eyes – eyes like her son's. 'He couldn't have. You're mistaken.'

Robyn looked at her notes. 'I understand you hold a spare key for Elliot's flat.'

'In case of emergencies, yes.'

'Was that your suggestion?'

Cheryl blinked again, face clouding with suspicion. 'I believe it was his idea. It was in case he ever lost his house keys. There'd be a spare set here.'

'Makes sense,' Robyn said.

Cheryl's lips twisted into a small smile. 'Kids, eh? Always losing things.'

Robyn pulled out a photograph. 'Do you recognise this picture?'

'It's of me.' Her eyebrows furrowed again.

'I understand you studied drama at university.'

'I took on a few roles after I left university, but I was out of work a lot of the time. I met Tom, got pregnant and gave it up. When Lotty was older, I became self-employed. Helped out on a few productions in Lichfield and around the area.' A bead of sweat formed on her upper lip. Robyn smiled again, rose and walked towards the photographs on the shelf, picking up one of Cheryl and her husband Tom.

'When was this taken?' she asked.

'About fifteen years ago.' Cheryl's fingers rubbed continuously at her wrist.

'You make a handsome couple. You ought to have been a model.'

Cheryl mumbled thanks. Robyn moved on to the next photo of an older Elliot with his sister. 'I see Elliot bears quite a resemblance to you.' She stared at Cheryl, who appeared to be folding into her chair. Robyn moved towards the woman and stood in front of the chair.

'You said you do your shopping online.'

'I have a laptop.' The words were barely audible.

'Mrs Chambers, I'm going to have to confiscate it and your mobile phone if you have one.'

Cheryl pushed herself forward. 'Go ahead. I haven't done anything wrong.'

'Then you won't object to us taking them away for examination.'

Cheryl folded her arms, defiance replaced subservience. 'You won't find anything on them.'

'Possibly not, but our technicians are very good at retrieving deleted information.'

Cheryl blinked several times.

'Mrs Chambers, think very carefully before you answer. Do you know this girl?'

Robyn held up a photograph of Carrie Miller.

Cheryl glanced at it. 'No.'

'This girl?' Robyn showed her the picture of Amber Dalton. Cheryl shook her head.

'How about this young woman, Siobhan Connors?' Again, Cheryl shook her head.

'I don't recognise any of them. Should I?'

'We believe they were all involved in online bullying.' Robyn studied the woman's reactions. Her face remained impassive. 'We think they bullied your daughter.'

'Are you here about Lotty, or these girls? I'm feeling pretty tired now and I don't think I can answer many more questions.'

Robyn sighed and dropped to her knees so she was facing the woman. 'In a way, we *are* here about Charlotte. We have good reason to believe Elliot was involved in abducting these girls and murdering at least two of them.'

Cheryl's reaction was slow. She blinked again, then said, 'Elliot wouldn't. He couldn't…' Her words trailed off.

'We believe he did. Your daughter was the victim of cyberbullying. She used an app that offers people the chance to meet members of the opposite sex, to get to know them, and maybe forge a relationship. Charlotte was picked on by these girls. She was too young, too naïve, to be using the app and didn't understand the implications. Elliot found out about it. He must have retrieved her phone when he discovered her body. He worked out what had happened and he's been getting to know these girls online, on this site, by pretending to be interested in them. All this time, he's been avenging Charlotte's death. He's guilty of kidnapping and murder. He'll go to prison for a very long time.' Robyn studied Cheryl's reaction. She swallowed a couple of times. She kept her eyes on Robyn's mouth, then spoke quietly.

'You're so wrong. My Elliot is a gentle, caring man.'

'You're his mother. You would believe that. I can understand.' Robyn gave a small smile. 'I'm sorry.'

Cheryl shook her head. 'No, he is. He hasn't a bad bone in his body. He's very sensitive. He adored Lotty. He wouldn't commit these crimes.'

Robyn passed over a fourth photograph. 'Okay. This is a picture of Florence Hallows, a thirteen-year-old schoolgirl whose mother is frantic with worry. Where is she, Mrs Chambers? I think you know. Did Elliot assist in her abduction?'

Cheryl growled, 'I've never seen her before. I've no idea what you're talking about. You're stressing me, and that's bad for my health. The pain gets uncontrollable when I'm stressed. I'll report you for this. I'll talk to your superior. You can't march in at this time of night and accuse my son of murder. Leave now. I must lie down. I can feel it flaring up. I need my pills.'

Robyn stood up. 'Where are they? I'll fetch them for you.'

'*Go away*. Take your colleagues and clear out of my house!' Cheryl picked up her stick and waved it in Robyn's direction. Robyn's heart thudded in her chest. She'd taken a risk riling Cheryl. For the last hour she'd listened to her instincts that told her Florence was being held captive at The Oaks. She'd established that Cheryl had been an actress and make-up artist. She had the skills to change her appearance and pass herself off as a younger or older woman, or even a young man. Before, Robyn had been so focused on the perpetrator being male she'd not considered Cheryl Chambers; yet now she was certain of the woman's involvement. She was a good actress, but her unconscious tells, like those subtle changes in a poker player's face, gave her away. Her face may have remained impassive, but the rapid blinking and slight tremor in her left eyelid had told Robyn exactly what she needed to know. Cheryl was behind the murders.

The laptop would yield Cheryl's internet searches even if she had deleted her browsing history. Dev Khan and Frank Cummings and Luke Sanderson would all be able to identify her as Joanne Hutchinson. She was not the feeble, sick woman she made out she was. All this would happen, but for now Robyn had to locate Siobhan and Florence. She prayed this woman hadn't harmed either of them. She held up the photographs of Siobhan and Florence.

'Mrs Chambers, these girls don't deserve to be punished like this. We'll make sure Siobhan is dealt with. We don't tolerate cyberbullying. As for Florence, she's a sweet girl. She isn't vindictive or cruel, and she didn't even know your daughter.'

Cheryl scowled. 'I told you to get out.'

'Let me take Florence home to her mother. Tell me where she is, please. Her mother is beside herself with worry. Don't put her through this. You know what it's like to lose a daughter.' In that moment, Robyn knew she'd overstepped an invisible line. The sneer on Cheryl's face scared her.

'Lose a daughter? You have no idea how it rips into your very soul, consumes your every waking moment and destroys you.' She sat up, her hands now on her lap. 'I… don't… know… where… she… is.' She stared at Robyn. Robyn cursed herself. She'd read the situation incorrectly. She'd believed she could coax the woman into handing over Florence, and now she'd blown it. She drew herself up, regained control of the situation.

'Sergeant Patel is going to conduct a search of the house, and then we'll take you down to the station. We're going to question you and Elliot further. Your son's still in custody.'

Cheryl's mood flipped again. 'Why've you got my son? He's nothing to do with any of this nonsense. Leave the boy alone. He's been through enough.'

Mitz answered a rap on the front door. Anna was outside, eyes huge. 'We've found a room hidden at the back of the garage. The car was blocking the door to it. There's something you need to see. We think it's a body.'

CHAPTER SIXTY-THREE

Robyn left Mitz watching over Cheryl and bounded outside. Anna accompanied her, the torchlight swinging back and forth as they trampled over to the shabby outbuilding. Anna's voice was hushed. 'There's a body hidden in a chest freezer. We can't be sure who it is and didn't want to touch anything.'

Robyn's heart skipped a beat. She was too late. She'd let the girls down. One or both were dead. She slowed, unwilling to acknowledge what she was about to see. Her lips were dry. She followed Anna's lead and squeezed past the vehicle. Ahead, a door was ajar. The room was small, and empty apart from the freezer chest humming quietly in the corner. Matt stood beside it. Robyn nodded at him and he lifted the lid. She peered inside. It was difficult to make out exactly what she was seeing in the light from the torches, but there was no doubt it was human. A thick plastic sheet was wrapped around the girl, whose face was almost invisible. Her eyes were closed, her lips blue-black. Robyn turned away. 'Call forensics, take Mrs Chambers to the station and get a team out here. I want the house searched from top to bottom.'

She gazed again at the frozen object before her, her heart heavy. *Too late.* Her pulse speeded again. There was only room for one body in the freezer. Somewhere there was another girl. *Please don't let this be Florence.* As the light spilt into the chest it fell on a piece of plastic tucked in behind the body. 'Matt, can you extract that, please?'

Matt lifted out a plastic freezer bag and held it under the beam of his torch. Robyn stretched a pair of gloves them over her hands and took it from him, teasing the contents apart. Anna gasped. The bag contained pieces of almost transparent human flesh – three rectangles of almost identical size.

'Give me some more light,' said Robyn quietly. Anna added the beam from her torch to Matt's. Robyn inhaled deeply and exhaled again – a long, sad sigh. Into each piece of flesh was carved one word – DOG. She passed the bag back to Matt. 'Put it back exactly as you found it,' she said.

She knelt down and studied the freezer. No grime or marks were visible, and there was an energy sticker that had not been removed on one side. She followed the lead back to the plug and noted it was white and unmarked. 'Does this freezer look new to you?' she asked.

'It isn't grubby, if that's what you mean. It might have been cleaned down,' Matt said.

'If it had been, this energy sticker would be showing signs of wear, or been removed. I'm thinking this is a recent purchase. A freezer in an outbuilding would have dust or dirt on it, especially on the plug. Nobody cleans plugs. We'll need to search for an invoice and find out when this was purchased.'

'Yes, guv,' said Anna. 'Can I ask why?'

'This is only supposition, but if her old freezer broke down last week, it would explain the disposal of Amber's body. Carrie's body was kept in cold storage for months until it was moved to the self-storage unit. I suspect Cheryl intended hiding Amber's body in the same freezer, but it stopped working and Cheryl had to dispose of the body quickly.' She looked up at the ceiling, shining her torch into the corners of the room where cobwebs hung low. She ran the beam along the floor. 'It's definitely not clean in here,' she said.

Anna's large dark eyes stood out in her pale face. 'Do you think this is Siobhan?'

Robyn looked again at the girl in the freezer and fought back the emotion threatening to overcome her. The body seemed a little too large to be Florence, but it was difficult to tell. Robyn wanted to rip open the plastic and confirm the girl's identity but she couldn't – not until the forensic team had arrived. She shut her eyes and shook her head.

'Anna, I honestly don't know.' For a moment she couldn't move or think. The fear that Florence was the girl in this freezer made her unable to concentrate or focus. She fought it. Florence had to be alive. In all probability this was Siobhan's body, unless there was yet another victim they had not identified. She dismissed that thought. This was Siobhan. Florence was still alive. She said the words over and over again to herself. If there was only one freezer, then Florence was probably alive. She steeled herself again. 'Matt, shut it back up, please, and come into the house.'

The burden of responsibility weighed heavily upon her, almost too much to bear. Another girl had died. She threw open the front door. 'Where is she?' she shouted, marching into the sitting room. Cheryl Chambers refused to answer.

Robyn tilted her head, eyes blazing. 'Where's Florence?'

Cheryl stared at her, then gave a chilling smile. 'You're too late.'

'So help me, if you've harmed her—'

'Boss, come away.' Mitz put a hand on her shoulder. 'We have work to do.'

Robyn was shaking – a mixture of anger and fear; fear that Florence Hallows was dead. 'You're right. Start searching the house.'

Matt entered with a clatter. 'I've called it in,' he said.

Robyn breathed deeply and regained her composure. 'Thank you. Would you please read Mrs Chambers her rights, then take her to the station?'

She drew Mitz into the hallway. 'Take a good look about but don't disturb anything in case any prints have been left by any of the victims. We'll need her laptop and mobile. Go into the attic and all the cupboards – anywhere you think a young girl might be hidden.'

Cheryl Chambers sat up tall and straight in the back of the car next to Anna. She threw Robyn one last smug look before the interior light went off and Matt drove away. Robyn stood on the doorstep, breathing in the cold air. The body in the freezer continued to immobilise her thought process. Although she felt responsible for the deaths she hadn't been able to prevent, she'd feel much more responsibility for Florence's. If anything dreadful had happened to the girl, she wouldn't forgive herself. Amélie had phoned her, told her about Florence walking to the station, and Robyn had brushed away her concerns without a second thought. She kicked at a stone. It flew a few feet and landed with a soft thud. She ought to have listened to Amélie. Hot tears sprang to her eyes and she blinked them back. Crying would serve no purpose. She had to find Florence.

A cold breeze made her shiver. She'd get a confession from Cheryl Chambers. She wouldn't let up until she'd extracted every piece of information from the woman and charged her with murder. She looked across at the innocuous outbuilding – a simple structure that housed a horrible secret. Cheryl had killed Carrie, kept her in the freezer and moved her body when she had the opportunity. She hunched her shoulders against the breeze. She had to think it through logically. Why hadn't Cheryl left Carrie's body in the freezer? It was a big risk moving her.

Robyn unclipped her torch again and walked across to the outbuilding where she stood next to the Zafira. She forced herself to concentrate. Had Cheryl emptied the freezer to make room for a second body – Amber Dalton? If Robyn's theory about the new freezer was correct, Cheryl had been forced to dump Amber's body and then used the new freezer for her third victim – Siobhan Connors. A tiny bubble of hope rose from somewhere inside her chest. Florence might still be alive and be held captive on the premises.

She returned to the house and began searching the sitting room for Florence. She pulled at the shabby chairs standing on faded rugs and dragged at the corners in the hope of finding a trapdoor under them. There was nothing. She tried moving a large cabinet away from the wall in the hope it hid a door. She tugged at it, her arm muscles straining as it shifted inch by inch away from the wall until there was sufficient space for Robyn to peer behind it. There was no door. Mitz called out Florence's name. A pang like a dull firework went off in her chest. It was hopeless. Florence wasn't here. She moved into the kitchen where she opened a wooden latched door that led into a dark pantry of shelves filled with jars and tins and plastic boxes. She shut the door again and wondered where else she should look, then heard Mitz calling her name.

'I'm in the cellar,' he shouted. 'Down the corridor.'

She followed the sound of his voice. At the end of the corridor was an open door and below, a dull orange glow from a single light bulb. She descended the steep steps, hanging on to a rickety wooden banister. Mitz stood in front of a chest freezer, his face a mask of anxiety. Her heart stopped. She'd been utterly and completely wrong. Cheryl's freezer hadn't broken down at all. She hadn't replaced it with a new one. Cheryl owned two chest freezers. *One for Siobhan and one for Florence.* Robyn's mind began to shut down. She would never forgive herself for this. She forced herself to speak.

'Open it,' she whispered.

Mitz pulled at the lid with both hands and heaved a sigh of relief. 'It's empty.'

She leant forward and breathed out, hands on her knees as if she'd completed a marathon. 'Thank goodness.'

Mitz walked around it and groaned. 'It's not plugged in. I should have checked before I called you down. I just saw the freezer and panicked.'

'I understand. You did the right thing to call me,' said Robyn.

Mitz held the lid up and examined it. 'The lid hinges are broken and it smells of bleach.' He wrinkled his nose.

'We'll get forensics to examine it.'

Robyn glanced around the room. Various plastic boxes were stacked against the wall. 'What's that?' she asked pointing at a helmet.

'It looks like a cycling helmet. That's one crazy headlight attached to it. You'd blind motorists with it. Somebody wanted to be seen in the dark.'

'Have you spotted a bicycle anywhere?'

Mitz shook his head.

Robyn crouched beside the first box and examined the contents. It held various clean rags and a fruit juice bottle filled with liquid. She unscrewed the lid and sniffed. 'Smells like antifreeze.'

'That's strange. Why would somebody pour antifreeze into a fruit juice bottle? Hang on a sec, wasn't Amber Dalton poisoned? Do you think it was with antifreeze?'

'Mitz, some days you astound me with your deductions. This bottle could well turn out to be a vital piece of evidence. Well done.'

'Thanks, but I'd rather have found Florence alive. I've checked all the rooms upstairs and the attic, but I can't find her, guv.'

'She has to be here, Mitz.'

The furrow between Mitz's eyebrows deepened. 'What if she's not here?'

Robyn digested his words. Then she recalled the look Cheryl Chambers had given her. The woman had definitely abducted Florence for whatever reason. Florence *was* here.

'We'll not give up yet, Mitz. Let's try outside.'

They left the house by the front door. Robyn shone her torch from left to right. She refused to leave without Florence. A squad car drew up outside the house. Tom Shearer got out.

'I was on my way back to the station when I heard this being called in. You got your murderer?'

'It seems that way.' The shivering had started again. She preferred to put it down to the cold air rather than the anxiety she was experiencing. She didn't want him to notice her shaking and, stamping her feet, walked towards him. 'Want to help me search the site? I'm looking for a missing girl called Florence.'

'Sure. I haven't got anything better to do, only going to bed for the first time in three nights. Besides, sleep is so overrated.' He shrugged.

She managed a weak smile. 'We found a room at the end of this garage. There might be more rooms like it in the other two outbuildings.'

Tom headed towards the nearest one, a tumbledown wooden shed, once used to house agricultural tools. Robyn moved towards the furthest away building, stumbling over stones and broken slabs. Mitz shone his torch ahead, searching for an entrance. The building was made of concrete with a tin roof. The door – a broken-down wooden pallet – was not as heavy as it looked. Mitz pulled it away and put it against the wall. Robyn wrinkled her nose. 'What's that smell?'

Mitz sniffed and pulled a face. 'Damp hay? Chemicals for putting on crops? This used to be a smallholding.'

Robyn sniffed again. 'It's a chemical. I think it might be bleach. Why would you clean a place like this with bleach? There's no floor as such and what there is has crumbled away.'

'To get rid of bloodstains?' Mitz's voice was solemn. His torch shone on a dark stain on the floor. Robyn knelt beside it.

'Could be blood. Difficult to confirm in this light. Are there any other stains? It might be a spill from an old engine – oil, a leak of some description.' Her words sounded hollow, even to herself. There would be no other reason to clean such a place other than to remove suspicious stains. Was this Florence's blood? A small vibration of fear tingled at the base of her spine.

Mitz trained the beam across the ground once more. Apart from the one patch, the ground was unmarked. Robyn rose, unsure of what to do. Fear of losing Florence was rattling her. She had to regain control or she'd never find the girl. This stain needed identifying.

'Make sure forensics check it out.'

Tom appeared and shook his head. 'I found a shed, but it only contained an ancient mower and some mice. It stank of mouse pee.' He wrinkled his nose. 'Pongs in here too.'

'Might be bleach too,' said Robyn. 'Does this look like a bloodstain to you?'

'Could be. Forensics will be able to tell.' Tom swept the room with his torch and shrugged. 'I don't want to state the obvious, but Florence might not be anywhere on the premises, Robyn. She might never have been brought here.'

Robyn refused to comment. Her instincts were right. They had to be. Florence had been transported to this house. They continued to search, their torch beams lighting the interior of the building like strobes at a nightclub. Robyn cursed. 'There's nothing. No door, no room, nothing. It's not like the other building where we found the chest freezer. Mitz, try the house again. Look for any hidden doors, cupboards, anything.' Her voice rose slightly. Her hand trembled.

Mitz left immediately but Tom hung back. 'I know you want her to be here, but you should steel yourself for a disappointment.'

'No. You're wrong. I'll find her.' She walked away before he could see the desperation in her eye. It was looking increasingly likely he was correct. He couldn't be. Florence had been in touch with Hunter. Like the other girls, she'd disappeared in or around Uttoxeter. *But she wasn't at the station.* She stilled the doubting voice. Florence had been seen in the main street. She might have been making her way to the station. The doubts continued. What if Anna was right and Florence, upset by the online comments, had run away, or worse still, like Charlotte Chambers, had taken her own life? She dismissed these thoughts once and for all and tramped across gravel and broken stones, her torch shining down the side of the building.

Tom shrugged and left her to it, joining Mitz inside the house. She clambered over a low picket fence into the back garden, now no more than grass and weeds. The damp seeped through her boots. She checked for wells, coal bunkers, an old children's playhouse, or anywhere that Florence could have been concealed, all the while shouting her name. She knelt on the damp ground and hunted under bushes, lifting branches, all the while praying silently that she didn't come across a lifeless body. At last, exhausted, and with freezing, wet feet, she admitted defeat. The weight of it threatened to drag her underground.

The moon had become more visible and its silvery light danced on the fields beyond. She marched down to the hedgerow. What next? She'd been convinced they'd find Florence, and so far their extensive search had unveiled nothing to indicate she was, or had ever been, at The Oaks.

An owl hooted loudly, startling her and making her spin around. As she did so, her torch beam swept across the back of the outbuilding she had checked with Tom, and across a wooden door. There was an entrance to the back of the building, yet when they'd checked inside there had only been a wall at the far end. Her mind suddenly propelled her into action. She sped to the door, and with trembling hands, felt for the handle and rattled it. It was locked. She banged on it and called out Florence's name. There was no response. *Too late? No, it can't be. Come on – think, Robyn.* She directed the beam of her torch along the building once more, searching it top to bottom, until she let out a soft gasp. There was a join where the building had been extended. This was without doubt the door to a secret room, out of sight behind the large building.

She raised her leg and kicked the door, a move she had repeated many times in the gym. It barely moved. Her hip groaned with the shock. She ignored the pain and kicked again, and again. The door gave only slightly. She yelled out for help, and within seconds Mitz appeared, racing towards her.

'The door,' she puffed. 'Help me open it.'

Tom arrived. 'Heard your screeching up in the bedroom. You can't half yell. Need a hand?'

Robyn growled, 'Just open it.'

Mitz and Tom pushed, kicked and pulled until there was a splintering of wood and the door collapsed into large pieces that clung to the hinges. Tom let out a loud grunt and gave it one last resounding kick that allowed Robyn to enter. She pushed through a heavy blackout curtain that fell to the floor in front of the door. The smell of bleach was more evident here and she wrinkled her nose as she stood in the doorway, shining light into the space. It was a bedroom, decorated with flocked wallpaper and containing a chest of drawers and a single bed pushed against a wall. On the bed was a small form under a sheet. She raced over to it, dropped down and pulled back a sheet to uncover Florence curled in a ball, face pale, eyelids closed, long strawberry-blonde hair around her head like a halo. The girl remained immobile. Blood pounded through her temples. *Too late?* She touched her neck, fingers searching for life. There was nothing. *Oh, Robyn, what have you done?* Her fingers shook. She lifted them and replaced them on Florence's neck. Mitz watched her, his eyes two huge discs. Tom shuffled and made small noises in his throat as if he were preparing to speak. She shot him a look. 'Don't say it, Tom.'

He cricked his neck to one side and the other, stared at the ceiling, tried not to watch Robyn fumbling for signs of life.

Finally, she found it. 'She's alive.' Tears brimmed in her eyes. She was overcome with a desire to hug the unconscious girl. A hand on her shoulder helped her regain control.

'Well done,' said Tom. 'I'm so proud of you. You were right.'

She leant into him, felt his strong arms around her. For a moment she allowed relief to flood her body. She heard Mitz calling for an ambulance. 'Couldn't have done it without your help.' She pulled away and turned towards Florence.

A flicker of a smile passed over his face. 'Sure you could. Now, if you don't mind, I need my beauty sleep. I'm off. If you need my report, tough luck. You'll get it when I come into the station tomorrow.' He raised his hand and returned to his squad car.

'Thanks, Mitz.'

Mitz grinned happily. 'Any time, boss. I can't tell you how glad I am that we found Florence.'

'Me too, Mitz. Me too.' She swiped at a tear that threatened to spill over her eyelashes. Her attention was drawn to the arrival of the forensic team who pulled into the drive seconds later. Robyn waited with the unconscious Florence. She hoped there was no lasting damage to her. The ambulance would only be a few minutes. She held the girl's hand and whispered, 'Wake up, Florrie. We all want you back home – me, your mum and dad, and Amélie. We all love you. Wake up, sweetie.' Although a weight had been lifted from her shoulders, she would still have to wait to find out if Florence was unharmed and able to regain consciousness. And there were still three dead girls whose families needed closure and justice. She had a duty to perform. Shearer might be going for some beauty sleep, but Robyn would work all night if she had to in order to extract a confession from Cheryl Chambers. She owed these girls that, at least.

CHAPTER SIXTY-FOUR

Florence looked a little groggy but was sitting up in the hospital bed. Christine and Grant Hallows were by her bedside. She managed a weak smile when she caught sight of Robyn.

'Hey,' she said.

Robyn went to the opposite side of the bed and, facing her parents, dropped down on the bed. 'Good to see you awake. You had me worried for a while.'

'And us,' said Grant.

'The doctor just told me she's fine.' Robyn smiled at the sleepy girl as she spoke.

Christine nodded. 'No damage, thank goodness. Florrie was given a strong dose of Valium. The doctor said it should soon be out of her system. She's staying in overnight to make sure.'

'We found that same drug in Cheryl Chamber's bathroom cabinet. It's what the doctor prescribed her for depression. We believe she used it to knock Florence out. Want to tell me about it?' Robyn looked at Florence. 'That's if you're up to it?'

Florence looked at her mother. 'I feel so stupid.'

Christine took her hand and squeezed it. 'Go on, Florrie. We don't think you're stupid. This is Robyn. She won't think any the worse of you either.'

Florence gulped back some tears. 'It all started when I joined Fox or Dog. I met a boy called Hunter and we got on really well. We messaged each other a few times and chatted, and I told him all about the horses and how I liked art and loads of stuff – music, films and all that sort of thing. We decided to actually meet up.' She sniffed, her eyes red-rimmed. 'I shouldn't have, but gave Mum a story about going home with Amélie after school on Wednesday, and arranged to meet Hunter instead. Now it seems such a dumb thing to do. It was only supposed to be for a couple of hours. I didn't think it would do any harm. I thought we'd have a walk, maybe a coffee, get to know each other more, and then I'd go home. Oh, Mum!' Tears welled up in her eyes. Christine made shushing noises and stroked her hair.

'It's the shock,' said Robyn. 'Take your time, Florence. You don't have to tell me if you don't want to.'

Florence snuffled noisily. 'No, I want to tell you everything. I skipped off art ten minutes early to go and meet Hunter at the station. I waited and waited for him but he didn't show. I was so miserable and fed up at being let down. I tried to message him on the app but he didn't respond. I thought he'd changed his mind about the meeting, or had been stringing me along all the time. I gave up and decided to go home. I crossed the car park to walk up the road and catch a bus when somebody came at me from behind, pulled my arms so I couldn't move them, and covered my face with a cloth. It stank. I kicked and tried to shake my head but I couldn't get away. It seemed to go on for ages. All the time, there was this awful smell. In the end, I went all woozy and fainted.'

Christine stroked her hair again. Florence gave her a small smile. 'I'm sorry, Mum.'

'What's important is that you're safe and okay. Isn't it, Grant?' Her husband put an arm around her shoulder.

'Too true,' he said and winked at his daughter.

Florence continued. 'I woke up in a bedroom, only it wasn't like a proper bedroom. It was really dark and cold in there. I tried to find a light, and while I was feeling my way around, I heard someone in the room with me. I thought I was going to be killed. I wanted to scream and run away but I couldn't. I turned around and there was a woman in the room with me. She told me not to be frightened, and that she only wanted to talk to me, and then she'd take me home. It was so weird. She wore a cycling helmet with a lamp on it. It kept shining in my eyes and I couldn't see her face. I was dead scared at first, but she kept repeating she wasn't going to hurt me, and even asked me if I wanted anything to eat.

'She told me I'd been really silly to sign up to Fox or Dog, but she was going to "save" me because it was an evil app. Then she mumbled some weird stuff about it being her duty to protect the innocent and hunt down the guilty. She'd been "patrolling", that's what she called it, and after she saw my profile picture she felt really bad for me because I had lots of dog emojis. She sat beside me on the bed and stroked my hair and hummed a lullaby. It was so bizarre. Then she got up and wagged her finger, told me I was very pretty and that I didn't need to go online to find a boyfriend, and I was to ignore all the horrible people.' Florence stopped. 'Can I have some water, please?'

Christine passed her a plastic cup. She gulped down a mouthful, her eyelids beginning to droop a little.

'A couple of girls had commented about me being ginger, and I got really annoyed. I knew they were only kidding, but I was so cheesed off I left a pretty rude comment on one girl's profile. I guess it was dumb to stoop to their level. Anyway, the woman in the cycling helmet told me that I should have let it go. She said it was too easy to become a bitchy bully like them and she didn't want me to be like that. Then she explained Hunter wasn't really a boy. *She* was Hunter, and that she'd enjoyed chatting to me. I was bright and cheerful and shouldn't worry about not being top of the class or having a boyfriend. She gave me a lecture about enjoying my life, carrying on with my painting and taking up a career in art or something similar.

'I asked if I could go home, but she became all huffy and said I hadn't learnt my lesson yet. I had to understand the Internet could be a dangerous place. She'd already confiscated my mobile and stood there typing a text to Mum. I got angry and told her to give it back and let me go. I jumped up from the bed and tried to snatch it from her. She grabbed my hand and held it tightly and laughed again. She said it was nice to have a girl with spirit again, then left and locked me in the room.

'I tried to kick the door down. I hammered on it until I was so tired I couldn't lift my arms. I gave up after that and went back to the bed. Soon after, she turned up with a mug of cocoa and some biscuits. "You understand now, don't you?" she said. I didn't know what she was on about. I agreed with her because I didn't want her to go nutty or anything. She seemed happier then and said I was a lovely girl. I began to feel really, really tired. I couldn't keep my eyes open. Next thing, I woke up in the ambulance.' Florence looked shamefaced. 'I was such an idiot.'

Robyn shook her head. 'We all make mistakes, but we learn from them. Believe it or not, I was young once and got into some right scrapes. I made up all sorts of stuff to sneak out and go and see a boy who worked in a butcher's shop. My mother didn't approve of him because he had a motorbike. She was terrified I'd have an accident on it.'

Florence laughed. 'You lied to your parents?'

'I'm afraid I bent the truth on a few occasions. I caught a lift from school with him one morning and we skidded going around a roundabout. It wasn't serious, but I scraped my leg and it ripped my new jeans I was wearing for the occasion. I learnt my lesson. We all do stupid things. Let's just say, it's best to run things past your parents before you go off and do them.' She patted the girl's arm. 'Anyway, I'm really glad you're okay.'

Florence sighed. 'Thanks, Robyn.'

Robyn smiled again. 'Get some rest. You'll have quite a story to tell the others at school.'

'I don't want to look like a saddo. I might keep quiet about it.'

'I know somebody who wouldn't think that. She's outside, waiting to visit you.'

Florence chewed at her lip and nodded. 'Can you ask her to come in?'

CHAPTER SIXTY-FIVE

David Marker handed Robyn the sheet of paper she'd requested. Detailed background checks on Elliot Chambers had revealed an important piece of evidence, and the medical report in her hand revealed Elliot Chambers had been admitted to a residential mental health clinic in Oxfordshire on July the seventh, and stayed there until August the twenty-seventh. Although the treatment itself couldn't be revealed because of patient confidentiality, it showed that he had begun receiving it while at Manchester University in late March, had been referred to an outpatient clinic in June and to the residential clinic in July. It appeared Charlotte's death had had a profound effect on his mental health. It also meant he couldn't have abducted or murdered Carrie Miller.

Robyn headed for the interview room with a determined stride. Inside, Cheryl Chambers regarded her coolly. Mitz was already in place. The solicitor next to Cheryl was one she hadn't seen before, a man in his forties with a terrible comb-over and a baggy suit that had seen better days.

'You know why you're here, Mrs Chambers. You've been charged in connection with the murders of Carrie Miller, Amber Dalton and Siobhan Connors, and the abduction of Florence Hallows.'

Cheryl sat back in her chair, arms folded, her face expressionless. Robyn continued.

'Traces of DNA discovered in a chest freezer in the cellar at The Oaks have been identified as belonging to Carrie Miller.

DNA samples and blood belonging to Amber Dalton have been found on the floor of an outbuilding and in the boot of a Vauxhall Zafira registered to you.' She looked up from her notes to engage eye contact with the woman, but Cheryl gazed steadily into the distance. 'The body of Siobhan Connors was discovered in a chest freezer purchased by you on Friday the twentieth of January, from Argos in Uttoxeter, and delivered to your home the following day, Saturday the twenty-first of January. Do you wish to say anything about this, Mrs Chambers?'

Cheryl blinked once. Robyn had expected nothing other than silence from her.

'Mrs Chambers, do you deny abducting Carrie Miller in July of last year?'

She looked up, but there was still no reaction from Cheryl.

'Do you deny murdering Carrie Miller by cutting her throat, keeping her in storage in a chest freezer, and then transporting her body in a trunk to Rugeley in a van hired in the name of your late husband, Thomas Chambers, where you arranged for her to be left in a self-storage unit?'

The solicitor kept his head down, avoiding Robyn's gaze, and shifted on his chair.

'Do you deny abducting Amber Dalton on the third of January, keeping her imprisoned in the outbuilding beside your house, and murdering her on Thursday the nineteenth of January, poisoning her with antifreeze? Do you also deny abducting Siobhan Connors and suffocating her, then placing her body in the chest freezer found in your outbuilding?'

Robyn let out a small hiss of annoyance. Cheryl was ignoring her questions. She tried one last one.

'Did you, on Thursday the twenty-sixth of January, abduct Florence Hallows and take her to your house, The Oaks, where you imprisoned her, against her will, in an outbuilding?'

Cheryl didn't flinch. Robyn sighed and shut the folder containing her notes. Mitz remained stern-faced. He knew what she was going to do. They'd discussed it before coming into the interview room.

'Look, Mrs Chambers. I'm not going to mess about. I have all the evidence I require to make these charges stick. We recovered the antifreeze used to poison Amber Dalton. We have found fingerprints, DNA and blood belonging to these young women. We *know* these were revenge murders for the death of your daughter, who was bullied online by these three girls. We came across Charlotte's profile on the Fox or Dog website. It's still there, along with the comments that were made about her.' She let her words hang for a moment, knowing they would resonate with Cheryl.

'There's no doubt as to what actually happened. We unearthed the mobile phones belonging to these girls that you used to send false messages to their loved ones and friends, in an attempt to pretend all was normal. Partial fingerprints are on those phones.' She waited for a reaction.

Cheryl blinked twice rapidly and swallowed.

'You didn't think we'd uncover them, did you? Putting them in cereal boxes was a clever touch.'

Cheryl shrugged slightly. Robyn was making headway at last. She was going to make this woman confess if it was the last thing she did.

'We know you were involved in the murders of these girls. I can only assume that by keeping silent you are protecting another guilty party, and that must be your son, Elliot. Your silence will only make matters worse for him; you see, we have evidence that implicates him in all of this. The trunk, containing the body of Carrie Miller, was bought and paid for by your son. His prints were found on it. Items of clothing worn by the person posing as Joanne Hutchinson were found in his flat. He has no alibis for the dates the girls disappeared and he's refused to talk about his whereabouts over the summer months of July and August when Carrie Miller was abducted and later murdered. He claims he was "chilling" at home which, quite frankly, is not an alibi. All the evidence points to his involvement, and we shall be charging him.' She gave a sad sigh. 'I understand why you're trying to protect him. You're his mother. It's only normal to do so. However there's no point, because in a few minutes he's going to confess to it. When I spoke to him before coming in here, he was at breaking point.'

Robyn gathered her notes, stood up and prepared to terminate the interview. She hoped she'd played it right. This was her only chance. 'I think we'll end it there, Sergeant Patel. We're clearly wasting our time here. We'll move across to interview Mr Chambers. Please have him collected from the cell.'

'Yes, ma'am.' Mitz stood up as well, and headed for the door. Only then did Cheryl speak. Her voice was steady and quiet. 'It was me. Elliot has no idea about any of it. Don't ask him any questions about Charlotte's death. It'll tip him over the edge again. It took months for him to get back to some semblance of normality, and even now he's still got a way to go. Charlotte's death was too much for him. He had to go into therapy after it happened and then into hospital. He can't talk about her. He has to pretend she's still there or he goes under. We kept his admission secret. We couldn't have his new employers knowing he'd spent time in a mental hospital. Imagine what would happen if his pupils found out. Now he's trying to make something of his life. Don't ruin that for him.'

Robyn cocked her head. 'You're telling us your son has no connection to these murders whatsoever? I find that difficult to believe, Mrs Chambers.'

The solicitor whispered something to Cheryl. She shook her head. 'It's no use. They'll convict me even if I plead not guilty. I can't let them involve Elliot.'

Robyn stood behind her chair. 'Would you like to continue this interview, Mrs Chambers?'

Cheryl nodded. 'Yes. You must believe me. Elliot had no idea.'

Robyn signalled to Mitz. 'Mrs Chambers, you are about to confess to three counts of murder. Do you understand the implications of that?'

'I understand.'

'Mrs Chambers, do you confess to the murders of Carrie Miller, Amber Dalton and Siobhan Connors?'

Cheryl Chambers took a deep breath and spoke clearly. 'Yes, I murdered them. They were responsible for Lotty's death. I wasn't going to let them get away without some justice.' She folded her arms, hands under her armpits.

'Believe me, I didn't set out to kill them. My intention had been to scare them. Frighten them so much they'd never think about online sites like this again, and most importantly, they'd learn that their jibes and caustic comments had resulted in the death of my girl.' She paused, staring hard at Robyn.

'Emotion does things to your head. It changes you. I'd never felt such incredible unhappiness. Not even when I lost my husband, Tom. Losing Lotty was the worst thing I'd ever gone through. I was so damn furious with myself to start with. So angry and then so sad, I wanted to die. I felt so alone. Tom was dead, Lotty was dead and Elliot retreated into himself. I couldn't get him to talk to me. As soon as Lotty was buried, he returned to Manchester. Couldn't even look me in the eye. I didn't know if that was because of the shock of it all, or because he blamed me for not knowing what was going on in Lotty's head – for preventing it from happening.' She stopped again, gathered her thoughts and began her confession.

'After the paramedics had taken Lotty away, I went into her bedroom. Her mobile phone was on her bed. I picked it up and turned it on. I don't know why. Maybe it was just to have contact with her – see her face on her photos – pretend none of it had happened. I don't know. I came across the Fox or Dog app almost immediately. It was on the home screen. I clicked onto it and saw her photograph. I soon worked out what had happened to my precious girl. When the police arrived to speak to me much later the following day, I told them Lotty didn't have a mobile or computer, that she did any computer work at the library. They didn't ask Elliot the same question, thank goodness, or he might have contradicted me.

'I knew why Lotty had taken her life. It was because of some website that claimed it would match up young people with members of the opposite sex. But instead, some cruel girls had broken her spirit. Words. Words wounded her, and burrowed into her soul. She died because of words. And what would the police have done about that? Given those bullies a warning? Shut down the website? They wouldn't imprison anyone, would they? Even though those girls were guilty of bullying my daughter to the point where she felt worthless and committed suicide, what justice would have been served? And is the punishment for this crime great enough?' Her eyes blazed with ferocity. 'I had to take matters into my own hands.

'Elliot buried himself in his studies, and pills from the doctor helped him through the ordeal. I had nothing to distract me from my pain. It grew and grew, driving me insane, and so I decided to trick these girls, meet up with them and somehow make them pay for what had happened to Lotty.

'I started with Carrie Miller. I created a fake account on Fox or Dog, using the name Hunter, and hoped she'd like my profile picture. Sure enough she did. We chatted regularly. She told me a lot about herself and how she hated her father's girlfriend. She was a cocky young madam, full of her own importance. At least, that's how she came across. She was so easy to manipulate. I told her lie after lie. In the end, she was convinced I was a regular nice guy who'd like to meet up. She messaged me late in the afternoon on July the twenty-eighth, saying she'd had a major row with her dad's girlfriend, Leah. I invited her to come and spend a few days with me at a music festival with a few friends. She jumped at the chance. She arrived at Uttoxeter station where I was hidden from view beside the car park. She made her way to the bus stop and stood there, facing up the road, waiting for him. I only had to wait a few minutes for the passengers to disperse. I approached her from behind, knocked her out with chloroform and dragged her to my car. I put her in the bedroom at the back of the first outbuilding. I'd fixed it up while Elliot was in the hospital and made it into a proper room. I'd decorated it to look like Lotty's. I even used the same wallpaper that's in her room.' She sniffed back a tear and continued.

'I was going to keep Carrie there a few days or a couple of weeks until she was scared rigid and had learnt the error of her ways, then let her go. I had to disguise myself, of course, so she'd never be able to tell who had abducted her. I used the cycling helmet to train a light on her at all times so she couldn't see my face, and whispered a lot. I can do accents and voices, but keeping up a male voice is difficult. I can only do it for short bursts. I wanted her to tell the police she'd been kidnapped by a man. That would deflect any attention or suspicion from me.'

She paused and stared at the mirror opposite her. From the other side of the one-way glass Matt Higham, Tom Shearer, DCI Flint and Anna Shamash watched while Cheryl Chambers continued as if in front of an audience.

'I took her phone. It was obvious people would wonder where she'd got to. I was prepared to answer any text messages. As it was, only one person was concerned about her whereabouts – a girl called Jade. I made up some ridiculous story about running away with a boy, and she fell for it. I kept Carrie doped for a while. I put Valium in her drink. I hoped she'd realise the enormity of what she'd done. I showed her the photograph of my Lotty but she didn't understand. I told her how the comments had driven Charlotte to take her own life, and do you know what she said? "No one takes that sort of thing seriously. It's just banter. That's what happens these days. You get dissed by someone and you diss them back. It's no biggie." What's that supposed to mean? She wasn't sorry at all for her part in it.'

Cheryl shook her head. 'It isn't acceptable, is it? She seemed to think it was normal behaviour and hang the consequences. Anyway, I'd decided it was time to knock her out and drop her off. So I took her some drugged food. I think she must have worked out I was drugging her water to keep her quiet, and had been tipping it away, because the wretched creature was lying in wait for me behind the door. When I went in she pushed me over and ran for it. The tray landed on the floor and a glass broke. She was disorientated and fell over a few feet away from the room. I caught her. She struggled and lashed out. I had a piece of the broken glass in my hand. I don't remember picking it up. She screamed. I wanted her to shut up. I didn't think. I just jabbed the glass into her neck.'

Behind the mirror, Anna winced.

'I wrapped the bed sheet from the room around her neck, but it kept on bleeding. She died quickly. I bought some huge plastic bags from the local DIY store, washed off as much blood as I could, wrapped her in one, and then put her body in my chest freezer down in the cellar. I left her there and hadn't thought about moving her body until I received a leaflet through the letter box. It was for a self-storage unit at Rugeley. Elliot had brought home a trunk that was about the right size for her body, which he'd left outside in one of the outbuildings, along with some boxes of costumes, books, kitchen equipment and so on. Using one of Elliot's costumes, a wig and ample make-up as a disguise, I drove to Rugeley where I paid for a self-storage unit in cash. The owner was too distracted by his mobile to pay too much attention to me.'

Robyn held her breath. This was a thorough confession. There would be no doubt whatsoever about Cheryl Chambers's guilt. The woman continued.

'I hired a van in my husband's name. I'd kept his driving licence, and nobody even questioned me when I turned up dressed in one of his old outfits. I drove the van home, loaded up the trunk and her body, changed my disguise again, and drove to Rugeley. I gave a decent performance of a toffee-nosed woman who wanted to house a trunk of valuables from her soon-to-be ex-husband's prying eyes. I asked the man at the self-storage unit to carry the trunk to the actual unit because I couldn't lift it. In truth, I didn't want to be spotted on the CCTV cameras. As far as I was concerned, Carrie Miller wasn't going to be discovered for a very long time. My heart felt lighter than it'd felt since Lotty died. I'd freed up space in my freezer, which I figured I'd use again, this time for my latest online friend – Amber Dalton. I felt satisfied and content that I'd got some justice for my daughter.'

Mitz leant across the table, unable to remain quiet any longer. His voice shook with emotion. 'Mrs Chambers, those young women didn't deserve to die. They were unkind, but they never intended to harm your daughter. You didn't serve justice. Murder isn't a form of justice.'

Cheryl's eyes bored into him. 'You know the children's rhyme, "Sticks and stones may break your bones but words will never hurt you"? Officer, words *can* hurt. They can injure as deeply as a knife can, or be as deadly as a gunshot. Those girls killed my daughter with words. They deserved to die. I'm satisfied with their punishment.'

A tear slid down Anna's face. Mitz was right. The girls didn't deserve their punishment. She wiped it away before any of the others could see it. She focused on Robyn, who continued to question the woman relentlessly. Robyn would ensure proper justice was served. Of that, Anna was convinced.

CHAPTER SIXTY-SIX

Outside the church, the mourners gathered under a pale-blue sky. Colourful crocuses stood to attention either side of the gravel drive as people left, pausing only to shake the hand of the man by the gate. Maneesh Shah, Carrie's ex-form master, and Kevin Winters, the head teacher, walked side by side. Behind them were some fifty pupils from Fairline Academy, all in their teens, who had wanted to pay their respects to Carrie.

The service had been more uplifting than sad – Carrie's brief life was celebrated as best it could be. Her father, Vince, read out a poem about love and gratitude, his voice cracking at the last line. Jade North gave the eulogy and surprised them all by talking eloquently about Carrie's aspiration to break into the fashion industry, and telling a couple of amusing stories about her friend. The pupils had all left red single roses on the coffin until there was no wood to be seen; it was now in the hearse waiting to go to Derby crematorium.

Robyn had felt more than duty-bound to attend the service. Carrie had not deserved the punishment she'd received. Behind the bolshie mask was a girl who craved nothing more than love and attention. The collage of hearts on her bedroom wall had touched Robyn, and she wished Carrie had not tried to find love on such a cruel app.

She waited until the crowd in front of her had dispersed, then stood in front of Vince Miller. 'How are you bearing up?' she asked. He had lost weight.

'Okay, I guess. It's going to be a slow process. I still wish I'd phoned her and asked her to come home. I'll never forgive myself for turning my back on her.'

Robyn touched the back of his hand briefly. 'It wouldn't have made any difference. She couldn't have answered you. You know that.'

He gave a small nod. 'You're right. She was already dead, wasn't she? At least now I can lay her to rest.'

Jade, in a large black parka with a furry hood, appeared next to him. 'You coming back to the house later?' she asked, looking at Robyn. 'There's food for everyone. You'd be welcome.'

'Thanks, but I can't. I have to deal with something else. You were great today,' said Robyn. 'Your eulogy was beautiful.'

'I only said what was in my heart. Carrie was a proper friend. She looked after me. I'd have had a harder time at school if it hadn't been for her. She was like my personal guardian angel. When you knew her, she was a different person to the one she pretended to be. We all put on a front at times to get by. She was very good at it, but I knew what she was really like. She had a big heart.'

Vince agreed. 'It was a lovely tribute. I was so glad her friends from school came too.'

'Yeah,' said Jade. 'It was really good so many came. I put the word out on Facebook. I wish Carrie could have seen them all. She'd have been well chuffed. She loved being the centre of attention.'

Leah, who had been in conversation with the vicar, joined them and took Vince's arm, giving it a gentle squeeze. 'We'd best be going,' she said. 'We have to take her to the crematorium.'

Vince nodded at Robyn and headed down the path, looking older than his years. Leah had one arm around him and Jade flanked his other side like a female bodyguard.

Robyn turned to take one last look at the church, its huge wooden door now closed. The last time she'd attended a funeral it had been for Davies. That had been a quiet affair, with only a couple of his colleagues, his superior, Peter Cross, and close relatives – Brigitte, his ex-wife with her new husband Richard, pale-faced Amélie, and Robyn, his fiancée. Ross had accompanied Robyn, clung on to her when her legs refused to support her. The coffin was bare of tributes, as had been requested. The service had been very brief, with one hymn – 'I Vow to Thee My Country'. She hadn't been able to sing. The tears had filled her eyes and blocked her throat. The vicar had said a few words about the man who'd given his life to protect his country and how they should all be proud of him, and she was proud of him, in spite of the gaping wound in her heart. A small cough made her turn around.

'You ready to leave, guv?' Anna was standing behind her.

'Yes. And thanks for coming, Anna.'

Anna gave a slight shake of her head. 'I wanted to. I had to. You understand, don't you?'

'I do. Now, how about we stop off on the way back to the office and grab a box of cakes for the team to cheer ourselves up?'

'Best get a couple of extra large ones for Matt, guv. It might stop him scoffing all the biscuits.'

CHAPTER SIXTY-SEVEN

Robyn stood beside the aviary in Stafford Park. The budgerigars chirped and flew from side to side – a blur of blue, yellow and green feathers swooping excitedly before settling on perches. She turned to face Ross who had just arrived, causing the kerfuffle.

'And who is this?'

'This is Duke.'

The Staffordshire bull terrier pup looked up and wagged its tail, tugged at its lead and fell on its backside.

'He's payment for searching for Siobhan Connors. I didn't want to take Lauren's hard-earned cash from her, especially as I didn't find her friend alive. Jeanette's been saying for ages we should get a dog. It's part of her plan to make sure I keep up my daily walks. Engaging little chap, isn't he?'

The dog chewed at Ross's shoelaces while he talked. 'Well done on cracking the case. I gather Cheryl Chambers confessed.'

'Once she believed Elliot was going to be convicted for the murders, she couldn't stop talking.'

'And Elliot had no idea of what she'd done?'

'None whatsoever. She said she killed Carrie unintentionally. She hid Carrie's body in a chest freezer in the cellar and moved it to the self-storage unit to make room for her next victim. With Elliot at the mental health clinic, she didn't try and trick Amber until he was more settled and had begun working at Delia Marsh School. Knowing Elliot was out with friends in Lichfield, she persuaded the girl to meet at his flat on the third of January. She had his front door key and waited there for Amber to show up. She drugged Amber using Rohypnol, carried her to the car parked nearby, and drove to the outside bedroom at The Oaks.'

'Why didn't Amber become suspicious when a woman instead of this chap, Hunter, opened the door?'

Robyn stared at the girls sitting on a bench, chatting. Florence was bearing up after her abduction. She'd had a few days off school and had patched up her differences with Amélie. The sound of their laughter carried over. Duke's ears pricked up at the sound.

'Cheryl used to act, and spent years in the theatre. She had a large supply of wigs and make-up and used them to disguise herself. In the half-light of the flat, she confused Amber long enough to drug her.'

'She can't have been right in the head,' said Ross.

'That's one way of putting it.' Robyn thought again about the interview with Cheryl Chambers and the lengthy confession that had left Robyn drained. The woman had shown no remorse about the lives she'd taken, or for those who would be left to grieve. Her words had been delivered like lines that had to be learnt but devoid of expression and emotion. She'd explained her plans went awry when the chest freezer containing Amber's body broke down. She'd foolishly panicked and driven Amber's body to Cannock Chase, dragging her to a secluded spot, a dip in the ground, and covering her with leaves. She'd shrugged as if it was of no consequence. Robyn had thought of Florence and it had taken all of her willpower not to grab the woman and shake her hard.

'And Siobhan?' Ross pursed his lips. 'I feel I ought to tell Lauren the complete truth.'

'She tried to lure Siobhan in the same way as the other girls, but Siobhan refused to meet up, and told Hunter she was going to try and make up with her boyfriend, Adam. Cheryl couldn't let it go so easily and began waiting outside Siobhan's flat, hoping to get an opportunity to abduct her. It happened on Friday the thirteenth when Siobhan walked to the station for a night out with Lauren. Cheryl tailed her in her car, and as soon as she realised Siobhan was headed for the station, she went on ahead to make sure the coast was clear. Then when Siobhan appeared she called the girl over to her car, claiming she was lost. Siobhan leant in to hear what Cheryl was saying. That was the moment Cheryl hauled her inside the car, restrained her and covered her mouth with a chloroform rag, much like the one she used on Florence. She took Siobhan's phone, answered Lauren's text message, and even had the forethought to ring Tesco, pretending to be Siobhan. She managed to give a convincing performance of a distressed Irish girl. It was enough to keep anyone from searching for her. Never met anyone quite as cold and calculating as her.'

'Where did Florence fit into all this?'

'It was Elliott. He told his mother about the rampant bullying at his school. He wanted do something to eradicate it and discussed writing a play about bullying and putting it on at the school to draw attention to the problem. Cheryl had already been watching the Fox or Dog site since Charlotte's death, and after he told her about the kids at his school, she narrowed down the search to cover the Uttoxeter area. She wanted to make sure none of his pupils were using the site, and if they were, she wanted to ensure they didn't get victimised. Her intentions were actually good. She left positive comments on lots of profiles where there were dog emojis. When she saw Florence's profile, she decided to warn her off the site – do what she couldn't do for Charlotte.' She looked across at the girls still giggling and chatting.

'She thought she could teach Florence a valuable lesson — one that would warn her off such apps in the future.'

Ross shook his head in dismay. 'As I said, she isn't right in the head. That's no way to teach anyone a lesson.'

'I agree. Cheryl was adamant she intended driving Florence home the night we found her. She was drugged with Valium so she'd have no idea of where she'd been held captive, and Cheryl was going to leave her outside her house, but we showed up and messed up her plans.'

Ross breathed in deeply. 'Crazy. People can be so crazy.'

'Life can screw people up. It can turn them crazy. Charlotte's death was too much for Cheryl to handle.' Cheryl Chambers had fooled them into believing she suffered from fibromyalgia. She'd thrown them off the scent. Robyn had made some serious errors during the investigation and almost got it wrong. Was she losing her touch?

The girls were watching something on Amélie's mobile and giggling. There was a little warmth in the sun and daffodils were pushing up under the trees in Stafford Park.

'Bet you're glad that's all over,' said Ross.

Robyn gazed at him, a half smile on her face. 'It's never really over though, is it? There'll be more cyberbullying, more hurt, more sadness and more murders. It's never over for people like us.'

Duke stood up and let out a whine. 'As long as there are people like us, there'll be less of it, and we have to think about them,' he added, nodding in the direction of the girls. 'They're the future. We have to try and make it as decent a future as we can. Now, stop brooding. You promised to buy us all dinner at McDonald's, and this little chap would like an extra-large burger.'

Robyn laughed. 'You know they say dogs can look like exactly like their owners…'

'Don't even go there,' said Ross, pulling at the lead.

She gave him a warm smile and then called the girls.

'Amélie, Florence, come on. Ross needs feeding.'

Robyn waited as the girls wandered across, arms linked, heads down, and deep in conversation. Ross was right. They were the future.

CHAPTER SIXTY-EIGHT

Back home, Robyn lifted the post from the doormat – an electricity bill and an A4 manila envelope postmarked London. She threw them on the kitchen worktop while she made a cup of tea and considered going to the gym. She had the rest of the day off to look forward to. As she waited for the kettle to boil, she opened the larger of the envelopes and pulled out a photograph. Time stood still. Blood rushed into her ears and her mouth dropped open in surprise. The photograph, taken at what appeared to be an airport, was of a dark-haired man in spectacles wearing a nondescript dark-grey suit and carrying a worn satchel. Unaware that he was being photographed, he was rubbing at the stubble on his chin as he waited beside a rack of magazines.

Robyn couldn't assimilate what she was seeing. The man in the photograph was without any doubt, her fiancé, Davies Hilton. What made her gasp was the date stamp at the top of the photograph. The picture had been taken at three thirty on the fifteenth of March 2015. She read the date stamp again and again. Her brain could make no sense of it. It couldn't be correct because at three thirty on the fifteenth of March 2015, she had been in a hotel room in Marrakesh and had just received the news that Davies had been killed. She checked the photograph again. Could it have been Photoshopped? Was it some cruel hoax? Her mind drifted back to that morning…

*

The first call to prayer wakes her. Davies is half asleep, his arm over her shoulder, holding her to him. She feels him stir and gives a smile. It had been worth joining him in Morocco. It is as beautiful and exotic as he promised it would be, and later today, on the roof terrace of this incredibly romantic riad, she'll reveal the news she's been keeping secret, that he's to be a father.

She never visits Davies when he's on a mission. It's forbidden, and ordinarily he never divulges his destinations, but this time he has.

'It's only a casual meeting with an informant. Nothing dangerous. I'm not even sure it's going to take happen. I'll probably kick my heels for four days and come home. Come on, Robyn. Marrakesh is amazing and you'd love it. It's a fascinating city. Why not come along with me?' he'd said. At first she'd refused, then she'd changed her mind. It would be a wonderful place to share the news of the life growing inside her.

As he wakes more fully, he draws her even closer to him and murmurs in her ear. 'Morning, gorgeous. If I didn't have to make that trip across the Atlas Mountains, I'd stay here all day with you. I'd really hoped it wasn't going to take place. Still, it's only one little meeting and then the rest of the time is all ours again. Any chance you'll still be here when I get back?'

The love she feels for him balloons inside her. She couldn't love him any more than she already does. 'I'll be here.'

'In that case, I'll make sure I get back early, in time for some pre-dinner passion.'

He nibbles on her ear. She feels warmth filling her every cell. She can't wait for the evening when they'll have something very special to celebrate.

She lifted the photograph once more and examined his face. It was without doubt Davies. He was in the same outfit he'd worn the last time she saw him: a beige jacket, pale shirt and blue jeans, and wearing his usual dark-rimmed, square-framed glasses. Yet Davies had headed for a village outside Ouarzazate, a three-hour trip on the other side of the Atlas Mountains. How could he be at this airport?

She studied the magazines on the rack in front of Davies. They were in English. Was he at a British airport? There were no other people visible or any other clues as to where he might be. She inhaled and scrutinised it again, her eyes straining to pick up anything that might identify his location. Then she spotted it. Hidden behind the rack and almost out of view were some souvenirs from the region, mostly blurred apart from one – a red double-decker bus, bearing a Union Jack flag. Davies was in the UK.

This was simply not possible. He'd left Marrakesh at five o'clock that fateful morning in an open-top jeep driven by Hassan, a man with jet-black hair and shining white teeth.

She closes her eyes and breathes in the scent of orange blossom that drifts through her open window. It's wonderfully cool inside the riad and so calm. When Davies returns she'll tell him what her body has known for a while; he's to be a father. The tentative knock at the door interrupts her delicious thoughts. She checks her watch. It's three thirty p.m. She rises from the bed, heart thumping. He's early! She races to the door and throws it wide open, expecting to see the face of the man she adores. But it isn't him. It's Peter Cross, Davies's superior. She's confused. How does Peter Cross know she's here? He answers her unspoken words.

'Davies called me. He told me you were here. In case things went wrong. He wanted to keep you safe.' His face says it all. His words confirm her worst fears.

'Robyn, I'm so sorry. 'There was an attack on several vehicles near Toufliht, at the foot of the Atlas Mountains. One of them was Davies's.'

'No.'

He gives a sad shake of his head. 'He didn't survive. He died immediately.'

She raises her fists and brings them down on Peter Cross's chest, hammering with all her might. He calmly gathers her hands in his own and holds them tightly.

'I'm truly sorry. He was one of my best men. He'll be a huge loss to all of us. You'll need time, Robyn,' he says. 'We'll all need time.'

She returned her attention to the photograph. It had to be a fake. She examined it once more with the magnifying glass then turned it over. Written on the back were three words, 'Fact not fiction.'

Her heart thumped so loudly it was all she could hear. If this was authentic, then Davies did not die that day. For twenty-two months she'd harboured a tremendous guilt – she'd believed that by travelling to Marrakesh she'd somehow blown his cover, and because of that he'd been tracked down and murdered. This suggested otherwise. Who could have sent it? And, if Davies was alive, why hadn't he contacted her? He was supposed to love her. What about his daughter, Amélie? He wouldn't have put the child through such upset.

This wasn't real. Her mind couldn't fathom the significance of the photograph, nor the implications. She'd lived through almost two years of hell. She'd mourned him and cried for him. She'd had a breakdown after his death and a miscarriage swiftly afterwards, brought on, she believed, by distress.

Robyn headed to the sink, ran the cold tap and splashed water onto her face while her mind turned somersaults. What was she supposed to do now? Search for Davies? And if he was alive, should she welcome him back with open arms and forgive him for such treachery and deceit? No. He couldn't mess with people's emotions like this, no matter what reason he had. Possible scenarios bounced in her head. The Davies she knew wouldn't deliberately allow his loved ones to suffer like this, so had he been captured and unable to reach her? Surely Davies wouldn't knowingly have put them through such pain – would he? There had to be a good reason for this. She pressed her forehead to a cupboard, steadying her hands and taking long deep breaths to steady her heart. If this photograph proved he was alive on March the fifteenth, was he still alive, and if so, where was he now? *Damn him! How could he do this to them?* Angry, hot tears filled her eyes. She put her head in her hands and let them flow.

LETTER FROM CAROL

Dear everyone,

My thanks to you for purchasing and reading *The Missing Girls*. I really hope you've enjoyed this case. It is, to date, the one I've most enjoyed writing. I find with each of the books in this series, I'm becoming closer to the characters, especially Robyn, who now has a personal case to investigate. She's in two minds at the moment and isn't sure whether she should pursue this. By the next book, she'll have made up her mind. What do you think? Should she look for Davies? Do you think he's alive?

If you'd like to hear about the next book, sign up to my mailing list below. Your email address will never be shared and you can unsubscribe at any time.

www.bookouture.com/carol-wyer

My inspiration for the book came from a friend whose son was being bullied at school. He'd recently had a major operation, leaving him physically scarred on his face and head, and the kids at school tormented him about it. The bullying continued at home when he accessed his social media accounts. Fortunately, his mother worked out what was happening, saw the head teacher and, dissatisfied with their response to the situation, removed the boy. Now he's content at a new school and is flourishing, but not every story has such a happy ending. I've always been aware of the negatives of social media, but my research for this book turned up some extremely disturbing cases of cyberbullying, and apps that are being used by youngsters without their parents' knowledge.

I hope *The Missing Girls* serves to highlight some of the difficulties and dangers our young people face by being unmonitored online, and the terrible effects bullying and cyberbullying can have on them.

I'm beginning to like DI Tom Shearer, but the second he lets his guard down he puts it back up again. He assures me he's a decent bloke underneath all that bluster, but we'll have to see if that's the case.

And my favourite character, Ross, now has a new love in his life – Duke! Several of you have written to say Ross ought to have his own series. Watch this space.

If you enjoyed reading *The Missing Girls* please would you take a few minutes to write a review, no matter how short it is. I would really be most grateful. Your recommendations are most important.

I love hearing from my readers, so if you'd like to get in touch, you can find me on Twitter, Facebook or through my website.

Carol x

www.facebook.com/AuthorCarolEWyer

twitter.com/carolewyer

www.carolewyer.co.uk

ACKNOWLEDGEMENTS

I'm having an ace time writing this DI Robyn Carter series, and really loved writing *The Missing Girls*. Although the book has my name on it, there's a huge amount of teamwork to make each book happen. My thanks to my marvellous, cool, calm and collected editor, Natalie Butlin, who kept my ramblings under control, and to Kim Nash, my fantastic publicity manager, who kept my spirits lifted. Thanks to everyone at Bookouture: Oliver, Lauren, Claire, Kate and the rest of the team.

Thanks also to all the bloggers and reviewers who take time to read my books and spread the word about them. You are too many to mention here, and I would hate to miss any of you out, but I am extremely grateful to each and every one of you, more than you'll know.

Heartfelt thanks to my Facebook Smile Team who support me on a daily basis; you are a fantastic group of people and I'm hugely fond of you all.

Finally, a huge thank you to you, my readers, for not just reading my books, but for emailing me, messaging and staying in touch on social media. On those long nights when I am heavy-eyed and struggling with a plot or character, you keep me going.

Made in the USA
San Bernardino, CA
31 October 2017